He read my mind.

My every desire.

My every need.

MY EVERY FEAR...

continued . . .

"*Midnight Rain* is dynamic romantic suspense."

—*Midwest Book Review*

"This thriller has just about everything you could ask for . . . suspense, intrigue, a broad brush stroke of the paranormal, and topped off with a great romance that makes it sizzle. To put it bluntly, this was one heck of an absolutely riveting suspense/paranormal romance—totally awesome! Such an adrenaline rush, I could have jumped out of my skin. Bottom Line—This is a superb, fascinating ride of a suspense filled romantic thriller. Do yourselves a big favor and find this book for a great read by an author who I predict has a fabulous future in front of her."

—SuspenseRomanceWriters

"Lisle explodes onto the suspense scene with a book so chilling and a voice so original that she's sure to become a major player. Creepy and thrilling, this book is truly unforgettable."

—*Romantic Times*

"Though this is her first foray into romantic suspense, Lisle proves herself a master. . . . Her story does everything right. Lisle has also created one of the creepiest bad guys to come along in a good while—Michael could give Hannibal Lecter lessons. *Midnight Rain* is the first in what I hope will be many more thrillers from this very talented author."

—BookLoons

last girl dancing

Holly Lisle

AN ONYX BOOK

ONYX
Published by New American Library, a division of
Penguin Group (USA) Inc., 375 Hudson Street, New York, New York 10014, USA
Penguin Group (Canada), 10 Alcorn Avenue, Toronto,
Ontario, M4V 3B2, Canada (a division of Pearson Penguin Canada Inc.)
Penguin Books Ltd., 80 Strand, London WC2R 0RL, England
Penguin Ireland, 25 St. Stephen's Green, Dublin 2,
Ireland (a division of Penguin Books Ltd.)
Penguin Group (Australia), 250 Camberwell Road, Camberwell, Victoria 3124,
Australia (a division of Pearson Australia Group Pty. Ltd.)
Penguin Books India Pvt. Ltd., 11 Community Centre, Panchsheel Park,
New Delhi - 110 017, India
Penguin Group (NZ), cnr Airborne and Rosedale Roads, Albany,
Auckland 1310, New Zealand (a division of Pearson New Zealand Ltd.)
Penguin Books (South Africa) (Pty.) Ltd., 24 Sturdee Avenue,
Rosebank, Johannesburg 2196, South Africa

Penguin Books Ltd., Registered Offices:
80 Strand, London WC2R 0RL, England

First published by Onyx, an imprint of New American Library,
a division of Penguin Group (USA) Inc.

First Printing, July 2005
10   9   8   7   6   5   4   3   2   1

PUBLISHER'S NOTE
This is a work of fiction. Names, characters, places, and incidents either are the prod-
ucts of the author's imagination or are used fictitiously, and any resemblance to actual
persons, living or dead, business establishments, events, or locales is entirely coinci-
dental.
    The publisher does not have any control over and does not assume any responsi-
bility for author or third-party Web sites or their content.

For Matthew

ACKNOWLEDGMENTS

In the writing of this book, I had wonderful help with my research into police detection, exotic dance, and the world of Army Rangers. For this help, as well as for assistance from my first-draft readers, I would like to thank:

Raymond E. Foster, the REAL POLICE Forum members, Jennifer Worthington, Charles Liverhant, Exotic Dancer Forums members, Robert Santa Maria, Salem, Russell Gifford, Jim Woosley, Frank Andrew, Scott Bryan, Jean Schara, Sheila Kelly, Emory Hackman, J. Patrick Garey, BJ Steeves, Linda Sprinkle, and Bob Billing. If I've missed anyone, I apologize deeply.

And to Claire Zion, for magnificent editing, and Robin Rue, for magnificent agenting, my warmest and happiest thanks.

And the mistakes in this, of course, are all mine.

AUTHOR'S NOTE

While I have done my best to be true to the work of detectives and to actual police procedure, the Atlanta HSCU is my own creation.

chapter 1

Deep-blue satin bustier, blue satin G-string, carefully applied makeup that covered and filled in the gapped half-inch incisions over each jugular vein. A halo of night-blossoming jasmine around a shining fan of long, silky brown hair. Sweet brown eyes, open, unblinking, beginning to dull and cloud.

The makeup over the abraded wrists and ankles hadn't covered as well this time as it had for the last two girls. This sweetheart had fought harder. She had been especially fun to hurt. To possess. Finally, to kill. But the makeup? Not good.

The photographer, still crouching, spread the dead dancer's legs wider, into a lewd pose. Appearances mattered. They told the story—pretty, wicked, filthy girls and the three friends who gave them what they deserved.

Click. Flash. One Polaroid slid out into a latex-gloved hand, and—click, flash—another. A third. And, quickly, one last lovely shot, because the photographer was working in a public place, and those flashes could bring attention. But everyone needed one final souvenir of this adventure.

That's what friends were for.

*   *   *

Heading up the back steps of the Special Crimes building, Jess felt like she was walking into a cathedral. She was on her way to the home of the Grand Old Men of Murder.

For the last eleven years, her goal had been to become one of the Grand Old Men, not all of whom were old, not all of whom were men. Because what all the Grand Old Men had in common was that they were the best. They got the toughest, most baffling, most frustrating cases. They got the murders no one else could solve. Becoming an HSCU detective touched at the very heart of the reason she had become a cop.

Jess knew her chance of reaching her goal was better than the odds of winning the jackpot in the state lottery, should she ever decide to play. But not much.

HSCU consisted of twenty detectives, two lieutenants, and one captain in charge of the unit. You had to have already been the best just to get a chance to apply. The waiting list stretched on forever.

And yet Jess had received word the night before that she was going to be on loan from her own Major Crimes robbery unit, and that she would be reporting to HSCU for as long as she was needed, starting first thing next morning.

No word about why. No explanation beyond a mention that she had been asked for specifically, and a comment that the HSCU team had a tendency to show up for work early, and she probably ought to be there half an hour before the official start of shift.

Jess figured she had this one chance to make a great impression. So she'd dressed conservatively, in her best suit. She wore a navy silk blazer specially cut to fit comfortably around her shoulder holster, and a lean, just-above-the-knee skirt in nubby silk. She'd put her hair in a French twist. Skipped the jewelry, skipped makeup beyond a bit of lip gloss. Wore her good watch with the leather band and the sweep hand. She looked professional. Respectable. Solid.

Every choice she'd made that morning had been an agonizing decision. Each one had felt momentous. In the end, she'd been too nervous for breakfast.

She felt like she was auditioning for a job seven years before she could hope to qualify, and she didn't even know what they were going to ask of her. Why did HSCU need *her?*

Jess came out at the top of the staircase into a wide corridor. Junk food and drink machines stood immediately to her left on the landing. Beyond them, the corridor stretched before her, with dark speckled linoleum and walls painted mustard yellow, fluorescent lights humming and flickering overhead. Doors to the left and right bore brass plates: Rape Special Crimes Unit, Robbery Special Crimes Unit. The third door left was Homicide Special Crimes Unit. HSCU.

Jess walked up to the HSCU door, swallowed hard, and opened it.

Industrial gray cubicles lined the side walls. A few windows on the back wall let in the first glimmerings of dawn. The gray file cabinets beneath those windows had seen better days. Maybe, she thought, eyeing them uncertainly, better decades. In the center of the open area between the two rows of cubicles, a big wood table squatted—pitted, scarred, and ugly—surrounded by a lot of comfortable-looking and surprisingly modern swivel chairs.

And though she was over half an hour early, the place was hopping. Detectives sat in their cubicles thumbing through thick notebooks or typing at computer terminals or talking on phones. Two detectives sat at the table in the center of the room, suit coats off but holsters on, sleeves of white shirts rolled up, papers and three-ring notebooks piled in front of them, coffee and candy bars scattered around them in drifts. Behind them stood a tall detective wearing a silk suit.

All three men at the central table looked up at the sound

of the door thudding shut behind her. And there was Jim Hennicut. Same shaved head. Same military bearing, same lean runner's build. Grinning at her.

"Princess Grace. We meet again."

Her heart felt a little lighter.

"Jim," she said, and returned the grin. "Are you the reason I get to be here?"

He stood and nodded. "We needed someone with your skills and your intangibles. I vouched for you."

Jess had done the hooker walk as an undercover cop on a couple of trick task forces for Jim back before she'd made detective. She didn't like undercover, but the experience had been useful—and she'd been good at it. Jim had made her better. Her theater background from high school and dance school had come in handy, as had her looks. But Jim had taught her how to fade into the scene, which was not something anyone in theater ever tried to do. Jim had lived and breathed the job back then, and his zeal had benefited everyone who worked with him. She'd become a chameleon, and johns had flocked to her. One of them had intended more than sex for pay, however, and had without warning grabbed her by the throat and dragged Jess through the window into his SUV, speeding off with her, intending rape. She'd had to get him under control while her backup scrambled like hell to reach her.

Her abductor had turned out to be a serial offender. Jess's observations had been critical in obtaining search warrants, developing lines of questioning, and eventually offering testimony that had helped convict him of the rapes of more than twenty women in the area.

Jess had made detective not long after that performance. Jim, seeing his own zeal and sense of mission in her, had been one of her staunch supporters in that promotion.

"So I owe you again," she said.

Jim, fifty, still married to his work, and, if rumors were

correct, recently divorced for the third time, said, "You make your own breaks, Gracie."

Jess rolled her eyes and smiled at that nickname. It had dogged her throughout her career, but it wasn't insulting when Jim said it.

"My name is actually Jessamyn Brubaker," she said to the other two detectives. "I prefer Jess."

"And yet *everyone* calls you Princess Grace," Jim said.

Jess sighed. "But you're the only one who does it to my face."

Jim laughed and turned to his colleagues. "See, she looks like Grace Kelly. And when she *wants* to"—and here he rolled his eyes—"she has these finishing-school airs."

Jess looked at Jim sidelong, and saw that he was laughing at her embarrassment. "Someone long ago once told Jim he was amusing." She looked him in the eye and said, "Whoever told you that lied to you, Jim." She kept a straight face while she said it.

Jim snorted. "Like I said, finishing-school airs. Anyway, this is Captain Howard Booker, supervisor of HSCU."

Booker, the standing detective in the good suit, nodded to her.

Jess studied him with interest. Fiftyish, she decided, very tall, with a short-cropped Afro going to gray, coffee-brown skin, and dark, watchful eyes. She leaned across the table and shook his hand. He had a thin hand, long spider-leg fingers, a good grip. She said, "It's an honor to meet you."

Booker smiled politely. "Thank you for coming out this morning," he said. His voice, high and reedy, wasn't the voice she'd expected.

The captain excused himself, leaving Jess with Jim and the detective she hadn't met yet.

Jim said, "And this is Charlie Sweeney. My partner.

Charlie has a wife problem." Jim winked at Jess. "He's still married to the one he started with."

Charlie didn't laugh. "Only two more years of you," he said to Jim, then reached across the table, smiled at Jess, and shook her hand a little too hard.

She guessed that Charlie was a few years younger than Jim. He had a bodybuilder's physique, a street cop's brush cut that made him look younger from a distance, and a wary, seen-it-all gaze. Short, stubby, wide hands with a lot of hair on the backs.

Jess asked Charlie, "Is Jim still leasing child brides on the two-years-and-trade-'em-in plan?"

"You really do know Jim," Charlie said. "Glad you could join us, Jess." He would have sounded like Darth Vader, if Vader had come from Georgia. "Welcome aboard. They tell you anything about our little mess here?"

Jess rolled her eyes. "Yeah. Two things. Dress nice. Be early."

Jim laughed. "That's all I gave them. We're trying to keep this case from landing in the papers with hundred-point headlines, though it's going to eventually. It would be a very good thing, however, if it did it about the same time we solved it."

Jess took a seat beside Jim, across from Charlie. "So what do you have? And how can I help you?"

"What Jim and I have," Charlie said, "is probable serial homicide. We have three victims so far that we know of. The first was murdered eight months ago—white twenty-one-year-old Mila Petushka, stripper at Goldcastle Gentlemen's Club. Then two months ago, same MO, Bernadette Chevalier: white, twenty-three, stripper at Goldcastle Gentlemen's Club. And finally, three days ago, Gloria Houseman. Twenty-one. Also white. Stripper at Goldcastle Gentlemen's Club."

"Correct me if I'm wrong," she said, "but I thought serial killers were careful not to take their victims from the same place each time."

"You're not wrong," Charlie said. "But that's only one of the irregularities with these murders."

Jim nodded. "The first known body was found eight months ago on a softball field pitcher's mound in Rhyne Park in Cobb County, and the Cobb County Sheriff's Department picked it up and started working it. The second known body was discovered four months ago on a picnic table in the pavilion at Pinckneyville Park in Gwinnett County, and the Gwinnett County Sheriff's Department started working *that* case. Both bodies were found within hours of death; the killer left them very prominently displayed. The third girl landed in a flower bed on a bit of green south of the zoo in our very own Grant Park three days ago, which was when the Atlanta PD got involved. However, the officer responding to the call happened to have a friend on the force in the Gwinnett Sheriff's Department who'd been talking about their stripper find, and our officer realized that his body fit the same MO. So he did some digging, located the other case that fit his parameters, triangulated the killer into the heart of Atlanta based on the body dump locations, and passed the three cases on to Homicide/Robbery. And they, in turn, passed everything they had on to us. They don't have the manpower to expend on this. We do."

Jess nodded. HSCU ended up with the cases that would run the overburdened zone homicide departments into the ground. It got the cases that crossed jurisdictional lines or had multiple victims, extended timelines, celebrities on either end of the bullet, or other complications.

"I'm guessing we assume we haven't located all the victims?" she asked.

Charlie sighed. "Good guess. After we were brought on board, the FBI and the Georgia Bureau of Investigations showed up, of course. To the *great* joy of all involved," he added with a snarl. "Though the FBI and the GBI are in enough of a pissing contest with each other over territory that they might leave us alone to get some goddamned work done. Before he locked horns with the GBI investigator over turf, though, our Feeb consultant gave us a profile. Killers are—he says—white males, late twenties to mid-forties, neat and well organized, college-educated and working in well-paid white-collar or executive jobs."

"Killers? Plural? Serial *killers* working together?"

"We'll get to that," Charlie said, voice grim. "The killers are planning the killings, are meticulous in the handling of the bodies, and are unlikely to leave us any crime scenes in the future. All three known victims were murdered else-where and dumped in locations that involve police organizations which historically have not worked well together."

Jim said, "So the killers have given this some thought. To this profile, we can add that crime MOs are identical—and all have the marks of organized killers who have had time to work out their method. We aren't getting the prac-tice kills, before our murderers had their kit together or had all the elements of their fantasy in place."

"But . . . more than one serial killer working together. That's not unheard-of, but—"

Charlie cut her off. "There are three of them," he said. "*That's* unheard-of. We have trace for a blond guy, a red-head, and a brown-haired guy."

"Christ. And the GBI *and* the Feds," Jess muttered.

Jim and Charlie made identical growls, and Jim said, "Oh, yeah. Everybody wants to get a dick in this one. But it's Booker's job to entertain the Feebs and Geebs. So far, he's been on top of it."

Jess thought for a moment. "The profiler give any sug-gestions on how long these guys might have been in busi-ness?"

"Years, probably." Jim sighed.

Jess frowned. "Three killers working together. That doesn't work too well over the long haul. They will have made mistakes. Over a period of years, one or the other of them will have been stopped, taken in for questioning, maybe arrested for something related to a victim. Serial killers almost always have close calls for years before justice catches up with them. And with three of them, one or the other should have turned state's evidence on the other two by now."

Charlie gave Jim a meaningful look and said, "Okay. *Now* I believe you."

Jess was curious about that comment, but not all that curious. She was used to being doubted, written off as a Barbie doll with a gun. Police work was still very much a man's world. She'd found that excellence was the best defense against prejudice, so she strove to be excellent. But excellence had to be proven face-to-face, so she ended up winning her colleagues over one by one. She didn't let it bother her. Much.

"Those thoughts have crossed our minds," Jim said, ignoring Charlie's remark.

"Any chance it's one killer, and that what looks like evidence . . . isn't?"

"Well, there's always a chance, but it doesn't seem like the best chance. First off, forensics has cleared the semen samples of any lubricant or spermicide traces."

"Which would make semen obtained from condoms unlikely," Jess said.

"Yep." Charlie glowered down at the stack of murder books. "Second, fiber and hair samples from three assailants are consistent across all of our known victims. The possibility of lab screwups exists, of course. Or that the actual killer reacted violently to either seeing the victims having sex with multiple partners, or as a follow-up to being a participant himself."

"That would work," Jess said.

"Not as well as you might think. We are keeping that possibility open. But see . . ." Charlie sighed.

Jim took over. "The MO on each of these is ugly. Signs on each girl of bondage, forcible rape, and torture before death. According to the medical examiner, death is by exsanguination, with the dancers hung upside down by their ankles while their jugulars are cut with surgical precision."

"Good God," Jess murmured.

"That's not all. Postmortem, the bodies are washed, hair is done up, makeup is applied, and the victims are raped again by each participant. As a final step, the girls are dressed in stripper costumes and removed from the scene of the crime to various dumping sites."

Jess sat there for a moment, staring down at her hands, feeling sick. She took a long, slow breath, looked up at Jim, and said, "All the surviving samples, then, are postmortem."

"Right. Same three men every time. So Mr. Fucking FBI assures us we have a three-member serial-killers' club on our hands."

"You don't like Mr. FBI?" Jess asked, managing a small grin. FBI intervention in his cases had always been a major sore spot with Jim.

"He's a pompous ass who keeps waving his doctorate in our faces like it's a bigger dick. And if he says, 'That isn't the way we do things at Quantico' one more time, we're going to show the arrogant prick how we do things in Georgia." Jim paused and glanced over at Charlie, who nodded, assumed an exaggerated, menacing expression, and cracked his knuckles slowly.

Jess laughed.

Jim said, "Charlie and I hate the serial-killer-club scenario, for the reasons you mentioned and more. But we haven't been able to come up with anything else that works."

"Here—have a look." Charlie passed Jess the three murder books, one labeled *Petushka,* one labeled *Chevalier,* and one labeled *Houseman.* Each was a thick ring-bound notebook with a photo of the victim taken when she was still alive on the cover, and pages of daily work on the investigation, lab results, witnesses questioned, and other details inside. Jess skimmed the daily work, then pulled the crime-scene photos.

They weren't at all usual for murder victims. All three women were completely dressed, albeit scantily. G-strings, high spike heels, bustiers. Dressed for work, Jess thought.

Each girl's features were composed. Eyes open, no sign of distress, anguish, or fear. Makeup was unmussed. So was their hair. None of the girls had visible wounds. No visible blood. The ligature marks on wrists and ankles were almost invisible, as were the small, neat incisions over each jugular. Jess could see where makeup had been applied as a coverup for the injuries, as well as cosmetically.

Each victim was pretty. Good figure, good face. Each was young. Each had been posed in a magazine-centerfold position.

Jess looked up and frowned. "What kind of makeup was used on these girls?"

Charlie sighed. "Your basic drugstore brands. We got lab results and I went out to see where I could find the brands listed. *Everybody* has them. We had some hope that we'd find something exotic or expensive that we could track, but no chance. If the store has 'Dollar' or 'Mart' in its name, all this shit is there."

"This is a complicated case," Jess said, looking over the

murder books. "But you have everything well in hand. So why do you need me?"

Jim, who had been staring at the victims' pictures, turned to Jess. "Because you've worked undercover. You were a damned good cop when I worked with you. You've maintained an excellent record as a detective since. Your one shooting was righteous; your marksmanship records are top-of-the-line. Your partners and your superiors praise your work without reservation. We've been through your packet, looked over your commendations and your background. Plus, you used to dance." He smiled a little. "Something you never bothered to mention to me."

"Never seemed much point," Jess said. "I was going to make dancing my career. But I ended up doing this instead."

"Any chance you've kept up with the dance?"

"I use ballet as part of my daily physical training regimen. Minimum of an hour a night, four nights a week." She smiled a little, and lied a lot. "One of those inexplicable obsessions, you know?"

"For us, it turns out to be a good thing. Good obsession. You have the skills we need. I'm hoping you're still fairly calm about gender issues, because if you aren't, in about three seconds I'm going to get myself sued for sexual harassment."

Jess laughed. "I'm still me, Jim."

"That, too, is a good thing. Glad to hear it. Then—and please don't take this the wrong way—you also have the look we need. You're pretty. You have a good body. And unless things have changed, you move well in high heels."

Jess was putting two and two together. "You want me to go undercover as a . . . a *stripper?*"

Jim and Charlie looked sidelong and shiftily at each other, and Jim said, "Neither the captain nor the department would approve that. The department would like you to go undercover as a drink server at the club. A . . . you know . . . waitress."

And then there was a long pause.

A very long pause.

And Jess looked from Jim to Charlie and back to Jim and said, "The *department* would . . . but a stripper would have access to people and places that a waitress wouldn't."

Both of them nodded, saying nothing.

"And we're talking about a serial killer, and about a case that looks to get really ugly," Jess continued.

Again, the nods.

Jess got it. Jim trusted her. Trusted her enough to keep her mouth shut about something that needed to be done, and that couldn't be done officially. Trusted her not to blow the whistle on him and Charlie even if she walked away. And she trusted Jim enough to know that she could turn him down for this assignment—this unspoken request—and he would still be there for her. Because what he and Charlie were asking without asking was big.

Big enough that she couldn't sit there and flat-out say, "I'm in," because she didn't know if she had what it took to do what they needed her to do.

She stared at the murder books. At the pictures of the dead dancers.

"How good would my backup be?" she asked, and she wasn't asking how quickly help could reach her if she got into trouble dancing on the stage or working out on the floor. She was asking, if the case went bad and she got in trouble for acting outside of department approval, if anyone would be there to act as a safety net. If the captain would cover them, if anyone would stand up for them.

"Very bad," Charlie said bluntly. "All three of us would die on this one."

"You already have your twenty," Jess said to Jim. "You're risking your pension on this?"

"We're looking at the tip of an iceberg, Gracie," he said. "Ugly fucking iceberg. I can feel it. What else am I supposed to do? Be a good boy, dot my *I*s, cross my *T*s, let these girls keep dying?"

She looked at Charlie.

"I'm only two shy of my twenty," he said. "My goal in life is to get my pension in two years, retire, and move to the country so I can get to know my wife and the kids again. But I'm with Jim. Some cases, you do what you have to do. Of course, we aren't the ones who would be flashing our tits in the face of a serial killer, so we have the perspective of the chicken looking at a bacon-and-egg breakfast. All we have in this is eggs. The one who's being asked to contribute the bacon has the right to decline without prejudice."

Jim nodded again. "You're *my* first choice. Our best choice, I think. But you are not our only choice."

Those pretty, blank, dead faces stared up at her, and, like Jim, she knew they weren't the only ones. More dead girls were waiting to be found. More live girls were waiting to die.

"Phew . . ." Jess said under her breath. Get up on a stage, take off all her clothes, have strangers touch her, even if only to slide money into a G-string or a garter.

And dance her way right across the part of her life that she'd been hiding from everyone.

Jim didn't know. Charlie didn't know. Jess didn't talk about Ginny. It hurt too much. But this case . . .

"How is this going to run?"

Charlie started to say something, but Jess saw the captain heading their way again. She gave her head a microscopic shake, and Charlie's face let her know he'd gotten the warning. "We're putting together a multicounty task force. The captain is coordinating. GBI and FBI will be in the way, no doubt—we'll work around them as we can and with them as we must. However, the undercover part of the operation is small, because there's no way we can make it any bigger. We've commandeered the personnel in an ongoing Vice undercover sting who were already working inside the club—and they're pissed, of course, but murder beats vice in the poker game of life. And serial murder is the royal flush of hands."

Jim said, "So there will be Vice cops around snagging DNA samples out of trash cans and off sidewalks and anywhere else they can legally get them, ferrying them outside to our pickups. We couldn't get a bartender or a deejay in place, though we tried. We have you as our inside eyes with the dancers and waitresses. You'll wear a wire and stay in deep cover. Once you're in place, you won't come into the station, and when you're . . . working . . . you'll have three undercover guys in a surveillance van who will be taping everything you say and anything anyone says to you, and who will also get help if you run into trouble. You'll only call us when you're alone or with your partner. The only other people who will know who you are will be our bouncers—you'll meet the off-duty guys later today. Also, Bill the Tech Guy, who will fit you for your wire." He cleared his throat. "*And* your partner, of course."

The captain had been listening in. Now he stopped beside them and leaned on the table. He said, "You're going to help us with this, then, Detective Brubaker?"

"Pretty sure I will," she said.

"Excellent. One less thing to worry about." And he walked away.

Jim waited until the captain was out of earshot, then said, "He did not want HCSU to get this case. He deeply resents the likelihood that it's going to generate negative publicity for the unit. I think he would be happiest if we could prove the three cases were unrelated and send them back to their original departments."

"The full resources of the department—" Jess started to ask, and Jim cut her off.

"—will *not* be spent," he said, "on solving the murders of three strippers who, early evidence suggests, may have also been prostitutes. And who are all white, which, since it looks like we're dealing with serial killings, suggests three white killers killing white women."

Jess sighed. "Which, inside the Perimeter, makes it a minority crime of no threat—and therefore no importance—to the majority."

"Bingo," Charlie said.

"This case is a loser all the way around, then," Jess said.

Charlie shook his head. "Don't get me wrong—if we solve it and generate favorable publicity for HSCU, we're golden. We solve it, and you're made as one of the Grand Old Men, Jim'll get his Detective Three and go on to greater things, and I'll have a chance to keep my fingers locked on the ledge long enough to get that pension." Charlie's weary eyes tracked the path of the captain as he walked into his office and closed the door, and he added, "But we don't solve this . . . well, we were chosen for this case because it won't break Howard's heart to sacrifice us."

Jess sighed. "Inner-Perimeter politics?"

Jim shrugged. "You know how it is. He's political, he and the mayor are great friends, he's new to the department, and we weren't his picks. He'd be just as happy to have an excuse to replace us with guys who were."

"I'd sort of forgotten, actually," Jess said. "I've been outside the Perimeter the last eight years. Different ball game. Well, same ball game, but National League rules, not American League. Go Braves. Rah."

Jim and Charlie both laughed.

"Most serial murders remain unsolved for years before the killer is caught—and they generate bad publicity for the departments working them the whole time. So basically,

I'm on a sinking ship," Jess said. "If I sign on, my best odds are that I'm going to lose my career over this—that we aren't going to solve it, and that the three of us are going hang as scapegoats."

"That's it."

She gave Jim a tiny smile. "And I was your *first* pick?"

Jim shrugged. "Figured you'd bring something solid to the team. And, since our only assets on this are us, we'd *very* much like to solve it. Charlie and I want to still be employed on the other side of this case. We think you can help make that happen."

Jess nodded. "You mentioned a partner. Who would be . . . ?"

"Well, along with putting in a special request for you, Charlie and I have called in a . . . private consultant," Jim said. "An old friend of ours. We've worked with him before. We're paying him out of our own pockets. He's going to be sticking close to you in his role as a customer, and you're going to get friendly so you can sit and talk to him without raising suspicion. And so you can . . . um . . . pass things to him from time to time."

Jess studied Jim and Charlie. Their eyes had gone all hinky, and they looked like they were trying to slip something past her. She knew Jim—he had a hell of a poker face, and it had just fallen apart. So this made her all kinds of suspicious. "The bacon is getting a bad feeling about this," she said. "Well, a worse feeling, anyway. What *kind* of things?"

"Notes. Items you pick up—bits of costumes, stuff lying around backstage—nothing that could be useful as evidence. Just . . . things that belong to the women who work there."

This sounded completely wrong to Jess. "Guys . . . what are you doing here? What kind of consultant is this?"

Jim's voice dropped lower. "A psychic. He won't be

contributing in an official capacity, of course. He's off the record."

Jess rolled her eyes and stared at the ceiling. "Jee. Zus. Christ. You're *shitting* me." She kept her voice low, but it was an effort. "We're working a serial killer case, we're tiptoeing down the wrong side of a very fine line, we already have everything to lose . . . and we're going to take a side trip to woo-woo land?"

"The psychic is solid."

"A solid psychic? Who is best friends with the reliable politician, no doubt. So when this turns into a media circus, we're going to make sure we have the clowns right up front."

Charlie said, "I get the feeling you're not crazy about psychics."

Jess looked sidelong at Jim. "You were *there* the night all of us watched that nutjob destroy our credibility on the Bleeker case. We had a good, solid, case, and that monster *walked* because the defense found out the department had used Madam Whassername, and they dragged her in to testify on *their* behalf. She killed us with the jury. Shadow of a doubt? She was a whole fucking eclipse."

She turned back to Charlie. "'Not crazy about' is too mild a term. I loathe . . . I despise . . . I *detest* psychics. I like good police work. I like rational thought. I like good science—forensics and DNA evidence and careful note keeping. Preserving the chain of evidence—very big on that. I like using all my senses to put the pieces together into a sharp, coherent picture that a goddamned shitweasel defense lawyer can't pull apart by floating the case out in front of a jury and discrediting it."

Jess heard herself getting loud, and noticed a couple of heads in cubicles turning her way. She took a long breath and lowered her voice. "Pardon me. That should be *Mr.* Shitweasel Defense Lawyer. Must remember to show proper respect to officers of the court. But the second Mr. Shitweasel Defense Lawyer dangles fucking Madam Griselda communing with the spirits for the benefit of the police in front of our twelve upstandings, all our credibility goes *right* down the shitter."

Charlie laughed and told Jim, "Yon Princess Gracie hath a potty mouth, m'lord."

Jim sighed heavily and told Jess, "If it makes you feel any better, Hank is going to hate you, too."

"Hank? Your psychic is named *Hank?* Hank the Psychic?" Jess couldn't help herself. She snickered, but then shook it off. Because this mattered. Because psychics screwed up cases and discredited detectives and made shit up after everything was over when they were talking to the press. With their hindsight a hell of a lot clearer than their foresight, they told the goddamned reporters that they'd told the police way back when this started how to solve the case, but that nobody would listen to them. And they got in the way during the case. And they made juries roll their eyes and wonder, if the cops were consulting psychics, why anyone needed cops.

And psychics were frauds, too—money-grubbing scammers out to wring every last cent out of desperate people who had run out of other options. Yeah, Jess had a chip on her shoulder about psychics. But it was a well-earned, perfectly legitimate chip.

The psychic, on the other hand . . .

"*He's* going to hate *me?* Why? And who the hell would go to a psychic named Hank?"

"To answer your second question first, only Charlie and me," Jim said, and Jess didn't miss the quiet determination in his voice. "Hank doesn't do psychic work professionally. Right now, he teaches martial arts and self-defense courses. The psychic thing is something he does only for us, by special request." Jim rolled a pen back and forth over the table with his palm, hesitating. "As for why he's going to hate you . . . you're pretty." He took a deep breath and said, "You may have good reasons for hating psychics, but I guarantee you Hank has equally good ones for hating pretty women. In spite of which, the two of you are going to have to work together, because we need both of you. Furthermore, we need both of you to pose as friends—platonic friends—because that will give him a reason to be there every time you're there without raising suspicion, and will still let him circulate around the dancers and waitresses."

Friends. Oh, good. Jess understood that she was not in her house, this was not her party, and she was a guest who could be removed for bad behavior and replaced by one to whom this case did not matter so much. And Jim was giving her a shot at getting into HSCU. It wasn't a good shot, maybe, but sometimes a bad shot was the best shot you got.

There was more to it than that, of course. She was driven; she had been driven for every day of the thirteen years since her world fell apart. This case had all the earmarks of a loser, a disaster, the reef upon which she could wreck her career. She had a clear, simple out. She could say, "No, thanks," and walk away, and nobody would think the worse of her. She might not have another shot at HSCU— but she wouldn't be flushing eleven years with the APD down the tubes, either.

She wanted to say no. It would be the smart thing to do. It would demonstrate that she had developed a reassuring instinct for self-preservation in the last few years.

Instead, she said, "All right. Bring on the clown. I'd work with Bozo himself to be a part of this case."

"Thanks, Gracie. That's all I ask. I have to make a phone call," Jim said. "Go ahead and look over the files; pay special attention to our interviews."

Charlie stood, too. "I'll leave you to read, Jess. And

thanks from me, too. If you have any questions, I'll do what I can to answer them."

Twin six-year-old girls, blond and blue-eyed, sat breathlessly beside their mother as the curtain went up on Firebird *and the dark, low notes from Stravinski's score shivered out over the audience. The Prince crept onto the stage, into the evil ogre's forest, and discovered the glorious Firebird, and the little girls sat silent, enraptured, won over by dancers who—weightless, glorious, gaudy and beautiful—flew and spun and leapt across a stage transformed into a bewitching universe. The fairy tales unfolded one by one, lovely and magical, and as they watched, the sisters' hands met and fingers intertwined, and the two of them breathed as one.*

When it was over, Ginny, the elder twin by eight minutes, turned to her sister, Jess, and said, "We have to do that."

And Jess said only, "I know."

chapter 2

Jess looked over the murder books. Stared at the pictures, read the interviews, studied the forensics reports, the crime-scene diagrams, the previous detectives' notes, and Jim's and Charlie's notes—not much of their stuff, yet, of course, because they hadn't had these cases for long.

I don't want this case, she thought. *I don't.*

A hand dropped on her shoulder, and she jumped.

Jim said, "You managed to miss all the strip-club action when you were in Vice, didn't you?"

"Yeah. I only did the hooker walk," she said.

"Okay. Well." Jim put a scrawled address on the table in front of her. "You and Hank are going to go to a couple of strip clubs tonight so that you can watch how things work. I want you to go over now and get to know him. Tonight, get out, watch the dancers, watch the club scene. See what you'll be doing, get a feel for the atmosphere in these places, and start figuring out how you're going to work together."

"All right. I'll go look."

"Hank will be in Goldcastle posing as a friend of yours whenever you're working. We want you to get to know the girls who dance there as well as the other employees. And the customers. You'll be wired, and we'll get everything anyone tells you via the wire. Aside from talking everyone up, you'll be providing materials for Hank to read. He'll let you know what sort of things to look for, and how to obtain samples. Tomorrow we'll do your permits, fit you for your wire, create your fake driver's license and Social Security card and carry-concealed permit and all your other goodies, decide on your name, and work out your backstory. The day after, you'll go in and apply for a job at Goldcastle. If you don't get it first try, we have backup plans—but the club is short on dancers right now. Rumors have evidently started to spread, and Goldcastle is running great big ads in every help-wanted section in town. Odds are good they'll give you a shot."

Jess started to ask Jim another question, but Jim said, "Go meet Hank first."

She looked down at the address he'd given her, mentally placed it, and raised an eyebrow. "Cheshire Bridge Road? Not a great neighborhood."

"Good place for a dojo, though. He lives above his business."

She started to make a smart-ass comment and stopped herself before the words escaped. "On my way," she said instead.

Jim said, "Seriously—find a way to get along with him. He's a good man. Get to know him, get past your problem with psychics. We need to break this case quickly—get you into Goldcastle, solve this, and get you back out before any of us get caught—and both you and Hank are going to be in a position to help that happen." He walked her to the door and said, "This thing is only a loser if we let it be a loser. You and I have turned other losers around. We can do this. You shine on this, Gracie, and you'll be one of the Grand Old Men before you know what hit you."

Jess tucked the slip of paper into her jacket and said, "Thanks for giving me the shot, Jim. I won't let you down."

*   *   *

The dojo was a converted storefront in a seedy strip mall, stuck between a Korean restaurant and a store selling adult clothes and novelties. It had the usual yin-yang sign painted on the center of the glass, and above it KAMIAN MARTIAL ARTS painted on the glass in red and black block letters. No teaching style mentioned, which Jess found odd. Generally, martial-arts places would announce that they taught judo or karate or whatever with a giant illuminated sign that sprawled across the storefront. Maybe he couldn't afford one of those signs, she thought, and got out of the car and strolled up to the door.

Hank Kamian had a list of classes and times posted there. Beginner. Intermediate. Women's self-defense. Advanced. Law enforcement. Translucent white rice-paper screens fitted inside the windows provided privacy to those inside. A few cars were scattered through the parking lot—mostly old. None of the stores in the strip mall seemed to be doing a brisk business. In that parking lot, Jess's shiny white Crown Vic looked exactly like what it was. She was going to have to make a point of driving her personal anytime she went to Kamian's in the future. Good covers had been broken by way less. Time to start thinking like an undercover cop again.

Kamian didn't look to Jess like a breathtakingly successful businessman, but first impressions could be deceptive. And no matter what Jim said, the dojo probably fronted for some mystic psychic-crap-of-the-Orient shtick anyway.

Jess walked through the door into a makeshift lobby. She saw a small desk, phone, signup book, a rack full of Japanese-style uniforms in black, and two cabinets with different kinds of gear and belts of various colors. Nobody at the desk, though. Behind the lobby, a solid wall and the sounds of thudding and grunting, and a deep voice issuing curt, quick commands.

A little shiver uncoiled low in Jess's belly. God, that was a good voice. She had always noticed two things about men first: their voices and their hands. This was one of those voices that rippled through her like the low notes of a well-played cello. She felt her skin prickle, and stared down at her arms. Goose bumps.

She waited in the lobby, but no bell had rung when she came through the door, and no one seemed to be interested in heading out to see what she wanted. After a few minutes, she kicked off her shoes and put them in one box of the shoe rack beside the door, then walked back toward the sounds of bodies whooshing through the air and crashing back to earth.

Six men and three women occupied the room. They wore black uniforms, black belts, no patches or badges. One man had his back to her—he was the one with the voice, and he was issuing commands. The others were throwing one another and attacking one another with amazing precision. There were some big guys, and some small women. But everybody was doing the throwing, and everybody was doing the flying. It looked rough and painful. And impressive.

She didn't recognize the style.

She stood quietly, and the people facing her ignored her completely. The man with his back to her ignored her, too. She was okay with that, actually. She didn't have anywhere else to be, and she was impressed enough by what she saw to think that she might be interested in adding some of the moves to her regular workout.

Besides, some of the men made for nice scenery, including the one in front of her, who along with his excellent voice had very good hands. Muscular, nicely veined, sturdy, with squarish fingertips. He had a nice set of shoulders, too, and hints of a great ass, though in baggy black judo jammies, it was hard to tell.

She wasn't shopping, but it was always fun to look.

Since he was the one in charge of the class full of black-belts, she guessed the man leading the class was Hank Kamian, the person she had come to meet.

The class went for a good ten minutes before he said, "Break," and everyone stopped and bowed.

Then, and only then, did one of the men say, "You have a guest, sensei."

And the man in front of her turned, and she had two impressions of him, one right after the other. The first was a stupid little thrill as his face came around and she caught a quick glimpse of a chiseled jaw, Roman nose, and gorgeous dark eye, and the second was shock as he came the rest of the way around and she saw that something horrible had once happened to the other half of his face.

And she thought, *Meet the eyes; don't stare.*

It was like looking at two people. He'd had a lot of very good reconstructive surgery, but it had been good surgery on massive damage. He still bore scars from it. The scars weren't as visible, though, as the immobility of the right side of his face when contrasted with the mobile, vital left side.

She bowed—force of habit from too many years in too many dojos—then held out her hand and said, "Jess Brubaker. Jim sent me over," and felt his hand clasp hers. Warm. Strong. A good, good hand. A good voice. A great body. And that face. She couldn't help but wonder what his story was, and at the same time, she didn't want to know what his story was. Because the story might make him someone she could like, and she didn't want to like him.

She gave him a polite smile and thought, *He's a psychic. Concentrate on that.*

She'd seen a flicker of surprise in his eyes. That vanished quickly, though, as he looked her up and down as if he were a food critic presented with a bad meal. "Hank

Kamian," he said in the voice that gave her goose bumps. He released her hand. "I have another twenty minutes on this class. I'd like to finish it out, if you don't mind, and then you will have my full attention." His voice was polite. Cool. Distant. All-the-way-to-the-moon distant.

"Not at all," she said, feeling irrationally hurt by his dismissal. "You mind if I watch?"

"No, ma'am. Not as long as you keep off the mats."

And he led his students back into hand-to-hand techniques, then two-on-one defenses, and then a flurry of stick fighting. And then into a cooldown.

Jess had recognized some jujitsu in the fighting style, and some Kempo, and maybe some karate. But it was an odd style that looked to her like something Kamian might have developed on his own. It looked efficient. And fierce. Nice combination of offensive and defensive moves, of upright and grappling styles.

Kamian turned to her once the class filed out, and said, "How much did Jim tell you?"

"I know what I'll be doing. And that I'm way out on a ledge with this. Not a lot of assets, whole lot of liabilities. All he told me about you, though? That you teach martial arts, which I could have figured out on my own, and that you're a psychic."

And that you hate pretty women, she thought. But she didn't throw that in.

She had to make a concerted effort not to reach out and touch the scars along his right cheek and jaw. Time had silvered them to the point where they were less noticeable than the stillness beneath and around them. She would guess Kamian had had some of his jawbone rebuilt. Probably his right cheekbone. The right side of his mouth didn't move much when he spoke, and the muscles on the right side of his face seemed almost frozen.

Kamian sighed. "Shrapnel," he said. "From a grenade. Quite some time ago now."

Jess jumped and met his gaze. "What?"

"My face. You were wondering."

"I apologize, Mr. Kamian. I hadn't meant to stare."

"You weren't staring. But your focus was on the left side of my face, which is what polite people do rather than stare at the right side."

Yeah. He probably did get a lot of that. "What happened?" she asked, deciding she might as well get it over with.

"Beyond the fact that it was military and classified and I don't do that sort of work anymore—nothing I can talk about."

Jess nodded. Which meant that he could have been Special Forces of some sort, or black ops, or regular service, or God only knew what else.

So why was he teaching martial arts and sidelining as a psychic consultant for the cops?

Jess said, "I'm here so that we can get to know each other. This will be an initial give-and-take, an opportunity for each of us to feel that we're on solid footing working with the other." She withheld a sigh; she didn't think she was good enough at mind games to pretend she was happy about what was coming, but she could at least be polite. "So that we have something to work with when you take me around to strip clubs tonight—"

"When I *what?*"

Jess stopped. "Jim told me that was the plan."

"Then that will be fine, Detective." Hank looked annoyed, but it was the sort of annoyance that expressed itself in chilly politeness.

Jess frowned. "Mr. Kamian, clearly you dislike me. That's fine. I have to admit that I don't like . . . psychics. So we're both starting with a disadvantage in working with each other. But I don't see why that has to be obvious. Do a little acting. *Pretend* you like me. I'll do the same."

His mouth twitched at the left corner. "Pretend. Sure. Guess I'll go buy a sugar-daddy suit for tonight."

"Sugar-daddy suit?"

"Some rich-stiff silk crap that will make everyone think they know why you'd be willing to be seen with me."

Jess tipped her head to study him. "You have a great body. Good hands. A terrific voice. A face with . . . character. The fact that you're a flake isn't visible, so why couldn't I be your girlfriend?"

"Flake?" He laughed, but it wasn't a friendly laugh. "Nice line otherwise. Very smooth."

Jess shrugged. "Jim told me he needed both of us on this case—not that we had to like each other. But you know why we're doing this, right?"

"Jim was very clear about why we're doing this."

"Then dress like a normal guy and pretend you like me. Or don't. You want to treat me like shit, I'll pretend I'm the sort of woman who gets off on that, and we'll do our jobs *that* way." She suppressed an unprofessional burst of anger. "I can't imagine how Jim thinks a psychic will help us, but he does. And I trust Jim. He and I go back a lot of years. So I'll work with you, and I'll get along with you to the extent you get along with me." She kept her body relaxed, though her hands wanted to clench into fists. She was angry, but she was also a professional in a line of work that didn't tolerate emotional outbursts. "But you remember *why* we're doing this, and then you remember that, whatever job you're doing for Jim, your *other* job is to not fuck up our case. Because we get only one shot to put this case together and prosecute it; if the case is ruined by *anything,* including things I do or things you do, the killers will walk, and no one can touch them on any of these murders again. Ever.

What we're doing here *matters,* Mr. Kamian. And we won't get a second chance to do it right."

"I'm not going to screw up your chances of catching these guys," he told her. "And I'm not going to turn this series of crimes into some sort of self-promoting media circus, either, which is what you're worried about, right? Jim and Charlie are the only people who know that I do the . . . ah . . . psychic thing, and I only do it for them, to give them a little extra edge from time to time. Jim knows about me because he's been a friend of mine for quite a few years, and when I fell across the psychic talent, I had to tell someone. He was the guy I trusted."

Jess maintained her appearance of composure. "Well, now I know, too."

"Yeah," he said. "Now you know. But you're not going to tell anyone, right?"

"Not a chance."

She wouldn't, either. She had no intention of admitting to anyone that she was partnering up, however temporarily, with a self-designated psychic.

Hank sighed. "So I'm supposed to take you to strip clubs tonight."

"So says Jim."

"I'm not a frequenter of the strip-club scene. There are some in this neighborhood, though."

Jess rolled her eyes, which she knew wasn't terribly professional. But . . . please. "Some? Close your eyes and throw a rock. And nothing personal, but this is a crap-ass neighborhood. The strip clubs *here* are going to be shit-holes."

Hank looked startled, but only for a second. "Darlin'," he drawled, "I'm guessing you didn't spend much time in Vice."

"As little as I could manage."

"Right. From my days in the army, I can state categorically that *all* strip clubs are shitholes," he told her. "Some of them just have prettier furniture."

She grinned a little. And then she cocked her head to one side and said, "Army, huh? I still have a couple of friends in the army. What was your MOS?"

"Eleven-BV." And when she raised an eyebrow, he translated, "Ranger infantryman."

"Rangers. Wow," she said, and for a long moment she didn't say anything else. She was impressed. She tried fitting the Rangers thing with the psychic thing, wanting to figure out which part of him would be the part she would be dealing with—the part she admired or the part she detested. At last she said, "Well, I'll take your word for it on the strip clubs, then. The one I walked into back when I was in school was awful, but I figured it was a bad example."

The second it was out of her mouth, she wanted to take it back. He was staring at her like she'd just said the most fascinating thing in the world. "You? Went into a strip club in college?" He chuckled and touched the back of her hand with his fingertips again and asked her, "Why?"

She almost couldn't breathe. She pulled away from him, feeling her muscles locking up, feeling her heart starting to race. She glanced down at her watch and said, "Look at the time," and with that pulled her keys out of the hidden pocket in her suit jacket. "I'll meet you back here, shall I? Since your last class for the day is at seven, why don't we say eight tonight? And I'll be dressed appropriately for going to sleazy places." She knew she sounded exactly like a society matron being panhandled by a bum. But she couldn't stop herself.

She stalked to the front door, grabbed her shoes, and was outside getting into her car before he even had a chance to respond.

*   *   *

Hank was discovering he could not have been more irritated at Jim. A friend would have warned his buddy about what was coming. A friend would not have dumped this icy Viking on him and expected him to deal with her.

Jess Brubaker was Hank Kamian's nightmare, and what was worse, Jim had to have known that when he chose her. Because she was another tall, beautiful blonde, and when Hank looked at Jess, he was right back in Walter Reed again, discovering his brand-new psychic gift of psychometry—of knowing hidden truths about people by touching them or things they had touched—by holding the hand of his beautiful blond fiancée and discovering all the different men she'd been screwing while he'd been fighting for his country overseas and sending most of his paycheck back to her.

Hank looked at Jess, and she wasn't the blond bitch. She was . . . He didn't know what she was. Something different. Someone honest. But looking at her sent shivers running up and down his spine.

He stood staring after her, the echoes of everything that question had set off vibrating like little explosions from his fingertips straight into his brain. And his gut.

"Hell," he whispered.

When Hank first saw Jess, he thought he'd known what to expect. He knew the type: beautiful, self-centered, bitchy, unfaithful.

When he shook her hand, he discovered he'd been wrong. She felt straightforward and solid to him. And she wasn't repulsed by his injuries. She was startled. Interested. Curious. Surprised.

But not repulsed.

And with that second touch, he'd discovered that she hadn't been kidding about liking his voice and his hands, either. Or about hating the fact that he was a psychic. She'd been flat-out honest with him, which was something he'd come to believe women were incapable of being.

Her honesty was bad, because she was beautiful in a careful, frostily perfect way. But that second touch also insisted she was nowhere near as frosty on the inside as she was on the outside. And his body was entirely capable of thinking wicked thoughts about this stranger who'd looked at him and almost liked what she saw, while his mind knew that pursuing those thoughts would be disastrous.

He walked to the phone, thoughtful. Called HSCU, asked for Jim, and waited.

And when Jim got on the phone, he went straight to the heart of the issue. "You bastard. You had to pick her?"

Jim said, "Hated her that much, huh?"

"Actually, I sort of liked her," Hank said. "I didn't want to, but I did. But . . . man . . . watching her walk in here was like reliving my worst nightmares."

"She has qualifications for this that would make your jaw drop," Jim said.

"Maybe so. But I thought fucking Liseé had materialized, first glimpse I caught of her."

"She doesn't look anything like Liseé," Jim said.

"Same height, same coloring, same build. The face was completely different, of course, but after what happened in Walter Reed, I don't react well to that combination. I was . . . cold."

"Don't be. Jess is honest, she's dependable, she's not looking for anyone to give her any free rides. When I worked with her, she was just one of the guys. Not a bullshit bone in her body."

Hank rubbed his temples and leaned his head against the wall. "I know. I felt that. There is something not right about her, though—which is the real reason I called. Not sure if it's a problem. Figured I'd run it by you."

"Shoot."

Hank said, "We were talking about tonight's work, and my uninspiring neighborhood, with its walking-distance strip clubs. She mentioned in passing having walked into a strip club while she was in college. I followed up, thinking it was kind of funny—and all the color drained out of her face, and she turned into the ice Viking and stalked out of here. You have any idea what I fucked up?"

"Yeah. I know what it was." Jim was silent for so long Hank started to think their connection had been cut. Then Jim said, "It relates to the thing that killed her dream, the incident that changed her life. The reason she's a cop. But it isn't my place to tell you, any more than it would be my place to tell her that you were blown up saving the life of one of your men, or how your fiancée financed her acting career." He paused. "Or how you had to fight to get your life back."

Hank sighed. "I understand." If he closed his eyes, he could still feel the shrapnel ripping into him. He could feel the warmth of his own blood, the heady, floating feeling of bleeding out. Could hear the chopper blades pounding the air, the medics shouting at him to hang on, to stay awake. Could remember the surgeries, the nurses, the doctors, the pain.

A handful of years and endless surgeries let him walk, move, chew, and swallow. Allowed him to walk on the streets in daylight without little kids screaming at the sight of him and bursting into tears. The surgeries, though, couldn't fix him up well enough that he would ever be a Ranger again—and being a Ranger had been the only thing he'd ever wanted.

So he knew about the death of dreams. About pain in the past kept inside, and pushed out of sight. He knew about searching for meaning in the ashes.

Jim said, "She'll tell you when she's ready. Or she won't. She's never talked with me about it, and we've been

friends for years. I only know because I've read the deep
digging someone along the way did and filed in her jacket.
I can only tell you that she couldn't be more motivated to
solve this case."

Hank said, "Then I won't push. If she tells me, she tells
me."

Jess hadn't handled that at all well. She'd fled, which
was ridiculous. If she hadn't been such an idiot about her
exit, she might have hoped for a graceful recovery—some
blasé story that brushed close enough to the truth that it
would satisfy, but dull enough to make the issue never
come up again.

Instead, she'd managed to send up a flare the size of
Texas regarding her dance-school years and the whole
strip-club issue.

And she had never done that before. Had never faltered
regarding the details of her past. She didn't think Jim knew
about Ginny. If he did, he'd never said anything. None of
her partners had ever known. A lot of cops followed up on
cold cases in their off time, and Jess was, as far as any of
them had known, only doing what a lot of others did. She
didn't talk about the case, she didn't leave notes around,
and she didn't let her investigations into her sister's disappearance interfere with her on-duty work. Her department
psych evals had never shown anything wrong, so she'd
never had to discuss those formative events with the department's psychiatrist. She figured she'd had no trouble
with anyone because she was so good at compartmentaliz-
ing things.

Until today, when something fell out of the box.

What did that mean?

She walked to her car, unnerved. She didn't know what
to make of Hank Kamian. He wasn't at all what she'd expected. She'd disliked him on principle before she met him,

and after standing in a room with him and talking to him, her principles remained. She simply wasn't sure they applied to him.

He didn't *seem* like a psychic.

He'd been a Ranger, for godsake. He was someone real. Someone who knew about the line, and who'd made his stand on the right side of it. He seemed like someone she could like. A lot.

She ought to turn around, walk back into the dojo, and say, "Look, I don't have anywhere I'm supposed to be right now, and I'm sorry I reacted so badly. Can we go someplace and sit down and we'll figure out how we're going to work together and see if we can get to know each other enough to understand what our roles are going to be with this job?"

But she didn't do that. She wasn't ready to go back in there and talk to him.

Why?

She almost felt like she was afraid of Hank Kamian, and getting into the Crown Vic and driving toward home, she explored that a little. She was going to have to work with this man in a situation that put her safety at risk. She had to know what buttons of hers he was pushing and why he was pushing them.

She wasn't physically afraid of him. In no way did she think that he would turn on her or hurt her. Not least because he was a friend of Jim's, and Jim would not have put her with someone who would turn vicious.

She wasn't unnerved by the way Hank looked. The scars had been startling, but they hadn't been disturbing. She considered his appearance for a moment. As she did, a quick image of a friend's old Kevlar vest flashed in her mind. The vest had a taken some lead, and he'd shown it to her afterwards. The bullets had torn it up. But not him. And that, she thought, was Kamian's face.

He'd taken some damage, but it hadn't destroyed him.

And that made him interesting. Oddly attractive. Certainly not repulsive.

But . . .

In light traffic, getting home hadn't taken too long. She pulled into her apartment complex and parked her car in her reserved space and sat there staring up at the dingy four-story building.

She could afford better, but she'd never gotten around to looking for better. The only person in her life was her, after all, and all she had was her work.

She closed her eyes.

"Jess?"

"Yeah, Ginny?"

They'd been doing arabesques together in the garage their father had renovated so that they would have room to practice without destroying the house. They were sixteen, not quite ready for pointe yet, wanting pointe so badly, but already hearing their dance instructor explaining to their mother that both of them were too tall. That they would never be anything but chorus dancers in the ballet. That they had the talent and the fire and the beauty to win lead roles, but . . .

Ginny said, "You heard what Dame Gerta said, right?"

"I heard."

"You going to stick with ballet?"

Jess had sighed. "I suppose the chorus wouldn't be so bad. But I've been thinking maybe theater. Or modern."

Ginny had nodded. "I've already decided to switch to modern. I don't have the voice for theater. And I already know I want lead roles. I've been looking at the North Carolina School of the Arts. I think I could get what I need there."

Jess sighed. "I thought we were both going to try to get

into Harrt School. It has one of the best dance programs in the country."

Ginny shook her head. "Be practical. You want us to endlessly be fighting each other for parts? I don't. You take one school, I'll take the other, and we won't each be competing with our double for every single slot."

"I wanted to be your roommate, though."

"I know," Ginny had said. "It would have been fun. But this is about the two of us being dancers. For real, up on the stage. With lights, and music. And applause."

Jess opened her eyes and stared up at the four-story apartment.

She and Ginny had figured it all out. Then fate threw Jess's new path before her as clear as a broad highway in midday. She'd had no choice. She became a cop, with her goal from the very first to make detective.

On patrol, and soliciting johns on the Tricks Task Force, and at the bar when she celebrated making detective with her new partner, she'd privately shared every moment with Ginny, and with a pain that Jess never admitted to anyone.

At the beginning, even after the dream of dance was dead and buried, Jess had still tried to have it all. She'd seriously dated a nice man, a man who could have been worth marrying. She'd gotten engaged, and she'd struggled to be everything to him and everything to her work at the same time. But she'd discovered the same truth a lot of other women had already discovered: Having it all was a lie. She could be an overworked cop and a frazzled wife and a mother who never saw her kids. Or she could choose to do one thing with everything in her, and make the sacrifices that took. Every path she followed meant turning away from all the other paths.

It was the same for everyone. Life had costs, and to live, she paid, just like everyone else.

So as she'd walked away from dancing, she walked away from the dream of marriage and children. She said good-bye to any hope of a normal life lived among good people; traded it in for a life lived amid criminals and their crimes.

Years later, she didn't know if she even believed in good people anymore. One thing she'd found, first as a uniformed officer and then as a detective, was that in almost every situation, almost everyone lied. She trusted other cops. And not always them. She never looked at civilians without wondering what sort of games they were running, what nasty secrets they were hiding, who they were hurting and how.

She was disillusioned with humanity. She didn't have dreams anymore. She had work instead, and the single goal that stretched out in front of her like an open maw that would never be filled. *Save them.* The innocent few, the helpless, the victims of the cruel, the violent, the insane, the evil.

Sitting in that car looking at her life, she abruptly realized why she was afraid of Hank Kamian.

He made her realize there was more to life than work, which was a deep, dark truth she had spent years avoiding. And she wasn't sure she could deal with that. Not yet. Maybe not ever.

Some dreams were better off dead.

chapter 3

After her odd exit, Hank wasn't sure what to expect, but Jess was right on time arriving at the dojo that evening. She got out of her car, and he shook his head at her idea of dressing for a night of sleaze. She was wearing a denim shirt with the tails out, and a short denim skirt, and high, high heels that would put her right at eye level with him. Her hair was loose, and it fell in neat lines to her shoulders. She had nowhere near enough makeup on.

Except for the shoes, she failed spectacularly to look trashy. The makeup would have to be half an inch thicker, the skirt four inches shorter, and the denim shirt a whole lot more unbuttoned to get her to that point.

She looked good, though. She had great legs. Long, muscled, tight, sleek, tapered. He'd always been an ass man, and he was deeply appreciative of good tits—but he could get behind a great set of legs, too. He considered himself well-rounded that way.

"Good evening, Mr. Kamian. Are you going to say anything, or are you going to glare at me?" she asked.

"Um . . . could we drop the 'Mr. Kamian, Detective Brubaker' thing? I wasn't glaring, I swear," he said, embarrassed that he'd been staring, and at the same time relieved that she'd misinterpreted it. "You look very nice. Though the denim shirt isn't really club wear," he added.

"Club wear doesn't offer a lot of places to hide a weapon," she said. "And . . . yes. Call me Jess."

"Hank," he said. "And thanks." He sighed. "I'm sorry about . . . whatever I said this morning—"

She cut him off with a wave of her hand. "I'm sorry I let it bother me. I didn't have a great time in school, and right around that time I ended up walking away from something I'd spent my whole life to that point thinking I wanted. I don't like to dwell on it, and I don't like to talk about it."

"Then I won't bring up your educational experiences again."

He wouldn't either. Not directly, anyway. But he was for damned sure going to find out what she had going on inside her head.

She said, "Thanks." He noticed that she was studying his outfit. He'd gone with tan slacks, loafers, and a dressy shirt that he'd had to go out and buy for the occasion. He told himself he wanted to look like a typical strip-club customer, but he'd known even as he'd thought it that it wasn't true. He could have gone into any of the clubs on his list for the night wearing a scruffy shirt and jeans, and as long as he paid, they'd have let him through the door.

He was dressing up because of her.

"We ought to go in my car," he said.

"You don't like my ride?"

She had a '69 Pontiac Trans Am, original paint—white with blue stripes—that was in good shape, and he was tempted to drool all over her ride, even if it could have used a good bath and some fixing up.

"*Good* car," he said. "But you don't get to drive us to strip clubs."

She laughed, conceding the point, and strolled around to the passenger side of his car, a nondescript older Nissan that he'd hung on to because it was reliable and he hadn't been trying to impress anyone. He went to open the door for her, and noticed that she walked like she'd been born wearing five-inch heels. He didn't get it. In his experience, only women who spent a lot of time in heels that high could walk in them gracefully, and, also in his experience, very few detectives traipsed around in stilettos.

More mystery, more proof that something was going on with her that she'd kept secret from everyone who worked with her. And maybe even from herself.

That smooth high-heeled saunter did fascinating things to her ass, though.

It was going to be a long night.

He drove her one block from his dojo to the first place on Jim's recommended list, a dive currently named Kat's Place. Hank paid the cover to the bouncer, who took the money while trying to look down Jess's shirt.

Inside, they bought the requisite drinks and carried them to a table along the side wall facing the door. The interior of the place was typical for the area: dark, grimy, loud. The girl onstage at the moment was about three quarters of the way through the first dance of her set—she still had on a miniskirt and a G-string, but nothing else. She was one of the ones who thought she could strut around the runway, wiggle her ass a little, and flip her hair a lot, and men would go wild for her. Hank sized her up in about two seconds and dismissed her, noticing that most of the customers had done the same. He and Jess engaged in a brief, almost wordless struggle over who got the chair facing the door. "I'm armed," Jess finally whispered in his ear, and he conceded the strategic seat.

They bought their required second round of drinks from a dancer working the room. And Hank watched Jess studying the dancer on the stage. "She sucks," Jess said after a minute.

"She might," Hank said. "She sure as hell isn't earning a living wage with her dancing."

Jess made a face at him. "Any idea how often this place gets raided?"

"This is the fourth club in here in the last two years. The previous three were shut down for violations. They're *lovely* neighbors."

"The 'new owner, new name' scam, huh?"

Hank nodded.

Like the majority of Atlanta's strip clubs, Kat's Place featured complete nudity. Nancy Sinatra's "These Boots Were Made for Walking" blared out of the speakers, the girl onstage stopped wriggling and started walking, and Hank and Jess stared at each other in disbelief. "Theme music," Hank muttered. "Notice the shiny latex boots. Notice the walking."

While Nancy sang, the wriggle queen stomped up and down the runway, stripping to the skin like she was undressing at the doctor's office. She grabbed her breasts a few times and flipped her hair. Ground her ass against the pole. Walked some more.

Jess muttered, "Pathetic," at the same instant that some drunk up toward the stage bellowed, "Flash me the poop chute, baby."

And the dancer turned her back on the audience, spread her legs wide, gripped her ass cheeks, and bent over.

Hank suffered a brief flashback to medical examinations in the army.

"Jee-*zus,*" Jess muttered.

"Like I said, I don't do strip clubs. But I'm told this is the worst one that's conveniently close. Jim suggested this place and three others as covering the gamut of what's available in this town, and put them in order from worst to best. We'll never have to leave Cheshire Bridge Road, and we'll get to see the full range of what's out there. From the wild days of my youth, however, I don't think you'll find that the best one is any classier overall."

"No?"

"No. What you have here is a room full of testosterone with nowhere to go, being played for money by women who wouldn't give one of these assholes the time of day outside of these doors. Doesn't bring out the best behavior in anyone."

Nancy and the boots finished to almost no notice, to be replaced by a skinny girl with enormous fake tits and about as much enthusiasm as the first dancer. Better taste in music, though. Metallica's "Memory Remains." For that, at least, Hank could forgive her.

And then Jess said, "Aw, shit."

He followed the direction of her gaze and saw that the girl who had been onstage was now strolling between tables, still wearing the boots, as well as a thong and a nearly see-through robe. The girl was flipping her hair at a customer, who said something completely drowned out by the pounding beat of the music. And the man shoved money into the thong, and the girl leaned close and pulled open the neck of her robe, and the man licked her nipple. The girl laughed and stood up, and the customer did, too, and she led him by the hand toward the very, very dark corner where Jess and Hank sat.

Hank glanced over at Jess.

"What's wrong?"

She wrinkled her nose in disgust. "If we stay, we're going to watch laws being broken in a depressingly grimy fashion. I have no intention of breaking cover. This isn't my gig anyway, and to be honest with you, I'd rather pass."

"Yeah," Hank said, glancing over as the couple got situated. "Watching strangers having bad sex isn't my idea of an evening's fun, either. Let's go."

*   *   *

Jess followed Hank through three different strip clubs after Kat's Place. The clubs had a lot of surface differences—as they moved up Hank's list, they found places with better lighting, friendly waitresses hustling drinks with winks and flirty little laughs, and dancers who had real talent. The clubs that looked like they were staying legal and weren't merely fronts for prostitution had more real dancers and fewer butt wrigglers, and Jess found herself studying the dancers' styles and their moves, and being impressed by the best of them. The pole work, when done well, was as athletic as any of the things she'd done in ballet. One dancer flipped upside down on the pole and held her body in place, completely inverted, while she did a split in the air, and finished it off with a little leg swing that spun her around the pole upside down.

The good dancers made eye contact with the customers. Smiled. *Looked* like they were having fun, whether they were or not. They spent as much time doing floor work as they did on the pole. Jess wondered how many of them were students paying their way through college, or single mothers supporting kids at home.

Some of the dancers engaged in far more physical contact with the customers than any city permit would approve. And some were cheerful beauties who chatted with customers, and stopped to talk, and did no-touch lap dances, but managed to hold the line.

The customers in the better places—the ones operating within the law—seemed to pay more attention to the rules, though Jess could see that it was basically the dancers who were left to enforce them. The customers looked and they yelled, they drank, they bought drinks for the dancers and lap dances from them; sometimes they applauded. They still called out crude suggestions to the dancers.

Even in the fancier clubs, though, Jess caught glimpses of the occasional girl taking money to be touched. Or kissed. In one club, the floor managers walked the main room with laser pointers, flashing them on dancers and customers caught in compromising acts. The little red dots served as a warning to everyone: Yes, we're watching; yes, we're counting; three and you're out. Occasionally a customer would go too far and get talked to by a floor manager in a bad suit who invariably looked like he worked for the mob.

The last place Hank took Jess to was Gazelles, upscale and elegant on the surface, with gorgeous furniture inside, chandeliers, paintings on the walls, a painfully expensive cover charge, and a massive man in a tuxedo showing them into the entertainment lounge.

They took seats away from the stages, and as best they could with the interruptions of loud music and nearly naked women dropping by to see if they needed anything, Jess and Hank followed Jim's request that they get to know each other. They made small talk that avoided any discussion of Jess's work or Hank's reason for being asked to consult. They talked about the dojo instead, the last books they'd read, physical fitness. When Hank discovered that Jess shared his passion for staying in shape, they got into a discussion of martial arts, dance and its value to combat-type situations, and training techniques . . . and they forgot for a while that they didn't want to like each other, and that they were sitting in a strip club getting background for undercover work.

Finally, though, Jess remembered that the city was paying for her and Hank to experience sleaze Atlanta-style, and she returned her attention to the club. And Gazelles proved that Hank's assertion about no strip club being classy was true. In Gazelles, the featured dancers came out in evening gowns that suggested Bob Mackie's career direction after he quit designing for Cher, and took them off in surprising and creative ways. They put on a good show. In between sets, waitresses brought drinks and chatted with customers, and flirted and giggled and suggested to the men sitting with dancers that maybe they'd like to buy the girls drinks. Dancers, dressed in robes or partial costumes, also chatted up the customers, sat at tables with some of them, did table dances for some of them—dancing not on tables but on the floor in front of the chairs of the customers. However, Jess noted that from time to time a dancer would disappear with a patron into a private room.

Even for those who stayed in the main room and followed the rules, it was the same old game. Booze to numb the customers and make them pliable, the illusion of sex to get them to loosen their wallets, and likely more than the illusion if the price was right and the girl was willing. A steady flow of cash in one direction, a pretense of interest and caring and the lure of sex in the other. No amount of lacquered furniture and oil paintings could pretty that up.

"You look miserable," Hank said, taking her hand, and Jess nearly jumped out of her skin. Pulled her hand away. Because she had been thinking of Ginny. Because this had been Ginny's life. Not for long. Just long enough for the damage to be done.

"I hate this," Jess said. "It's all . . . pretense. And people using each other."

Hank gave her an unreadable look. "Some people only want pretense. Only want to use. Or be used. If you try to give them something real, they run away." He was staring into her eyes. "That . . . that isn't you, though."

"No," she said. She yawned, and glanced at her watch. "Good God, Hank. It's four in the morning. I've been up all day."

He said, "Me, too. I wasn't watching the time." He shook his head. "Company got too interesting."

"It did." Jess smiled a little, realizing that Hank had been surrounded by enormous bare breasts all night and he'd given them cursory glances and then returned his attention to her. He had been interesting to talk to. He seemed like a good, solid man. Someone worthwhile, though neither he nor she had crept anywhere near a personal conversation. He gave off a good feel, though—and Jess couldn't see anyone who'd been sharp enough to be a Ranger being a waste of skin.

So what the hell was Hank doing shilling psychic crap at Jim?

Hank watched Jess drive out of the parking lot. Watched until her taillights vanished from view. When he was sure she was gone, he let himself into the dojo, locked it back up, then trudged up the back stairs to his place. Alone. He was very conscious, for the first time in a long time, of being alone.

Of getting undressed alone. Of getting into bed alone.

Jess had been good company. Smart, funny, open, blunt, occasionally crude. She was gorgeous, but she was unconscious enough of her own beauty that he could forget about it too. Could treat her like a friend, a colleague, someone who wasn't an object.

And then he'd suddenly realize that he was swapping war stories with the most beautiful woman he'd ever spent time with, and all of a sudden he'd lose track of what he was saying, and catch himself watching her drink or laugh or smile.

He wanted to take her to bed, of course. That was a given. He was male, she was female—and a particularly good example of the gender to his way of thinking—and they were both warm and breathing. He'd been celibate for a very long time. So of course he wanted to get her naked.

But lying there in the dark, staring at the ceiling, he was mostly seeing her laughing, hearing her voice as she leaned over and murmured shocking comments about the dancers

and the customers in his ear. He found himself smiling at
her observations about the people around them. Loving the
way she appreciated his own tales of life as a martial arts
instructor, and later, when he felt more comfortable with
her, about life as an army Ranger. She'd had her own good
stories, too. She'd been tested by fire. She was tougher than
she looked.

And if, as he replayed the evening in his mind, her
clothes kept mysteriously disappearing, if he found himself
wishing she were in bed beside him—that he was holding
her, kissing her, running his hands over her breasts and
hips, feeling her legs wrapped tight around his waist,
driving into her while she thrashed and screamed—that
didn't mean anything.

Did not mean anything at all.

He wasn't going to get involved. Not now, not ever. It
wasn't worth it, he didn't need it; he had his mission, and
the mission was enough.

Jess woke to the alarm going off at noon, sighed, and
rolled out of bed. She had to be back at HSCU by three to
get all the paperwork done for her cover identity, and to be
fitted for her wire. And before she went in, she had a fair
amount of uncomfortable, awkward shaving to do, a
process she did not anticipate with any pleasure. The problem with the shaving was that all of it had to be done in
places where sharp things didn't belong, and she chanced
surgically altering those places in the process.

On Jim's advice, she had a halter top and a pair of Daisy
Dukes in a bag along with makeup, hair spray, and other
things she'd need to transform herself from Jess into a cred-
ible exotic dancer. She threw in the stiletto heels she'd
worn the night before because they helped her feel the part.
Undercover work was all about being someone else, and
good undercover cops could become someone else with lit-

tle more than posture, movement, and attitude. Jess, knowing that her life could depend on how convincing she was,
wanted to practice the stripper character for Jim and Charlie to make sure she would be able to carry it off.

She wore as few clothes as possible, because Jim had
told her Bill the Tech Guy was going to be in there to set
her up with a wire. It wouldn't be the wire she was going to
use, though. It would be the wire that they would put together to keep Captain Booker happy and off everyone's
case—the one a waitress could wear under the skimpy
Goldcastle waitstaff costume. *Not* the one a stripper could
wear while dressed in nothing but a G-string and shoes. Jim
promised her Bill already had that one finished.

She dragged into HSCU on time, weary but game, carrying her goody bag.

Charlie was dummying up her undercover ID—driver's
license blank, permit to serve drinks, permit to perform in a
strip club, a couple of other goodies.

Jim noted her bleariness, and said "Late night?"

"Four A.M. We closed the place down. Guess I'll have to
get used to those hours." She waved the brown paper bag in
front of him and said, "I've got my stuff here. Didn't want
to drive to work dressed like this, though."

"Good plan. Go get changed. Do whatever you're going
to do to look the part. Charlie's setting up for you over
there." He pointed to the southeast corner of the big room,
behind one of the two lines of cubicles. "There's a bathroom back there for you to change in, and we'll keep the
traffic down to Charlie, me, Bill—and you."

Jess sighed. "I appreciate it. I'm going to have to go public with this look—and less—but I'd rather not do it
today."

"I understand."

In the bathroom, she shed her jacket, holster and gun,
blouse, bra, work shoes, skirt, hose, and underwear. She put

the badge on top of the pile of clothes and shivered. She felt more naked without the badge and the gun than she did without the clothes. She thought she could have strolled around in a thong with no problem if she had her badge clipped to one side of it and was wearing her shoulder holster.

She sighed, and slipped into the shorts, the tube top, and the stiletto heels, put on heavy eye makeup and dark lipstick, and, after studying the sleek lines of her hair, teased it out into a fuller, wilder look and sprayed it in place. She probably ought to get extensions. Longer, tousled hair would better fit the part she intended to play.

She finished, put her other clothes, sidearm, and badge into the bag, put the makeup on top, and then stood staring at the door that led out to HSCU.

She swallowed, feeling her pulse pick up. God, she'd forgotten all about stage fright. She was about to be wearing a whole lot less than she was at that moment and strolling between tables full of drinking, rowdy men. She was going to be unarmed. She was going to be playing a part that was her deepest personal nightmare.

And she had to look like she was having the time of her life.

Best start trying on the act right then.

She took a deep breath, pasted a bright smile on her face, and got ready to open the door. Stood there, frozen, willing herself to move forward. And sagged against the plaster wall, her hand suspended inches above the knob and the smile washing from her face into an expression of despair. With the cool plaster against her skin, she closed her eyes. This was too hard. She was thirty-four, for God's sake, and pretending to be part of a business that would have preferred everyone to be twenty-one and look eighteen. She had a good body and it was in shape. She had a good enough face. But she wasn't twenty-one, and no one was ever going to mistake her for eighteen.

And then, with her eyes closed, she could feel Ginny inside her head. Confident. Certain. Ginny would have known what to do. Ginny had done this, and had succeeded at it. And in a way, Jess was doing this for Ginny.

Senior talent show, three days before Halloween. Jess and Ginny holding their breath, ready to bound out onto the stage the moment they were announced.

A blue spotlight illuminated the center of the dark stage. "And now, Ginny and Jess Brubaker, with 'Ghost in the Mirror,'" the show's producer, Mr. Hamblich, announced.

The first dark notes from Mozart's Requiem shivered and skittered through the air. The girls had choreographed the dance themselves. They would be telling, in three minutes, the story of a girl being haunted by her own ghost. Jess was the ghost, wearing a tattered, shroudlike version of Ginny's white, diaphanous dress. Their mother had made the costumes—she'd been inspired.

Jess and Ginny were doing pointe work simply because they could. They were in top form; they were ready.

This dance, presented some months later, would win both girls openings in the dance schools of their choice.

However, in the eyes of the teenage boys who made up half of the audience in their high school auditorium, identical twin sisters in skimpy costumes and tights who not only mirrored each other's movements, but who at one point held hands and stared into each other's eyes, looked a lot more like the lesbian porn of their fantasies than the horror of a young woman coming face-to-face with her own mortality. Jess and Ginny's dance had been wildly popular. But for all the wrong reasons.

For the rest of the year, an unending stream of wishful males would be offering them money to watch "the next

time you do it." Would be inviting the two of them to par-
ties, but "only if you come together. Come. Get it?"

When Jess was ready to stay home and hide, humiliated,
Ginny encouraged her to hold her head up and keep going.
Thanks to Ginny, both of them made it to school every day,
smiled politely at their tormentors, and graduated just like
the girls who hadn't accidentally stimulated an unending
stream of idiot boys' lesbian-twin-sister fantasies.

So Jess caught her breath.

I can do this, she told herself. *I can do this better than*
anyone else could. I can do this because those dead girls
need me. Because this isn't about me at all. It's about them,
and about the job. The mission. About getting it done.

And the smile went back on her face, and this time her
hand made it all the way to the doorknob and opened it, and
she put on a dancer strut that came out of nowhere. She
swung out into the room of waiting men and did a little
twirl like the one she'd seen one of the good dancers do on
the runway the night before.

She heard the intakes of breath. From Charlie: "Omi-
gawd." A low whistle from Jim.

Yes, she thought. *I can do this.*

And she came to rest facing her audience, and found
Hank there with Charlie and Jim and Bill. When had *he* gotten there? Hank's eyes met hers, and she could see pain in
there, coming from somewhere she couldn't go.

Inside she yelled at him, *This isn't me. This isn't me. This*
is the job!

But she kept on smiling, and kept her strut, and did a little bow before walking over to get her picture taken. And
pretended the wary, suspicious look on Hank's face didn't
matter. Because this was the mission. And if she broke
when her heart fell out of her chest onto the floor, when she
wanted for reasons unknown to go over to a man she'd

barely met and explain herself, she would not be able to trust herself to stay in character when the situation inside Goldcastle got uncomfortable, when she wanted to arrest someone rather than to smile and wink and move out of reach.

Jim looked at her and nodded. "I knew you were the right one for this, Gracie," he said. "I don't know how I knew it. But you have layers." He shook his head, and laughed ruefully. "Whole lotta goddamned layers."

"All of which are in that brown paper bag in the bathroom." She shivered, shedding her stripper persona at last. "And which of you bastards turned the air conditioning up? God, it's *cold* in here."

The men around her saw the change, saw her shaking off the stranger's skin and becoming a cop again, and she could see them relax. Charlie laughed; Bill snickered. For a moment there, she had been alien to them, and they'd been tongue-tied, not sure how to react. But when she became one of them again, even in her outlandish getup, they could become themselves, too.

Charlie said, "We wanted you to be all . . . perky for your picture."

"You're supposed to take a picture of my face, dumb-ass," she said, laughing, not missing his meaning. Her nipples felt like rocks under that tube top—they had to be visible from space. She didn't know of any men who missed the presence of visible nipples beneath clothing. Men were wired that way, and she'd learned not to take it personally.

Charlie got the pictures. Bill brought in the wire and fitted her with one that lay beneath her right breast and itched like hell. He bitched at Jim for a while about the low output with the technology they had, and how they were going to need to have a lot of signal boosters hidden around the club. He and Jim agreed that they would have Hank place transmitter boosters around the inside of Goldcastle. Bill thought maybe the guys who'd been co-opted from Vice could place the boosters, but in the end they were not HSCU, and they were an unwilling part of the investigation, and Bill and Jim and Charlie agreed that "their Gracie" was their secret weapon. That she was strictly need-to-know. The Vice guys didn't need to know.

Jim vouched for Hank, who had experience placing hidden things. "Army Rangers," Jim said in a soft voice, and Bill did that little spine-straightening thing men did when in the presence of someone who had earned respect without question. Yes. Hank was their guy, too, even if he was not officially one of them.

Jess felt the same way. And she kept trying to fit her natural reactions to him into her well-earned loathing for psychics. It wasn't working. There were pieces of Hank that didn't match up.

When the photos were done and the wire was fitted and she was back in work clothes again, with her hair brushed out and the goop off her face, she got her assignment for the next day, which was to get a job at Goldcastle. Hank talked to Jim while Charlie put the finishing touches on Jess's ID kit; Charlie told her that for routine things Hank, in his role as her contact, would act as a go-between. He told her of two neutral places that she could meet with either him or Jim if she had to have a face-to-face.

"I've duped everything in your wallet that you might need. Credit card and bank card will work up to one hundred dollars in case you have a situation. Jim came up with your new name—he said he wanted to keep it simple. And your story is that your brother has non-Hodgkin's lymphoma and no insurance and you need a legal way to make a lot of money fast, which is why you want the job now. Further, you worked as a house dancer up north in Fayetteville, North Carolina. You danced in two clubs near Fort

Bragg—both of these went under years ago, so you won't
have to worry any unfortunate employers failing to remember you. You . . . ah . . . hung up your G-string after one
year of dancing, and retired until this came up."

Jess nodded. "That'll work." She looked from Jim to
Charlie. "But what if they don't hire me?"

"We'll worry about that then."

"All right," Jess said. No point second-guessing things
that she couldn't control. Her job was to give Goldcastle
every reason to want her.

"You are undercover from this point on. Go home, get
changed, memorize your new name and your story, fill in
whatever details you'll need to keep it consistent. I put together a short list of cheap rental places—you should get
one so that you can go home again once you're done with
this. You have enough cash in there for the first month's
rent at any of these places. Some of them, you get a dis-
count if you rent by the month."

"Real high-class places, huh?"

Jim smiled. "If you live in a real high-class place, why
do you have to work in a strip club to help your brother
out?"

Jess nodded.

Jim said, "Speaking of your character. You're in character anytime you're outside your own doors. Your badge
stays home, and if you carry, make sure it's your backup
weapon and not your police issue. And for God's sake, stay
away from anyone who could make you. At this point, our
serial killer could be anyone, and where Goldcastle is concerned, that anyone covers a very wide scope." He frowned.
"Got a neighbor who can feed your cats or goldfish or
whatever you have there?"

"It's not a problem."

Jim said, "Here are a list of places that rent by the day,
week, or month. Look them over; pick one. But get into

your place today. Move *before* you interview with Goldcastle." And then he told her, "Don't break cover at any
time, for any reason. We are, at this point, without any solid
theory regarding the identity of the killers, or killer, and
until we have *something,* the field of possibles is huge. The
Goldcastle employees are the usual sorts, but the clientele
consists of senators and sheiks and actors and sports
celebrities and old, rich men. Lotta foreigners, fair amount
of Eurotrash. And middle- and upper-middle-class locals,
too. If you catch the attention of the killers, we have no idea
what sort of resources they'll bring to bear to get to you. We
have every reason to believe they have good resources,
though—that these are not broke losers operating out of
their mothers' basements."

"Got it," Jess said.

"Not much chance Goldcastle will get raided while
you're there—Vice wants to get back in with its drugs,
prostitution, and gambling investigation once we get our
work done, and they want to keep everyone quiet and happy
until then. However, shit happens. You get swept in a raid,
Hank'll get you out," Charlie said.

"And if Hank gets swept, too?" Jess asked.

"We've already taken care of that."

Which meant either that Hank had fake cop ID for this
gig—which Jess found hard to believe—or that he had
something else under the table as his get-out-of-jail-free
card.

She was okay with that. In spite of the shaky footing of
her part in this, her people were behind her. She felt very
solid right then.

Of course, the weight of her Beretta and her badge at her
hip didn't hurt, either. It would be a little tougher to feel
solid when she was unarmed and wearing a G-string and
nothing else.

chapter 4

Hank hadn't been expecting what he got when Jess walked out of the bathroom door. He'd been expecting a cop in too little clothing, and instead he got a Vegas showgirl, all legs and big hair and bright smile. She'd looked like Jess. Mostly. But bad memories suggested she wasn't.

She'd become someone different. She felt like Liseé all over again. An actress hiding behind convenient faces. Someone who used men.

He waited until he had an opportunity to brush against her, lightly, just for an instant. "Jim said they're having you move into a by-the-week rental place," he said, but he only half listened to her response, which was something funny about strippers and dives. He managed to laugh appropriately. But his attention was fixed on the flash he got in the instant he touched her—of fear, embarrassment, awkwardness, pain . . . and a deep determination to do this thing she had to do to save lives.

Pain? This was more of whatever Jim had hinted at without ever opening up. Hank realized an awkward silence lay between them—he was supposed to have said something, and he hadn't. So he blurted out, "I'll go with you to look. Since you can't advertise that you're a cop, I'll debut in my friend role so that if any creepy neighbors who are watching you move in, they'll see you with someone big and ugly and mean."

Puzzlement in her eyes. He'd missed answering something that required an answer, then. Still, she flashed him a quick, genuine smile. "Thanks."

When she was done with Bill and Jim and Charlie, she and Hank walked out together. Hank didn't say anything. He didn't know what to say. He wanted to know where that pain of hers came from. And the determination, too. There was more to her than just a good cop determined to do a good job. There had been . . . what had Jim said? Layers.

Yeah. Whole lotta layers.

Jess kept pace with him easily. She wasn't talking either.

Hank knew eventually one of them was going to have to break the silence, but he had no solid basis for coming out and asking her, "Who hurt you, and when, and how?" He couldn't tell her how he knew something was wrong. He'd invaded private space inside her for no legitimate reason. They weren't friends. They weren't really anything— yet—and *that* question was far too personal for new work partners.

Out of nowhere, Jess said, "I'd like for you to show me some of the stuff you were doing in the dojo yesterday."

Which kicked Hank out of his reverie, and threw him a curveball. "You . . . what? Right. Sure."

"Because I've spent the last whole lot of years focusing on armed combat, and while I haven't let unarmed practice fall completely off my radar, I'm not sharp." She glanced over at him. Lovely face—she had a damned sweet face, soft and rounded, with very blue eyes and full lips. Kind of a sharp nose, he thought, but that gave her face strength it could have lacked otherwise. And her chin made no compromises. She said, "I'm going to be unarmed a lot of the time, and I had one nasty experience dealing unarmed with a real creep. Next time, I want to be ready."

He nodded. "If you haven't eaten, I'll take you some-place for an early dinner. Then we can check out that list of rental rooms, and after that, we can go to the dojo and claim the back room. I use it for cop classes mostly, but nothing is scheduled in there today."

"You'll still be working at the dojo during this?"

"I'll go in on the days you aren't scheduled to be in Goldcastle, but I have my instructors covering most of my classes until Jim doesn't need me anymore. So, no, I don't have to work today, but there will be days that I will, at least for a few hours."

"Thanks for giving me some of your time," she said. "As much as I can, I want to be ready for this thing."

He drove again. She was leaving the Vic at the station and driving only her personal until this was done. He could tell, from the look of longing that she gave the big white cop car as she walked past it to his vehicle, that she was not happy to be leaving it behind.

Her expression of misery when Jim and Charlie went over the whole "no badge, live undercover, backup weapon only" thing upstairs had been comical. It had made him want to like her, because he understood that part of what she was heading into so very well. The weapon, the badge, the clothes—they all became an extension of the self. In the hands of someone qualified, they became a rarely used but well-understood final solution to deadly problems for those who stepped into harm's way for the good of others. The weapon itself was the last resort, and never, never the easy solution. But it was, in some cases, the best solution. The ef-fective solution. A tool to draw the line between evil and good.

He'd been forced to lay down arms, to put away the uni-form, to walk naked back into the world, stripped of his mission and his mandate. He'd rebuilt himself into a weapon. Found new missions.

So to that extent, he understood her. Maybe he understood more than that, too. Or would, if he could uncover the parts of herself that she was hiding.

She directed him to her apartment.

When he pulled into the parking space she indicated, she said, "You can come up while I change. I won't be long, but you could get something to drink if you're thirsty. Or use the bathroom . . ."

"I'm fine," he told her, staying right where he was. "I'll wait here and watch people until you get back." He smiled a little, and nodded toward a cute young black couple running together, their German shepherd on a leash between them, and then to a tremendously fat man who was sitting on a bench beside the sidewalk with his head lolled back and his mouth hanging open.

"Yeah. I have some interesting neighbors," Jess told him, and then she was gone, running at an easy lope toward the closest building with her brown paper bag under one arm.

He studied her shoes, noting that the heels weren't all that low, and he wondered what sort of physical training she did to be able to move like that.

He had no interest in her neighbors, actually.

But he didn't want to go into her personal space. He didn't want to confront who she was away from being a detective—didn't want to see pictures of the boyfriend or the kids or the hubby or whatever it was that she had stashed away up there. Didn't want to meet her dog or cat, or see what kind of books she read or what kinds of games she played or what kind of furniture she sat in when she had free time.

He had a vested interest in her where work and mission were concerned. That pain of hers . . . that could well impact the mission. It was, Jim had said, why she became a cop.

He had no desire, however, to see who she was outside

that frame. He didn't want to find himself with a personal stake in her. He wanted to know her as a cop. He most definitely did not want to know her as a woman. Did not want to risk falling for another Liseé.

He didn't want to care.

Jess threw on jeans and a loose cotton shirt. She tucked her backup gun, a .38 Smith & Wesson Airweight, into its ankle holster, and strapped it on.

She pulled her real driver's license, her badge, and anything else that identified her as *her* out of her wallet, locked it all together in her lockbox with her police-issue sidearm, and filled her wallet with the fakes that Charlie had dummied up for her. She studied the made-up face with the big hair on those new IDs. She didn't look like herself. She looked like someone who was having fun, someone for whom life was one big party.

And then she looked at the name on the driver's license for the first time, and started swearing.

Grace Kelly Callahan.

"Sonuvabitch," she muttered.

Jim was going to have his moment of fun at her expense, apparently. She should have been more suspicious when Charlie told her that Jim had made sure she had a name she could remember.

So she was going to be Gracie for a while, God help her. She could admire Jim's logic; she was used to hearing the name, and knew when she heard it that it meant her.

But, dammit, she *hated* that nickname. And for the moment, at least, she was no fan of Jim's sense of humor, either.

Badgeless, with the wrong gun in the wrong place, and with somebody else's name attached to her face, she scrubbed her skin completely free of makeup, pulled her hair back in a ponytail, and tucked her shirttails into her jeans—tucking in a shirt was something that she hadn't done in years.

Naked. Fully dressed, she felt naked.

She hated it.

She practiced the bright smile in the mirror a couple of times, but she wasn't feeling any cheer.

Realizing that she could walk away from the apartment and never come back, and that not a single soul would be inconvenienced—not even a goldfish—did not improve her mood. A couple of her neighbors, who knew her to say hello but nothing more, might notice she was gone eventually. Maybe. No papers would pile up. The mail in the tiny, locking apartment mailbox down in the parking lot would fill invisibly, and when it was packed to capacity, her mail would stop coming equally invisibly. People would come out to turn off her services if she didn't pay them. But who would notice that? Her neighbors were home no more regularly than she was.

Walking out her door into the melting Atlanta summer, locking up, she was reminded again that this was not the life she'd wanted for herself. And then, because she was on a case that mattered to her personally, and because this case mattered so much, she pushed her dissatisfaction with her personal life out of her thoughts, the way she always did. She didn't have time for it.

The mission called.

Hank was still waiting when she jogged back to the parking lot. She slid into his passenger seat; it was a given that they would ride together while they worked out how they were going to signal each other and otherwise communicate during their mission. And she liked watching him drive; he was good at it.

But they didn't have much to say. Not yet, anyway.

Hank nodded as they passed Goldcastle on the way, and

Jess noted the neighborhood. Moderately better than the one that Hank lived in, but not spectacular. Some furniture stores, a handful of restaurants, and a sleazy little strip mall sat around the Goldcastle Gentlemen's Club, which had its own restaurant with side entrance—Sharra's—and a big parking lot in back. Goldcastle's was open for business, with a valet out front parking cars. The club had the parking lot tucked away out of sight, Jess knew, because most strip clubs did what they could to hide the presence of their customers from wives or girlfriends who might go cruising past. Goldcastle's was trying for an upscale appearance, but the look of the place did not give her a warm feeling inside.

Hank chose a twenty-four-hour diner that served all-day breakfast, located not too far from the club. "I want an omelet," he said. "Sometimes you just want an omelet."

"That works. This will still be breakfast for me, too," Jess said. "I woke up too late to eat." They settled into a booth at the back, and Jess ordered pancakes and bacon and a big glass of juice and hash browns and a couple of biscuits—this place called her breakfast "the Lumberjack."

Hank waited until the waitress was gone, then said, "You going to need someone to hold your hair back when you throw that all up?"

Jess laughed. "I do an hour or two of ballet a night, four or more nights a week. Plus katas in the morning before I go to work. Three trips a week to our training facility to lift weights. My problem is keeping weight on, not taking it off. I can't be a skinny little nothing. I have to be able to be physical, even though it's been years since I had to."

"You're a detective now. That's not a particularly physical job. Don't get me wrong. I'm all behind staying in shape. But . . ." He shrugged. "That seems like a lot."

He was right. Her obsessive nightly ritual with the barre and the cleared floor in what would have been the apartment's second bedroom was exactly that. Obsessive. She didn't do it because it contributed to her safety. She didn't do it because it was fun anymore. Those hours of dance were like penance. Like dancing on the grave of her dream. They were a painful reminder that she had turned her back on something she'd loved, to do something that kept her lonely. She thought she could have been happier as a cop if only she could have forgotten about the stage, and the bright lights, and the flow of body to music.

Everything she *needed* to do to be safe in the everyday run of her work, she could have done by keeping up at the firing range and working out in a dojo a few times a week with the other cops.

But something inside of her, some masochistic part of her, wouldn't let her let go.

She pushed that thought away. Told Hank, "Well, then . . . maybe I just like pancakes."

He nodded. "That's enough reason for a big breakfast." He frowned a little and said, "So . . . tell me about you."

"Not much to tell." She leaned back in the seat and looked out at the parking lot, at two young men who were loitering around a car parked in the far corner. "I do my job, I go home and sleep for a few hours, I go back and do my job some more. My work helps people, it gets criminals off the streets, and in a lot of ways it matters to me."

"That's good. I understand that. But if you don't mind me saying so, it sounds lonely."

"I have friends."

"Other cops?"

"Sure. Other cops and criminals make up the vast majority of the people I know." The kids in the parking lot looked up, saw her watching them, and faded away. She looked for another few seconds, then turned and grinned at him. "Not too interested in being friends with the criminals." The food arrived.

Stacks of it, most of them placed by the waitress in front

of her. Jess waited until the woman left, then said, "I'll be honest with you, Hank. You seem like a really decent guy. A hero. You have the dojo, you're teaching something valuable, and if you weren't doing that, I have no doubt you'd be doing something else worthwhile." She spread butter on her pancakes, then looked over the syrup selection and decided on plain maple. As she always did.

She poured the syrup on her pancakes, watched it fill the bottom of the plate, and put it back in the syrup rack. Looked him in the eyes. Frowned. "So why the hell are you shilling the psychic crap?"

Hank gave her a little smile. "Can you eat one-handed?"

"Sure."

"Then give me the hand you don't need, and let *me* tell you about you."

"I've heard all the vague, mystical nonsense you people spout—" she started to say, but he took her hand and looked into her eyes.

She grew very still inside. His touch—his fingers around her fingers, his warmth, his strength—surrounded her. His voice still made her shiver. She could have fallen into the depths of his eyes. She didn't believe in him, but she realized that she was tired of window-shopping. That she liked the way their hands fit together.

And she pushed that thought away.

Hank said, "You have three green dresses in your closet that you have never worn. And sometimes in the evening you go in and turn on the light in the closet and touch them."

Jess's heart thudded to a standstill, and for an instant she wasn't sure it would start again. This was not "You're lonely, and you yearn for fulfillment, and for someone to appreciate you." This was as specific as specific got, and while she was going to have to backtrack to see if there was any mundane way he'd gotten that information, at least now he had her attention.

"How did you know that?"

He looked at their hands touching. "It's a strong picture in your mind. What's more interesting is why you do it," Hank said. "You have a recurring dream about a green dress. About you, and a faceless man, and being someplace wonderful in an emerald-green dress. Your words— emerald green. But you don't think you have time for the man or all that he symbolizes: commitment, love, a future. Yet each time you find a perfect green dress, one that reminds you of the one in the dream, you buy it, promising yourself that if the moment ever comes that you can capture that dream, you'll have the one element of it that you can control."

Jess pulled her hand out of his. She had a lump in her throat and had to blink back tears, and suddenly she was afraid of him. He could see her. He could really see her— see the things she didn't let anyone else look at, see the things she didn't have the courage to look at herself. She didn't want to know any more about herself. She sure as hell didn't want him to know any more about her. She'd put away parts of her life that no one—*no one*—was ever going to think about again.

Hank gave her a sad smile. "Jess, I'm sorry. That was fresh in your mind, right up there on the surface."

She shook her head, not saying anything. She didn't look at him; she kept her head down and ate her pancakes and choked them past the lump in her throat, and she blinked to keep from getting tears in her food.

It didn't matter, she told herself. She shouldn't be reacting like this. The green dresses . . . they were a stupid game she played with herself. Nothing important. They were a little ritual she performed out of superstition. She knew when she bought them that she would never wear them, and she was okay with that.

She looked up at him. Smiled. "It's all right," she said. "Sorry about the . . . reaction. Clearly I haven't had any-where near enough sleep." She took a long sip of orange juice, and told herself to feel all right again. Steady slow breath. Separation of all the things that hurt from the sim-ple realities of living from day to day. Pain folded up, tucked away. There. Fine. Everything was back in the box, lid shut, and she was okay.

"That's all right. I didn't mean to upset you." He smiled a little. "I have to confess that I have my own ways of get-ting through being single and telling myself it's for the best." He shrugged. "I suspect if someone read me, that would be the first thing he or she picked up, too. It's . . . human nature, maybe."

Jess nodded. "So you're not married, huh? Ever been?"

"No. Long story. Boring, and not a lot of fun."

They sat in silence, with the voices of other patrons drifting around them, and the occasional click of a fork on a heavy dish.

And then, out of nowhere, Hank asked, "Why are the words 'Virginia' and 'stripper' so important to you?"

The floor fell out from under Jess. She felt like she'd been punched in the stomach. A wave of nausea rolled over her; unthinking, reacting, she pushed out of the booth and fled to the bathroom, grabbing the first stall and leaning there, hands against the back wall, bent over, gagging, try-ing not to throw up.

How the hell, how the hell, how the hell had he done that? *Oh, God.*

He acted like he didn't know. But suddenly she sus-pected that he knew a lot more than he was showing. That he was going to keep doling out these bombs until she con-

fessed everything. She felt naked in front of him. Dizzy.
Helpless.

Scared.

Everyone had secrets, she thought. Everyone had reasons for doing what they did—reasons that, after a while,
not even they dared examine. Her reasons were locked
away, and that bastard out there at the table had picked the
locks right in front of her, and opened the lid.

Her stomach heaved.

Virginia.

Stripper.

He knew, didn't he? And if he knew, who else knew?
Who else knew about Ginny? And who else knew about
how Jess had spent her free time for almost eight of her
years on the force?

At the table, Hank stared at Jess's empty place and wondered what sort of vein he'd hit.

Something big was going on inside that woman. She was
hiding something huge. Something that had beaten her until
it almost broke her. And it had to do with Virginia. With
stripping.

He had the feeling he ought to turn what he knew over
to Jim and Charlie immediately. Maybe they didn't know
about Virginia and strippers. Maybe Jess had some horrible
past as a stripper. She'd sure known the moves. Maybe
something terrible had happened to her, almost destroyed
her life.

If Jim had known about the stripper past, would he have
put her on this case? Probably not. If Jim found out, he
would drop Jess from this investigation, and bring in some
woman who didn't make Hank feel like he'd collided head-
first with a speeding train. That would be the course of action that would no doubt most benefit this case. And Hank.

And maybe even Jess, because whatever she had going on inside of her, she needed to deal with it.

One cell phone call, he thought.

Simple solution.

He looked at the cell phone in his hand.

Thought about the stricken, stunned look on her face as that relatively innocent question of his sank in.

And he thought, *Since when does a Ranger take the easy way out?*

He rose, walked back to the ladies'-room door, and knocked.

"You all right in there?"

She came out looking like hell. She was pale, had sweat beading on her forehead and upper lip, and yet . . .

She gave him a weak grin. "Underdone pancake," she said. "I'm all right now, though. And we have a whole lot of things we have to do today. Or at least, *I* have a whole lot of things. You really don't have to come along if you don't want to."

"And leave you to find a place to live while you're feeling like this?" She was going to tough it out. Whatever was going on inside that head of hers, she'd kicked it back into place again, and here she was, up and fighting.

Sonuvabitch.

How did he dislike a woman like that? He would have recommended her for promotion if he'd been her NCO. Well, once he'd gotten the truth out of her, anyway.

He said, "A cold wet cloth on the back of your neck will make you feel better."

"I'm okay. Really. I need some sort of fizzy drink while we drive around getting things done. That'll settle my stomach."

"This happen to you often?"

"Haven't thrown up in twelve years. And change," she said. "And *still* haven't."

He laughed. Sonuva*sonuva*bitch. "You have me beat by four. Came out of anesthesia on one of my last surgeries, nearly took out a nurse."

"That shouldn't even count," Jess said. "Anesthesia . . ." She waved anesthesia away with a broad sweep of one hand.

"My stomach insists that it counted." Why, talking about throwing up, did he keep seeing this woman naked? He was a normal man with normal urges, and puking didn't show up anywhere in his turn-on menu.

But.

There she was, naked all over, and he was hot and bothered and uncomfortably hard, with visions of the two of them in some amazingly creative positions, and in some shockingly public places. Restaurant table. Restaurant bar. Restaurant floor.

Well, it had been a while. She was hot. She was down-to-earth. She remembered how long it had been since she'd last barfed . . . and so did he, and he didn't know why that made her feel like a friend, but it did.

"Come on," he said, leaving too much tip on the table and picking up the bill. "You actually are looking like you might make it."

He bet if he got her into bed, he could get the truth out of her.

James Bond-ian scenarios of her confessing her stripper past in Virginia while clawing the sheets with her legs wrapped around his neck, the two of them magnificently hot and sweaty, her eyes glazed, her hair wild and tangled, him driving into her, her swearing to tell him everything if he just . . . wouldn't . . . stop.

Okay.

Now *he* really needed to sit down.

chapter 5

If their breakfast-for-dinner was a barely averted disaster, Jess had to consider it a fitting prelude for the rest of her day. Hank stuck with her while they drove around looking at horrible rental rooms. While he drove, the two of them managed to discuss how they could work together, and how they would communicate with each other. They devised a couple of hand signals so that she would know when he had something to tell her, when he had someone he needed her to check out, and when she had someone she needed him to check out.

She couldn't help noticing how carefully he avoided any hint of personal questioning after the incident in the restaurant.

So maybe he'd bought her excuse about bad food. Maybe he really didn't suspect anything.

Probably, though, he hadn't believed her. Maybe her reaction had given him some last bit of information he'd wanted, and he was going to say something to Jim. And then, for a while, her life would be awkward and uncomfortable.

She settled on the least horrible of the weekly places that had a vacancy. The studio didn't look all that secure, but the parking lot was lighted, the flimsy door at least had a decent lock, and she saw a black-and-white parked in one of the resident parking spaces near hers, so at least another cop lived close by. The studio was furnished—after a fashion—though she couldn't remember when urine-yellow Formica was a surface of choice for decorators. The table, the counters, and the cabinets were all variants of the same awful color scheme, with someone deciding that chartreuse for the bedspread and curtains made a perfect complement. A maid would come in a couple times a week to change the sheets and clean. There were a couple of lockable cabinets for personal things.

Jess didn't intend to bring much.

But she realized she did need Gracie clothes, and getting them would give her a good excuse to lose Hank. She found that she wanted very much not to be with him right then. Being with him was causing uncomfortable feelings she simply didn't want to examine.

He dropped her off at her apartment so that she could pick up her car, and he took off, leaving her to wallow in paranoia about what he might be thinking, and what he might know. She shopped for clothes that suited the character she intended to play, and picked up a few household items—a couple of aluminum pans, the cheapest four-place-setting plastic dinnerware set she could find, soap, shampoo, toothbrush, and toothpaste, and two good padlocks for the lockable cabinets. She didn't want to have anything in the place that she couldn't bear to walk away from.

She dragged her collection of bags into her new, temporary home. The furnished studio had been designed to give claustrophobes the willies, she decided. She dumped everything on the floor, debated searching out the public laundry room, and decided against it. Instead, she hung up the skirts and blouses straight out of the bag, and put the underwear in drawers.

Thongs and G-strings. *Ugh.* She was a huge fan of cotton high-cuts. She preferred coverage and comfort, and contemplating lace underwear actually *designed* to crawl up her butt filled her with no joy.

She put away her other purchases, then sprawled on the bed and stared up at the ceiling, cell phone in hand.

If she went to Jim now and told him the truth, she'd have a lot less to deal with than if Hank started talking. Odds were that Jim would be fairly understanding, even if he *would* almost certainly take her off the case.

The fact was that the whole reason she'd become a cop was to use the resources available to the police to find her sister. To let her detective's shield open doors that nothing else would open. To imply an official weight to pressure people into the truth. If it had all been to no avail, that didn't change anything. If, over the years, she'd transferred her failed mission into a relentless dedication to her work that benefited *other* people, that didn't excuse anything.

She hadn't become a cop for any noble reason. She'd become a cop out of pure self-interest. To find out the truth for her mother and herself.

And it had been for nothing. Ginny was still gone. Out there somewhere, maybe, but if she was, she was nowhere that Jess could reach.

Someone knocked on her door. She jumped a little, and yelled, "Who is it?"

"Jim!"

And her heart clogged her throat. Here it was, then. Hank had passed on whatever he'd discovered to Jim, Jim had put everything together, and now he was going to give her time in private to explain.

She opened the door and let him in, and for a moment he stood there staring around the single dimly lit room with an expression of horror on his face. "Gracie," he said, and his voice was a croak, "we gave•you enough money to get something better than this."

She shrugged. "This was the best of the places that would let me in today. Besides, it's temporary." She suspected as she said it that the place was going to be a lot more temporary than either of them had planned.

"It's horrible." He turned to his right. "Good Christ, the linoleum is piss yellow with bloodstains."

"It is not. That rusty brown is actually part of the pattern. Though I did get down on hands and knees to check."

"Did you wash with Lysol afterwards?"

"Thought about it." And then, because she wanted to get everything over with, she said, "What brings you by?"

"Hank told me which place you'd chosen, and gave me your room number—which is lucky, since you haven't reported in yet—and told me you two got some good work done today, but that I ought to come by here and tell you to move out immediately."

She raised an eyebrow.

"He didn't like this place any better than I do." Jim gave her a stern, fatherly look, then walked past her to the daybed, and leaned across it to look out the room's one window. He said, "This place is a nightmare. That fire escape looks like it's about to rust right off the building, and the alley below is completely unlit. And all this window has to keep it shut is a thumb-lock." He turned to her. "You know how often patrols have to come out here to deal with problems?"

"I figured frequently," Jess said. She was realizing that Jim probably hadn't come to grill her about any questionable use of police resources, and she started to breathe a little easier.

"Three or four times on an average night."

"Jim, while I appreciate your concern, this place was on your list."

"I didn't know it was this bad. I don't want to take the call on an officer raped and murdered where she slept." He sighed. "And as someone who likes you on a personal level, I don't want to see you get hurt."

"I'll be okay, Jim," she said, and smiled. "I'll do a little work to beef the place up. Add some motion sensors to the door and the window, peg the window into place. I won't get hurt."

He sighed. Then he turned back and said, "So what did you think of Hank?"

"He wasn't what I expected." She thought about it for a moment, then added, "I liked him a lot more than I thought I would."

"He's a good man. I'd trust him with my life. You can trust him with yours."

Jess nodded slowly. "I'm sort of figuring that out," she said at last.

Jim spent a few more minutes talking with her, but when he realized that she was tired, he made a polite excuse and left.

And Jess thought, *Whatever Hank figured out, he hasn't talked to anyone else about it.*

She realized she was going to have to be interviewed the next day, and she didn't know what would be required of her. So she spent a little time working out a dance routine, in case she was asked to audition. Showered, dressed in her own pajamas, flopped on the hard mattress, and at last drifted into uneasy, restless sleep, and a dream in which she was searching for Ginny again.

Hank stood in the dark hall, clutching two bags of breakfast, two cups of coffee, and a third bag containing the neat, James Bond-ian wire Bill the Tech Guy had dropped by Hank's place, along with the paraphernalia Jess would need to use it. Hank now knew how to wire an exotic dancer so she could strip down to nothing and no one would be the wiser. Which was kind of cool. Certainly more fun than learning how to place semtex for best effect, and maybe almost as useful.

He kicked at the door with his foot. Not too hard—it was a cheap, crappy door, and he wasn't quite scared enough yet to break it down. Didn't look like anyone had broken in. He knew that Jess had her gun with her in case someone tried. But she wasn't answering the door, and the place was too small for her not to hear him out there.

Then he heard fumbling with the lock, and after a moment she pulled the door open. She looked like she was sleepwalking.

"Deaf? Drugged? Or dead?" he said, feeling irritated that she'd been so slow to answer when his hands were full. But less irritated as he saw her.

"Bewildered, confused, and caught in the middle of a nightmare," she said, letting him in. She rubbed her eyes with the backs of her fists like a little kid, and yawned, and turned away from him to wander back into the ratty little studio. Her hair stuck out at all angles, and she wore a black T-shirt and a pair of honest-to-God flannel pajama bottoms with little duckies or something on them, and for a second his heart thudded stupidly to a standstill.

He'd managed to get through that dreary house-hunting trip with her the day before with nothing more than his hormones reacting. But looking at her, sleepy and scruffy and vulnerable, his heart and his body made all the wrong connections. That she was—or could be—someone special. That he might dare to risk himself again.

Thank God his brain was still functioning, and he recognized them as the wrong connections.

She went into her bathroom, but didn't close the door. He dumped the things he'd brought on the dinette and for half a second watched her putting toothpaste on a toothbrush. That was too intimate. "I'd tell you to get yourself something out of the fridge, but I don't have anything yet," she called, and leaned over the sink to brush her teeth. He noticed the way her breasts moved beneath that T-shirt, and the fact that her nipples were already wide-awake even if the rest of her wasn't.

To make himself stop watching her, he walked over to her front door to make sure she'd locked it—which she had—and, suddenly curious, he reached for her doorknob.

I'm not prying. I'm not.

And his fingertips touched metal, and he was drowning in a cold, empty sea. A girl, scared and desperate. Darkness. Endless, aching darkness, and no direction that offered the faintest hint of light.

Jess's nightmare ran through him, somehow tied into her waking reality. Hank couldn't let go of the doorknob quickly enough. The residual of Jess's dream left a foul taste in his mouth.

"I *brought* food," he yelled over the sound of running water. "Must have been some nightmare for you not to have noticed."

"Always is," she called back, though she did it with a mouth full of toothbrush, so it took him a second to figure out what she'd said. She rinsed out her mouth and spit in the sink, and that was no more attractive than when anyone else did it, and splashed water on her face, which was sort of cute, and turned off the water. "Nasty night." And she sighed, and came back out, rubbing a towel over her face. "You brought breakfast? Really? What's in there?"

"Ham biscuits. Cinnamon-and-raisin biscuits—you looked like someone who would like them. Couple of cups of coffee."

She grinned at the bags. "Hardee's. God, I love a Hardee's breakfast."

"None of this stuff is good for you."

"Not for the body, maybe. But it's damned good for the soul."

They sat down, and she polished off two ham biscuits and two cinnamon-raisin biscuits, and the entire huge cup of coffee, and leaned back and closed her eyes with an expression of ecstasy on her face. And sighed.

And some perverse little troll in the back of his mind saw her pleasure in food as sexual, and whispered, *You could make her feel better than that.*

So he asked the question guaranteed to make her stop looking so tempting. "Who was the girl in your nightmare?"

And her eyes flew open and her entire body stiffened. "What?"

"The lost girl. Who was she?"

Jess's gaze froze the air between them; her withdrawal from him had weight and shape, and flavored the air like bitter smoke. "I didn't tell you what I dreamed."

He looked down at his hands.

She said, "The touch thing."

"The touch thing," he agreed. "I touched the doorknob, checking to be sure that you'd locked the door. And I got pieces of your nightmare."

"You got more than you needed, then," she said, and started to back away from the table.

"The reason you hate psychics so much has something to do with that girl," he told her. "And with her being lost. It's all tied together in one ugly mess, and if we're going to work together effectively, and if we're going to trust each other—and you know we need to be able to do that—I *have* to know at least the bare bones of what happened. We're stuck in this minefield together, darlin', but you're the one with the map. At least tell me where the land mines are so that I don't step on them."

That steady, cold gaze of hers never wavered. "She was

my sister. Identical twin sister. Eight minutes older than me. Her name was Virginia Woolf Brubaker." And he thought, *Oh, fuck.* That's *the Virginia—not the state.* "Everyone called her Ginny. She was my best friend in the world, and then one day she disappeared."

She stopped looking at him. Stared down at the table instead, at the wrappers and bags piled there. She started playing with a wrapper, folding it, smoothing out the creases, folding it again. "When she and I were twenty-one, my father apparently decided that he was ready to be twenty-one himself. He emptied out my parents' joint savings account, took off to Mexico with his secretary, and left my mother a complete wreck. Ginny and I were both in dance schools. I was going to Harrt on full scholarship. She was in the dance program at the North Carolina School of the Arts, and my parents had been mostly paying her way. Which my mother couldn't afford to do once my father took off."

Jess looked out the window. "Ginny, being Ginny, came back to Atlanta to offer support to Mama. She was always resourceful, and when she couldn't find a job with a local troupe, she started stripping on weekends. Making good money, which she needed if she wanted to be able to pay her own tuition to get back to NCSA. She didn't like it much, but she would have done anything legal to get back to school." She looked down at the table again, and played with a biscuit wrapper, folding and unfolding it.

"She was working as a stripper when she disappeared," he said.

"Yeah. One day she was there; the next day, her apartment was empty and she was gone. She vanished from the face of the earth."

"So in a way, the case we're working right now is personal for you."

"As personal as it gets. Once I got my cop's shield, I

spent eight years looking for her, trying to find an answer for my mother. And for myself. Even once I realized that I was never going to find her again, I still checked databases from time to time to see if she'd resurfaced. And now . . ." She shrugged. "I couldn't bring her home. But maybe I can do something for these girls."

"She's the reason you became a cop. And then a detective."

Jess wouldn't look at him. He wanted to see her eyes, but she kept staring at the table. "She's the reason I did a lot of things. She's always been classified as a missing person. Back then, no one paid much attention to missing-persons files. The police couldn't find her, but she was an adult and had every right to take off—so they didn't look very hard."

"No signs of foul play?"

"No. She'd paid all her bills, given notice to her landlady, moved out. Some of the people she worked with said she'd gotten an offer to do a movie out in California."

Hank said, "You found that out when you went to your one and only strip club."

She nodded. "From the couple of people who were left who'd actually known her." She still wouldn't look at him. "I should have gone sooner. Most of the people who'd worked with her had moved on by the time I went. But I was young. What did I know? I didn't start looking on my own until everything else had failed. The private detective my family hired. The psychic I hired."

Well, yeah. Considering her feelings about psychics, he had a good idea what had happened there. "So how much did he take you for?"

"*She*. She took me for about six thousand dollars. Everything I'd managed to save over the years; my parents had always been emphatic about the importance of saving. Worse, though, was the endless stream of hope she kept feeding me and my mother, telling us we were getting closer, that we were going to get Ginny back." She looked out the window, lips pursed.

He sat there, putting things together. Playing with the pieces, seeing how they fit. "So then you turned your life upside down. Became a cop. Made detective. And . . . then what?" He rested his hand over hers, and her humiliation and anger and self-hatred poured into him. "Never told any-goddamned-body about your sister, that's for sure. So what did you do?"

"I stayed in Atlanta so she could find me if she came looking. Kept myself in the phone book under my own name. Kept hoping that she'd show up one day with a nice husband and a station wagon full of nieces and nephews for me to get to know. That at least one of us ended up happy. And I looked for her. Used every resource available to a cop to find her."

"You still looking?"

"Not so much. I still check databases. But I ran out of leads a long time ago. I've finally convinced myself that she's gone. That I'll never know what happened to her."

"You're carrying so much guilt. Her disappearance wasn't your fault, though. You know?" Hank said.

And she looked down at the table again. "I think a lot of it was. I think if I'd come home, too, she would have had a backup. Someone to watch out for her. She was the more reckless one of the two of us. I was . . . cautious. I would have seen something going wrong, maybe. I could have saved her from . . . whatever it was." She bit her lip. "But I didn't. I had my full scholarship, and Ginny had always been Mama's favorite anyway. So I let her go home and deal with Mama and all the fallout from that. And with finding her own way to pay for her school. I was upset about my father. Because I had been—or *thought* I was—his fa-vorite, I was too busy being selfish and sulking. When he left without saying a word—even to me, or maybe especially to me—I blamed my mother."

He reached across the table and rested a hand on the back of one of hers, stilling it from its restless fidgeting. This was the pain. It poured from her to him, unfiltered. This was pain and guilt and grief and loss. Enough to crush anyone.

But Jess had taken all that awfulness and worked around it. Maybe even used it to make herself stronger.

Jess's voice got softer. "I keep hoping that if I don't give up, someday she'll come home. God knows, he never did."

He wanted to pull her into his arms and hold her. Wanted to kiss her, and smooth her hair. Wanted to tell her that everything would be all right, that he was with her, that he'd make everything better.

But he wasn't going to make anything better. He was going to do this mission with her, and then he was going to get out of her life because he'd promised himself after Liseé's betrayal that he was never going to risk himself in the emotional war of involvement with a woman again. "I hope you find her," he said. "You deserve to." And then he changed the subject. "I brought the new wire. You don't by any chance have your belly button pierced, do you?"

She gave him an odd smile. He felt her gratitude for his abrupt change in the direction of their conversation. She said, "Not a chance."

"Bill said you'd have a lot easier time with this if you'd get it pierced. But in the meantime, he sent along some special glue, and a solvent to remove the glue when you're done with it. He told me to tell you not to sniff the glue or the solvent. Also, keep your window open when you use either, and put the wire on at least an hour before you need to be in public, because that's about how long the glue smell will linger on your skin."

Hank handed her the brown paper lunch bag, which

looked like it had been used for lunch a few times before it made its transition to carrying important things. Jess pulled out the new receiver, and her eyebrows rose. It was a sparkly sapphire-blue gemstone, with little metal loops and curlicues around the edges and a smooth metal back.

"Bill was excited about this; apparently he's been wanting to try making a mike like this one for a while. He said for today your transmitter can fit into your purse. Keep the purse in the same room with you, and the guys in the van will be able to hear you. I'll plant a couple of the signal boosters while you're interviewing. Once they're in place, the guys will be able to pick you up about fifty feet in any direction from any of them. I have some standard bugs for you to plant, too. Bill said you should make sure you put them in the dressing room, but also to put them anyplace else backstage where you think they might hear something useful."

"Haven't been able to get backstage at all, huh?"

"Not even once, I hear."

"I'll take care of it." She nodded, staring at the gemstone. "And I just . . . glue this to my navel?"

"So he says. He said the glue is waterproof, sweat-proof, and jiggle-proof, and that unless you want to leave bloody holes in your skin, you should always use the solvent to remove it. And that he thinks you'd be a lot happier if you got your navel pierced and let him solder a jewelry wire on for you."

He liked her derisive snort. "I'll pass on punching holes in myself, thanks."

"Didn't sound fun to me, either," he agreed. "I'd stick with the glue if I were you."

"God, please tell me that line was accidental."

He stared down at the remainder of his coffee and grinned a little. "I'd hate to have to lie."

They looked at each other across the breakfast table and

exchanged wry smiles, and that awful sense of rightness and belonging and familiarity washed over him again.

He needed to get out of there, call Jim, tell him to find someone else to squire Jess around and do the surreptitious readings on the customers and the employees.

Except no one else could. Jim didn't have someone else who could do what Hank did. And looking at Jess, Hank could bet Jim didn't have someone else who could do what she did, either. They were unique in what they had to offer, and without either one of them, the mission would have a smaller chance of success. Lives were at stake.

And so was honor. Hank intended to keep the promise he'd made to himself back when he found himself handed his honorable discharge: to find a way to make civilian life matter the way the Rangers had mattered. If he walked away from this thing because he couldn't deal with his emotions, he was done. He would be the quitter he had promised himself he would never be, and that he had promised the Rangers he would never be. He'd taken the Ranger creed, and being a Ranger was for life.

He rose, though, and cleaned off the table. "You want to get ready? We ought to be out the door soon. The listening post is going to be set up for you to go in at noon."

She glanced over at the clock and nodded. "Considering traffic, I guess I need to get ready now."

She rose and headed for the bathroom. "Give me . . . ten. Fifteen."

She yanked open a drawer, then a tiny closet door, pulled out clothes seemingly at random, and then ran for the shower. He glanced at his watch. Fifteen minutes? Not a chance.

The shower started and, an unbelievably short time later, stopped. Hank rechecked the watch. Four minutes? *Damn.* The blow-dryer whined to life next; she didn't spend much time on that, either. And then Hank heard silence, punctuated by the occasional thud. This would be where it all fell apart. The dressing. The makeup. The fiddling with the hair.

But 12.5 minutes after she walked into the bathroom, she walked out of the bathroom door, and she was somebody else. She was almost the somebody else he'd seen in the station two days earlier. But not quite. And this woman had never met the woman in ducky jammies who had answered the door.

Jess wore silk. A light, wispy, long-sleeved off-white silk blouse with the sleeves rolled up. He could see through it enough to tell that what lay beneath was worth seeing. He got a glimpse of sparkles, and serious curves. A tiny hint of glittery blueness at her navel. The fact that the blouse didn't cling to her the way that tube top had—and that he couldn't see through it well—made her more, rather than less, intriguing. Her skirt, very short and beige, looked like silk, too. Classy, in a weird way. Her legs were bare, long, perfect. They went on forever and disappeared beneath the little skirt, and the tightness in his pants argued fervently for following them wherever they went.

She wore what he'd always thought of as fuck-me pumps, heels that were five inches high and spiked. But the things were beige and closed-toed. If they hadn't had those spike heels, they would have looked at home with a business suit.

Her hair was up—the way he'd first seen it. Elegant, with some little sparkly comb thing holding it in place. She had a little makeup on. Not a lot.

He stared at her, not breathing too well, and she sauntered over to him, looked him in the eye, and smiled a devastating smile. She was an impossible combination of prim and wanton—the Madonna and the whore. "Hi," she said in a languorous drawl a little more pronounced than the "city Southern" she spoke the rest of the time. "I'm Grace Callahan. Call me Gracie."

And he thought, *It doesn't matter which of her I'm with, does it? The one in the jammies, the one in the blue cop suit, the one in the take-me clothes. It doesn't matter what's going on in her head, what's going on in her past, what she's doing now or what she's going to be doing in an hour. Because no matter who she is, I still want her.*

chapter 6

Jess called Goldcastle and talked briefly to one of the dancers, who said the dance manager was in but might be leaving soon, and if she wanted to interview, she needed to come on. And that she ought to come to the side door and ask the bouncer for Teri.

Hank drove her over, and Jess did her wire test from the passenger seat of Hank's car. Got the all-clear on her cell phone, took a deep breath, and said, "Walk me to the door."

"Don't want to find out the bouncer is too friendly on your first day?"

"Right."

"No problem," Hank said.

He walked her to Goldcastle's side door, but didn't touch her. Some big, hairy Neanderthal was guarding that door. "I'm here to see Teri," she told him.

He wasn't one of the undercover guys. He gave her the creeps.

"Dancer?" he asked, leering at her.

God, he was scary. "Yes," she said.

"Ri-i-i-i-ght. You go on in, sweetheart. And stop and say hello to me later. Buddy-boy back there can't come with you, though. He wants to watch the titties jiggle, he goes through the front door and he pays like everybody else."

Jess waved to Hank and called, "You going to wait in the car?"

"Nah," he said. "I'll go on in."

"I won't be long."

The Neanderthal watched Hank waiting to see Jess go through the door, and after a staring contest between the two of them that Jess didn't miss, he sighed. "Left corridor, straight back," the door guy said.

Jess nodded. "Thanks." She walked past the guy, feeling his stare on the back of her neck. But he didn't touch her when she passed him, and she thought she had Hank to thank for that.

The inside of the place was . . . well, the only word Jess could think of was industrial. The floors were bare concrete, the walls concrete block. Someone had painted all flat vertical surfaces a hideous shade of bargain-basement peach-gone-wrong—that paint had to have been on sale as a massive mixing error, because no one would choose that color on purpose. A fiftyish woman who might have been pretty once, but who now looked hard and worn, stood next to the stage door, fixing the back of one girl's gown. "You're ready," she said, and the girl nodded, and then at the sound of the deejay's voice over the intercom, went through the door. A second later, another girl, naked except for a black G-string with money still hanging from it like tree leaves and with her arms full of pieces of a fuchsia satin costume, hurried back toward the dressing room.

The older woman looked over at Jess and said, "Can I help you, honey?"

"I'm here to apply," Jess said.

"Dancer?"

"Yes," Jess said.

"I'm Louella. The housemom. You need to talk to Teri," the woman said. "She's out on the floor right now, but I'll see if I can track her down for you." Louella picked up a phone, punched in a three-number code, and waited. After a minute, she said, "Teri? Dancer back here wants a job." The housemom glanced at Jess and said, "Oh, definitely . . . I'll have her wait in your office? . . . Right."

She pointed with a thumb to the door with TERI on it in gold letters. "She says go on in. Give her ten."

Jess nodded, and went into the office.

Posters and photos decorated the walls, all of them of the same sleek, gorgeous woman, shown with varying colors of hair, and eyes of such a light brown they looked amber. Some of the posters were for triple-X-rated movies, some were featured-dancer promos, and some were simply glamour shots. Some of them had been taken when the woman was in her early twenties; in some she was as old as thirty-five, Jess guessed. Jess saw half a dozen names attached to those pictures, though all the movie posters identified her as Stormy FoXXX, with the triple *X* at the end of the name in bigger, brighter letters.

Along the left wall sat an enormous wheeled wooden trunk with a dress rack built on top. Sequined gowns hung on the rack along with a couple of risqué theme costumes. The name Stormy FoXXX decorated the battered lid, painted in large letters. Jess wished she could lift the lid and peek inside—perpetual curiosity was one of the side effects of being a cop.

The bookshelf behind the desk held some dance awards and a Miss Nude America award. Trophies, certificates. Framed photos ranging from a small one of the young woman surrounded by Shriners to a considerably larger one of her, somewhat older, striking a sexy pose while being carried through a surging horde of men on a bamboo litter by six muscular stud-muffins in Tarzan thongs. Studying that picture, Jess was reminded uncomfortably of a roast pig being carried to the banquet table. Or of virgin sacrifices.

She got engrossed by the photos and whatnots—enough so that she jumped when the door opened.

"My brag shelf," the woman said. "I retired eight years ago."

Jess turned and recognized the woman in the door as the one in the pictures. Her eyes, in real life, were less amber and more light brown. Her black hair fell loosely past her shoulders in tumbling waves, untouched by gray. Or maybe touched by a good hairdresser. She was still stunning, in her early forties but with an excellent figure shown to best advantage by a tremendously sexy red satin dress. She didn't look well preserved. She simply looked good.

Jess found herself hoping she held together so well at that age. "Grace Callahan," she said, reaching out. "Mostly Gracie."

The other woman hesitated for an instant, a puzzled expression on her face. And then she put her hand out and said, "Ekaterina Thomas. Call me Teri." They shook hands briefly. "I'm one of the owners, and the only hands-on one. I wear a number of hats—tour guide for prospective members, mediator for problems with irate clients, club promoter. But for your purposes, I'm the women's personnel manager. I hire and fire Goldcastle's dancers and drink servers and make out schedules."

Jess said, "Then you're the woman I need to see. I need a job." She smiled, waiting to be asked to sit down. But Teri didn't ask her. She stood there looking at Jess with a penetrating, critical stare that Jess found unnerving.

"You're twenty-seven? Twenty-eight?"

"Thirty-four," Jess said, and watched Teri's eyebrows lift slightly.

"Hold out your arms, forward together and with your wrists facing up."

Teri demonstrated the position she wanted, and Jess held out both arms.

Teri leaned forward and studied the skin of her inner arms from biceps to wrist. "No tracks. Good. Doesn't mean you're clean, and I'll tell you right now that if you get caught using drugs here, you're out. We don't require a urinalysis, but you're an independent contractor and we can fire you at any time for any reason. Where have you danced?"

Jess swallowed hard, remembering the details of her cover story and hoping she could sell it. "The Doll House and Carolina Girls. Both up near Fort Bragg in North Carolina. A lot of years ago. In college. I've only been a house dancer, and when I finished college and paid off my tuition, I quit."

Teri nodded. "You're in luck. I have some openings at the moment. Our minimum for any one dancer is usually three days a week, but considering our scheduling issues, even that's a little flexible at the moment. Your tip-out is fifty dollars, and we offer eight-hour shifts. You can work less, but you still owe the full tip-out. That covers the house and me, and community supplies like clean towels for the showers, deodorant, toothbrushes and toothpaste, and tampons if you forget yours. You're also responsible for tipping the deejay, Louella, and any drink servers you team up with to sell drinks. You already know that you can't ask a patron to buy a drink for you, but that a drink server can suggest that your client buy one for you—and that if you get your card punched with enough drink sales, you don't owe your tip-out?"

"I know how it works," Jess said.

"We offer lockers. Dancers who are here at least five times a week get their own. If you use one, bring a good lock."

"Personal belongings wander out?"

Teri gave her a sidelong glance and an amused smile. "Only if you don't bring a good lock."

"Got it," Jess said. And held her breath. She was going to do this. She was going to strip. If she chickened out at this point, she didn't think Jim would hold it against her.

But Jess stood there, eyes half-closed, thinking of Ginny. And, oddly, of Hank. She thought about how she would be letting everyone down, no matter what they thought, if she didn't go through with this—her fellow detectives, the dead girls, their families, the girls who would die if no one caught the bastards doing this. But Hank seemed as much a pressure pushing her to do this as her sense of mission or her obligations to everyone else . . . and *that* she couldn't explain. She didn't owe Hank anything.

She sighed. "What do I have to do to get myself on the schedule?" she asked.

Teri laughed grimly. "First, under no circumstance ask that question in those words when you go up to talk to Lenny."

"Lenny?"

"The club manager. He's a slimeball. He handles the nonentertainment employees, the money, ordering food and booze, bringing in high rollers. And if you say those words to him, he will convince you that only sexual favors will get you on our dance card."

"But you said you do the hiring for the dancers."

"I do. But Lenny has connections to the other owners. And he has a veto. I'll send Louella in with you when you go to tell him I've hired you. Do not go into the room with him before she does, and do not stay after she leaves. He's . . . a problem. And, as you know if you've done this before, this is not a job where anybody takes sexual harassment seriously. Once Lenny has okayed you, get out of there as fast as you can. Do not stay to hear any of his special offers. When you're dancing, stay down here or out on the floor in one of the two public rooms, or the downstairs private dance rooms—though I don't recommend them. If you accept invitations up to Lenny's office, you do so with the full understanding that I wash my hands of you and any problems you may incur. Are we clear on Lenny?"

"Yes."

"I stand between the dancers who are here to dance and all the people who would like to turn them into whores. Within that realm, I have enough financial clout to protect my turf. If you have problems with anyone—*anyone*—come to me. However, if you decide to step outside the house rules and I find out about it, I'll fire you. Right then, right there, without question."

"I'm fine with that," Jess said.

"Good, Grace. I'm glad to hear it."

Teri settled into her comfortable-looking leather chair. Crossed her legs, leaned back, steepled her fingers together and rested them beneath her chin. "Incidentally, you do not have to audition for Lenny. When he suggests that you do, tell him you've auditioned for me."

Jess nodded.

"On to the actual work, then. We are one of the few clubs in the area that does not offer full nudity. Because of that, we have to bring more to the table. First, Goldcastle only hires the best dancers. We fire butt wrigglers. Second, our dancers are focused on the customers. They are friendly, they smile, they are kind and courteous and clean, they make our customers feel special and welcome. *Legally*. The dance area is no touch, no excuses." Teri's voice went sharp when she said that.

Jess did not miss the implication of either the words or the tone of voice. Noting specifically that touch was off-limits in the dance area, Teri implied that the club had places that were not no touch, no excuses. Places outside Teri's turf. And Teri, part owner of the business, did not like this fact. To some extent, that put Teri and Jess on the same side.

"*My* hires do not work the Weekenders."

"Weekenders?" Jess asked.

"Goldcastle hosts big parties several times a year at our manager Leonard Northwhite's mansion. They are attended by the rich, the famous, the degenerate, and Lenny's dancers; they last all weekend long; and they are one of the big draws for the special upper-tier membership level. They are essentially orgies. I voted against them, I consider them a threat to the legitimacy of this club, and if I hire you, you will not be a participant in them."

"That's fine," Jess said. "They are not what I'm looking for in this job."

She and Teri sat there for a long, awkward moment, studying each other.

Teri seemed to make up her mind about something. She nodded and said, "Oh. We don't take dancers with tattoos. You have any tattoos?"

"No."

"Good. So we'll be hiring you. I'll pass on the audition today—I'm pressed for time and you have experience. I'll watch you your first time out on the floor and make sure you're dancing appropriately. If you have costumes, I can put you in this afternoon for a couple of two-song stage sets. Since it's . . . ahh . . . been a while since you've danced, I'm guessing you may not have costumes anymore."

"I don't," Jess said. "Before I invest, do you have any forbidden costume themes or dance routines?"

"A few, actually," Teri opened a drawer in her desk and pulled out a couple of photocopied sheets. "This is the list of house rules, set rules, costume rules, client rules, the schedule of tip-out breaks you get for selling drinks and how we recommend you sell them. . . ." She smiled a little ruefully and handed them across to Jess.

Jess dropped one of the pages, and while she was bent

over, planted a bug on the bottom edge of the modesty panel on Teri's desk.

"When I was dancing," Teri said, "everything was simpler. More disorganized, but simpler." Teri sat back in her chair and said, "I'm curious. Why are you doing this? Now?"

And Jess grabbed onto her story like a lifeline.

"I have a lot at stake," she said. "My brother has non-Hodgkin's lymphoma. At this point his prognosis is good if he can get treatment. But he has no insurance, and I want him not to have to worry about anything but getting well. So if I'm going to help him out, I need this job. It's the only work I could think of that I could do that would pay well enough to . . ." Her nervousness caught up with her, and suddenly she felt shaky. Her voice trembled, which worked well enough for selling her story.

Teri said, "I'm . . . so sorry."

Jess said, "Me, too. But I'm trying to take a practical, realistic approach. It seems better than crying."

"Good for you." Teri stood up, which Jess took as an indication that the interview was over. But Teri said, "You're going to have to go up and see Lenny the Worm in a minute, but before you go, I've been made aware of something in the last few days. A . . . situation we have. And while I've been instructed not to discuss the problem, I'm going to give you some unasked-for advice."

Jess watched her, wondering what was coming.

"This job puts women in vulnerable positions. You're here doing something worthwhile, and I admire you for that. So don't do anything that would make you less safe. Do not agree to meet customers alone anywhere. Ever. The same for employees. Don't ever let a customer hand you a drink. Take drinks only from the trays the waitresses bring, or directly from the bartender. And watch how much you drink; you're especially vulnerable when you're drunk.

Don't assume that you know anyone, or that anyone is safe. Walk to and from the parking lot with one of the floor managers and—if you can—with at least one of the other dancers, and all of you watch each other get in your cars. This is all simple common sense, and I wouldn't even bother to tell you, except there's a possibility that some of our dancers have . . . gotten in trouble . . . for failing to exercise common sense."

Jess nodded. "What sort of trouble?"

"That's what I can't tell you. I don't know for sure that the problems are related to this place, and until I'm sure, I'm going to have to trust you to simply acknowledge that problems could exist. And that your behavior can keep you safe."

"Thank you," Jess said. "I'm a very careful woman."

"I'm glad to hear that," Teri said. "I think you're going to do well here." And then she shook her head and chuckled. "Go. See Lenny. Take Louella with you, and don't let her leave you in there alone."

Jess walked out the door wondering exactly what sort of nightmare Lenny the Worm was.

Hank paid his cover charge and stepped out of the Atlanta heat into dim, cool air and a broad, extravagantly decorated foyer. The designers had been aiming for lush Victorian, but what they'd actually achieved was cheesy X-rated Victorian theme park: stained-glass lamps, polished brass rails, fat leather chairs. Victorian-style oil paintings covered the walls—but the subjects were skinny women with enormous breasts in positions no Victorian painter would have ever considered.

It wasn't the sort of place Hank would have voluntarily spent five minutes in.

"Welcome to Goldcastle Gentlemen's Club, sir. Is this your first visit?"

"It is," Hank said, ostensibly looking around the foyer but from the corner of his eye studying the greeter. She wore a blue sequined floor-length gown that prominently featured her breasts, and mostly hid the walking cast on her left leg. *Dancer*, he thought, *and one who'd had a mishap.*

She gave him a bright corporate smile. "Then let me quickly acquaint you with our facilities. As a nonmember, you are permitted in the downstairs area only. The downstairs area includes our excellent restaurant, our bar, and our world-class exotic dancers. Downstairs areas where you are not permitted will have a Members Only sign on the door. Upstairs is off-limits entirely. We have dancers in the grand ballroom to your immediate right. In the smaller VIP lounge to the right just in back of the staircase, our girls, excluding our feature acts, will dance for you privately."

"Features don't do private dances here?"

"They do for *members*. Also note that our house rules are quite strict. You may look at our dancers, but if you touch, you and the dancer will either receive a public warning, or, depending upon the severity of your infraction, you'll be removed from the facility. We are," she said, "a class establishment."

"Got it." Hank had to suppress a laugh. "What are the advantages of membership?"

"You would have access to our private gentlemen's smoking chamber with its wide selection of excellent cigars, beverages, and library; to our gaming room—we have several avid pool players, an enthusiastic poker group, and even a small group of chess players—to private rooms for members who wish to reserve them for meetings, parties, or simply personal entertainment; and to the upstairs dance room, of course, where our featured performers and select house dancers give special members-only performances. If you decide you would like to become a member, I can arrange a tour of the member facilities for you."

"Not today. But I'll keep it in mind," Hank said.

The greeter turned to someone else, and Hank quickly touched the place on the wood-and-brass podium where the woman's hand had rested.

And death was there, in the midst of a clamoring crowd. Thick and heavy and ugly, hunting already for its next meal, it was watching and looking and reaching out to fill the black hole inside of itself. He felt the poison of a vile, evil mind, and the pleasure it took in the terror and the pain of others clogged Hank's lungs and fogged his vision. He managed to let go of the podium and step away, wondering if the greeter could be one of the killers.

Then a new customer rested a hand on the podium. And a moment later, a fully clothed dancer sauntered out of the room to the right and caught the greeter's attention and leaned up on the podium with both hands to whisper something in the other woman's ear before she flashed Hank a come-hither smile and strolled back the way she'd come.

The podium was a touch point. From reading it, Hank could only know that one of the killers had been there. Recently. He could not assume that anyone near it had anything to do with the deaths.

People touched things. All the time, unconsciously as well as consciously. Hank had once been stopped in his tracks by a little boy in a store pointing to a toy on a shelf and asking his mother, "Can I see it with my hands?"

That was people—all of them. They saw things with their hands, even when they didn't know they were doing it. He stared at his own hands and acknowledged that some people saw with them more clearly than others did.

He headed into the grand ballroom, grabbed the first open chair, and sat heavily in it. He rested his hands on the table in front of him to stop them from shaking . . .

. . . and death was there, too. Lies and cleverness, lust and twisted love, perversion, hunger and rage.

Hank shuddered, smelling a faint, light perfume, thinking that was part of the vision, part of the horror that he was pulling in.

Until a pair of heavy breasts propped up by an architectural red silk bustier hove into view inches in front of his face, and somewhere above them, a voice said, "Hey, sweetheart, would you like a little company?"

She rested fingertips lightly on his shoulder.

And he felt death again.

Dark and hungry death, searching for a place to happen. Death, but at one remove. Death had touched this girl and left whisper-prints on her skin. Death had looked at this girl and thought, *Maybe, maybe, maybe later, but not this one right now. Not today.*

Hank leaned his head back far enough from the breasts to be able to see over them to the face. She was a pretty girl. One of the dancers. Her fake breasts were oppressive, but the girl herself still looked friendly, warm, unjaded. Didn't mean she was, but if she wasn't, the job hadn't left its marks on her face yet.

He smiled a little, trying not to let the queasiness he was feeling show, and said, "I'm waiting on a friend, actually."

The girl's smile became a bit more genuine; she looked almost relieved. "You're friends with one of the dancers? I can tell her you're here if you'd like."

Hank shrugged. "Not sure if she's a dancer or not." And when the girl looked puzzled, he said, "She came in to interview. I drove her because her car's in the shop."

"Well, sweetheart, if you'd like a little company while you're waiting, let me know."

She trailed fingers with long, fake nails painted blood red down his arm, and Hank said, "Maybe another time."

The girl nodded and sauntered off, her cherry-red miniskirt flipping and flirting with each swing of her ass.

It was a good ass. Not fake, like the breasts. Or the imitation of attraction the girl had projected at him. That stung—to see the friendly smile and feel the flash of distaste that lay underneath it in the moment that she touched him. The pain from that never wore off, because every time, it came from someone new.

Watching the dancer stroll away, Hank found himself thinking about Jess bursting out of that bathroom door in the station like she was claiming a stage she owned, with that huge smile on her face, wearing heels and short-shorts and a skimpy tube top, and he remembered the way her appearance had felt like a punch in his gut. She'd been projecting the same external cheer, while hiding dark emotions beneath it.

But none of those emotions had been distaste for him.

Hank leaned back in his chair, balancing it on the back two legs, watching the dancer on the main stage, whose athletic, high-energy performance was impressive. The greeter hadn't been overselling the talent of the dancers in the place, anyway. As he leaned back, he pretended to tip his chair too far back so that he had to grab the table to catch himself— and as he did, he reached under the edge of the table and placed one of Tech's signal-booster transmitters against the table's central post, out of the way of casual contact. A person who found it would have to be looking for it.

He was quick about placing it because he didn't doubt for a minute that he was being monitored from a security room somewhere in the building.

He set the chair back on all four legs and looked around as if he hoped no one had noticed him almost fall over.

A waitress in Goldcastle's blue-and-white French maid uniform strolled up to him and asked him if he wanted anything, and he said he'd take a beer in a bottle. She had the big smile, too. The bright attitude. The same faint air of "hustle" that he found so disturbing. And the same falseness.

She came back and handed him his drink and gave him that flirty smile and reminded him that the dancers would be happy to sit with him and keep him company if he asked them.

When he picked up the bottle she'd held, he felt it again. Death. But death distant, and uninterested. Death had touched the waitress, had looked at her, considered her, and had passed her by as unsuitable. Because death was watching someone else in the room, someone who more closely fit its appetite of the moment.

He caught glimpses of a personality behind the murders. Shapes of calm, of rationality, of amusement. The killer was orderly, organized. Hungry for the victims, enchanted by their beauty, angry at them, disgusted by them.

Cold washed down Hank's spine like ice, as the shape of the killer's passions came into focus. He had maintained a personal relationship with each of the dead women. Had loved each woman, and had convinced himself that love was returned until each of them demonstrated . . .

. . . what?

Hank couldn't catch it. Feelings of betrayal clung strongly, but the acts that had given birth to those feelings were lost in the sheer multiplicity of destructions.

Hank could feel more than three deaths. A lot more. Most of the dead women hadn't been dumped in parks. The park dumping was new behavior that came about only when the killer ran out of room in his preferred storage place. He'd kept most of the girls' bodies as souvenirs, someplace safe. Someplace that wouldn't betray him. Someplace close to him.

Six by six, Hank thought, and didn't know what that meant. It meant something to the killer. And it scared Hank.

He felt a lot of dead women in that echo. But he felt only one killer, and felt that the killer always worked alone. Which didn't fit the facts. Could there be another predator haunting this place? And what about the dead girls? So many—so many more than anyone had suspected. Had all of them come from Goldcastle? If so, how had no one noticed?

And then he considered women who became strippers. A lot of them had walked away from awful families or bad home situations. Many of them didn't have any contact with people who would be motivated to report them missing. A lot of them lived transient lives, traveling from club to club, across cities and states and even countries, often without notice—so that in many cases absences would be unremarkable even to friends. Some exotic dancers used dancing as a cover for prostitution. Some drank heavily; some did drugs. Hank, considering all of that, decided that, careful as the killer had been, he had exercised his greatest amount of care for keeping himself hidden simply by the victims he chose.

Jim would need to know all of this. So would Jess. She would be facing a practiced, experienced killer who was actively hunting for victims, who was a lingering presence in the club, who might be an employee. Who would see her before she saw him.

But Jess was likely to dismiss anything Hank told her as being tainted, simply because of the way he got his information.

He sat in a cloud, the touch of a monster cold in his veins, and wondered how he could make her believe in him.

chapter 7

"If you want me to leave, tell me," Louella said. "Some of the girls do."

Jess studied her through narrowed eyes and said, "Why?"

"The girls who, well, work with Lenny . . ." She looked away when she said that. "They make a lot more money than the girls who don't."

Jess could guess how. Lenny would be the guy who "arranged" things between high rollers and those dancers willing to provide what people in the trade euphemistically referred to as extras. She wondered if Lenny had been the target of Vice's undercover operation, or if he was a middleman for someone higher up the food chain.

She was . . . curious. With a cop's keen interest, she wanted to know exactly what sort of slug would crawl out from under his rock if she lifted it. There was always a chance that he was killing dancers who became a problem—but it didn't seem like a big chance. The crimes she was looking at didn't have the feel of anything that had been done to keep a business running smoothly. The killing had been the point for the killers, not some other motive.

She'd keep her eyes open, though. In case he was mixing business with pleasure.

Louella led her out of the concrete back rooms into the main club, through a wide, burnished-wood-and-brass lobby, and up a broad, curving staircase. Customers already on the premises looked her over, and though she wished desperately for a longer skirt, or pants and a heavy jacket, she remembered the part she was playing. She smiled at them—the showgirl smile, practiced in front of mirrors by dancers since dance began, and once learned, never forgotten.

And the men smiled back. Some leered.

Jess's queasiness returned.

Louella nodded toward the open door to the right of the landing, and raised her eyebrows in question.

"Don't. Go. Anywhere," Jess told her, sounding more desperate than she'd intended.

Louella smiled. "Not a problem, honey."

They went through the door together.

Lenny stood with his back to them, talking on the phone and flipping through a ledger.

"I brought a new girl," Louella said.

He held up an index finger. "Minute."

Lenny was big. Six five maybe, probably close to three hundred pounds, and most of it looked like it was still muscle. Blond hair going silver, a voice both deep and coarse, accented with last week's episode of *The Sopranos* and way too many mob movies patched over a lifetime of deep-fried Southern good ol' boy. He snapped, "No, Kasim, the house is short for the last week because we had a bunch of dancers quit. . . . How the fuck do I know? Someplace opened up that has a smaller tip-out, or that lets them have tattoos and piercings, or that gives 'em darker corners to screw in. They're goddamned flakes—*you* know that— and if you build a business that depends on goddamned flakes, sometimes your receipts are going to come back funny." A long pause. "Yeah, well, I'm interviewing one

now, so how 'bout you let me do my job?" He slammed the
phone down and turned around, looking pissed.

He might have been a good-looking man. But Jess hated
him on sight. He gave her the creeps.

Louella said, "This one's only here to get your okay,
Lenny."

And Lenny started to say something to Louella, except
that as he was opening his mouth, he looked at Jess.

He froze, and his face went pale and gray and sweaty,
and his breath rushed out of him in a whoosh. His eyes
widened and his jaw dropped. He scrabbled for his chair
with suddenly shaking hands—big, meaty, ring-bedecked
hands—and collapsed into it as if his knees wouldn't hold
him any longer, and for a second Jess wondered if she was
going to have to do CPR on the bastard.

He stared at her, saying nothing. He looked like he'd
seen a ghost.

"Have we . . . met?" Lenny asked, his voice shaking,
his face getting grayer and grayer.

"Not that I know of," Jess said. "I'm Grace Callahan.
I've been Hot Pepper, and Randi Lee, and Silver Jones, but
not for a few years now, and nowhere around here. I suppose you might have seen me a long time ago."

Jess watched Lenny the way wolves watched injured
deer. He looked like prey to her. He was limping, and she
smelled blood. But . . . from what?

"Good Lord have mercy," Lenny said. "I reckon I . . .
must have." The mobster voice fell away completely, and
for a moment he was someone else. Not the gangland
wannabe anymore. He was younger. Vulnerable.

Scared.

He stared at her with eyes that had, a moment before,
been hard and cold. Ruthless. Killer's eyes. But that hard-
ness had washed away. Lenny stared into Jess's eyes, looking for something he wasn't finding, and she would have

given anything to know what he wanted to see. Because that would have told her so much. Then he cleared his throat, and that questioning look slipped away, replaced once more by flat, dead, reptilian eyes. "Grace, is it?"

"Yes."

"Teri already cleared you?"

"Yes."

"Gimme your permit and your license. I know Teri told you the rules. The club has other opportunities too, and if you want to find out more about them, you come to me. But . . . not right now. I'm . . . not feeling so good right now," he said.

She handed him the IDs he requested. He photocopied them, punched holes in the photocopied page, and put it into a ring binder behind his desk that said DANCERS down the spine in big, carefully hand-printed black letters.

He handed her the license and the permit, and as he did, his hand touched hers.

She hid the shudder she felt, but not the look of loathing in her eyes. She saw his surprise, noted the way he backed up, and thought longingly of a couple of takedown moves. Not because she had anything on him. Simply because it would have felt good.

She didn't even take the time to put her IDs in her purse. She just said, "Anything else?"

"No. Not right now."

Out in the hall again, Jess caught her breath.

"That was . . . weird," Louella said. "I've never seen him look like he looked right then."

"I don't know what that was about," Jess said. "But it was creepy."

"Creepy is one of Lenny's specialties," Louella said as they walked down the stairs. "All the rest of his specialties are worse. Stay out of his way."

Jess nodded. "Those sound like words of wisdom to me."

"We're done for today," the housemom said. "Teri will call you to discuss the schedule. She'll have to look at it before she can give you definite times."

"That's fine," Jess said. "I'll have to run down a couple of costumes before I can start anyway."

Louella nodded. "I know some girls who are selling their costumes. If you'd like, I'll let them know you're looking. That'll help you keep your costs down." She paused. "Give you more for your brother, you know?"

Her brother. Apparently Louella had been listening at the door. Jess couldn't forget about her brother. Jess must have looked surprised at Louella's mention, because the housemom added, "I think you're very . . . brave, doing this for him. And turning down Lenny's specials, too. Knowing what you need the money for, I would have understood if you'd told me to leave. But I think it says something good about you that you didn't."

Jess felt like such a fraud. This was the part of undercover she'd hated. Fooling the decent people, making them think she was something she wasn't, in order to get to the bad ones. Louella seemed like a decent person. "Thanks. I'm . . . Don't make too much of it, okay? Lenny wasn't that hard to turn down."

Louella laughed. "He's persistent, though. He'll be back with offers."

Jess, at the bottom of the stairs, nodded toward the grand ballroom and said, "My ride should be in there waiting for me. Thanks very much for your help. I'll see you . . . well, whenever I make it on the schedule. And"— she dug into her ridiculous little purse for paper and a pen, about the only things that fit in there beside her ID and lipstick—"here's my cell phone number. You can give it to the girls with costumes and tell them they can call me."

Louella took the number and said, "Tell your brother we'll be cheering for him."

Jess nodded. "I'll do that."

Hank was sitting at a back table, a strange, sick expression on his face. He turned to look at her as soon as she came through the doors, and rose immediately. Jess had been planning to watch a few of the girls dance, just to get an idea of their routines, but the look in Hank's eyes suggested she shouldn't even ask.

"What's the matter?"

"I'm running late. When you asked for a ride, I thought you said this would be quick," Hank snapped, and Jess realized that quite a few people were watching the two of them: the bartender, some of the customers, a couple of dancers. "Did you at least get the job?"

"Yes. Don't know when I'll start, though."

"But you're done here for today?"

"Yes."

"Then let's get the hell out of here before I'm so late that I lose *my* job." He glared at his watch and stormed out a step ahead of her.

He was convincing. She'd give him that. He'd tipped her to the fact that his foul temper was an act with the comment about giving her a ride. But he was quite convincing as a pissed-off man kept waiting.

He didn't say anything else until the two of them were in the car, and they were actually back on the road. And then he said, "Give me your hand."

"What?"

"Your hand."

Jess reached over and put her left hand in his right one, and saw him look even greener than he had before.

"Now the other one."

She put her right hand in his, and she thought he was going to have to pull over.

"What—or who—did you touch in there?"

Jess started to blow him off with a smart-assed remark about psychics and stupid voodoo shit. But Hank had managed to convince her that he had *something* going on with his psychic tricks. So she closed her eyes and ran her mind back from the time she walked into the place. "Doorknobs first—the one at the side entry, then both sides of the one in Teri's office. Desk and shelf, Teri's office. Shook Teri's hand. Chair, Teri's office. Railing in the corridor that the dancers—and probably the other employees—use. Railing going up the steps to Lenny's office. Wall in Lenny's office. Lenny's hand. That was a bit less fun than squashing live cockroaches with my bare fingers, incidentally. The housemom's hand when I gave her my phone number. Railing on the other side when I was coming down the steps. The door frame on the way into the room where you were sitting. The exit doorknob on the way out." She sat very still for a moment, remembering, making sure she hadn't missed anything. "A table on my way through the back of the foyer to go up and meet with Lenny. I tripped on an Oriental rug and caught myself on the table edge."

"Shit."

"Why do you ask?"

He glanced over at her. "Because you touched the killer, or something the killer touched, and I was hoping we could narrow it down."

"I touched . . . You're kidding." She wanted to call him a fraud, or a fool, for making such a claim. Except he wasn't presenting this to her in the way the other psychic she'd worked with had. He wasn't closing his eyes and murmuring things like, "I'm sensing movement through the Veil."

Jess had bought that whole dramatic act when she was so desperate to find Ginny. She'd thought that someone would have to be a little different—a little odd—to have more than five senses. She'd wanted to believe, too, because she had run out of other hopes, and she *needed* something to believe in. She'd eventually realized the psychic was a charlatan. But she'd assumed that all psychics were like that one. Had Hank sounded anything like that previous psychic, she would have had no trouble blowing him off.

But he didn't seem to have an ounce of pretense in him.

She shifted a little sideways in her seat so she could look at him better. She had the scarred side of his face toward her. It was odd, but that side seemed more like the real Hank to her. "You can't tell which of them it was? See into their heads or something?"

"No. It doesn't work like that. I get . . . emotions and physical sensations, sounds and smells and tastes, sometimes an idea of physical location. Shreds of inner personality, but that might not match outer personality at all, and in this case is likely not to." He frowned. "A lot of it is physical sensation. It's hard to connect that to an individual person, but sometimes I can get a specific piece of information that's useful."

"What does it feel like?" she asked him.

"What?"

"Being psychic? What does it feel like to touch something and get impressions from it?" She watched his hands as he drove and shifted, and watched the way his feet moved over the clutch, the brake, the gas pedal. Comforting.

"Depends. Touching something happy doesn't feel like much of anything. Maybe a little buzz along my nerves, along with flashes of sounds and pictures, sensations, sometimes tastes or smells. Something nasty, though . . ." His voice trailed off, and he negotiated an intersection before picking up the sentence again. "When I touch a critical piece of evidence from a murder scene, it feels like . . .

pardon me"—he glanced sidelong at her before returning his attention to the road—"it feels like a bad case of shit cramps. Can double me over sometimes. Depending on what I'm touching, I can get the physical sensations of the death itself, the pain, the fear, the anger, the lust, the perversion, sometimes words and the screaming, smells and tastes—the killer and the victim in their final interaction all mixed together. It can be horrible."

Jess stared at him, trying to imagine voluntarily doing anything that affected her that way. "That sounds hellish. More like a disease than a gift, if you don't mind my saying so. Have you always . . . been psychic?"

He laughed a little. "No. Just since I got myself blown up. As for it being a disease—it seems that way to me most of the time, honestly. It gives me a lot of information I'd rather not have, all the time and whether I want it or not, and so far I haven't found it compensating me with little bluebirds of happiness elsewhere in my life to make up for all the awfulness."

Jess turned and looked out the front again so she wouldn't stare at him. "The injuries you got in battle *made* you psychic?"

His voice held puzzlement. "I'm not sure. I don't *think* it was the actual injuries. I had bad damage to my right arm and right leg, and extensive facial damage, but no brain injury. I didn't spend any time in a coma, and while everybody including me was sure I was going to die, I didn't die, even for a minute. No white light, no review of my life, no dead friends coming to meet me. From what I've since read about late development of psychic ability, I guess what caused this in me was the trauma surrounding the whole mess."

"The *physical* trauma."

She caught his shrug out of the corner of her eye. "Personal stuff, too. There was no joy in Mudville back then, no matter where I looked for it."

"That *sucks*," she said. "So why do you let Jim put you in situations where you have to deal with that?"

He drove in silence for a long time, and she could see him struggling with whether or not to answer her question.

"It's the mission," he said at last. "My mission. To stand up for people who can't protect themselves. To do the right thing, not the easy thing. I swore once that I would give my life to do that, and though I can no longer serve as a soldier, the oath is still there." He stopped at another red light, turned on the left turn signal, and said, "I still mean it—you know? So that's why, when Jim calls me and asks for my help, I give it. I would do it without charge, but Jim insists on covering the classes that I don't teach while I'm taking the time off."

Jess got a lump in her throat. How could she not believe in Hank Kamian? He might be a great psychic, or a lousy psychic, or just a guy who got sick to his stomach at crime scenes and mistook that for being psychic. She couldn't judge his qualifications; she had only his reading of her upon which to base any such judgment, and while that was impressive, she could not verify how he'd gotten his information. But all that was beside the point. She had no doubts that he was a good man.

He pulled into the parking lot of his dojo, and she said, "Here? I thought you were going to drop me off at my place."

"Later." He took the key out of the ignition, unlocked his door, and got out. He looked in at her and said, "First, however, you and I are going to go into the back classroom and do that workout we missed yesterday."

"Right now?"

"Right now. I'm going to be sure that you have all the tools you'll need to defend yourself in unarmed combat."

He took a deep breath and added, "I want to make sure you can kick ass stark naked if you have to. The monster who is hunting in that club has managed to gain the trust of every one of his victims. They've all had a close relationship with him. And he's played on that relationship to murder them."

"You feel one killer?"

"So far, yes. Only one personality. But one personality that has destroyed a lot more than three women."

"*They* weren't looking for a killer."

"Come on." He slammed the door and walked away from the car, leaving Jess to either sit in the heat or trot along after him.

She could use a workout, she decided, and followed him into the dojo.

He already had a black uniform pulled off the rack for her. "My donation to the cause," he said.

"I'm going to need a sports bra, too."

"Yeah, we have those. Look on those shelves. They'll be to the right of the belts."

Jess found a bra that would fit, and then debated between fighting in a rhinestone thong and skipping the underpants entirely, since Hank didn't seem to stock panties. She decided that nothing at all was preferable to doing kicks and throws with the thong creeping up her butt. She'd have to buy the uniform when she was done. But she would have done that anyway.

She changed in the public restroom, scrubbed the gunk off her face, pulled her hair back into a ponytail, and went out to join Hank on the mats.

In the front room, a women's self-defense class was in progress. The back room, though, they had to themselves.

"You ready?" Hank said.

Jess nodded. She'd always been very good at defending herself.

He did some standard frontal attacks, and she moved with him, diverting the force of each assault so that he went flying past her. He rolled gracefully out of her throws, and came at her again, using a slightly different attack each time.

She focused on defense, on form; she tried to keep her attention strictly on what they were doing. But every time she connected with him, and every time his weight and his heat moved past her, she wanted to touch him. Feel him. She didn't. But she wanted to.

"Nice," he said at last. "You have excellent form, and great live hands. Let's see how you do from behind."

Her mind went all sorts of wicked places with that, so much so that she missed her first grapple and he took her down. He let her right back up, though. "Pay attention," he said, his voice rough. "This is your life we're trying to save."

"I know."

The next time he grabbed her from behind, she broke his hold and escaped. As she did the next handful of times. She broke free from choke holds, arm pins, waist grabs. She stayed sharp. She fought hard.

She couldn't forget the sheer heat of him behind her, or the strength of his arms around her, or the occasional brush of his cheek, already rough with beard stubble, against hers.

When they were both sweating, he backed away and said, "Good. As long as you're paying attention, you're solid on the basics."

She laughed out loud. "The basics?"

He grabbed a couple of folded towels off of a stack in one corner, wiped his face and neck with one, and handed her the other. "The basics," he said.

She took the towel he gave her and wiped the sweat

from her face. "That's a whole lot of years of experience, and working with the best trainers in the APD."

Without warning, she was flat on her back on the mat with his full weight on top of her, with her arms pinned at her sides and his powerful thighs and calves locking her legs into place.

"I know," he said, staring into her eyes. "The person who is doing this," he told her, his voice even and careful, "finds a way to befriend his victims. He wins their trust. And when they trust him, he kills them. Or he and friends kill them. Either way, you have to stay alert. Every. Single. Second. You didn't, and now you're in trouble. So. Get me off of you."

His voice, his weight on her, his heat, his power, the musky male scent of him mixed with the clean sweat of their exertions, sent signals to her body that bypassed her brain entirely. Jess didn't think at all, didn't even know what she was going to do until she did it.

She kissed him. A full, open-mouthed, tongue-probing, rip-my-clothes-off-of-me-and-take-me kiss, freighted with years of repressed hunger and yearning and desire to be touched that she'd walled off. Her lips touched his, and the floodgates inside of her opened, and as their tongues collided and as her body arched up to meet his, he relaxed a little.

She got her feet under her and with one sharp, hard movement flipped him over, so that she was on top, he was on the bottom.

And she was still kissing him. She lay atop him, her legs wrapping around the outsides of his, her heels hooking under his thighs to pull them up to cradle her buttocks.

He let go of her wrists, and interlocked his fingers with hers. And he kissed her back. Passionately. Wonderfully. His lips searched her mouth, her jaw, the line of her throat, the tender space where her neck joined her shoulder. He nibbled, he licked, he bit, he sucked, and she whispered, "More. Harder."

Her nipples beneath the uniform felt like pebbles, and her breasts tingled; her body ached to feel his skin on her skin, to lift her hips over his straining cock and plunge down onto him and wrap him in her and feel the two of them slide together, to feel the hard, heavy thrust as he pounded into her and their bodies crashed together as she rode him, as they lost themselves in each other.

She wasn't wearing underwear. It wouldn't be all that hard to make it happen.

She shuddered as he rolled them over again and covered her with his body. She could feel how hard he was, how ready. She wanted him. Right then. Right there.

He cupped her face in his hands and kissed her, but the kiss was gentle instead of passionate. He said, "We can't do this, Jess," and his voice held the same urgency she felt, the same wild hunger.

"Yes, we can," she told him.

"Think about it."

And she lay beneath him, feeling desire burning her from the inside out, and she disconnected her mind from her body. She'd had plenty of practice at that.

Why couldn't they do this?

And she knew the answer to that question.

They couldn't pursue each other because they were work partners with a critical job to do. Because people's lives depended on the two of them having their focus on their work, and on both of them doing one thing and doing it well. And on that one thing they were doing well *not* being each other.

Hank had said that Jess was going to have to stay sharp. To keep her mind on what she was doing every second, she couldn't have it drifting off to him. If she lost her focus, someone else could die. If she lost her focus, *she* could die.

She looked him in the eye, and took a deep breath. "Can I hate you for being right?"

"Not as much as I'm going to hate myself; I guarantee it." He kissed her lips once more, lightly, and pushed off of her. "We still need to finish our workout," he said. "I want to make sure you get the advanced stuff. Better that you have it and don't need it than need it and don't have it."

Jess nodded and rose. And they got back to work.

chapter 8

The next morning, Teri called to tell Jess she'd be starting on the day shift tomorrow, starting on days and alternating a week of days with a week of nights.

"I have you on six days, off one, and then on six nights. I figure since you're trying to raise a lot of money quickly, you'll want a lot of hours."

"Thanks," Jess said.

"If you need a different day off than the one I've given you, of course, or if an emergency crops up, you can trade with the other girls."

As soon as they were done, Jess's phone rang again, and she didn't recognize the name on the caller ID. It showed a real name, though, and not that somebody was blocking the caller ID. So she answered anyway.

"Is this Gracie Callahan?" a female voice asked.

Jess almost said no. And then she remembered that people from the club were going to be calling her on that phone. "I'm Grace."

"Delaney Mills," the woman said. "Louella said you wanted to buy some costumes."

"Desperately. I'm supposed to start work tomorrow, and I don't have anything."

"I have a lot. You want to come over and take a look?"

"You mind if I bring a friend with me?" Jess said, not wanting to meet with anyone from the club alone.

"Not at all," Delaney said. "My boyfriend will be here with me."

Jess got the address, called Hank to find out when he would be free to go with her, and called back to let Delaney know when she would be by.

Hank drove. Neither of them said much the whole way over, though. It was the sort of awkward, painful silence that Jess would have welcomed when questioning a suspect. Sitting next to a man she almost couldn't bear to keep her hands off of, though, and with the urge to blurt out any-thing—anything—to make it end, that silence was hell.

Delaney's house was small, neatly tended, in a neigh-borhood euphemistically referred to as "transitional," which meant that property values were on the way down and the drug dealers hadn't shown up yet, but were ex-pected at any minute. The owners of some of the houses on the street looked like they were setting up feeding stations for them.

Delaney answered the door with the boyfriend, who was big and muscular and menacing, glowering behind her. Everyone exchanged names, and then Delaney smiled. "Nice to meet you, Gracie. Come on in." The boyfriend and Hank went off to watch ESPN, and Jess and Delaney headed into the spare bedroom, where Delaney had a closet devoted to her costumes.

Jess flipped through the hangers. "These are great. Which ones are you selling?"

"*All* of them."

Jess turned to study her. "Why?"

"You're working at Goldcastle, right?"

"Going to be."

"You've heard about the missing girls?"

"No. I heard there might be some sort of problem, but not what it was."

"I haven't heard anything solid. Just that maybe a couple of girls who worked there were murdered. Maybe. But . . ." She shrugged. "I've had a few close calls stripping, you know? I have a good boyfriend. I have a little money in the bank. And it seems to me like maybe it's time to move on. Set up a dance studio, maybe, or do some modeling, or . . . something."

Jess bit her lip. "You're smart, I think."

"And you still want to buy my costumes, which makes you . . . what?" Delaney asked. She smiled when she said it, but Jess caught a tinge of worry in her eyes.

"Desperate," Jess said, and trotted out the lie about her imaginary brother, feeling like a shit when she did it.

Delaney looked sympathetic, and worried, too. "Be careful."

"I will," Jess said, and went back to perusing the clothes on the rack.

"I made the best money with the cop costume and the nurse one," she added.

Inwardly, Jess cringed. She wasn't going to insult the police uniform, even in an unofficial version. She said, "I was looking for something . . . happier, I guess."

Delaney had accumulated a broad selection of costumes. She had a fairy with iridescent wings, a sexy witch, a cheerleader, a Catholic schoolgirl, a firefighter, a cowgirl with chaps that Jess thought looked cool, a Chicago-style gangster with a tommy gun, a nun with wimple and rosary, a French maid, a sequin-laden princess, and a jungle girl. She also had a collection of gowns.

"If you're working at Goldcastle, you'll have to have gowns for evening wear—you can do all costume sets during the day, but you have to do at least one gown set if you're on nights. Some of my gowns are one-size-fits-most, so they'll work for you, but you're a lot taller than me, so you'll have to have a seamstress work on the hems if you get them."

Jess nodded, looking at the gowns. She pulled out a black one that had a halter top, no back all the way down to what Jess guessed would be butt crack, and in the front, a four-inch opening that started at the cleavage, then took a sharp turn to the left and ran down the left thigh. The only things holding it together were a rhinestone clip below the bust and another at the hip point. Jess, looking at it, thought it would be terrifying to wear something that a good wind could remove.

Delaney said, "That's a really good one. It's easy to come out of, and easy to get back into, and the guys loved it."

And Jess remembered that getting out of the damned things was the whole point.

She and Delaney settled on the cowgirl outfit, the jungle girl, the princess, and three gowns: the black one, a red one that was basically little patches of red material held together by lots of spaghetti strings, and a white one that actually provided good coverage. It reminded Jess a lot of the gown Audrey Hepburn wore in *Roman Holiday,* without all the sashes and official ribbons, and it came with long white gloves and a tiara. And best of all, it had about six inches of hemline tucked up underneath. Jess figured those ought to be enough. At least to get started.

"Remember the closed-toe shoes," Delaney said as Jess and Hank were leaving. "Goldcastle won't let you dance in open-toe shoes; something about keeping down injuries. You can't ever wear a watch, either."

"Thanks," Jess said.

"And get those grippy things from Wal-Mart to put on the bottoms, or you'll bust your ass on the main stage. The floor right around the pole is unbelievably slippery."

Jess grinned. "Got it." She paid Delaney in cash.

Delaney's voice dropped. "And watch your back," she said as they all walked out to the parked cars. They stood in Delaney's front yard at noon on a hot, sultry Atlanta summer day, and Delaney looked both ways before speaking, as if she was afraid something was going to jump out and grab her. "There really is something . . . nasty . . . going on there. I got wind of it and left—didn't have to be told twice. I've never been one to figure that all the awful stuff in the world couldn't happen to me."

"Thanks," Jess said, and meant it. There were, after all, decent people left in the world. "If I didn't have to be there, I wouldn't. But I'll be careful."

"They were nice people," Hank said on the way back. "Her boyfriend was scared shitless for her—that somebody was going to come after her. They're taking a huge financial hit because she quit dancing, but he's relieved."

"I liked her," Jess said. "She was scared for me."

"You should be scared for you, too."

"I'm the person who's going in to fix things."

"Right," Hank growled. "Tell me how that makes you bulletproof."

Jess started to tell him that no bullets had been involved—and managed to shut up just in time. She knew what he meant. She didn't have to correct him. And he was right. Delaney was right, too. She *did* have to be afraid. There was something about Goldcastle that set off all her alarms, something innately horrible and wrong about it. She was tempted to write off the feeling as being her reaction to strip clubs in general, but she couldn't. The exotic-dance industry seemed cold and hard to her, but at least the other clubs she'd been in didn't leave her feeling like something was creeping up behind her.

"I *will* be careful," she said.

Hank didn't look at her, but he nodded. "I know you

will. And I'm going to do what I can to help you be more careful."

In the few hours she had left, Jess bought a bunch of thongs, picked out music, worked out dance routines, and did her own costume modifications on the red and the black gowns. Sparkly fringe and a glue gun stood in for sewing skill. It was "any idiot can do this," but when it came to sewing, Jess *was* any idiot.

And then she woke to the alarm clock blaring, and she lay there realizing that in a few hours, she was going to have to take off her clothes in front of a bunch of guys who were spending their lunch hour away from the office wishing for tits and ass, and she wanted to roll over and go back to sleep.

But she got up, showered, glued the disguised microphone to her navel, shaved everything, washed and dried her hair, brushed her teeth, and tried to think about inconsequential things. She put on jeans and a T-shirt because she didn't want to look like a dancer when she drove to the club; she stuck the black gown, a couple of thongs and a G-string, a pair of sweatpants for warming up and cooling down backstage, and the cowgirl outfit into her kit bag. She also tossed in a pair of black patent-leather pumps with four-inch heels and grips on the soles. She found that she could get all the rest of the costume gear—the toy six-shooters, the low-slung gun belt, and the lasso—into the bag. But not the hat.

She sighed, and tugged on the high-heeled, fringed cowboy boots that would be what she danced in when she wore the cowgirl costume. Then she scooped all the makeup she'd bought into the bag, jammed the cowboy hat on her head, and swung out the door. She stopped off at Hardee's for breakfast, had three ham biscuits, and did not succumb to guilt.

Then she drove herself to Goldcastle. She was early, but one of the handouts Teri had given her stated that as long as she got in before eleven, she could warm up on the stage. The club was open from eleven A.M. until four A.M., but dancers were permitted in early. Jess called the surveillance van on her cell phone as she drove past it, told the undercover guys she was ready to go live, and they turned on her mike. Hank would finish placing the transmitter boosters when the club opened to customers, and the UC guy said sound checks inside the club had gone well for them so far. So she did the mike test, they said they had her loud and clear, and she headed in.

There was a different gorilla at the employee door this time—still not one of the undercover guys, but not the one that made her skin crawl, either. "You're early," he said.

She nodded. "First day. I wanted to test out the floor and the pole and the stairs and make sure there wasn't anyplace where I'd be walking around in the heels and break my neck."

"Good plan," he said. "We had a girl fall off the main stage doing a swing around the pole a couple of months ago, and she broke her leg in three places."

"Shit."

"Tell me about it." He opened the door for her. "Hey, good luck on your first day." He had a nice smile. She hoped to hell he wasn't the killer, because she thought he seemed like a decent enough guy.

She had the dressing room to herself, and found an empty locker. She planted one of her bugs, then got out the costume she wanted to practice in. She had to do a dress rehearsal of the whole thing. She'd realized on her way in that if she couldn't take her clothes off while in front of an empty room, she was going to fall apart in front of a roomful of rowdy, shouting, hooting men.

Jess stripped down to skin and started putting on the

cowgirl costume. She started with a fringed red thong and matching fringed bra that she'd picked up at a local adult shop, then added Delaney's furry black-and-white cow-spotted chaps, gun belt, and the silver six-shooters that had bright orange caps over the muzzles so no one would mistake the pretend status of the weaponry. She added the furry cow-spotted vest and bright red fringed glovettes. She shoved the hat on, and slipped back into the cowboy boots. And then she locked her stuff away.

She went out to the stage, wishing she'd thought to bring a tape recorder with her music on it so she could try out her act to the music.

She knew her dances well enough. She stood behind the stage door, ran her announcement through her head, put the smile on her face, and strode through the door and out onto the stage.

It was dark. Chairs were up, a few safety lights were on along the baseboards, but the stage itself was a black sheen in a black cavern.

And she felt like the darkness was watching her.

She wasn't alone, she reminded herself. There were undercover guys in a van outside. But if the killer was in the place, she was vulnerable in ways she couldn't even bear to think about.

She had to find a light switch . . . but maybe she should not worry about rehearsing on the actual stage.

And then the lights came on, and Jess's heart came to a full stop. Blinded, she stood there hoping Lenny's hand wasn't the one on the switch.

A woman's voice said, "You'd kill yourself trying to practice up there with the lights off."

Teri.

Jess breathed a sigh of relief. "God. I didn't realize when I came through the door that the lights would be off in here. It scared the piss out of me."

Teri laughed. "I'll bet."

"You always come in this early?"

"Not a chance. I still keep dancer's hours by preference. I'm a natural night owl. But you said you were going to be here to try out the stage before we opened, so I figured I'd better be here too. Some of the boys get in early, surprisingly. Lenny's one of them."

"Thanks, then."

"You have your music and everything?"

Jess said, "Sure."

"If you want to run through one of your sets, I'll be deejay for you, so you can get a feel for everything."

"I have time for a full four-song set?"

"For now, do one fast and one slow." Teri was in jeans and a tank top, with her hair pulled back in a ponytail. Like Jess, she wore no makeup. And Jess thought she looked even better that way. More relaxed. Happier.

"I'll get my music."

When she came back, Teri said, "Doing a full dress rehearsal, huh?"

"I wanted to get the bugs out of the routine. No surprises, you know?" Jess laughed. "But to be honest with you, I was mostly concerned with the shoes."

"With reason." Teri studied Jess's music. "Tim McGraw's 'Real Good Man.' 'Hard on the Ticker,' also Tim McGraw. Alison Krauss and Union Station's 'Let Me Touch You for a While'—hmmm, haven't heard that one. And Faith Hill's 'Breathe.' Heard *that* one plenty of times. Which two do you want?"

"Give me 'Real Good Man,' and 'Let Me Touch You for a While.'"

"You got it. The cowgirl getup should work for you." Teri grinned. "The boys here like cowgirls. Go on back, and I'll call you out."

In a four-song set, the first song would be the stripping-to-the-bra-and-thong song; the second would be her fast pole dance—she'd toss the bra at the end of that. The third would be her slow pole dance, and the last one would be the floor song, where she would do the slowest, most erotic moves while lying or crawling on the stage. She was going to have to condense all of that.

Jess stepped backstage and waited beside the door, trying to figure out where to modify for a two-song set. While she stood back there, the sense of being watched didn't leave her, but she felt better knowing she wasn't alone in the place. Or, more precisely, that she wasn't alone with Lenny. Or the as-yet-faceless man—or men—who'd murdered at least three Goldcastle dancers.

Teri gave her an intro, and this time when Jess burst onto the stage, cowboy-sauntering and with thumbs hooked into an imaginary gun belt, striding in her boots like she owned the Wild West, she had music going and lights on, and the grand ballroom didn't feel creepy anymore. But it felt twice as cavernous.

She faltered.

No one watched her but Teri—but even so, it was the idea of the thing.

Jess looked into Teri's steady gaze, and her stomach knotted and her mouth went dry. She had mentally prepared herself for the performance aspect of this. Had worked out and practiced the moves, figured out how and when she would come out of the costume. She knew that she would be able to give a knockout technical performance that showcased her dancing and her body.

But she had to get naked in front of a stranger—right now—and connect somehow, because getting naked and making the connection were the tools that she believed would bring the killers to her. And she was there to overhear conversations, and she was there to find connections between the victims and the killers. But most of all, in her own mind if nowhere else, she was there to draw the killers away from innocents and to her, to get her shot at them. To take them out.

To do that, she had to be a convincing stripper. She had to connect with Teri.

Any good cop was a good actor. It was as much a part of the job as knowing how to question suspects and comfort families, how to protect the chain of evidence, how to uphold the law and still stop the bad guys. In Undercover, Jess had learned acting in the school of life or death. And she was good. But this situation combined an awkward act, an awkward audience, and huge stakes.

She steadied on jangling guitars, a steady drumbeat, and Tim McGraw's voice. Sexy voice with a down-home twang.

Wild ride, she thought. Play with the fantasy.

Which would have been a hell of a lot easier had she been into the stripper fantasy, and not a cop trying to get into position to stop a probable serial killer. Jess, dry-mouthed, tried for a sexy smile, and fought for inspiration because the music wasn't doing it.

She swung her hips and spun around, grabbed the prop chair from the back of the stage and straddled it, gave Teri what she hoped was a smoldering look, felt the connection fizzle badly, and fought to take herself out of the huge, empty, rattling room, out of the awkwardness of the situation and into something hot and sexy. Into a fantasy *she* could believe in. And somehow . . . somehow, about ten to fifteen eternal seconds into the dance, with her body moving and the drumbeat taking her away, Teri faded and Hank was there. The shape of his powerful hands. The line of his broad shoulders, the slope of muscular forearms that tapered to strong, lean wrists. Jess heard his voice instead of the music, and imagined undressing for him. She smiled broader, relaxing; felt the drumbeat rock and stomp, and dove into it with him. Saw the two of them sweaty and naked together. Felt his lips on hers, hot as Atlanta in July, and she spun and shook, swung around the chair, made eye contact, flicked off clothes with practiced ease. As if she'd been doing it forever.

Tossed the hat behind her and shook her hair free.

Slowed down as McGraw gave way to Krauss, slid around the pole, shimmied and stretched, with Hank the invisible world around which she moved. She remembered to put dance things in there, but mostly, she was in a place where she and Hank were doing all the things she wanted and couldn't have.

She heard the words of the song, and to Hank she whispered, *Just let me touch you for a while.*

She could feel him with her. Jess played peekaboo with the bra, swung on the pole, finally tossed the bright red fringy bra behind her onto the back stage, and ended up kneeling at the front of the stage, knees far apart, hands resting on the inside of her thighs with her arms squeezing against the outsides of her suddenly bare breasts, smiling, smiling.

At Hank.

As the music ended.

Jess's vision of Hank vanished with the last note, and instead, she saw Teri studying her with interest.

"Yeah," Teri said after a long moment. "Okay—Alison Krauss definitely goes on the recommended list. As for the rest, I think you'll do all right. However, you want a little constructive criticism?"

"Sure," Jess said. She got up and started scrambling after her costume—put the bra and the vest back on, and immediately felt better.

"I had you pegged as a wriggler, figured we were probably going to be sending you out the door. But you've clearly got a solid background in classical dance. The problem is, Gracie, that anything that comes from ballet or modern or jazz dance doesn't work in this venue. You know how to move, but you're going to have to stay in character. You can't just wiggle your ass or crawl around the stage making kissy-faces at the guys. But on the other hand, if you put in that ballet-ish jump you did, the boys aren't going to know what to make of it. Same with the butt-tucked ballet posture you fall into by habit. Ballet posture is lovely, but we strippers stick our asses out. The boys like asses."

"It's been a few years," Jess said.

Teri laughed. "Honey, don't lie to me. It's been never. You're one hell of a quick study, but nothing you say is going to convince me that wasn't your very first time taking your clothes off onstage. You're in a money bind, and I respect the hell out of you for putting yourself on the line like this for your brother. But you have never stripped before in your life."

Jess sighed and sat back on her heels, her back leaning against the pole and her arms wrapped around her knees, and thought, *Busted.* "No. I haven't. Do I still have a job?" She felt sick to her stomach. She could have blown this, in spite of everything. Without Jim and his good cover story, she *would* have blown it.

Teri strolled back over to Jess and handed her back her music. "We're short on dancers; you have the motivation to get good at this; you had some really fine moments up there if you can string them all together. And you have a look we can use." Teri shrugged. "In spite of a rough, rough start, you showed real . . . promise. Kick the ballet out of it and you'll have 'em drooling all over themselves."

"I was hoping all those years of classical dance would let me make the transition easily."

"It gave you the body, and stage presence, and athleticism. But ballet isn't about sex, whereas stripping is *all* about sex." Teri leaned her elbows on the edge of the stage. "I'll give you the most useful single piece of advice I got when I started in exotic dancing. Pretend the pole is a man. And pretend your hands are his hands. Because that's sure as hell what every guy out there is going to be pretending when he's watching you. That he's the pole, and everything you're doing to it, you're doing to him. And that he's touching everything you're touching."

Jess sighed and considered that for a long moment. "Okay. I can see where, in that context, ballet moves aren't going to do anything for anybody." She ran through her routine in her mind, substituting jumps and spins with places where she could run her hands up and down her thighs or play peekaboo with her breasts. Drop on the floor on her stomach, maybe, arch her back, and swing her legs forward into a side split, then go to a standing position by keeping her hands on the floor and her back arched and bringing her legs in, lifting up that way. That was going to pull the hell the out of her inner thighs.

Whatever. It'd look good. And at least she'd be getting something out of all those years of dance and all those hours of martial-arts work.

Jess stood, and Teri said, "By the way, Grace . . ."

She didn't say anything else, and Jess arched an eyebrow.

"Don't lie to me anymore, okay? A good working relationship has to be based on *mutual* trust."

Jess felt like a heel, knowing she was *still* lying. "Okay," she said. "I . . . needed this job. And I didn't think you would hire me if I didn't have experience."

"I might not have," Teri said. "Which would have been my loss, I think."

"It would have been Jim's loss," Jess said, deciding on the spur of the moment that if she was going to be stuck being Gracie, then her fictional brother could by God be named Jim.

Teri's mouth twitched in a half smile. "Yeah. I guess there is that, isn't there?" And she held out a hand. "So . . . we're good?"

Jess took her hand. "We're good."

From the main door into the ballroom, Lenny's voice floated into the room. "Well, isn't that sweet?"

And Jess thought, *Thank God I'm not alone in here.*

Hank stopped by HSCU headquarters before he went on to Goldcastle. Jim was back in his cubicle when Hank tracked him down.

"Problems?" Jim asked.

"I'm nervous," Hank told him. "About Jess. About her vulnerability up on that stage. The killer is a regular presence in there; I could feel his touch all over the place."

"You got all the transmitters and bugs planted?"

"I will by the end of her shift today. And the guys you have in place in there won't be connected in any way. Plus Goldcastle has plenty of security cameras in there, and big goons who watch them."

"We have you in place, too. She's not alone."

"Backstage she is."

"Only the dancers go backstage during work hours."

"Can't be sure of that. I get the feeling that, at least after hours, the killer has been back there."

"You mean killers," Jim said. "So you're leaning toward insiders? That fits what we have."

"You might have evidence for more than one person involved, but I only feel one killer. An employee, or a club member using an employee who may or may not be in on what's happening," Hank said. "Only one personality behind the deaths. And someone who has killed a lot of women."

Jim leaned against the corridor wall and hooked his thumbs into his pants pockets. "How many? Ballpark."

"Two . . . maybe three dozen. Maybe more." And then he paused, closed his eyes, and whispered, "Six by six." He looked up at Jim. "The killer keeps thinking 'six by six.' So . . . maybe thirty-six?"

Jim pursed his lips and shook his head. "Yeah. Yeah, yeah. I knew this was bad. Anytime I start munching Rolaids, I know I'm in the middle of something nasty. And I realized this morning that I'm up to half a bottle a day."

Hank nodded. "Your own psychic barometer."

"Isn't worth much."

"Better than nothing." Hank said, "More than *she* has. And I'm afraid that Jess isn't going to be prepared for what the killer throws at her. She's met him. Maybe touched him. Definitely touched something he touched."

Hank watched the blood drain out of Jim's face. "She didn't say anything."

"She isn't sold on my ability to read this stuff. She's been polite about it, but she's not going to hang her reputation on anything I tell her. So I wouldn't have expected her to."

"But *you're* sure."

"Getting there."

Jim stood up straight and rubbed the stubble on his shaved scalp. "Well, this was always a possibility. A near certainty, really. We put her in there to get information, she's in the tank with the rest of the fish. And she's a real pretty fish. Shark's going to want to take a shot at her, too."

"She have anyone watching her when I'm not with her?" Hank asked.

"We only have her covered at work."

"Cover her at home, would you?"

"We can't, really. We're stretched thin on this already. But she's a big girl. One of the most focused cops I've ever known. And one of the best. She'll be okay."

Hank decided that he could be her guardian angel. He could keep watch over her away from work, as well as in the club. Or maybe spend extra time at the club, even when she wasn't there, finding out who was killing dancers. But all he said was, "All right. I'm sure you're right."

Jim looked at him, then looked away and made a disgusted noise. "I would never have thought it, but you are the most pitiful excuse for a liar that I ever met. Which is fine. It's the liars who are good at it who make my life hell." He grinned. "All right, my ass." And then he said, "I'm not going to ask you what sneaky little plan ran through your head. Just don't fuck up the case. And don't screw up Jess's cover."

"I know all that. I don't want to see her . . . hurt."

Jim said, "Me, either. That's why I'm looking the other way."

chapter 9

Backstage, a couple of the day-shift girls had arrived by the time Jess got through a quick shower in the dancers' locker room. They occupied seats along a mirror, putting on makeup, working with their hair, and adjusting costumes. Both were brunettes. One looked a lot like Crystal Gayle, with huge blue eyes and hair almost down to the floor. The other one was pert and short and cute. The pert one looked up and smiled when Jess walked in, and tapped the other on the shoulder. The long-haired girl looked over, nodded acknowledgment, and went back to fixing her hair.

"You're one of the new girls," the pert one said.

"Grace Callahan," Jess said.

"That your real name or your stage name?"

"Real. My stage name is Summer." This part of undercover was going to really drive Jess up the wall. She had to be Grace in here and Summer out there and make sure she didn't let any of the details of her Grace identity slip to the customers, because exotic dancers had to protect themselves from potential stalkers even at the best of times. Summer would need a story of her own, but everyone would know it was a tissue of lies.

When Ginny and Jess had talked about stripping, Ginny had said, "They ask me if I'm a college student, or an actress, or if I'm a nurse or a dental hygienist or whatever. And I ask them what they *think* I do. And when they tell me, I tell them they're right. Because if they say they think I'm really a secretary during the day, well, that's their fantasy. That some uptight girl who works in an office during the day might really be this wild stripper on the weekend. Or they want to think I'm the college girl they wanted so much to get into bed with. Or maybe a single mom trying to make it on my own. I'm whatever they want me to be, and they leave happy, and I leave with a lot of money."

Jess shook off the memories of Ginny, and returned her attention to the two women in the room.

"My real name's Millie Hantumakis," the perky dancer said. "But call me River. Everyone else does, and it's easier to keep everything straight that way."

"I'm all for easier," Jess said.

"And she's Cree," River continued. "While she's dancing anyway."

"Hi, River," Jess said. "Hi, Cree."

Cree ignored Jess.

"She's deaf," River said. "And she already has her hearing aids off because they're big and they get in the way once she starts on her hair."

Jess felt her eyebrows starting up her forehead, and got her expression under control. "Doesn't that make it hard to, ah . . . do this job?"

"No," River said. "She's amazing. She picks music with a good bass beat, and goes by the vibrations. The guys love her. And she reads lips really well, so what with the loud music out there, she follows conversations with the guys a lot better than most of the rest of us do."

Which made sense.

Jess got back into the cowgirl costume.

"I did a cowgirl for a while," River said. "Too many pieces to take off."

Jess grinned. "I considered that a plus, actually."

River was pulling on the parts of a schoolgirl uniform. Lacy little ankle socks, a very short pleated plaid skirt over a plaid thong, a plaid bra with sequins along the top and over that a white shirt and a school tie. "You been doing this long?"

"I've been *dancing* for a long time. This is my first day stripping."

River looked startled. "Um, nothing personal, but . . . aren't you kind of old to just be starting out?"

"Yeah," Jess said, putting on eyeliner. "I had a sudden need for a whole lot of money, and this was the only legal way I could think of to get it."

River took a seat at the dressing table and started applying makeup. "You get in trouble with a bookie or something?"

Jess gave a rueful laugh. "Jesus. What is there about me that makes people think gambling problem? My brother's in the hospital, and he doesn't have insurance. I'm going to see if I can raise enough money to pay his bills."

"I'm sorry," River said. "Me, I do it to keep a roof over my head and my kid's, and so I can get time off to go to her school plays and stuff."

"You have a kid? In school? You don't look old enough."

"I got pregnant in high school," River said. "Dani's father turned out not to love me quite as much as he said he did once that happened. He offered me money for an abortion, and my mother tried her best to talk me into taking it." Her voice got soft. "At the last minute, I didn't go through with it. I couldn't kill my baby. And every day since, I've been glad I didn't. She's the best thing that ever happened to me."

Jess said, "I can't imagine. I don't have kids."

River said, "Dani changed my life. I learned how to be responsible, how to think about someone besides me. It's

"Sure it is," Ginger Rose said, rolling her eyes, and left the dressing room.

Jess's surprise must have shown on her face, because River said, "A lot of girls claim it's their first time. Mostly to the guys, though. The guys like newbies, and sometimes they tip better when they think you've never stripped. But you really look like you've never done this before. Honestly, once you get out there, it's a whole lot easier. The waiting is the worst part. You'll be great."

The bottom fell out of Jess's stomach. "Thanks," she said.

When Ginger Rose returned with a belly-dancer costume, however, Jess decided to ignore the redhead's previous derisive comment. She said, "Give your ex-boyfriend another thought. When you go home, take a couple of big, muscular friends with you. You don't need to be a statistic, and if you walk into your house and discover that you're alone with a pissed-off ex waiting for you, you could be."

Ginger Rose started pulling on the borrowed costume. She turned to look at Jess. "This from experience?"

"Yes," Jess said, not elaborating.

Ginger Rose stared at her face in the mirror. "Don't worry about me and Stan. He's a goddamned bastard. But all three of my brothers are over at my house right now helping him move out. And when I say *helping,* you should imagine Stan's shit flying out onto the grass in pieces. I guarantee you my brothers are a big, *big* help. I called them at work on my way over here, and every one of them said they'd take a couple hours off to make sure I went home safe." She looked over at Jess and frowned. "And you don't have the right coloring to borrow makeup from, dammit. You know how hard it is to find makeup that goes with red hair?"

"Unfortunately, I do," Jess said. "I was a redhead for a while once. It was too much trouble."

"You do blond well, though. It matches your skin and your eyes. I can't be a blonde. It just makes all my freckles stand out."

"You're a natural redhead?" Jess asked, looking at the shocking red of Ginger Rose's hair and doubting deeply.

"Yeah—but not this red. Red hair gets darker when you get older. I was a carrot when I was six, but now if I don't mess with it, it's mostly brown, except when I'm in the sun. Which, the way I burn, is about never." She patted Cree on the shoulder, and Cree looked over. "May I borrow your makeup?" she asked, enunciating clearly so that Cree could read her lips.

"Sure," Cree said. "Anything you need." She did a good job of modulating her tones and her volume; Jess wondered if she'd always been deaf, or if her hearing loss came later.

Jess sat there for a few more minutes, staring at herself in the mirror. She put on the hat, took a deep breath, and gave herself the dancer smile. *I've already found out things we needed to know,* she told herself. *They need me here. I can make a difference in this investigation.*

She looked at the clock and sighed again. *First time for everything,* she told herself. *It's only skin. It's dancing, and you know how to dance. Smile a lot, make eye contact, don't do the ballet thing. The pole is a man; your hands are his hands.*

And don't throw up onstage.

Jess curled on the bench seat in the bay window in her tiny room, listening to two of her three apartment mates arguing about the number of calories in a quarter slice of pizza, and whether it would be better to eat a quarter of a slice each and keep it down, or eat two or three pieces and then purge it.

She shouldn't have roomed with other dancers, she thought. She didn't need their neuroses as well as her own.

She watched the rain sliding down the window and said, "We have a bad connection. You're doing *what?*"

"You heard me. Stripping," Ginny said.

"Oh, my God. Does Mama know?"

And Ginny had managed to sound incredulous. "Are you insane? It's bad enough I'm doing this. You think I'm going to tell her how I'm making my money and then hear about it for the rest of forever? I'm desperate, Jessie. I'm not crazy."

"Surely there's something else you could do."

"Of course there is," Ginny had said. "But not anything that's going to let me take home three thousand dollars a week, which is what I'm getting right now. It's temporary, Jessie. I'll have enough money to pay my tuition for the next year, and then I'll be done. I'll join a troupe somewhere, or start auditioning for roles in musicals. But she can't pay my way." For an instant, Jess caught a tone of jealousy as Ginny said, "And I didn't get a full scholarship."

Jess sighed. "I'm sorry, Ginny. You should have. You're wonderful."

"So you won't tell Mama?"

"No," Jess said. "I won't do that." She'd paused and taken a deep breath. "What's it like?"

The line fell silent for a moment, and then Ginny's voice came back, bemused. "It's horrible. Men touch you, even though they're not supposed to. They ask you to let them do things to you that would just make your jaw drop. They act like the biggest favor they could do for you is take you into a dark corner and screw you over the back of a chair."

And then she laughed. "And at the same time, it's wonderful. When you're onstage and the lights are on you, you can see them admiring you. Wanting you. Lusting after you. You're this goddess, and they're your worshipers, throwing money at you and begging you to be with them. You're all-powerful. It's . . . like a drug. The applause, the apprecia-

tion. Some of the men are really nice. I sit and talk to them, and they have such sad lives at home. They're so grateful for my attention."

"It sounds like a weird job," Jess said.

"That's not the half of it." She laughed. "Just be grateful you'll never know."

Hank was almost the first customer through the door when Goldcastle's opened, but the lunch crowd was large. He found himself a place right up against the stage, and settled in with the beer he was going to pretend to drink and a lunch special brought to him by a waitress from the restaurant who was taking orders from an abbreviated lunch menu in the ballroom. Corned-beef sandwich, fries, soggy pickle. None of it was very good, but then Hank supposed most of the guys who were eating in the grand ballroom didn't pay much attention to the food.

The deejay dropped the volume on the rock music he'd been playing and did an intro for a girl named River. A cute, young-looking dancer in a school uniform with a plaid skirt, lacy ankle socks, and high, high heels came skipping out to something hideous, yet horribly appropriate, by Britney Spears.

While River danced, Hank split his attention between her and the men watching her. The early crowd looked like a mix of guys on lunch break from offices around town and out-of-towners. It was tempting to look at the sleazy guy in the back and think that he was suspicious. Except that the victims gave every sign of having trusted the killer, and Hank would bet there wasn't a girl working at Goldcastle who would willingly go anywhere with Raincoat Bob back there.

Second song. Equally bouncy, equally bad. Some other teenage singer. Someone really needed to sit down with this River girl and discuss good music, and what it wasn't. But the dancer was up at the pole, naked except for shoes, socks, and a plaid thong, and Hank had a job to do.

He fished a five out of his wallet and held it up, and when the dancer swung over to get it, he stuck it into her thong at the hip. She flashed him a big, bright smile, and he could have been hurt by the shiver of distaste he felt underneath it. But he was looking with his fingertips. Seeing with his hands, and what he saw when he touched her was that she had a kid at home. Little girl. A decent home situation, a lot of love. Just the two of them, plus the dancer's mother. River bore no taint of the death that was all over this place. The poison had not touched her.

She did two slow songs after that, but Hank's attention was on a couple of dancers in short, see-through robes who had started circulating among the tables, talking with customers, letting the men buy them drinks, doing table dances.

He'd need to connect at least briefly with each of them, to see if he could get a feel for whether the killer was present, to see if he was hunting one of them. If his touch was fresh. Because if the killer was in the house right then, it would narrow the suspect list to something manageable.

And then Jess came out, and Hank almost couldn't breathe. He actually hadn't seen her in any of the costumes she'd bought. She was smiling, her hair swinging loose to her shoulders, her bright red cowboy hat framing her face, and she moved like . . . like . . .

He couldn't think. He had no words. He was watching her, sort of hearing the music in the background but not in any meaningful way. He was lost in longing, knowing that he had turned her down and walked away from his chance to touch her. She was looking at other men, smiling at them, deftly flicking the vest off and tossing it behind her, playing with the guns at her hips, shimmying out of the gun belt, tossing away the chaps.

And then her gaze connected with his, and it felt like he was the only man in the room. The only man on the planet. She was undressing. Undressing, exclusively for him, her gaze locked on his, her smile suddenly secret. Private. Between just the two of them. He stared at her body. At her breasts as she let him glimpse them, then hid them away, and his body ached to feel her against him. To touch her, to hold her, to make love to her.

He'd had her in his arms. He'd felt her kiss, felt his body cry out for her touch, and he had pushed her away. He could see what he'd missed, and right at that moment, he was wishing to hell that he wasn't missing it. And he had told her that the two of them weren't going to happen. Couldn't happen.

The world was full of fools, but he was the fool who turned her down. He was *that* fool.

Guys waving money at her drew her attention away from him, and the connection between the two of them broke. She was gone, and he wanted to go pound into the floor the men who had taken her away from him. He watched her dancing for them, taking their money, smiling when they shouted to her. He watched as the music slowed and her dance became sexier, and he didn't even have to use his imagination to see him and her in bed together; he watched as the music slowed more and she moved from the pole to the floor.

And he saw the other men looking at her, their eyes as hungry as his own, and jealousy ate into him. He wanted to touch her, and pulled a bill out of his wallet, and waved it, and she crawled over to him, smiling, and whispered, "How am I doing?"

It was all he could do to get the word "Fine" past the lump in his throat.

He slid the bill into the side of her thong with all the

other money that was there, and the shock of the story that his fingertips told him made his knees weak.

"He's here," he said loud enough that she and the mike in her navel could both get the words, but no one else. "He . . . he's been watching you. He *touched* you."

The smile on her face never wavered. "Then we'll find that sorry sonuvabitch," she said, and crawled away, to take someone else's money, to smile in someone else's eyes. To do the job she was here to do, which was nothing like the job she looked like she was doing, Hank remembered. Finally.

Behind him, two waiters suddenly moved from seat to seat at the bar that bellied up to the stage, bringing complimentary coffee in Styrofoam cups, offering a cup to any man who wanted one. They were the Vice guys, Hank realized, who had been forwarded his tip about the presence of the killer from the officers working the surveillance van.

These inside guys had the sweet job—handing out the cups. Some poor rookie in plainclothes, however, would be out by the trash in back, waiting to go Dumpster diving should any discarded cups come his way. And around the front of Goldcastle, just outside the door, another plainclothes cop would be hoping some of these guys would carry those cups out with them, then toss them in the trash, in plain sight. So that he could pick them up. DNA the legal way.

More than once, Jim had bitched about what a pain in the ass the fine art of collecting untainted evidence was. Hank was watching the start of a long, slow chain that wouldn't bear fruit for weeks. If ever.

But it was a start, wasn't it?

Hank stopped watching Jess, and started watching the faces of the men around him, trying to catch some glimpse of the killer. Because the killer was right up there against the stage, right where he could touch her, right where the residue of his sick hunger could linger.

And any of the faces Hank saw could have been the guy. Staring at Jess the way they were, they all looked like a bunch of perverts. He could have gone around the stage kicking the shit out of every man there and he wouldn't have lost a minute's sleep.

Which was *why* he and Jess couldn't get involved, he told himself. He was ready to kill complete strangers for looking at her, and he'd only kissed her once. Imagine what would happen to his judgment if the two of them were actually sleeping together. If they were involved. If, God forbid, he fell in love with her.

Her set ended and he caught a glimpse of her hurrying off the stage, and then the deejay did a big lead-up to a firecracker redhead in a belly-dancer outfit, and Hank realized that someone backstage could have touched Jess before she came out. Were there any men back there? Security guys or bouncers or boyfriends, maybe?

Then he remembered that Jim had told him the UC guys couldn't get back there during work hours because it was absolutely, unconditionally, no-exceptions dancers only. Otherwise Jess's participation in this thing would not have been so critical.

The harem girl had gotten rid of only the veil when Hank waved his money at her. She shimmied over to him, and all he could think was that next to Jess, she was invisible. He slid the bill into her costume.

Without warning, violent, nightmare horror washed over him, so brutal and so sick that Hank sagged back into his seat, lost in the killer's rage. She was next. *This* girl—this dancer—she was going to die this night. He knew which park the killer was going to dump her body in, and that the killer had a stage set. For her to dance on. One last private dance, after pain and torture and abuse. Everything was ready.

Tonight, Hank thought. Tonight.

The ferocity of that fresh rage, the bastard's intense feelings of betrayal, and the hunger to degrade, destroy, pervert, hurt, and then slaughter, tore Hank up inside.

He got to his feet, fled into the bathroom, and puked, his head hanging over the bowl, his hands on the stall to either side. Bad. This was bad—as ferocious, as horrible, as any crime scene he'd ever touched.

The restroom attendant was watching him when he came out of the stall wiping his mouth on a strip of toilet paper. "Are you all right, sir?"

Hank raised an eyebrow. "Yeah, sure. I usually toss my lunch like that, don't you?" He washed his hands and face, cupped water in his hands and rinsed his mouth out with it, and took the towel the man offered him. "Something I ate didn't agree with me."

"Something you ate . . . here?"

"That's why I was here," Hank said. "Lunch and titties."

"I'm sorry, sir. If you tell your waitress—"

"Don't worry about it," Hank said. "I feel fine now."

"Yes, sir." The guy started to ask him something else, then stopped. "Are you a member?"

"No."

Hank got out of there as fast as he could. He headed back to his seat, but his beer was gone and someone else was sitting in his place. He took a table along the back wall and called Jim.

Jim picked up on the first ring.

"I got the next victim, Jim," he said. "He intends to kill her tonight, dump her body in Piedmont Park." Hank swallowed against another wave of nausea and closed his eyes for a moment. "Dancer named Ginger Rose. She's on the stage right now."

"You sure? Tonight?"

"Positive. At least as positive as I can be. This one hit me so hard I tossed my lunch."

He was having a hard time hearing Jim over the noise of the club. The girl was dancing to "Genie in a Bottle," and with the way he felt, the music was drilling straight through his skull. But he thought Jim had told him to hang on.

Jim came back to the phone a moment later and said, "Our guys in place have her, and they'll hand her off to mobile surveillance when she leaves. We won't let anything happen to her."

Hank managed a mumbled, "I hope not," but he was still so weak, so sick—still shaking so badly—that what actually came out of his mouth had to have been incoherent.

Jim's voice in his ear was calm and reassuring. "It's okay. We're ahead of the curve on this one, Hank. We can save this girl."

chapter 10

Jess leaned against the wall in the dressing room, her hands shaking, her whole body weak from a combination of nerves and exhilaration and embarrassment. And fear. Mustn't forget fear.

The killer had been out there, had seen her dancing, had even touched her, and she had looked into those faces and smiled her smile and hadn't seen anything in even one of the men out there that she could point to and say, "He's it. He's the one who's killing them."

They'd been a bunch of relatively clean-cut guys in suits or work shirts and loosened ties, as well as one guy she was almost sure was an actor on a TV series that filmed in Atlanta. He'd had a dancer right up close to him, but he'd still put a big bill in Jess's G-string. She checked.

One hundred dollars from him. The rest were ones and fives. Mostly ones.

A dancer who'd been out on the floor poked her head in the dressing room door and said, "Jason Hemly wants to meet you."

Jess closed her eyes. Jason Hemly was the actor's name. God. She so very much did *not* want to go hang out with actors and pretend to be who she wasn't. But she would.

Soon. "I'll be out in a little bit," she said. "I need to . . . catch my breath first. And change."

"I'll tell him," the girl said. And with an envious glare that personified the darker side of the early twenty-something, cheerleader-gone-wild persona of most of the Goldcastle dancers, she flounced off.

Jess started pulling the money she'd made out of her G-string and dropping it into the front pocket of her bag. Teri leaned in the door. "Caught your act from the doorway— just for a minute. The modifications you made worked well."

"I'd say," Jess said, counting money. Not including the hundred-dollar bill she'd made from the actor, she had already earned back her fifty for the day's tip-out, and a little more. Surely it couldn't be that easy.

"I'll be going, then," Teri said. "Just wanted to congratulate you on a good debut."

And Jess looked up. "You have a minute?"

"Sure."

"In your office?"

Teri's smile died. "Of course."

Jess followed her down the hall, into the office, and closed the door behind them.

"Problems?" Teri asked.

"Just one really big one. You didn't tell me that the problem this place was having was with dancers being murdered."

Teri sat down and sighed. "You heard."

"Word gets around. I would have liked to have heard from you. That's the sort of information a woman wants to have *before* taking a job. I'm not going to do my brother any good if I'm dead."

"Have a seat," Teri said, and Jess sat. Teri sighed again, heavily, ran a hand through her hair, and stared at her desk. "As far as I've been able to figure out—and I had to identify one of the bodies, and the police have been around asking questions, of course—there have been three girls murdered in the past year," she said. "All three were dancers; all three were employees here, though I cannot say with certainty that all three were employed here at the time they were killed. And I have no way of knowing if they were also dancing at other clubs, or if what happened to them was even because they were dancers."

Jess sat there, listening. Waiting.

"I'm sorry I didn't tell you," Teri said. "I should have, I suppose."

"Yeah," Jess said. "You should have told me."

"I was in a bind. Still am. We are short fifteen dancers on our roster. Fifteen. All of those fifteen but one quit when the rumors started, and the rumors have continued to keep most prospective replacements away."

"All but one?" Jess studied Teri, watching for tells that would suggest deception. "So if fourteen quit, what did the other one do?"

"Got killed," Teri said, not meeting Jess's eyes. "To stay in business, we need a full roster. A lot of people depend on us keeping our doors open so that they can pay their bills. Or in your case, someone else's bills." Now she looked up at Jess, and she seemed defiant. "It's my job to keep our roster full, to make sure people get paid, that nobody starves. We don't get paid if the boys don't spend it. And the boys like variety."

"So does the killer, it would seem."

Teri took a pen from her desk. "I'm hoping Goldcastle isn't the link. I really am." She played with the cap of the pen.

Jess realized that Teri already thought Goldcastle was the link. Teri didn't want to believe it, Jess decided, because money was at stake, a lot of it hers.

"You look stressed out," Teri said.

"Bad case of nerves," Jess told her, still watching. "About halfway through my set out there, I almost panicked and ran off the stage."

"But you didn't. You were solid. And very fresh. You were putting something out there the customers really responded to. You're still tucking your butt too much when you move, though."

"Dammit. I thought I'd fixed that."

"Most of the time you have. You'll get there. And I think you can fill seats for us, Grace. I'll definitely be keeping you on the schedule. And on the weeks when you do nights, you'll make even better money, and get more exposure."

Jess laughed. Her laugh sounded hoarse in her own ears. "What?"

Jess said, "How much more exposed could I be?"

Teri chuckled. "Well, yes. There is that. But that isn't what I meant. Evenings, we have some genuine movers and shakers in the audience. People who could get you the sort of work that would make you a feature dancer—someone we could headline. Having seen how quickly you've caught on to this, I have to think that you could do it. You'll have to move fast if you want it, because of your age. At this point, you have a very short shelf life. But you can make a lot of money in a couple of years if you're careful about how you spend it." She leaned back and spread her arms. "And then you can invest it, and let your money work for you. That's what I did."

And you're looking at a lot of that money vanishing into the ether if this club goes down the tubes, aren't you? So you'll tell your dancers to be careful, but you won't tell them why.

All she said, though, was, "Well, I guess I have to believe you about the big shots. There's an actor out there right now who sent someone back to tell me he wanted to meet me."

Teri sat up straight. "Really? Who?"

"Jason Hemly."

"Then go. Go! He's gotten a couple of our girls on his show as extras, and one even got a small speaking part. Those are credits we can use, Grace."

Jess hesitated.

"Hurry," Teri said. "Get out there before he gets distracted."

He'd had second and even third thoughts about it, but finally Hank decided that he'd drop by Jess's place rather than go straight home. And take food, because she wasn't going to feel like shopping on the way home, and she'd had nothing in her cupboards.

So he was leaning against her door, starting to get worried, with grocery bags scattered around his feet, when she came out of the stairwell and spotted him.

Jess gave him a weary, grateful smile, and Hank found himself thinking again that he would have to be *that* fool—the one who'd turned her down.

"Long day." She sighed. "Thanks." And she opened the door and led him inside.

He had the irrational urge to hug her; it seemed so much like the right thing to do. Instead, he said, "I'll cook while you change."

"You cook?" She looked surprised, and at the same time intrigued.

"I eat; therefore I cook."

She said, "Give me ten minutes," and headed into the bathroom.

He didn't let himself think too much about the fact that by this time tomorrow their joint assignment would be over. The stakeout team would get the killer—or killers—tonight. And once he and Jess finished whatever debrief HSCU required, Jess would be heading back to her regular job, and Hank would be back at the dojo, with no reason to call her or drop by with food. If he wanted to change his mind, this would be his last chance to do it.

Except he *could* call her after they were finished working together. And that way, they wouldn't be jeopardizing the mission. Wouldn't be screwing anything up by being so drawn to each other.

Really, though, their part of the thing was done. Because he had found the next victim before she was dead, because the police were going to be there to step between the girl and her would-be killer, because HSCU would have the bastard dead to rights, and arrest him, and that would be the end of it.

Hank listened to Jess in the bathroom showering, and imagined her wet and naked. That proved to be an awkward line of thought, leading as it did to her wet and naked and beneath him. So he focused on how relieved he was that she wouldn't have to take off her clothes in front of a big room full of drooling perverts anymore, and that led to his being possessively relieved that he wouldn't have to share her.

Usually Hank loved to cook. Right at that moment, however, it gave his mind too much time to wander. He preheated Jess's crappy little oven, started a base sauce of tomato paste, tomato sauce, and a dollop of water simmering in her sauce pot, and got water boiling in his own stockpot—which he'd brought with him because he did not think Jess was a woman who would own a stockpot. Then he went to work crushing garlic and dicing tomatoes and rolling dried oregano off his palms into the sauce and adding a little extra-virgin olive oil and a pinch of salt and a bit of the garlic to his nice, crunchy loaf of Italian bread. The garlic bread went into the oven, and the diced tomatoes, more garlic, more olive oil, and another bit of salt went into the sauce.

The shower stretched a lot longer than Jess's predicted ten minutes

The water was already boiling and the pasta nearly done when she came out of the bathroom in a big, fluffy terry-cloth robe, her hair wet and pulled back, her face scrubbed free of makeup. "Sorry I took so long. One shower wasn't enough," she said. "I got out, but then I had to get right back in again. And I need . . . stronger soap. Or . . . Lysol or something." She shuddered a little. "Maybe after supper I can take another shower. I keep feeling strangers . . . touching me." And then she stopped dead, and sniffed the air with an expression of utter ecstasy on her face. "Ooooooh, what *is* that?"

"Garlic bread, sauce, and pasta," he said. "Basic stuff, but I'm hungry and I figured you would be too. This is quick and simple."

"Quick. Oh. Wow. It smells like that, and it's quick and simple? When you said you cooked, I thought you meant that you knew how to microwave or something."

"I eat; therefore I cook," he repeated. "I don't like microwaved food."

"Who does? Where did you learn this stuff?"

"My mom's Italian. We lost the language, but we kept the food."

"Thank God," Jess said so fervently that Hank laughed. "After the day I had, I can't think of anything that would fix things better than real food."

He turned to her. "Don't talk about work. It'll ruin your appetite, and I'm making a *lot* of food."

"A lot of food. Can I keep you?" she asked. Her tone was joking, but there was a little flicker in her eyes that suggested the joking would end if he said yes.

He turned back to the stove and stirred the pots. "You don't like psychics, remember?"

"I could make an exception in your case." And just like that, all the joking was gone from her voice.

Hank swallowed hard. He was willing to make exceptions in her case, too, he realized. Was willing to take chances when he'd sworn to himself that he would never do that again. Willing to believe.

Was he stupid? Gullible? Setting himself up to get his heart broken?

Yes, probably.

He poured the pasta out of the stockpot into a colander he'd brought, shook it hard—a lot harder than it needed. Poured a little of the sauce into the bottom of the empty stockpot and let it sizzle a bit, and then dumped the pasta back, and poured sauce on top of it. Stirred it around so that all the pasta was well coated, took out two plates, and pulled the bread from the oven.

"I bet," Jess said quietly from right next to him as he put the baking sheet on a pot holder, "that this place has never smelled this good before. Ever."

He turned, and her face was inches from his. She went up on her toes and kissed him on the lips, and before he had a chance to respond, pulled away and said, "Watching you, all I could think was that I had never seen that done before that well."

All the blood in his brain fled south. He didn't have enough left to feed rational thought.

He muttered, "Thank you," and turned back to the bread—already sliced, all set to go into in a bowl of its own.

He heard her sigh, felt the air get empty all around him as she moved away.

"I . . . While we eat, I have some things I want to . . . Dammit." Words weren't working for him. He didn't punch anything. But he thought all inanimate objects ought to be grateful that he didn't want to look like an ass in front of her, because he wanted to put a fist through the wall. He left the half the bread on the sheet, the pot of rotini pasta covered on the stove, and went after her.

Grabbed her wrist, turned her around, pulled her into his arms, and kissed her until his head felt like it was going to explode and he was sure he'd forgotten how to breathe.

"All I want to do is touch you," he said into the side of her neck, and felt her body molding itself to his.

Showered, she was clean of the residue of the day—he could feel no echoes from Goldcastle on her skin, no darkness anywhere. Beneath his fingertips, Jess shimmered with heat and lust. "You have on that robe, and all I can think is that there's one lousy tied belt between me and that body of yours. I want . . ." God, he wanted things he didn't even dare say. He wanted everything.

"Touch me," she whispered. She undid the belt of her robe, and in that same simple move, undid any last resistance he might have mustered. He groaned, and slid his hands beneath the thick terry cloth and along her sleek skin. His fingers sought out her curves, and at the same time, they told him the truth of her desire; that she had no hidden agendas, no secret deceptions. He felt no doubt in her. All he felt was that she wanted him as completely and as hungrily as he wanted her.

He had not thought he would ever feel that. He gave himself up to her, lost himself in the moment, thankful only that it existed and not daring to look beyond the instant they inhabited to the wide abyss of the future.

He tangled his hand in her hair and pulled her head back and growled, "Kiss me." She wrapped her body around him and leaned up into his kiss.

Her hunger consumed him. One hand released her hair, slid down her back and caught her waist, and the other curved under her bare buttock; he hiked her up so that she was at eye level with him, and she wrapped her legs around him, locking her ankles together and tightening her thighs. He groaned, and pulled out of the kiss to search her face for an echo of his own desperate desire. "I want all of you, Jess. Now."

She shivered. "Take me," she said. "Right now."

She began to tug his pullover off; he put her down long enough to fish his wallet out of his back pocket before stripping out of pants and underwear and shoes and socks at top speed. He didn't want her to see his scars. And most of the right side of his body was nothing but scars. But she smiled at him, ran her hands over both sides of his body, and never flinched or looked disgusted. He reached into his wallet and pulled out a condom. "I told myself today that we weren't going here. But I still bought condoms along with the groceries."

"Well," she said, "you're psychic."

"Maybe more than I thought." He rolled the condom on, then caught her arms and braced her back against the dining room wall. She smiled at him with eyes gone heavy-lidded and lifted her legs around his waist, and he plunged into her.

She cried out, but he had no chance to wonder if he'd hurt her; she tightened around him and locked her legs around his waist, pulling him deeper into her. He paused at the pleasure of him in her, at the softness of her breasts crushed against his chest, at the soap and skin scent of her as he pressed his face against hers, at the way she arched against him and moved with him.

He held himself still within her, and again stared into her eyes; he was stunned, shaken, almost afraid. "God, oh, God," he whispered, needing proof that this wasn't a dream. "Are you real?"

"Are you?" she asked. "Take me hard."

They understood each other—he could see it in her eyes. They'd both been in the darkness for a long time. Had both been dead inside, and they were staring at each other, discovering that they weren't dead anymore, but both were afraid to be suddenly alive again only to discover they were alone after all.

He moved inside her. A slow, careful withdrawal, a hard thrust that made her gasp.

"Yes," she groaned.

He did it again, and felt the pleasure in her, his fingertips reading her hunger, her yearning for the force and the ragged edge of his rough need, and the breathless wonder of her nearly drove him over the edge. Her body went rigid and her head went back and she screamed in wordless release.

His breath sobbed out of him as she groaned, "Yes, more." He tightened his grip on her, pounded into her harder, faster, and she dug fingers into his shoulders, arched and writhed, screamed, "Harder, harder," while his muscles and skin went molten, incandescent, and the connection of him to her, him in her, them together as one grew brighter and brighter until he shut his eyes tight against the light of her, and even then she burned behind his eyelids like too much sun.

He felt like he was going to shake apart, like he was going to explode from the inside out . . . like he was going to disappear into smoke and flames and pleasure too intense to comprehend. She collapsed against him, boneless, and he carried her to the daybed without pulling free of her, and carefully he laid her down on it, and moved over her.

"Look at me," he whispered. "Be with me."

She opened her eyes. Touched the sweat on his forehead and looked into his eyes and smiled, and whispered, "You're wonderful."

He shuddered, and she touched the scars on his face lightly, and her eyes went feral as she said, "Give me all of you. Everything."

"Yes," he growled, and she lifted her hips to collide with

him hard and fast, and she watched him through half-closed eyes. He lost himself in her ferocious wanting and luxuriated in the pleasure in her murmured urgings—until control eluded her and her head tossed and her eyes shut of their own accord, her fingers locked onto the covers, and this time he let himself go all the way, holding nothing back, crashing faster, harder, deeper into her until they exploded together, shuddering, lost and found at once, and they fell together, exhausted, exhilarated, thrilled.

Slowly and carefully then, he lowered himself onto her. He stroked her lips with a finger, and brushed his cheek against hers.

"You had all of me from your first touch," he whispered.

They managed to get back to supper while the pasta was still warm, at least. Jess wished she could remember more of how it tasted, but at that point food was nothing more than fuel to get her and Hank to the next round. They ate, they laughed, but as soon as they were done, they were back in bed. And then on the floor, somehow, and then in the shower.

At one point, she said, "You know, we're doing a terrible job of keeping this thing between us platonic."

And he laughed a little and said, "I know. But it's okay. The guys are on a stakeout right now, at the house of the woman who was going to be the next victim. They're going to get these bastards tonight."

"You're sure?" She was startled and hopeful and worried all at the same time. She wanted the case to be solved, but she didn't want to not have Hank around every day, every night, all the time.

She couldn't get enough of him. If she could have fused the two of them into one person, she wouldn't have had enough of him.

Finally, in the small hours of the morning, they lay side

by side in her daybed, tangled together because they didn't have enough room for anything else, and because even exhausted, they still wanted to be touching.

"You're amazing," he whispered. "I can't believe someone before me hasn't staked a claim to you. Or at least managed to hang on to you."

Jess lay back and closed her eyes. "I . . . ah . . . there was only one other man. We were serious about each other. I thought it was going to be forever. But my work got in the way, and I couldn't give up my work."

"One. You mean . . . that you were engaged to or married to or something, right? Not that you've been with."

"That I've been with," she said.

He shook his head, looking puzzled. "Recent breakup?"

"No. A long time ago."

"Jess . . . why? You're beautiful. You're wonderful. You wouldn't have to be alone."

"I've never cared much for promiscuity. Sex for the sake of sex I could manage all by myself. So I did. I figured I'd make love with someone when it was making love. When it mattered."

He wrapped his arms around her and pulled her close. "You don't know me. You don't know much about me at all. So . . . why me?" His voice sounded so hoarse. "Why me, of all the men in the world?"

She touched his lips. She couldn't promise him anything. Odds were that when this case was over, the two of them would walk away from each other, because her work came first, and he wasn't the sort of man who could be second. Or who *should* be second.

Maybe she shouldn't have done this. But she hadn't wanted to resist him. Of all the men she'd ever known, he was the only one she had to have.

She didn't know what that meant. She said, "Because you matter. I don't know where we're going; I don't know if this is something that can last. I have no idea if I'm right for you. But you're right for me."

He wrapped his arms around her, held her close. And then suddenly he rolled away from her and growled, "Fuck," and rubbed at his eyes.

"What?"

"Tears," he said. "Shit."

Jess's throat clogged, and for a moment she couldn't quite catch her breath. She couldn't think of anything to say. So she held him. And then he rolled over and held her. Jess drifted toward sleep, her body cradled against his. They fit. They fit like they were both pieces of a two-piece jigsaw puzzle. Like in all the world only the two of them could ever go together so perfectly. She had never felt so safe, or so good.

And as she teetered on the edge of dreams, she heard his voice in her ear one more time, a low murmur that she just barely caught before she faded entirely.

"Please tell me I get to keep you."

chapter 11

Hank brought in a paper from the newspaper rack outside of her apartment when he came back with her Hardee's biscuits. He wished he'd seen it after breakfast; now his appetite was gone.

"Hey," she said, when he came through the door. She spotted the biscuits and smiled hugely, and walked over and threw her arms around him and kissed him.

Half of him wanted to scoop her up in his arms and haul her back to bed, and the other half wanted to run with her down to his car and get them the hell out of Atlanta. "God. I was sure they were going to wrap this up last night," he said. "Maybe we should have held out a little longer."

She frowned. "No. No. No. Not holding out was the best thing that's happened to me in ages. I wouldn't go back and undo last night for anything."

He put the newspaper down in front of her.

STRIPPER KILLER STRIKES FOUR TIMES?
EYEWITNESS OFFERS IDENTITY OF POSSIBLE SUSPECT

"The killer left the body right where I told them he would," Hank said. "Jim promised they were going to keep her safe."

Jess leaned over the article, reading. Frowning. He watched her scanning the paragraphs, and saw her freeze at one point as a look of pain washed over her face.

"What?"

" 'Following notification of the family, the victim has been identified as Millie Hantumakis,' " she read. And then she looked up at Hank. "That was *River.* I talked to her. She was really nice to me, and she had a little girl; she was stripping so she could make enough money to live on and still be able to go to her daughter's school plays and PTA meetings, for God's sake." He could see the shine in Jess's eyes that betrayed tears, and could see her blinking them back. All the life and color drained out of her face. "River had heard about the killings. She was talking about picking up and moving, getting out of Atlanta." Jess looked down at the paper, lips pressed in a thin line. "She should have."

"Which one was River?" he asked.

"You saw her. She came out first yesterday. Had on a schoolgirl uniform."

Hank had a sudden sharp memory of the short, bouncy, dark-haired girl with the awful taste in music. "*Her?*" he said. "Not the redhead in the harem costume? You're sure?"

"Positive."

But the killer hadn't touched River. Not recently enough to show up for him, anyway.

But that was the problem with trying to read living people. Influences overlaid each other quickly, as people hugged, shook hands, brushed past each other, washed and showered, moved and changed focus over and over. The focused intent in the touch of the killer a few hours earlier could disappear in the events of an ordinary day.

Conversely, inanimate objects—and corpses—held on to impressions. Sometimes for a very long time.

Hank closed his eyes and rubbed his temples with one hand.

"Piedmont Park," he said. "Where I told Jim the guy was going to dump her body. But the girl who the killer wanted called herself Ginger Rose. When I touched her, I got a clear image that she was going to be the next one. And I read the killer's decision to dump the body exactly where he did."

"Is this thing of yours an exact science?" Jess asked. "Have you made mistakes before?"

"Of course I've made mistakes. I'm as prone to misconception and error as you are. Or anyone else is. My fuckup has never cost someone else her life, though. And I never cost some kid her mother." Hank put the biscuits on the table. "There's a dead dancer on the bridge, right where I said she'd be. But she isn't the woman I said she would be, because the cops were watching the wrong girl all night. Because I told them to. How did I screw this up so badly?"

"Maybe you didn't. You said . . . Ginger Rose. I remember her. Her boyfriend had just gone apeshit on her. Maybe that's what you were sensing. Maybe he intended to kill her, and you saved her life by having the cops watch the place."

"That's possible only if her boyfriend is the same killer who's slaughtered the other dancers. I waved Ginger Rose over, stuck money in her costume, and got so sick from the feedback of the murderer that I had to go throw up. When I came back out, I called Jim and told him what I'd discovered."

"Wait, wait, wait. You touched her costume? *Only* her costume? Belly-dancing costume? Kind of an *I Dream of Jeannie* thing? Blue?"

"Yeah."

"*That wasn't her costume,*" Jess said. "That costume be-

longed to River—Ginger Rose's whacked-out ex-
boyfriend diced all of *her* costumes in an attempt to force
her to quit. So River let her borrow a costume she wasn't
going to wear."

"And I touched the costume, not the girl. Because inanimate things give me more accurate readings. I sent everyone in the wrong direction from the very start," he said,
feeling sick. "It's my fault that girl is dead."

"It's the killer's fault she's dead," Jess said. She returned her attention to the article. "You realize that it
wasn't good investigative reporting that broke this story,"
she said.

"What?"

"This reporter was tipped. Maybe by the killer."

"I didn't get that far in the article. Why do you say
that?"

"Couple of things. First, the reporter notes that he was
first on the scene. Which right there means somebody
called him. No reporter merely happened to be walking
through Piedmont Park to stumble across a fresh body at
five in the morning. *With* a photograph. Second, he says
that his source states that police, state, and federal agents
are already investigating three similar killings. And when
asked, the FBI confirmed this. How about a nice 'no comment' next time, guys?" she muttered under her breath.

"Not happy with the FBI?"

"Not so much. We were trying to keep the fact that there
was a case quiet long enough to maybe slide in under the
killers' radar. And now . . . well, there's no chance in hell
of that, is there?"

He had, for one horrible, stupid instant, an urge to tell
her she was really cute when she was mad. Sanity pre-
vailed, however, and he pulled her into his arms and
hugged her. "You'll get them. *Him*. Dammit, Jess, every-

thing I get is telling me this is one killer working alone, not three."

She sighed and slid her arms around his waist. "Maybe. One would make a hell of a lot more sense. It doesn't fit the *facts*." She squeezed tighter. "And I'd love to say that I knew we were going to get him. But most serial killers aren't caught, you know. If it comes to it, we'll roust the devil out of hell looking for this one."

"You're exactly the woman to do it," Hank told her.

She pulled away from him, and he felt a pang of loss. "I need to call Jim and find out what's going on. Give me . . . say . . . half an hour, okay? And then I'll update you on what he tells me."

Hank nodded. Jess sat at the table, cell phone in hand, and called in. Hank turned on the tiny television supplied with the furnished studio and surfed to local news.

And there it was. A wobbly picture of a body in Piedmont Park, taken from a distance with a telephoto lens. Yellow tape fluttering in the breeze, detectives and forensic technicians and two guys with GBI in big letters on the backs of their jackets, and one guy with FBI on the back of his jacket, all inside of the perimeter. More cops and a throng of bystanders on the outside. A crush of reporters doing stand-ups around one edge. This guy was back a bit and had found something high to stand on, because he was the only one who actually had a shot of the body.

Hank suddenly realized the cameraman was up a tree, following the "If it bleeds, it leads" dictum by getting as much of the horror of this thing as possible on camera for Mr. and Mrs. John Q. Public. The reporter was in voice-over. Then the shot changed, and the studio face took over.

"Breaking news—a local celebrity has been connected to this murder by an eyewitness," the male hairdo said. "Jason Hemly, who plays bumbling Dr. Bob Buckley in the hit sitcom *Heartthrob,* was identified leaving the scene of the crime this morning after allegedly dumping the body. Local police received an anonymous phone call shortly after the body was discovered, stating that before dawn this morning, Mr. Hemly was seen carrying a body wrapped in black plastic bags out of his home, and putting the body in the trunk of his car."

The scene switched to another telephoto shot—this time of the driveway of a gorgeous mansion, where police had just opened the trunk of a black Mercedes, and with gloved hands were carefully lifting out two lawn-and-garden-type bags that had been taped together to form what looked like a body bag, even from a distance. One detective ran into the scene carrying something small in a clear plastic bag. Whatever it was caused a flurry. Hank suddenly realized the detective was Charlie, and the one with his back to the camera looking through the trunk was Jim.

Hank wasn't even hearing the hairdo's commentary anymore. Jess came over and stood beside him, watching. "Guess that explains why they aren't answering their phones," Jess said.

The camera then zoomed into a close-up of the handsome Jason Hemly, wearing pajama bottoms and no shirt, in his bare feet with his hair mussed. He stood on the walk with an expression of horror and bewilderment on his face. A dapper man in a dark suit got out of his Mercedes, walked past the police to Jason, shook his hand, patted him on the shoulder, and then turned to watch the police.

"Harmon MacAree. Premier defense attorney to the rich and guilty," Jess muttered. "What a surprise."

Hank glanced over at her. "You want to go in?"

"Can't. I'm deep undercover. Until I hear different— which isn't going to happen until they slow down enough to answer their phones—I'm not supposed to be seen anywhere near any of this. For now, I'm an exotic dancer. I have no legitimate reason to break my cover."

"How about because they found the killer, the body bag, and something that had Charlie looking happy at Hemly's house?"

"The only information I have to go on right now is that we're looking for three killers. Jason might be the redhead. He might also be an innocent man being framed. It's my job to presume the latter is the case until evidence proves otherwise."

"So you'll still be going in to dance today?"

"If I don't hear from Jim or Charlie . . . or *somebody* . . . between now and then, yes. I have my job. And as best we can tell, even if Hemly *is* guilty, there's still a brown-haired killer and a blond killer out there watching him right now on their own televisions."

Jess didn't hear from Jim until she was already showered, dressed, and driving in to Goldcastle.

"You've seen the coverage, of course," Jim said by way of preamble.

"Nobody on earth has missed the coverage. How does Hemly look for it?"

"He does a very nice innocent act," Jim said. "But then, he gets paid to know how to act like a nice, goofy, good-hearted guy, doesn't he?"

"'That's the act," Jess agreed, shifting lanes. Traffic was horrible. "How's the evidence?"

"Found the dead girl's missing earring right outside Hemly's back door. Found the homemade body bag in the trunk, with hair and fibers. Found bloodstains, old *and* new, *in* his trunk. Found cord of the sort the ME has been telling us the killers have been using to bind the victims' ankles before hanging them upside down and draining the blood out of them. The cord is also bloodstained, and was in Hemly's body bag. Based on all the goodies we found outside the house, the judge was kind enough to grant us a rather broad search warrant for the inside, over the loud protests of Hemly's hired shitweasel."

"That's Mr. Shitweasel to you and me," Jess said, feeling good all of a sudden.

Jim laughed. "It is indeed."

"So . . . what the hell happened? One of his buddies turn him in?"

"Mr. Hemly had the misfortune to have dumped the body when he was not as alone as he thought. A young homeless man, who had found himself a place in Piedmont Park where he could sleep unbothered by either chicken-hawks or cops, was awakened by the sound of someone talking animatedly nearby. Apparently Mr. Hemly talks to his victims while he is posing them for display."

Jess stopped at a red light and readjusted her headset on her cell phone. The mike never seemed to stay where she wanted it.

"A homeless guy was reliable enough to act on?"

"Didn't hurt that a friendly source inside WSB-TV tipped us that the station was investigating a phone call the local police department received, stating that Mr. Hemly looked like he was carrying a body out his back door at around four A.M." Jim chuckled. "We called, the dispatcher on duty confirmed that they had received that call, but that it had come from a public pay phone."

"That's not good."

"In that neighborhood, everybody has big lawyers. I'm willing to consider that our tipster didn't want to be the focus of attention. Or maybe to explain why he was up at that hour."

"Hemly's back door is visible from the neighbors' houses?"

"It is, surprisingly. He has a big wrought-iron fence, some landscaping. But those big houses are all on small lots, and we figure any of the inhabitants in any of three

separate houses could have had a clear view of him haul-
ing our dancer out his back door, and two others might
have had a view from one or two windows. It could have
even been someone driving down the street. We have people going door to door right now, but so far we haven't
found anyone who will admit to placing the call."

"How would they even have seen anything? Stuff isn't
too well lit at four A.M."

"Hemly's place is. He has motion sensor lights. *Everybody* around there has motion-sensor lights." Jim sounded
happy. "Plus, his landscaping includes a fair number of
solar-powered lighting fixtures along walkways and foun-
tains. He might as well have dragged her out the back door
right in front of *Candid Camera.*"

"His security tapes give you anything?"

"He doesn't have a security system that includes
video."

Now Jess smiled. "*Really?* Big, rich star like him, and
he has no videotapes of potential stalkers or thieves or dis-
gruntled nutcases? That's oddly suspicious."

"It's good, Jess. It's solid. Our two tips were shaky, but
they're panning out pure gold."

Jess pulled into the parking lot of Goldcastle and
sighed. "Speaking of gold. I'm now in the parking lot at
Goldcastle. It's mobbed at this hour of the day, incidentally. I see the guys in the van across the street, so I'm
guessing you still want me here."

"Yes. Hemly may give us the other two guys. But if he
and his lawyer are going to push the innocent plea, he'll
hold out as long as he can. The other two might lie low, but
we can't count on that. And you might be able to get us
some corroborative evidence on Hemly. Girls who had
contact with him, how he behaved, where he took them . . .
you know the drill."

"I know the drill," Jess said. And stopped. "Hey. How is

it nobody was watching the park? Hank thought it was covered."

"Yeah—that was a bad miss on our part. The girl we were watching never left the house, so we never activated the park team. We're short on man-hours, but long on cases." Silence on the other end. Then, "Who knew, huh?"

"Hank, I guess. Signing off for now, Jim. I'll get you what I can."

She checked in with the surveillance team, did a mike test, talking into her belly button. She had the portable test transmitter hidden in her trunk. That way she didn't have to worry about carrying it around so she could test, but no one would see it lying on her seat.

The guys in the van were good to go. So she hauled her kit bag off the passenger seat and swung into the side door of the club, feeling almost elated.

Until she saw the first little cluster of dancers. They were standing along one wall, whispering. Crying. Talking about River, and whether anyone knew whether her little girl, Dani, was going to be able to live with the grand-mother.

Everything snapped back into sharp focus for Jess. If they had one of the guys, fine. But she and her colleagues weren't finished. A young mother was dead, two killers still roamed free and unidentified, and none of these girls could consider themselves safe.

When Jess got to the dressing room, Ginger Rose was already there. "You heard?"

Jess nodded. "Nothing *but* on TV this morning."

"I know. I can't believe it. I can't imagine Jason want-ing to hurt River. They'd gone out a couple of times, you know? River said he was a perfect gentleman. Took her out to nice restaurants, got along great with her daughter. She'd been so thrilled to be dating . . . well, you know. A star."

Jess nodded again. The guys in the surveillance van parked outside had to be doing a hula dance right about then. Previous repeated contacts with the victim, a relationship of trust built up. Yes.

"Were they still dating?" she asked.

"No. Jason never dated anyone for very long. He claimed he was actually deeply in love, and was trying to get over a broken heart after the woman he loved dumped him. So for the girls he dated from here, he was good for maybe two or three dates."

"And after he slept with them, he moved on?" Jess asked.

"No. He really was a gentleman. He never had sex with any of the girls he dated—at least not that I know of."

Because that wasn't what got Jason Hemly off. Right. He sounded like a lust killer. Most common sort of serial killer, for whom the combination of sex and torture and murder was the big thing. And if he was into a steady diet of perversion and blood, straight sex with his intended victims beforehand would probably not do much for him at all.

In two or three dates, he could find out what he needed to know about his victims. How to get them to go where he wanted them to go, say what he wanted them to say to make sure that no one would suspect they were meeting with him.

"Are you up to going out?" Ginger Rose asked. "Teri has been back here twice trying to get more girls out on the floor, but . . ." She waved a hand at the empty room, then blew her nose and wiped her eyes. "We can't go out like this."

"I can do it," Jess said. "I . . . yes. I'll go out."

She changed quickly into a thong, miniskirt, sequined bra, and see-through blouse, and went out to work the floor until time came for her to do sets on the stage.

The place was even more crowded on the inside than it had looked on the outside, and the floor managers with their little laser penlights had their hands full with grabby customers. Jess did table dances, focusing on men with brown or blond hair.

She drifted by Hank from time to time, brushing against him and touching one of his hands casually. He kept giving her the all clear signal that she hadn't run up against the killer yet.

And then Jess heard raised voices out in the foyer. She drifted toward the door without being too obvious about it, and got a good look at Teri arguing with Lenny. Teri had both hands full of Lenny's shirt, Lenny was pulling at her wrists, and they were snarling at each other, oblivious to the stares of employees and customers alike.

"You stay out of the dancers' area, you pervert. You have no business back there. Not now. Not *ever*."

"I *wasn't* back there."

"You're leaving things in the dressing room again and I'm not supposed to figure out it was you? How stupid do you think I am?"

Teri pushed him away, breaking her wrists free from his grip in the same sharp movement. "You go back there again, I'll make sure you're gone from here, Lenny."

Jess slipped out of sight, worked her way over to the deejay, and said, "How about something a little faster and more upbeat? The girls backstage are just wrecked, and it isn't too easy for us up front, either."

He nodded.

The next instant, she felt two hands grab her ass and slide around front under her skirt.

"Still love the deejays, hey, Andi?"

Lenny's voice. Her first instinct was to back up under him and flip him on top of the table in front of her.

But—for the moment, at least—she was a stripper. Not

a cop. She was playing sweet and mostly helpless and maybe a little . . . scared. She broke his hold without seeming to expend any effort, turned, and said, keeping her voice low, "I'm Gracie. Not Andi. I don't even *know* anybody named Andi."

And Lenny gave her a creepy sort of I-know-your-secret smile, and whispered, "Right. And back when I was a deejay, you weren't sliding down my fireman's pole every goddamned night." He was staring at her. "I loved you. *Loved* you. And you loved me. I don't know what happened that night, Andromeda, or why you let me think you were dead for so long, or . . . I don't understand anything. Not even what I thought I understood. But I know you. And if you've come back here now, I figure it can only be because you love me, too. Because we were meant to be together after all."

Jess had to rest a hand on the table beside her. Suddenly there wasn't enough air in the room; suddenly everyone and everything around her looked fuzzy and her legs wobbled and her mouth dried out so that she had to fight to form words.

"Andromeda?" she whispered.

"He's so cute, Jess," Ginny said over the phone. Jess couldn't help but smile at the happiness in her sister's voice. "Tall and blond and handsome. He was a football player in high school until he broke a leg. Oh, God, he's such a bad boy, too. I wouldn't have thought it was possible, but he talked me out of my clothes the first time we went out together."

And Jess had asked, "You guys . . . did it?"

"We did. We do. Oh, Jess, you won't believe it. Sex is better than anything you can imagine. And he's so . . . Wow. He talks about us in five years, and what our kids

will look like, and he's so . . . romantic. A romantic bad boy. Imagine."

Jess was trying to get her mind around the fact that Ginny was having sex with someone. They'd promised each other they weren't going to, that they were going to stay focused on dance until they made it. But Ginny's plans had derailed. "Has Mama met him?"

"You are crazy. He thinks my name is Andromeda, and that I'm an orphan. There's no way I'm taking him home to meet Mama. She'd explode."

Which had not sounded terribly promising to Jess. "What does he do? What's his name? Tell me everything."

"He a deejay at the club where I'm dancing. His name is Mitch. Mitch Devon, but it ought to be Mitch Divine."

chapter 12

Mitch Devon. The most romantic guy in the universe. Versus Lenny Northwhite, red-faced, middle-aged thug.

Jess had never met him, but she knew Devon had fallen off the face of the earth not long after he had established an airtight alibi for the time frame in which Ginny had disappeared. He'd never resurfaced anywhere. Jess had checked. She'd been watching.

She tipped her head and made her eyes go wide and tentatively whispered, "Mitch?"

He smiled. It wasn't the dead-eyed smile of the shark she'd met upstairs. This was a tender smile. Sweet. Gentle. "You really didn't recognize me?" he asked.

When Ginny first started dancing, she told Jess she'd gotten a cheap fake ID identifying her as Andromeda Callisto. The ID probably wouldn't have been good enough to fool a state trooper, but it had been good enough for the club where she'd wanted to dance. Ginny had been old enough to work at the club; that wasn't the problem. She'd obtained the ID because she never wanted anything about the stripping to get back to her mother.

And this . . . this *monster* had known Ginny as Andi, had told her he loved her, had won her trust.

I don't know what happened that night, Andromeda, or

*why you let me think you were dead for so long, or . . . I
don't understand anything. Not even what I thought I understood.*

His words. Mitch Devon had provided a very solid alibi
for his whereabouts for the entire day and night between
when Ginny was last seen, and when Jess and her mother
realized she was missing. That alibi had included being
publicly visible, both to friends and to detractors, for the
entire time in which Ginny could have gone missing.

And yet . . . he'd said, *I don't know what happened that
night.* Jess had to find out which night.

He'd said, *why you let me think you were dead.* What the
hell was that about? Was that her worst nightmare come
true?

And now he was looking at her like a long-lost love
come back to him.

"I . . . can't talk to you right now . . . Mitch. Lenny."
Jess put a little stammer into her voice and a little confusion
on her face. "I have to work right now. I . . . need the
money."

He nodded. An understanding nod, but confident, too.
Like he'd been sure all along that she was going to give him
what he wanted. "We'll get together later to talk."

She nodded.

"My place," he said, and Jess shook her head. Much as
she wanted an opportunity to look around inside his home,
she didn't want to end up dead in the process. If Lenny got
crazy, backup that was stuck outside a locked door might
not be able to get to her in time. She'd meet with him in a
public place first, judge the level of danger, maybe get
enough info to get a judge to issue a search warrant. If that
didn't work out, she would think about accepting his invitation to his home.

So she said, "At dinner, maybe."

"We can have dinner at *my* place." He smiled. She

caught an edge of Lenny in with all that sincere, sweet Mitch, and felt a shiver slide down her spine.

"I'm not ready for that yet. You and I need to talk about a few things first, and . . . No. Fast food will be fine."

His face told her he was hurt. She needed to get away from him. "I have to get back to work now," she said, and flirted her way back over to Hank as quickly as she dared.

She leaned down and whispered in his ear, "Find a way to brush your hand against my ass without getting caught by the floor managers. I have a bad suspicion I got grabbed by one of the killers."

Hank stared at her. He stood up slowly, moved behind her, saying, "No, thanks—I'm going to pass on a lap dance right now," and as he brushed past her, ran his fingertips lightly across the curves of her butt, beneath her skirt.

She shivered again, turned on by his touch in spite of herself.

She pivoted to say something to him, and found him one step past her, bent double with his hands around his gut, his skin gone so gray and sweaty she thought for a moment he might be having a heart attack.

She grabbed one arm and tried to help him stand up straight. "Should I call nine-one-one?"

"Bathroom," he said through clenched jaws.

The combination of Hank's skin color and Jess helping him along cleared a path through the crowd. She couldn't ask him what she wanted to know—if this reaction was caused by touching her, or if maybe he'd gotten something from the shrimp he'd been eating.

Sick. He'd told her that sometimes what he felt with that sixth sense of his made him sick. She'd figured he was exaggerating, the way she would exaggerate by saying she was starving, or that a headache was killing her.

From the look of him, she had to confess that if this was

what he'd meant by sick, he'd severely understated his reaction.

Hank managed to drag himself to the sink, where he threw
up so severely that the bathroom attendant fled the room.
Hank retched, and heaved, and sagged against the cool mar-
ble of the bathroom counter, and since the attendant wasn't
there, grabbed one of those hand towels the guy usually
passed out to patrons. He soaked it and rinsed his face.
Rinsed out his mouth.

The killer had touched Jess. But it was more than that.
He'd chosen her as his next victim. She was the one he
wanted, she was the one he intended to have. He'd finished
digging her grave already; Hank could see the long, shallow
rectangle, smell the dirt, almost feel the shovel in his
leather-gloved hands. *Six by six.* Graves filled over years.
That was six by six, and Jess would fill the last one.

The perversion, the hunger, the rage. They pulsed
through Hank's blood and tainted the air he breathed and
scared Hank worse than he had even been scared in his life.
He'd read edges of the killer before. Side glimpses. That
one nearly direct connection through the costume. But this
touch—it was still hot. Fresh.

Directed at someone he loved.

The attendant came running back in, accompanied by a
floor manager.

"Sir, do you need an ambulance?" the floor manager
asked.

Hank, still leaning on the counter with water washing
the last vestiges of puke out of the sink, said, "No."

"If you've had too much to drink . . ." the manager
started, but Hank held up a hand to stop him.

"I haven't. I thought I got hold of some bad food in here
yesterday," he said. Talking was hard; the images, the visu-
als, the clear pictures of Jess already dead, being tossed

naked into a hole and buried. "Now I'm not sure what it is about this place."

He cupped his hands in the running water, rinsed and spit, and stood up. His legs felt weak, he was shaky, and his skin alternated between being too hot and too cold. All of his scars felt like they were on fire.

"Shall I have someone bring your car around for you, sir?" the manager said. "Or will you need to have a cab take you home?"

Implied in those questions was the clear but polite notice that Hank would be leaving.

Well, if he left, the surveillance team would pull Jess out, too.

At the moment, he could only think that was a good thing.

"I . . . I'm well enough to drive," he said. "Give me a minute to get cleaned up."

The floor manager seemed relieved that Hank wasn't going to give him a problem. Hank handed the man his car claim tag, and the manager left to see that it would be waiting for him.

Jess was waiting outside the door for him, clearly worried.

"I'm sorry to scare you like that, Gracie," he said. He leaned against the wall for support. "I'll be sure to come back and see you again soon. You take care, now."

He gave her the "trouble" signal that they'd worked out. She nodded and said, "I hope you're feeling better soon. We'll miss you."

She headed back to the floor, to sit down and start talking to another customer. Hank left, frantic that he was letting Jess out of his sight for even an instant.

"So what do you enjoy?" she asked the brown-haired executive sitting across from her at one of the little tables.

He grinned a little. "Making money, mostly. I go skiing in Aspen a couple times a winter. I have a place in Nassau where I go to get away from it all. Another out on the coast."

Every word out of his mouth made her think he was a dull jerk, and a pretentious one at that. But Jess responded with a big-eyed, dewy, "Wow. That must be wonderful. What do you do?"

"I own a software company. We have a video-games division and a business division—and frankly, the games are currently outearning the productivity software about twenty to one. We have a huge hit on our hands right now with *Attila, Lord of Chaos*, where you play as Attila the Hun, and your goal is to conquer and pillage the known world."

"Sounds fun," she said, still smiling. She suddenly knew who he was, though. Wayne Alton. Atlanta's best-known software mogul. And he might be a jerk and he might be dull, but he was being utterly honest about all his money. He'd been in the news a few times, as family groups tried to get his games off the shelves because of excessive violence. *Attila* was supposed to be the worst of the lot. She wondered if his follow-up was going to be a game allowing the player to become Pol Pot, or Idi Amin, or maybe Torquemada. *Nero for a Day,* maybe.

And she kept smiling.

He talked about his work, about how the games his company developed in-house were actually educational tools that permitted teenagers and adults to explore the historical horrors of bygone days in full color and at first hand, and how what he was doing made people aware of the pure hell that was most of history.

Jess thought that if he'd wanted to do that, he could have made a game in which the players tried to stop Attila. Not *be* him. She didn't say anything of the sort, though. She oohed and ahhed and nodded and smiled.

He paid her for a lap dance, she danced, he kept his hands to himself, and she thanked him and moved on.

And suddenly Teri, looking frantic, burst out of the back door and waved to her.

Jess hurried over.

"Call from the hospital. Take it in my office."

So this was how they were going to pull her out. She ran to the phone, kept in character. "This is Gracie."

"This is Dr. Smith," Jim's voice said. "Your brother has had a relapse, and we need you in here immediately to sign papers. This is an emergency. Can you come in, or do you have someone else we can call?"

"I'll be right there," she said.

She turned to find Teri right behind her. "Is everything okay?"

"No. I have to leave right now. I'm sorry to leave you in the lurch—"

Teri waved it off. "Is he going to be all right?"

"Dr. Smith said it was an emergency. I'm guessing that means they don't know."

Teri pursed her lips. "Go on. We'll do fine here. Tell your brother we're all thinking about him."

Hank was at her apartment when she arrived. "Change and come on," he said as soon as they were through the doors. "I set up a meeting with Jim and Charlie—we need to talk about what I discovered today. It may be the break they've been looking for, and all four of us need a chance to talk it out."

Jess threw on jeans, a T-shirt, and running shoes over the spangly bra and thong. "I'm ready."

She saw Hank swallow hard. "You've had a rough two days," she said.

"You don't know the half of it." He cleared his throat and watched her pick up her handbag. "You were right to suspect Lenny. His touch, the killer's touch: same thing. And, worse, you're supposed to be next. I could see the 'six by six' image I've been hearing in my head, Jess. I could see you lying in a shallow grave with someone shoveling dirt on top of you. It was as real for that instant as you and me standing here right now. Six by six—it means graves. The killer has thirty-six graves hidden away somewhere, with the last hole in the square already dug and waiting for you."

Jess rested a hand on his shoulder. "It's not going to happen, Hank. I'm not a helpless stripper. We know who this killer is." By unspoken agreement, they put the subject on hold as they headed out her apartment door and down to Hank's car.

But once in his car, she said, "There's more, though. Lenny thinks I'm my sister, Ginny. He asked me why I let him think I was dead for so long." She turned to Hank and frowned. "He said he isn't sure what happened that night."

"What night?"

"That's what I have to find out," she said. "Hank, what are the odds that I'd get put on this case and end up running into someone who knew Ginny? What are the odds that the same man would be our prime suspect in the deaths of other women? If you're reading that 'six-by-six' thing right, maybe thirty or so other women. Jesus—could it be a co-incidence? Have I finally found Ginny's killer?" Her throat tightened and she blinked back tears. She fought to put some distance between herself and this possibility. She couldn't let herself get bogged down by emotion; if Lenny was Ginny's killer, her personal involvement and her emotion, however justified, could throw off her judgment and lead her to do something that would destroy the case.

She cleared her throat and got a grip on herself. "His real name isn't Lenny Northwhite. It's Mitch Devon, and he was the deejay at the club where my sister danced back when she disappeared. Even more suspicious, she was dating him. She was head-over-heels in love with him."

"And the police back then didn't check him out?"

"Sure, they checked him out. He had an airtight alibi that accounted for every minute in which she could have been killed. He was deejaying a long-weekend Hugh Hefner–type party at the club owner's mansion as some sort of promotional thing for the club. It was attended by all the rich and influential men in Atlanta who could be dragged away from their lives, and a bunch of strippers and booze and drugs, and they partied around the clock from Friday night through Sunday night."

"And Ginny?"

"He wouldn't let her attend the party. She'd complained to me about it at the time—that her boyfriend was going to be having all this fun and she wouldn't even get to see him for the whole weekend. And she didn't, either. Everyone who attended the party was certain that she hadn't been among the dancers there."

"So he was always in the public eye, and she was nowhere near him."

"That was the story."

"Funny. He has an airtight alibi this time, too. That's one of the things that has Jim so frustrated."

They pulled into the parking lot of an all-day buffet, and Hank led Jess into one of the private rooms. Jim and Charlie were already there.

Both rose when she came in. After greeting one another, everyone sat down. One of the servers appeared, carrying a gallon pitcher of sweet tea and a stack of clean plates.

Jess wasn't in the mood for food right then. Apparently Hank wasn't either. Jim and Charlie were already eating.

"Hank told me Lenny Northwhite has an alibi for the night of the murder," Jess said.

"He does," Jim said. "Charlie."

Jess turned to stare at Jim's partner. "You?"

"I staked out his place; Jim and one of the other guys watched the dancer. We figured Lenny was our most likely candidate."

Hank said, "Why?"

"Because Lenny has records as Mitchell Devon Leonard—his birth name, as Mitch Devon—the name under which he worked as a club deejay for a number of years—and as Leonard Mitchell Northwhite, which is a combination of his last name and his mother's maiden name. He's been arrested for breaking and entering, a string of sex-related complaints, and a lot of shady financial crap. Nothing that got him put away, but he has money and a good lawyer he apparently keeps busy."

"And both the breaking and entering and the sex-related crimes suggest at least the capacity for sex-related murder," Jess said.

"Right."

"I didn't know about his aliases until today," Jess told them. "But I have something I need to talk to you about. My twin sister went missing thirteen years ago. She was stripping at a little club called the Palomino X to earn her tuition back to dance school, and she started dating Mitch Devon about a month before she disappeared."

She was watching faces. Neither Jim nor Charlie looked surprised when she mentioned her sister, though both looked stunned when she told them about Ginny and Mitch.

"You guys knew about Ginny?"

"Everyone knew you spent all your free time investigating something," Jim said. "I took a couple of days and backtracked some of your file requests. It didn't take me all that long to figure out you were looking for your sister."

Charlie nodded. "He told me before you joined up with us, because he thought I needed to know. We only knew the basics, though."

Jess sat there, frozen, disbelieving. She thought of all the careful tiptoeing around her real work, of making sure she never let her personal mission interfere with her job, of making sure she never let the loss of her sister intrude into similar situations. She'd been the consummate professional. And they still knew? They knew? "Why didn't you say something?"

Jim said, "I thought it was pretty clear this wasn't something you were willing to discuss. It didn't affect your work, as far as I could see. It sure as hell didn't affect your competence. So why would I say anything?"

She stared at her hands, thinking that if she had known someone knew and that what she was doing wasn't a problem for him, if she had been able to discuss her unending, heartbreaking search with someone, maybe she would have done better dealing with it.

But that had been her fault, for keeping her problems to herself. She couldn't blame Jim or Charlie or anyone but herself that she'd dealt with this alone.

"You wouldn't. You were right not to," she said at last. "I would have brought it up if I'd been ready to talk about it."

Jim said, "Okay. Then let's get back to this. How did you find out Northwhite's real name?"

"He told me. He thinks I'm Ginny."

Jim and Charlie turned to stare at each other, frowning.

Jim moved mashed potatoes and gravy around on his plate for a few seconds. "Hank called me and told me he's dead sure Lenny is the killer, and that you're his next planned victim. So far, what I'm hearing makes that sound like a real possibility."

Jess nodded.

"But you clearly think Northwhite killed your sister."

Jess nodded again.

"How could he have killed her and still think you're her when he looks at you?"

"I don't know. And that's what he says, too. He doesn't understand. When I walked into his office that first day, though, and he looked at me, I saw a man who was looking at a ghost. He was . . . petrified. That's the only word for it. He just fucking turned to stone."

Charlie asked Hank, "You're sure you read this right? Lenny touched Jess, you touched Jess with nobody else in between, and you read Lenny."

Jess said, "He wasn't watching me walk through the crowd toward him. But no one touched me after Lenny did."

"All right. We need to get past Lenny's lawyer, who so far has fielded and blocked any requests for us to meet with Lenny, in his place of business or ours. Lenny has the best possible alibi for the night of the latest girl's death, but we still have three men and three separate hair colors on our fourth victim—blond, redhead, and brown. Two secretors and one nonsecretor, like the other three times. This girl died in exactly the same fashion as the previous three known victims."

"Lenny's in on this," Jess said.

"We'll keep someone on him," Jim told her. "Right now, though, the evidence we can use is contradicting the evidence we can't use. I've worked with Hank on these things enough to be sure that when he says the killer touched you, the killer touched you. But I can't take Hank's reading to a judge. So. You know who to watch. Watch him. Give me something I can use."

From Jess's studio, Hank called the dojo and made sure everything was running all right. Jeni, his part-time secretary, answered on the fourth ring. "Hey, sensei," she said when he identified himself. He could hear the laughter in her voice. She called him sensei only when she had good news.

"I'm not going to be in for a couple of days. So I'm checking to see how things are going."

"You wouldn't believe. This story on the serial killer broke, and we are all of a sudden hip deep in young women wanting self-defense training. We had six sign up yesterday, and eleven more today. It's like a blondes-and-boobs beauty contest in here. You're going to have to set up a special implants-only class."

"They're dancers."

"*Strippers.* Lots of them. Mike already volunteered to take the overflow. Then Crunch said he'd teach that class for free. I'm just waiting for Wills to hear Crunch's offer and appear with a box of chocolates and a dozen roses for me if I'll schedule his name in. It's been a *gooood* day for us, sensei."

"Figures," Hank said.

That was the business. People came to him *after* something horrible had already happened. But better they learned to protect themselves late than not at all.

"So how long are you going to be out?" Jeni persisted.

"I don't know. I have something major I'm working on right now, and I cannot be there."

"You're really Agent Double-Oh-Six, aren't you? James Bond's boss."

Hank laughed politely, told Jeni to let Mike take the receipts and cash to the bank, and to go ahead and set up a class for the dancers and to give it to Kevin, *not* Mike, and hung up.

The secret-agent question rang in his ears. What he had in mind was a little more secret-agent than either Jim or Charlie would have liked.

He intended to get himself invited into Lenny's office, and following that, to see if maybe he couldn't wrangle an invite to one of the infamous Goldcastle Weekender parties that Lenny hosted at *his* mansion these days.

Hank wanted to feel things out. And in the meantime, he intended to keep an eye on Lenny for a while. See where he went and who he went with, find out what he did, try to get a read on the location of Lenny's plot of graves, in six neat rows of six graves each.

Off the phone, he turned to Jess. "Are you going to be all right here?"

"I'd be better with you," she told him.

He shook his head. "I'm going to be doing a couple of things you shouldn't know about."

Jess shook her head. "Don't. If you collect any evidence in an illegal fashion, it will be fruit of the poisoned tree. It will kill our whole case, and the bastards who did this will walk scot-free. If that happens, they can shout that they did it from the rooftops and we won't be able to lay a finger on them."

"Jess. Stop. Jim has been beating me over the head with the rules of legal evidence collection for years. I'm not going after anything but observations and impressions. I'm not going to be eavesdropping, and nothing I find will ever show up as evidence to be haggled over. I'm not going to screw up your case. You need to trust me."

He sat down beside her on the bed and wrapped an arm around her. "I know that the possibility that Ginny is somehow a part of this mess makes it worse for you. You're going to get justice for her. I'm going out now to do my part to see that happens."

Jess nodded, not saying anything. Guilt radiated from her like heat from an oven; it made him feel like he was smothering, like his lungs would catch fire if he breathed too deep.

"Jess?"

"Yeah."

"Why do you blame yourself for her death?"

Jess gave him a nervous smile. "You know, when I'm

down, I think I might start insisting that you don't touch me except when you're wearing rubber gloves."

He kissed the top of her head. "Wouldn't make a difference. I routinely work gloved when I'm reading for Jim and Charlie, so I don't contaminate fingerprint evidence. Now, though, I want you to tell me about the guilt."

She leaned her head against his chest and he pulled her close. "I should have left Harrt when things got so bad for Ginny. I should have come home and helped Mama get over what my bastard father did to her. I should have found a job that would have helped Ginny raise money. We should have both done other things for a while." She made a funny little noise in the back of her throat. "It all seems so trivial now. Dancing. But I had my scholarship, and I wasn't going to walk away from it and see *my* dream go into the toilet, too."

He tightened his arms around her. "Dreams are never trivial."

"Is a dream worth dying for?" Jess whispered. "Because it's what Ginny died for. She died because she had to be a dancer." He realized that she was shaking. Crying, but without any sound.

"No. She didn't. She died because she crossed paths with a killer. Probably a serial killer who had been specializing in dancers already. She died because she was in the wrong place at the wrong time, and she met up with the wrong man."

"If I'd only been with her—"

"Shhh. You could have done everything differently. You might have done everything better. I don't know. But you don't know, either. You might have simply found out that Lenny was really into twins, right before he killed you both." His own what-ifs slammed into him again, and for a moment he could smell the baking dust at midday, see the explosion, catch the sound of it as pressure in his ears that became a sudden white eruption of pain. And silence. Everything in silence, and then darkness. And then faces over him, up close, and blood and friends and fear: a war movie that had run in his head so often the images were faded around the edges, scratched, worn thin.

"You won't do a single thing in life that you couldn't have done better somehow. Not one. That's the bitch of life. It ain't a rehearsal, darlin'. You make it up as you go and you do the best you can. Maybe once in a while, you'll be good enough that you won't have any regrets. That's what you hope for." He pulled back from her, lifted her chin, and looked into her eyes. "But most of the time it isn't what you get. You did what you did. Now you're doing what you're doing. We both are. We're giving it the best we have, the best that's in us. We'll get through this. And we'll make it count. Right?"

"Yes," she said. She breathed in deep. Gave him a shaky smile. "Yeah. We *are* making it count. You and me."

Mostly it was the light. Pale, greasy gray. It made every-one in the department look like zombies. Jess sat across a battered, institutional desk from a detective with tired, old eyes. He was missing the first joints of two fingers on his left hand.

"I'm sympathetic, Miss Brubaker," the detective said. "I am. It's hell to have a loved one go missing without a word. But you have to understand, we have a witness who saw her get on that bus. We have no suspect. We have no body. We have no sign of foul play, and every indication that she had, or at least believed she had, a movie role waiting for her out in California. We did investigate, but we cannot con-tinue to expend the resources of the department on your sis-ter's missing-persons case. I have over thirty murders on my desk alone right now, and I'm no busier than anybody else." He reached across his desk and patted her hand. "I

spent a fair amount of personal time tracking down what I could on your sister. But I have to start focusing on other cases now. I'm sorry. I truly am."

Gray on gray on gray—the detective who had been so kind, and who was now kindly sending her on her way; Jess who felt ancient and all used up at twenty-two; the air she breathed; everything. Gray sinking into the inescapable depths of sea-deep black, and her sinking with it. Dead but still moving. A zombie. All of this was her fault. Ginny would not have gone anywhere had Jess been here. Jess had always been the sensible one, the planner, the shaper who turned Ginny's wild flights of fancy into workable realities.

"There has to be something someone can do."

The detective sighed. "A friend of mine left the force a few years ago. Went private. If you'd like, I'll give you his number, and tell him you're going to call."

Jess took the scrap of paper he proffered. Snowy white in a sea of gray, crisp black scrawling out a name. A number.

"I'll call," she said.

chapter 13

"You're the guy who's thrown up twice in here," the floor manager said.

Hank stood inside the foyer, faced off against the floor manager he'd seen earlier that day, the greeter, and an extra floor manager who'd sauntered over when he saw the first glorified bouncer moving fast to head Hank off.

"I have to apologize for that," Hank said. "It wasn't Goldcastle food after all."

Eyebrows raised.

"My girlfriend found out I was coming here. She's . . . jealous. She knows I always add a little bump to my beer." He pulled out a flask in his hip pocket, waved it under their noses. "My preferred single-malt whiskey, which you don't stock. The bitch loaded a beautiful bottle of Talisker with Antabuse she bought off the Internet, and since lately I've only been drinking it here—because at home I get Talisker with nagging, and here I can have Talisker and beautiful women—I come in, I drink my drink. And then, thanks to that bitch, I throw up."

Now the floor managers and the greeter were looking at him with odd sympathy.

"Girlfriend?" one said.

Hank shrugged. "Ex, now. Who needs that?"

"Truly," the other said.

Hank said, "Next few days, while that crap clears out of my system, I'll be in here buying drinks and not drinking them." He sighed and shrugged. "Is Lenny still here, by any chance?"

The late-coming floor manager had walked away. The one who helped Hank make a speedy exit earlier in the day said, "Why?"

"Because I want to talk to him about becoming a member. A friend of mine is a friend of his. He goes to some of Lenny's Weekenders, and he told me I *have* to join."

"The Weekenders are by Lenny's invitation only."

"I know," Hank said. He was wearing a rich man's casual clothes. Docksiders, elegant tan slacks, an open-at-the throat cotton knit pullover with a carefully discreet logo. He was wearing the diver's watch, the fine leather belt. The outfit had set him back more than he would have spent on any ten other changes of clothes. But it showed off his build and his scars in equal measure. Suggested not merely money, but old money. He'd decided he was old money new in town, setting up a branch of his stock brokerage. He knew enough about stocks to sound coherent discussing them. He'd never considered them an interest, but a man trying to turn a veteran's disability pension into a business nest egg learned how to invest.

"You know how much a membership costs?" the manager said.

And Hank smiled. "I wasn't worried about it."

"Let me see if Mr. Northwhite is still in his office," the floor manager said. He picked up the house phone, turned his back on Hank, and after a moment said, "I have a prospective new member . . . friend recommended him . . . Weekenders. Right." He turned back to Hank. "Who's your mutual friend?"

Pointed in his direction by Jess, Hank had talked for a

few moments to Wayne Alton, a new-money bastard with old-money friends. Hank, well-enough dressed even then to pass as someone Wayne might associate with, had waxed rhapsodic about the club, and Wayne had said the public entertainment was nothing compared to the private member perks. He had, in fact, told Hank that for real fun, he needed to get himself invited to Lenny's Weekenders.

"Wayne Alton," Hank said.

The floor manager passed this on, and turned to Hank a moment later with a friendly smile. "Mr. . . . ?"

"Vines," Hank said.

"Mr. Vines. Please come upstairs. Mr. Northwhite will be happy to talk with you."

Lenny sat in his office, a pampered king in a fine throne room. Hank noticed the appointments—oil paintings, leather chairs, a teak desk polished to a high gloss and empty at the moment of anything that resembled work. Hank followed the floor manager through the door and promised that, no matter what he touched, or what he discovered, he would not allow his body to betray him so completely a third time.

He knew he was going to have to shake hands with the bastard. He was going to have to brace himself. Because he had to get as close to this guy as he could. He had to get the images—where the bodies were buried, where Lenny and his friends committed their crimes, who did what. He didn't know how much he would be able to get from a touch. He didn't know how much he could take. The poison pouring out of Leonard Northwhite from when he'd touched Jess had been worse than anything Hank had ever felt.

But he had to do this. Every connection he could make would move Jess a little farther out of this bastard's reach.

Lenny stood. He was a big guy, one who clearly still worked out. He carried a little fat around his middle, but

Hank, studying him, didn't see Lenny as either slow or weak. In a fight, Lenny would be a challenge to take out.

"Lenny, this is Mr. Vines. Mr. Vines, Mr. Northwhite."

Lenny held out a hand and smiled, and Hank smiled and reached out to shake that hand, bracing himself inside and hoping he didn't look like that was what he was doing.

And . . . nothing.

They shook hands.

Lenny and a couple of other guys, all on the same girl at the same time a few hours earlier. Lenny banging a dancer on top of his desk only moments before the floor manager showed Hank in. The dancer was still hiding in the office, Hank realized. Under Lenny's desk.

Hank let the connection slip deeper, and in an instant was flooded with foulness. He got Lenny breaking a window and climbing on some girl in the dark, raping her at knifepoint. Lenny raping his sister—that was big in his mind, a lot of times, a lot of ways. Lenny skimming, extorting, stealing, bribing. Lenny with lawyers. Lenny providing important people with their darkest desires: bondage, leather, branding, whips and chains, slavery, virgin sacrifices that included real rape, though not murder afterwards. And hidden cameras everywhere recording every little bit of sin and wickedness, because first and foremost in Lenny's mind was that if he went down, everybody went with him. Lenny, therefore, jail-proof.

But no matter how deep Hank forced himself to dig, he couldn't find Lenny with a six-by-six-grave grid of dead girls. That wasn't there. Nor Lenny draining the life out of a screaming, pleading girl. Hank found faint whispers of death and guilt and bewilderment a long time in Lenny's past, but that was overlaid by . . . Jess. Hunger, desire, weirdness and heat and perversity all wound around a massively twisted image of love. But Lenny didn't want Jess the way the *killer* wanted Jess. He didn't want her dead.

"Call me Lenny," Lenny said, squeezing too hard before he let go of Hank's hand.

"Hank."

Lenny sat, and Hank followed suit. Hank felt like someone had blindfolded him and spun him in circles a dozen times. He didn't know where he was, he couldn't understand what he was feeling, nothing connected, nothing worked.

Lenny ran a hand over the corner of the desk where he had so recently nailed one of the dancers. The spot, Hank thought, was probably still warm. Lenny said, "So you're a friend of Wayne's?"

"He told me about your Weekenders," Hank said. He wasn't going to get what he wanted out of Lenny, because it wasn't there. But now that he was sitting in the office, he couldn't say, "You know what, I've changed my mind," and leave. He wanted to leave. "And he told me I hadn't lived until I'd gone to one."

"Only our Gold Reserve members are invited to Weekenders; did he mention that?"

"He didn't mention requirements; I didn't ask. Requirements aren't usually a problem for me."

"If he even mentioned our Weekenders to you, they probably won't be." Lenny said, "But so we both know you know, an annual Gold Reserve membership is twenty-five thousand dollars. The Weekenders are only one of the special privileges. If you actually make use of all we offer, the membership can be . . . well, *quite* a bargain."

Hank said, "Are invitations to Weekenders automatic at that membership level?"

"Oh, of course."

Hank gave Lenny a shifty smile. "All right, then. Do you accept . . . ah . . . cash payment?"

Lenny said, "Of course. You could pay in cash?"

Hank smiled. "Of *course*. It will take me a day or two to do it neatly."

Lenny looked interested. "What's your business?"

"Investing."

Lenny said, "Not too many investors end up with scars like yours, if you don't mind me saying so."

"I was in the military before I became an investor. My family believed in the discipline and . . . connections . . . that military service offered."

"The Citadel, West Point, a commission, getting to know future senators and congressmen and like that?" Lenny asked.

And Hank lied easily. "Almost exactly like that. With a few surprises thrown in." He dismissed the experience with a shrug.

"Surprises. Yeah. Shit happens nonstop, far as I can tell," Lenny said. "Looks like you landed in more than your share."

Hank rose. "It was a long time ago, and isn't much of a factor in my current life." He nodded politely. "I'll give you a call in a few days, if that's all right."

Lenny stayed seated, his hand intermittently reaching out to touch the corner of the desk again. "I look forward to hearing from you."

Hank Vines, millionaire stock manipulator, walked out of Lenny's office and trailed his hand down the rail. He could feel death's touch there. It was old, vile, horrible . . . but overlaid by a steady stream of other touches.

But Lenny . . . Lenny had touched Jess earlier in the day, and he'd been a horrifying serial murderer whose next victim would be Jess. Tonight, though, he was a monster of a different kind. But not a killer. Not *the* killer.

Hank could think of three explanations. Lenny had an identical twin. Or Lenny had a split personality, and the part of him that killed women was submerged at the moment.

Hank didn't like either explanation.

The third was that Lenny had a buddy who stayed close. Close enough that he and Lenny had shaken hands not too long before Lenny touched Jess.

That one, he thought, was probably gold.

When Jess picked up the phone and found Jim on the other line, she said, "Do you know what time it is?"

"When has that ever mattered to you or me?" Jim said, and chuckled, sounding positively gleeful. "Two in the morning and this is worth it. Our boys and girls hit the fucking mother lode at Jason Hemly's house."

"Define mother lode."

"In a very nicely hidden storage space cut into the back of the closet in Jason Hemly's master bedroom, we found Polaroid pictures of eleven different girls, some of them still alive and handcuffed to a stripper's pole, some dead and lying in shallow graves. None of them have shown up on missing-persons reports anywhere. Each is tagged with a neatly typed label giving the girl's name and date of death. The killings cover the past twelve years. Along with photos, we also uncovered a stash of necklaces, rings— including class rings with names or initials—earrings, lockets with photos, little clippings of hair, and intimate apparel."

"I'd call that a mother lode, too." She shook her head. "That's terrifying. He's made a career of being a likable guy."

"It worked for him for a lot of years."

"You say . . . eleven? Not including the four we've found, or including them?"

"Not including them. These are all new. We have to figure that the other two killers might have some souvenirs, too, or maybe that Hemly has another storage space that holds more evidence."

"How about bodies?"

"Aside from those dumped in parks, nothing. And Hemly's not admitting anything. We say, 'We found your photo collection,' he says, 'What collection?' We say, 'We found your souvenirs.' He says, 'What souvenirs?' We say, 'We have you, we know you killed them, we have hair and semen samples on you, we have four bodies, we have pictures and you're *still* going to say you're innocent? That you don't know anything about this?' And guess what he says?"

" 'Talk to my lawyer' would be my first guess," Jess said.

"You'd think so, wouldn't you? But we went down and told him what we'd found in his place, and Hemly—get this—said he wanted to talk with us. I've just now stepped out of interrogation. He insists he's innocent, has never hurt anyone. His swimmers floating around in four dead girls in the city's freezers, and he's claiming innocence."

Jess said, "That's almost good enough to make *me* buy an insanity plea."

"Hemly dragged his lawyer in. The lawyer is pulling his hair out. Saying, 'You don't have to answer that question, I recommend you don't answer that question, you should stop talking now,' and Hemly is ignoring the bastard. He's going on and on about all the girls he dated at Goldcastle, and how they were all crazy about him, and always wanted to date him because he was such a great guy." Jim said, "Come to think of it, he might be building an insanity defense, with his own lawyer as star witness."

"So Hemly is still lacking an alibi?"

"In the case for which we have eyewitnesses, he remains without alibi. We are still trying to track down his whereabouts during the other three murders for which we have bodies."

Jess could hear the smile in Jim's voice. "Good news,

then. One down. Two to go." She grinned a little. "Thanks for the call. You were right—I wanted to know."

She was almost asleep again when someone bumped against the door to the hall, and she heard the doorknob rattle. She stared at her travel alarm clock. It was almost three A.M.

Soundlessly, she grabbed her gun and crept to the door and looked out the peephole. It might be Hank, she thought. With grocery bags or something.

It wasn't, though.

Lenny had been bent over, putting something in front of her door. He stood, looked both ways to make sure he hadn't been observed, and walked back down the hall toward the elevator.

Jess held her breath. Should she call a bomb squad over to the house? Lab techs?

Staring out the peephole, she saw Lenny step into the elevator. Watched the doors close. The second they did, Hank erupted from the stairwell and ran toward her door, grabbed whatever Lenny had placed there, and ran like hell back toward the stairs.

Did he see a bomb? What the hell?

Jess kicked into running shoes, grabbed her cell phone and handgun, and, still dressed in a tee and flannel pajama bottoms, took off down the hall after Hank.

"Hank! Wait!"

She raced down the stairway, spotting what looked like flower petals as she ran.

At the bottom of the stairwell, she hesitated for an instant, seeing Hank heading for the far, deserted corner of the community parking lot. She ran the other way, planning on stopping Lenny—but he was already getting into his car when she made it around the corner of the building.

She would break cover if she threw herself in front of the car and pulled her weapon on him to stop him.

But she didn't need to. An unmarked car pulled out of the parking lot just an instant behind him, and the cop riding shotgun gave her a nod as they drove away, tailing him.

Jess swore softly, thumbed the safety on, and jogged around to the far parking lot to join Hank. She caught up with him as he crouched a reasonable distance away from the objects he'd taken from in front of her door.

"You think he left a bomb?"

Hank was staring at the shadowy items lying on the pavement. "No. But I didn't see any point in taking chances."

"You were following Lenny?"

Hank looked at her and raised an eyebrow.

"Well, yeah. Stupid question."

Jess called Jim. "Hey," she said when he picked up. "We have a problem. Lenny Northwhite just stopped by my place and left goodies of an unknown nature at my door. His tails are on him, but we have the evidence right here. You want to get some techs over here?"

"What did he leave?"

Jess moved closer and squinted. "It *looks* like a heart-shaped box of candy and a bouquet of flowers. But considering who dropped it off in front of my door at three in the morning . . ." She let the sentence hang.

"Hank's with you?"

"He wasn't. But he is now. He was apparently following Lenny around."

"Oh, Christ." A pause, then a heavy sigh. "I'll be there."

Jim hung up, and Jess clipped her cell phone to the neck of her T-shirt, then studied Hank. "You have any theories on what Lenny was doing here?"

"Yeah. I think that a pervert who thinks he's in love left anonymous candy and flowers for the woman he thinks he's in love with."

Jess walked over to his side and stared at him. "And the

part about planning to kill me would be . . . what . . . the next phase of his love plan?"

"I have conflicting readings on that, Jess," Hank said. "What I got right after he touched you was very clear. It told me he was the killer. What I got tonight . . . Well, it seems to be equally clear that he isn't."

Jess let that sink in for a long, long moment. "What?"

"I went in and talked with Lenny tonight. As a prospective member of the club. Had a recommendation from a current member and everything. It was all very civilized, we shook hands. . . ."

At last Hank turned to look at her. "There was nothing in him of the monster I feel in that club, Jess. He's a sick fuck, and he wants you. A lot. But I couldn't find the part of him that wants to kill you. That wasn't there. I touched him, and neither you, nor 'six by six,' nor any of the poison and the pain-lust and the death-hunger that permeates the club were there."

"It was there when he grabbed my ass."

"I know," Hank said. "I'm not arguing. It was there; it's not there now. The best I can suggest is that he and the killer are buddies, and they shook hands before he came in to play grab-ass with you."

"He might have. He was out of my sight for a few minutes. But he knew something happened to Ginny," Jess said. "He had a part in it. I think he killed her, and I think he killed the rest of these dancers. He fits, Hank. Right down to being blond, he fits."

"I know. I'm telling you what I feel, and I know what feelings are worth compared to evidence. I can't make you believe that I'm right. My gut tells me that *you're* right, by the way. But all Jim's evidence—and now my hands—tell me you're wrong." He shrugged, and turned back to look at the box of candy and the flowers. "When I touched him, I couldn't find the monster inside of him. And, dammit, I looked."

Jess said, "There are things that can throw you off."

"I know. Lately it seem like there has been nothing but. I assume the dancer owns the costume she's wearing and another girl dies. Simple mistake. I'm missing something here, too. Something big."

Jim's car pulled into the parking lot. No lights, no sirens. "Charlie's on the way," he said, getting out of the Crown Vic. "Got the bomb guys coming, got a tech team coming. We're going to be quiet, keep the lights and sirens off."

Jim was studying the two of them with interest. "No rest for the wicked, eh?"

chapter 14

Jess, working the lunch shift, saw that computer-boy was back, sitting right up against the stage, grinning up at her with a dollar bill in his hand. Wayne Alton. Multimillionaire. One dollar.

That seemed about right.

The music thudded and Jess swung around the pole and did an impromptu slide over to him, crouching with legs spread wide, breasts thrust forward. He had that look on his face—that glazed-eyed look that most of them got when presented with a steady stream of tits and ass. This was not the best face men had to present to the world; if she had to deal with this every day, she would hate the whole gender. A lot of the dancers did.

"Sit with me when you're done," Alton said. "I want to talk to you."

She flashed him the dancer smile, nodded, picked up a couple more ones and a five being thrust at her by other men, and then went back to her dance.

Hank had a seat at a dance table back from the stage. When she looked at him, he wasn't watching her. Instead, he was studying the other men in the room, a bothered expression on his face.

She understood it. She felt the same bewilderment. After

Jim and Charlie and the bomb squad and her tech team and her roses and chocolates had all made their grand exit from the parking lot (with the roses and chocolates, bomb-free, bound for a fate as test materials in the police search for fibers, DNA, fingerprints, drugs, and other goodies), Jess and Hank went to bed together.

They didn't have fun, though. Instead, they'd debriefed.

Hank had told her exactly what he'd discovered when he touched Lenny, right down to Lenny's blackmailing of some of the city's key officials.

After hearing him out, Jess thought the Weekenders—which were what the Vice team had been trying without luck to infiltrate—likely held the key to the murders. Somewhere in the middle of all that kinky sex and blackmail, someone was getting a little extra. Hank had given Jim and Charlie the short version of what he'd read on Lenny. He would be going into the station after her shift was over to read a few items that belonged to Jason Hemly, and to give his impressions on items taken away from the Millie "River" Hantumakis murder.

Jess, weary as hell, thought maybe she would drag the surveillance team along to meet with Lenny. Because he knew something about Ginny. He had answers that Jess wanted. And no matter what Hank said, Jess thought Lenny was the key to this thing, all the way back to the very beginning.

She finished her set and went backstage.

"Hey, Gracie," Teri said. She was standing in the doorway of her office. "You look beat."

Jess gave her a weary smile. "Long night."

"Those can be fun."

"This one wasn't. Someone left anonymous flowers and candy in front of my door, and I figured with all the stuff going on, I'd better call the police. The guy who left them knows where I live, and he's leaving things."

Teri looked worried. "Do you have a friend to stay with? A family member, maybe?"

Jess laughed. "The police asked me the same questions." She shrugged. "I'll figure something out."

"You have to get a gun, honey."

Jess raised an eyebrow, looked down the hall at the other dancers, then back at Teri. "You think there are any girls here who aren't carrying? I don't. And I'm sure as hell not the exception."

Teri looked relieved. "Just . . . don't get caught then."

Jess grinned. "I'm legal. Carry-concealed permit, regular range practice and everything."

"Good for you. It's a relief to find a woman who takes her own defense seriously." Teri sighed, and sagged against her peach-painted office door frame. "Gracie?"

"Yeah?"

"Come talk to me once you're done with your shift, okay?"

"Sure. Am I in trouble?"

"Anything but."

"Good. I'll be there, then."

A few minutes later, showered and changed into one of the miniskirts and another see-through blouse and front-closing bra, she was out on the floor with Wayne.

"I wanted to ask you out," he said without preamble. "You're so beautiful and so sweet, Summer. Let me take you to dinner, okay?"

Jess looked at him and smiled brightly and said, "The way things are right now, we've all been instructed not to date men we meet at work. I'd love to take a rain check though, Wayne."

"The way things . . . are? With the killer?" Wayne shook his head and laughed. "That's funny. I'm a computer geek—nobody's going to mistake me for some psychopath."

Well, they might now, Jess thought.

"Seriously," she said, still smiling, "once the police are sure they have all the killers in custody, I'm sure Teri will lift our work restrictions."

"Teri?" Wayne said. "She's the one who's telling you girls you can't date customers? Teri and I are old friends. She'll vouch for me."

Jess rose. "I'll be talking to her later, darlin'. And I will absolutely, positively ask."

"Wonderful," he said, and when she stood up, he stood, too. He took her left hand and squeezed it and kissed the back of it. "I need to get back to work now. I came in here especially to see you," he said, and winked. "But I'll be back tomorrow."

Jess wandered over to Hank, flirting and teasing all the way, careful not to touch anyone with her left hand. She trailed it down his arm, murmuring "Read," in his ear at the same time.

"Sick," he said. "Really sick. This guy is into S-and-M. He's done some bad, kinky, weird, fucked-up things."

"He our guy?"

"No. Who is he?"

"Wayne Alton, software mogul."

"Ee-yeah. Got a brief feel for him yesterday. Ugly."

"This job sucks," Jess murmured, and pulled back, flashing him a bright smile. She moved on.

The dead girl lay faceup in a parking lot, prettily posed in an empty parking space. This strip mall didn't get much traffic, so she would probably be there for a little while before someone came along and found her.

They should be pleased when they did. She looked . . . lovely. She wore green lace, green patent-leather shoes, green silk stockings. They went very nicely with her deep green eyes, her pale pink lips, her soft honey hair.

The killer snapped four quick Polaroids, smiling. This was, after all, a moment worth remembering. And sharing.

Hank's cell phone rang. He glanced at the caller ID. Jim. "Yeah?"

"Got a body. Want you out here for this one. It doesn't quite fit the previous MO, but it's close. I want to see if you can get a quick read on whether or not we've picked up a copycat. Could save us a little time."

"Tell me where."

Jim gave him the address.

Hank looked around for Jess, spotted her talking to the redhead he'd thought was going to die, and waved Jess over.

"Hey, darlin'," she said. "You looking for a lap dance?"

He realized they were being watched. "I have to run, Summer. I know I told you that I wanted one today"—he fished a twenty out of his billfold and handed it to her—"but work called. My partner needs me to check some figures before he runs them with a new client. It's . . . kind of an emergency."

Her smile never wavered, but he could see the sharp intelligence. She nodded. Tucked the twenty into the waistband of her skirt. "Good luck with that," she said. "We'll make time for your dance another day." She tapped the bill. "You're paid in advance." She said, "I was off in a few minutes anyway, so this will be good for both of us."

He headed out the door. The guys in the surveillance van would have heard that they were her only backup. They would make sure they kept her covered, would be ready to break down doors if they had to. Of course, as long as she was actually in the club, she was safe. And when she left . . . well, she was a competent cop. She would be fine.

But he didn't feel good about leaving her alone in there.

*   *   *

Jess returned to her conversation with Ginger Rose, who was quitting. "The place is giving me the creeps," Ginger said. "I'm not the only one out of here, either. The money won't do it for me anymore. Cree already quit; Jade quit—"

Jess knew Cree was the gorgeous deaf dancer, but Jade? "Jade is . . . ?"

"She's been on nights since you started. You probably haven't met her yet. Japanese, about so tall, absolute firecracker. She's probably the most popular house dancer in the club."

"She one of Lenny's?"

"Not a chance. Guess I should have specified. She's probably the most popular dancer in the club who isn't turning tricks on the side."

Jess considered that for a moment. "How is Teri taking this?"

"Not well. Everyone said she about exploded when Jade told her she'd found a place at Studz. She's been a bit better about some of the other dancers jumping ship, but Teri had been trying to fix Jade up with some acting jobs in pornos. Teri has those movie connections, you know, and she saw Jade as a big feature draw for Goldcastle."

Jess nodded, and Ginger Rose said, "Anyway, Gracie, I just wanted to tell you good-bye. I'm out the door in ten, and I won't be back."

"Not telling Teri in person?"

"Not sure I have the guts to tell her at all. I'm not as important to her as Jade was, but I do all right. I sell so many drinks I can't even remember the last time I had to pay my tip-out. I don't want to leave her. But I want to leave *here*."

"Good luck," Jess said. "For what it's worth, you're probably doing the right thing. Leaving, that is. Be really careful out there."

Ginger Rose patted her shoulder and said, "You, too.

And tell your brother Cree said she wished him luck. Jade, too. She heard about him from some of the girls. And give him a hug from me."

Without warning, Jess had tears in her eyes. "Yeah," she said, blinking them back. "I'll do that."

She liked these girls. She wished she could do something that would magically make their work safe, or give them skills that would let them earn the same money without the daily immersion in this sleazy, dirty world where they were risking their lives and their safety every day.

She turned away and headed in to talk to Teri, who was probably not going to be in a great mood, and who was probably going to ask her to pick up extra hours. Meanwhile, if Jess had read Hank's code correctly, the police had found another dead dancer.

Jess wondered who was dead. If she'd known this girl, if she had met her. Maybe talked to her. Maybe liked her.

She sighed and, since she didn't feel like walking back through the ballroom and fending off attention she did not want, she went through the foyer, past the staircase, and back toward the private dancing rooms and the other backstage entrance.

"Hey, baby," Lenny murmured in her ear.

Jess jumped and turned. How the hell had he moved so quietly?

He'd been standing right behind her. "You looked great out there today. Nobody was ever as good a dancer as you." He smiled.

His eyes were focused on her, intent. He didn't look threatening. He looked like he was trying to be charming. But he took a step forward, and she took a step back.

"It's been a long day, and I didn't get any sleep last night."

He frowned. "You shouldn't be losing sleep, sweetheart. What's wrong?"

"Someone left candy and flowers in front of my door, and the police were there for hours investigating."

Lenny looked startled. "Investigating?"

"With dancers being murdered, I didn't think having someone I didn't know following me home and finding out where I lived was a good thing."

He smiled broadly, crossed the distance between the two of them in one quick step, and pulled her into his arms. He kissed her, a wet, openmouthed, tongue-probing kiss that almost made her gag. "I'll take care of you, baby. I can keep you safe from anyone out there. You come home with me, sweetheart; we'll put you right back on that fireman's pole, hey? Pick up where we left off."

"Where we left off? You mean with you thinking I was dead? We have a lot of ground to cover before we go anywhere near picking up where we left off."

He let go of her. "Yeah. One of these days, you're going to tell me what the hell was up with that. It wasn't fucking funny." He was suddenly cold. Angry. "You look like you're in a hurry to go, and I guess I'm not in as good a mood as I thought I was. So you go ahead on, and I'll see you tomorrow. If you think you can manage to show up alive, that is."

And he turned and stalked away.

She stared at the goose bumps on her arms and felt the hair standing up on the back of her neck.

If she thought she could manage to show up alive? Was he threatening her? What the hell had just gone on?

She had to take a deep breath before going into Teri's office and dropping into a seat without being invited.

Teri raised an eyebrow.

She debated the relative virtues of telling Teri what Lenny had done, and decided that her cover would survive considerably better if Teri heard it from her, rather than the greeter or anyone else. Gracie wasn't a fighter, but she would not tolerate being pawed by Lenny. And Jess was playing this as Gracie. As Jess, after all, she would have kicked his nuts through the roof of his mouth. So she said, "I was coming in here through the private dance entrance. And Lenny came out of nowhere and grabbed me. And kissed me."

Teri frowned. "He *what?*"

"Grabbed me and kissed me."

"No warning?"

"He told me how much he liked the way I danced, if you consider that a warning. I sure didn't."

Teri's eyes narrowed. "You haven't gone up to his office to work out any little deals with him?"

"Good God, no."

She slammed the side of her fist onto the top of her desk and looked away. "Damn him. He's out of control."

"This happen often?"

"Not with *my* girls, it doesn't." She blew out a sharp breath and turned back to Jess. "I'm sorry, Gracie. I'll take care of him. He won't bother you again."

"Thank you. I really appreciate it."

Teri leaned back in her chair and said, "In light of . . . recent adventures, you might not be in any mood to hear what I have to say."

"That doesn't sound good," Jess told her.

Teri looked down, a smile tugging at one corner of her mouth. She lifted one shoulder in a shrug. "I'm not in a line of work that's particularly conducive to friendship," she said. "Most of the dancers here are little more than children. The handful of adults tend to be bitter. They're heading into a future where they're not going to be able to count on their looks anymore, and only beginning to catch on to what that means while they realize that they never planned for that time." She sighed and looked up. "You're . . . different. You haven't been living this life, it isn't what you're looking at long-term, you haven't . . . Well. You haven't sold your soul into this business, for lack of a less melodramatic term."

Jess nodded, cocking her head to one side. "Okay . . ."

"You seem like someone who would be good to have as a friend, and I could really use a friend right now. I have no one to talk to. No one."

Jess said, "Me?"

"You're . . . smart. Thoughtful. A genuine grown-up. I'm looking at losing a fortune right now, and realizing I'm connected through this place to something horrible. I'm realizing that at least one person I liked and thought I knew has done things so brutal that I can't even imagine them." She rubbed her temples, an expression of pain on her face. "My life is suddenly not going the way I'd planned. And I don't know how to fix anything. And I just thought, well, maybe it would be nice if you and I went out for coffee sometimes. Maybe . . . shopping, if you like to shop. I need someone to talk to. And I imagine you do, too, with everything you have going on."

"Coffee sounds good," Jess said.

"You want to, then?"

If you're going to talk to me? Tell me the secrets of this place and the people in it? Damn straight, Jess thought. All she said was, "Yes. I think that would be very nice."

"Want to go now?"

Jess had not held a conversation with a woman who was not a cop, a criminal, a victim, or a potential witness in about ten years. She wasn't sure if she remembered how casual conversation between women worked. Teri seemed nice enough, and Jess liked her for watching out for her dancers and for working so hard to keep at least one part of Goldcastle straight. It was hard to equate Teri the businesswoman with Teri the porn star.

Right at that moment, Jess wanted to get out of the club,

find Hank, fall into his arms and let him work the magic that took her away from all the world's awfulness. She was exhausted, her bizarre night had segued into an equally bizarre day, and if she let her eyelids slide closed, she could feel Hank holding her, could hear him whispering to her, could almost let her legs wrap around him and . . . yes. Well.

But Hank was working with Jim and Charlie. Another dancer was dead. Teri might be able to tell Jess something about this situation that she needed to know. And even if Teri couldn't, she might know something that would send the HSCU detectives in the right direction. Besides, right at that moment, Jess sure as hell didn't feel like approaching Lenny about having a public-place dinner together.

"Sure," she said. "I'd love to. Let me get changed and I'm out of here."

Hank stopped off at the dojo and dug into the back of his closet for his duffel bag, which contained a graft compression mask and shirt that he'd worn in his last round of surgeries. He'd tossed the bag in there when he first bought the dojo and hadn't moved it since. He probably shouldn't have even kept the compression mask—but he thought it was important to remember where he came from. Sometimes it was easy to forget how well he had things compared to how they had been even a handful of years earlier, and the presence of those bandages warded off any temptation to indulge in self-pity.

But since he was undercover in Goldcastle and couldn't allow himself to be identified with Jim and Charlie when the killer might be watching—and since serial killers had a tendency to flit around the background of the scenes of their crimes, looking for a little extra bang for their buck— Hank figured he might as well put the old gear to use. People could think he was a burn victim. That would work. So long as they wouldn't be able to connect him with the guy sitting right up against the stage at the strip club, he was happy.

He was tempted to call Jess to make sure she was all right. But she might be doing something as Gracie that a call from him could compromise. He decided to wait, and see her when he was done with this business for Jim and Charlie.

The heat shimmering off the pavement made the scene of the latest body dump gruesome. The coroner had removed the girl's body right before Hank got there—traffic had slowed him down and the cops had to get her on ice fast to preserve evidence. The heavy, sickly sweet stink of death still clogged the still, humid air, though. It and the awful heat slammed Hank as soon as he stepped out of his car. The heavy elastic of the old-style fitted compression bandages didn't help matters any. The bandages had always been hot even in cold weather. Jim spotted him and waved him over. "Haven't seen that *face* in quite some time."

"Didn't want the wrong person to recognize me," Hank said. "Don't tell me any more about what you've got here than you already have." He could see chalk marks inside the yellow-taped crime scene. "Tell me where you want me to read, and I'll give you what I can."

"I marked off three squares for you on the pavement," Jim said. "Those were areas that had good contact with . . . well, things."

Hank nodded, walked along the line Jim pointed out to him, and crouched beside the first white chalk-drawn square. "Here?"

Jim was right behind him. "Yeah."

"Everybody else out of earshot? I can't see a damned thing down here."

Charlie looked sick. Hank, shaking his hand, had gotten flashes of exhaustion, depression, a desperate desire to be done with all of this, and gone to some shining lake with his wife and kids. This thing was haunting him, chewing him up a day at a time, a piece at a time. Charlie had a daughter the age of most of these girls, Hank realized. Early twenties. He was looking at these dead girls and seeing his oldest kid.

Charlie set a tape recorder on the ground next to Hank. "You're clear all the way around. Go ahead."

Hank rested the fingertips of his right hand lightly on the ground inside the square.

And he got dozens of women's touches, worries about price, quality, one that doubted the beadwork would stay on. But none that belonged to a killer and none that belonged to a woman who had just been killed.

"This feels unrelated to the crime," Hank said. He passed on the comments and concerns he felt, and said, "I don't know how this relates."

"It was a handbag," Jim said. "Matched what the victim was wearing. But it was empty. Might have just been a prop—something that the killer bought but was careful not to touch." He frowned and wrote something in a notebook. "Move to the next one."

Hank duckwalked two steps forward, touched down in the center of the second square.

"Girl talking. Laughing. Very excited about being in a movie. The killer's touch is stronger here than the presence of the victim, but this isn't a lust killing. This is . . . strange. There's no hint of violence in this scene. The girl is laughing. Happy. And then she isn't there anymore."

"What about torture? Rape? Fear? This girl was *murdered*. Almost identical to the MO we have on the other four." Charlie wasn't looking at Hank when he asked. He was staring down at the little chalked squares, seeing what had been there before the police bagged the evidence and hauled it off.

"Inside her own head, the victim wasn't murdered," Hank said. "She was there, and then she just went away. The last thing I have from her is excitement about her career."

"But you feel the killer here."

"Strongly. Same killer. Completely different motive. This is just . . ." Hank closed his eyes. "Just . . . shit. Confusing as hell. Let me try the third spot."

All three of them moved again.

Hank put down his hand, said, "Impressions on square three—nothing whatsoever on the girl. The killer is clear here. Putting down something that is supposed to send the police in the wrong direction. He thinks it's funny as hell. The girl is dead for the same reason. Because she doesn't fit. Because he thinks someone may be getting close to the truth, and this is a game he's not quite ready to end yet."

He opened himself to more of that touch, and at the back of it, he found Jess again. Jess, who was the real target. The one the killer was waiting for, working toward. In the back of the monster's mind, Jess already lay in a grid of six by six, brutally murdered. "Omega . . . and alpha," he said suddenly.

"What?"

"He thinks of Jess as Omega. And . . . alpha. But not." And then it hit him. "Oh, hell." He stood and wiped sweat out of his eyes. "Alpha isn't Jess. Alpha is her twin sister, Ginny. That's why the killer wants Jess. She's been working her way toward this bastard since she became a cop, only he spotted her first. And he wants to make her the closing act of his current collection."

"It's got to be Lenny," Jim said. "Got to be. He was the sister's boyfriend way back then. And here he still is, same business but a different name, hitting on Jess, following her home. Closing out a chapter."

Hank said, "I've read Lenny. The person I'm feeling isn't him."

Jim said, "No. No. I would have agreed with you before, but no. Not now. Things are clicking with Lenny. We have two fingerprints on one of the victim's shiny blue patent leather shoes this time, and I'm betting that Lenny rings our bell."

"Not going to be Lenny," Hank said.

"Tech was supposed to run the prints first," Charlie said. "If it's Lenny, we have several complete sets of prints on file for him since he stepped up from juvie crime. We should have a hit by now."

Jim made sure Hank was looking at him, and cut his eyes sidelong at Charlie, and Hank saw a flash of worry cross Jim's face. Jim plastered on a cocky grin and said, "Going to be Lenny. I'm in for ten," and he stared at Hank. Willing him to get this fake jocularity.

And Hank did get it, because he could see Charlie sinking fast. This bet, this black humor, was about getting Charlie's mind off what they were doing, this hell they were in the middle of, where Charlie was dealing with girls the age of his oldest kid—pretty girls like her, only badly dead and dumped like garbage.

Hank said, "All right. Ten. I'll go more if you want. It isn't going to be Lenny."

Charlie looked at them both. Gnawed the inside of the corner of his mouth. "I'm not betting on this one. But I like Lenny for this whole thing. He fits. Hank seems too sure, though, and I'm saving every penny I get for retirement, which cannot get here fast enough."

"Bullshit. You're a cheap bastard is all," Jim said. "But since you're the guy with nothing to lose, you make the call."

Hank watched Charlie call in to HSCU, heard him say, "Charlie here. We got a positive ID on those prints?" He grinned a little, looked at Jim, then Hank, then back to Jim. "Got it. Thanks." He cut the call. "We have a winner."

"It was Lenny," Jim said. "Ha!"

Hank waited.

Jim glanced from Hank to Charlie.

Charlie said, "We *also* have a positive ID on the prints."

Jim said, "Charlie, you prick, get it out or I will not be responsible for my actions."

Charlie managed a small grin in Hank's direction. "You hear what he did to me the last time he wasn't responsible for his actions."

"Habanero sauce in your sandwich." Hank turned to Jim. "It's that sense of humor, incidentally, that has earned you three divorces."

"I guess news travels fast." Jim had managed to kick Charlie out of that dark place where too much death and too much horror would send a man. He'd provided a distraction, thin though it was. Hank had to admire Jim for pushing Charlie away from the edge of the pit. Charlie actually smiled as he said to Jim, "It's not Lenny. You owe Hank ten bucks, you arrogant know-it-all. But . . . you remember the computer millionaire whose hot little housekeeper charged him with sexual harassment and a couple of bigger goodies last year?"

"The case settled out of court," Jim said. "Gag orders on both parties, records sealed. She was after his money, but she had to have had something on him, to walk away with stack of green I heard she got."

"Maybe she had a lot more on him than anyone thought. The prints on the shoe were his."

Hank said, "You two talking about Wayne Alton? The game guy?"

"Yes," Charlie said.

Hank said, "He's in Goldcastle a lot."

"He is indeed," Jim said. "Has dated a whole string of the girls. He's very popular. *Everybody* loves Wayne."

Hank said, "I did a couple of reads on him, Jim. Wayne loves S-and-M and girls in cages. He likes to date fresh new dancers and see how far into kink he can drag them. So I'd guess not everybody loves him."

"We know about his hobbies. Thanks to Wayne hitting on Jess hard yesterday, we did a file on him. Neither one of us has slept since this thing broke, and Charlie's wife is sure now that Charlie's a figment of her imagination, but we have met the real Wayne, and he is a freaky, creepy, sick son of a bitch."

"He's not the killer, though," Hank said.

And both Charlie and Jim turned to stare at Hank with expressions of pure exasperation. "Is your killer sniffer broke?" Jim asked.

"I read Wayne. When I did, I got all the creepy and freaky you could ever want. But . . . the monster who's killing the dancers has a shape. A presence. I touch something he's touched and it's like this black plastic bag slides down over my head. I can't see, I can't breathe, I feel the panic of more scared, dying women than I can count and this cold inside of me that defies description. I get queasy; my gut wrenches." He stood there thinking about it for a moment. "It's as clear to me as a fingerprint is to you."

"But we can admit fingerprints in court," Charlie said.

"I know. All I can tell you is, I'm as sure that Wayne Alton isn't the killer as I was sure that Northwhite's fingerprint wouldn't be on that shoe." Hank said, "I'm heading over to Jess's place. I'll update her on what I got, and see what she came up with after I left. I'll take a message if you want."

Jim said, "I'll call her tonight to give her the brief. We'll set up another meeting after we get more info on this latest girl, but we don't need to bring her in again just yet. We still don't even have a name on this one."

"I'll tell Jess."

chapter 15

"Try the Costa Rican Chocolate Blend. All their stuff is wonderful, but their Costa Rican Chocolate Blend is the best coffee on the planet."

Jess, standing at the counter in the little coffee bar beside Teri, said, "I should never drink the best coffee on the planet. Most of the time, I'm in places that only offer the absolute worst coffee on the planet. My taste buds don't need to get their hopes up." She scanned the menu and shook her head. "I should get something decaffeinated anyway. I haven't been sleeping worth shit since I started this job. My plans when I get home today are a long shower, a long nap, and then straight to bed."

Teri laughed. "God, I understand that. Between coming in early and leaving late, I manage on five hours of sleep most days. Sometimes less." She was studying Jess's face. "You know what? You look good even without makeup. Not exotic or glamorous or anything. But . . . good."

Jess was a bit startled by the observation. "Well . . . thanks. I generally don't wear makeup," she admitted. "It makes my skin itch. Besides, I'm comfortable with my own face."

Teri smiled. "It's nice seeing women with their real faces. We don't often, you know? We don't often show our own faces, either. We're always in disguise—because when you think about it, that's all makeup is. Us pretending to be something we aren't."

"I suppose." Jess got decaffeinated black something-or-other with a stupid name, plus a giant cookie, Teri got a cup of her favorite, and they took a seat at one of the little tables. "I never thought about it much. I'll use lip gloss because it keeps my lips from getting dry. Dancing aside, I don't bother with anything else."

They drank their coffee for a moment, neither saying anything. And the coffee was, unfortunately, very good. The mere memory of it was going to make the swill at the police station taste even more gruesome, something she would not have thought possible. She took small sips, closed her eyes, and smiled.

"I was right about all their coffee being good, wasn't I?"

"Beyond a doubt. You come here often?"

"It's one of my favorite places."

They looked out the window, and out of the corner of her eye, Jess saw the surveillance van slide into a parking space not too far away. It had circled the block twice before finding an opening, and Jess was worried that Teri was going to say something important while they were out of range.

Jess leaned back in her chair, put her cup on the table, and said, "You sounded down earlier."

Teri gave a bitter laugh. "I am down. Goldcastle has the customers coming in, so the money is still there, but a lot of our recent traffic has been gawkers. Sightseers. I've noticed a lot of our regulars missing, and who can blame them, considering the news? If they come in, they take a chance of looking like suspects. Plus, we're losing dancers left and right. Things are going on upstairs that I have no control over, and Lenny is . . . God, I cannot even begin to describe my problems with Lenny."

Jess sipped her coffee and waited.

"Well, some of Lenny I clearly don't have to describe."

Jess took a bite of the cookie, and raised her eyebrows in silent agreement.

And Teri sighed. "I'm afraid of him. I'm afraid he has something to do with the girls who have died. He's . . . well, in private, he's very, very scary."

Jess said, "In what way?"

Teri looked down at her hands and shook her head. Jess realized the other woman's hands were shaking. Teri seemed to realize it at the same time and hid them on her lap. "I don't want to talk about it. It's mere speculation, and speculation is nothing I want to be a party to. Innocent people get hurt that way, and I don't want to contribute to gossip." And then she flushed, and said, "Not that I was suggesting that *you* would gossip if I said anything."

Jess put a reassuring smile on her face and said, "I wouldn't," in her best sincere voice. "And I understand you not wanting to speculate about someone when you don't know anything is definitely wrong. I think that's admirable." She created a carefully timed pause with a sip of coffee, and said, "The world would be a better place if all the people who suspected things took the time to find out the truth, and all the people who knew the truth told it."

She caught a flash of guilt and fear in Teri's eyes, quickly hidden. Yeah. Teri knew something about Lenny. She was afraid of Lenny, vulnerable to him somehow. Maybe he was blackmailing her, though Jess had a hard time imagining anything a man could use to blackmail an ex–porn star.

If Teri would just tell Jess, Charlie and Jim could get the lovely search warrant to Lenny's mansion that would give them this case. And Lenny. And maybe, at long last, Ginny.

But Jess needed to find the right approach to Teri, who was careful and now a bit edgy, and who looked like she would spill her guts if tipped the right way, or shut down completely if pushed.

No pressure at all, Jess decided, would be the best approach.

"How are you going to handle the staffing, since people are quitting?" she asked.

Jess could see Teri breathe out, relieved. "Cut our nightly tip-out, bring in new girls—though we aren't getting applicants like we were."

"Well, no," Jess said. "I'm not surprised."

"Are you going to stay?"

"I've thought about leaving. I'd be crazy if I hadn't, wouldn't I?" she asked.

Teri's rueful shrug was her only reply.

"And at this point I could move to a different club, I suppose," Jess said. "But I have some regulars who tip well now, and Jim has more expensive tests coming up, and I really can't afford to stop." She smiled at Teri. "Plus, you're there. I'm impressed by the way you take care of your dancers." And then she got her hook. "Lenny's a problem, though. I'd thought about going to the police about him, but really, I'd bet anything he was the one who left the flowers on my doorstep. And kissing me in the hallway against my will was . . . Well. But if I go to the police and charge him with those things, nothing is going to happen to him. You know that. And I'm afraid involving the police without having enough on him to get him locked up might just piss him off."

Teri nodded. "It would, I think."

"Do you think he's killing the dancers? Do you think I'm in danger?"

Teri sighed heavily and clenched the cup in her hand, knuckles white. "Oh, God. Jess, I think he might be. And you might be in danger from him. I don't know. But . . . no. I can't talk about it with you." She looked into Jess's eyes,

and Jess spotted the sheen of unshed tears. "I can't." Teri
rose. "I have to go." She tried to give Jess a reassuring
smile, but her lips trembled, and after just an instant, she
turned away. In a strangled voice, she said, "Whatever you
do, stay as far away from him as you can."

And she fled out the door and across the street, almost
running in her haste to get away.

Jess stood up, staring after Teri. She could have chased
after her, but she didn't. No pressure.

Instead, she cleaned off their table, wondering all the
while exactly what Lenny Northwhite was holding over
Teri Thomas's head.

What the hell was Lenny Northwhite's connection to
Teri Thomas? She had a feeling that she and Hank and Jim
and Charlie needed to find out. Fast.

Hank thought she looked too tired when she stepped out
of the elevator. He walked down the dingy hallway to greet
her, picked her up and swung her around and kissed her,
and felt her sag against him.

He could feel the killer on her, but only from a distance.
At one remove. She had touched something the bastard had
touched. He breathed a little easier. Not much, but a little.

"You look beat."

"I am," she said. "God, I am. I did not think today was
ever going to end."

"Me, either." He put her down and wrapped an arm
around her waist and walked her back to her apartment
door, where he'd left bags full of good things waiting. "But
I'm cooking. So long as you promise to stay awake at least
long enough to eat."

"Promise. What did you bring?"

"Be surprised."

She unlocked the door and let them in. "I have to get a

shower," she told him. "Have to. Lysol, Clorox, lye—there has got to be something that will wash that place off of me."

Hank wanted to tell her that not going in there anymore would do the trick. That her being out of the line of fire, away from that place, when she was the killer's next target—and special target, at that—would do a very fine job of keeping her slime-free. And alive. He didn't want to forget the importance of her being alive.

"I do have some ideas on that," he said, and sounded grimmer than he'd intended to. "But go shower, and I'll get some of this stuff started, and we can talk while it's cooking."

She almost lunged into the shower. He could understand it—probably better than most, he thought. She was carrying the residue of the touches of men she didn't like, wouldn't want to associate with, and under other circumstances wouldn't even go near. They were touching her with thoughts in mind that ranged from the merely pornographic to the horrifyingly perverse—and those impulses and wishes and desires clung. If they didn't, he wouldn't have anything to offer the cops. Or anything that made him want to drown himself every time he ended up in the middle of a crowd, or riding a public bus.

There were some sick fucks out there, and a lot of them were congregating around Jess. Including the one who wanted to kill her.

Yeah, he could see that he wasn't going to be able to put this business in perspective anytime soon.

But he could at least be calm talking about it to her.

He heard the shower running, and her moving around.

It was hard to forget that she was naked in there. Hard to look at baking potatoes and good thick steaks and salad greens and bread and think about cooking dinner. Hard to keep his mind away from the hours he'd been watching other men watch her, watching the bastards imagining her being with them. And the whole time, he'd known what she felt like, how she moved, how she responded—and he didn't want to share her. Not with their hands pushing money at her, not with their eyes looking at her, not with their minds thinking things about her they had no business thinking.

He wanted to protect her. Wanted to keep her safe, and that had nothing to do with her being a cop in a risky job, and everything to do with him being a man in love.

Good God. *Not* in love. Not that.

He sighed. From his second bag, he pulled out a small bouquet of bright yellow carnations with red tips, which smelled good and looked nice in the vase. And which he could identify by name; he'd never been a flowers kind of guy. He'd learned the basics—orchids, roses, daisies, carnations—and he stuck with them.

He wasn't quite sure what he was looking for from Jess, but when he was making his way through Publix studying slabs of beef wrapped in plastic and stacks of spuds, looking for exactly the right ones, flowers had been a part of the picture in his head. Candles. Wine.

Something small and shiny with a diamond attached.

He closed his eyes, swearing under his breath. That *wasn't* what he wanted. This thing had happened between the two of them too fast, and all of a sudden he was thinking of forever? No. No, flat, not-a-chance no.

He didn't know Jess well enough for forever. He'd barely met her. She was a good woman. She was someone he could love. But he didn't love her. Not yet.

He stared at that little arrangement of carnations.

He *could* see the two of them together forever, though. That was the problem. He was thinking about a romantic evening followed by a great time in bed, and at some point talking her into at least coming to stay with him until this mess was done—or at most getting out of it because she was in danger, dammit—but some conniving bastard deep inside of him that had been keeping his mouth shut was pulling strings Hank hadn't even known he had. The little man in the control tower was directing Hank the Big Dumb Sucker to flowers and good bottles of red wine and priming him to open his mouth either before or after the great sex tonight and say something monumentally stupid.

Like, *Marry me*.

Hank wrapped the potatoes in aluminum foil, stuck them in the oven, and set the timer. Forty minutes, and then they could finish up on the bottom rack while the steaks broiled and the wine breathed. The salad was the work of three minutes. Maybe five. Hank didn't want to tear the lettuce until they were ready to eat it.

He heard the shower cut off, and his heart slid into his throat.

The little guy in the tower didn't seem to have all that bad an idea. He ran it through his head, examining it. *Marry me, Jess, and let's be happy and wonderful together for the rest of our lives. Marry me, Jess, so that I can see your smile every morning when we wake up and every night before we turn out the lights. Marry me, Jess, because you're the only woman I've ever known who looked at me and saw me, not scars, right from the first. And I might be a big dumb sucker, but I'm not so dumb that I think that's going to happen again.*

Marry me, Jess, because I love you.

And there it was. He could tell himself till the sun came up that he didn't love her.

But he did.

From the bathroom, thumping. Jess was graceful when she walked, and graceful when she danced, but getting dressed in that tiny bathroom, she sounded like two dogs fighting in a cardboard box. He grinned, wishing he could watch.

He was smiling when she walked out the door. She looked clean-scrubbed, fresh, rested. She was everything he had ever wanted in a woman and a lot of things he hadn't even dared to imagine.

"Hey, darlin'," he said. "Potatoes are baking. We have a little time."

"Time is good. Baked potatoes—*not* microwaved?"

"You know my opinion of the microwave."

She grinned at him. "That I do."

He considered going with the wine and the flowers and the getting down on one knee and making a fool of himself, but they were both on empty stomachs, and dinner was cooking, and he had the whole business of her being the next victim to discuss with her. It would be really unfair, he thought, to ask her to come live with him, or marry him, and then break it to her that he wanted her to get out of this investigation. Something inside of him insisted that she would look at this as his attempting to manipulate her. She'd see it as cheating.

He wasn't a cheater. Never had been. So he'd do this in order.

He said, "I called the surveillance team to figure out when to look for you. Lump says you met with Teri after work? Get anything good?" Lump was Dan Lumpkin, who was heading up the surveillance-van team.

"I'm still processing it." She pulled up a bar stool on the other side of the counter and watched him. "She's hiding something big about Lenny—I'm trying to figure out if anything anyone else has said to this point would tell me *what*."

Lenny. Lenny. Where the hell did Lenny fit into this?

"How about you?" she asked. "Called in on the new dead girl?"

"She wasn't part of the series," he said. He stuck the steaks in the fridge, moved the bags out of the way, and came around the counter to sit on the other bar stool. "She looked about the same, and she'd been killed in the same way. The things done to her after death, also all the same." He turned at right angles to the counter so that he could look straight at Jess. "But she was a decoy. The killer was trying to make it look like he'd moved on."

"Moved on?"

"Here's what Jim and Charlie managed to find out about today's victim: She was twenty-six years old; her name was Bethany Hertz; and she'd been stripping as a hobby for a mere three weeks. Her full-time job was as a radiologist at a local women's clinic. Apparently, noticing that they weren't meeting a lot of men at work, she and three other girls decided to participate in an amateur-night topless contest, and she won some sort of prize. The club where she participated was more than happy to have her back as a twice-a-week regular."

"So she has no ties to Goldcastle," Jess said.

"Not a one. No links to anybody in it. She barely has ties to stripping. She had Wayne Alton's fingerprint on the back of her shoe—"

"Wayne Alton! The creepy computer-game guy?"

"Yeah. Him. As far as they were able to tell, Bethany never met Wayne Alton before her death. And, of course, Alton has never been to the clinic where she works, either."

"And yet she's dead, and he killed her."

"He and the still-missing blond assailant. Jim said they had fibers, semen, and head and body hairs that appear to match every other case."

"Okay. I can see—to some extent—why she wouldn't quite look like part of the series. But she's dead, and the same people killed her in the same way."

"Not quite. I could feel the difference—I could feel the intent. Which was to put people off their trail. But Jim and Charlie put together a whole list reasons why she didn't fit.

Her body was dumped in a public parking lot in the middle of the day, and the treatment of the girl before death was completely different."

Jess leaned forward. Frowning. Intent. "How?"

"She had the same postmortem bath-and-makeup ritual, same post-cleanup rape. But the medical examiner confirmed what I felt. Nothing—absolutely nothing—was done to her before death. He couldn't confirm the other thing—that this girl never suffered. I can't explain it, but she missed her murder. So that's a big difference."

"I'd say."

"The fact that she wasn't raped or tortured premortem actually fits with what I felt about the killer choosing a victim almost at random, just to throw us of his trail, and to divert attention from you."

"Because if she isn't from Goldcastle, then it looks like the killer has changed hunting grounds."

"Right."

Jess closed her eyes and rubbed her fingertips against her forehead. "But you still think I'm the next real target?"

"You're the *last* real target, Jess. You've been chosen because your sister Ginny was the first victim. I keep feeling this alpha-and-omega thing, every time I connect with the killer. After you're dead, he's planning on picking up shop and moving to some other location. You fit this six-by-six thing he has going, and you're omega."

Jess laid her face in her arms on the counter and said nothing.

"Jess?"

"Give me a minute. I know I've considered that Ginny might have been early in his series. But that she was the first, and I'm supposed to be the last . . ." He heard her choke up.

"Breathe, sweetheart. Breathe. I'm here." He ran his hand over her back, stroking, rubbing her tense muscles.

She flooded him with her pain, her grief, her sense of loss. He caught images of her with a girl who looked just like her, of friendship and love and of the huge gaping hole her sister's disappearance had left in Jess's life. And he could feel, too, a swelling fury that raged into him like the back-blast of a wildfire.

Lenny. She wanted to rip Lenny to shreds with her bare hands.

"Breathe. Breathe, Jess."

Muffled, her voice still sounded like agony personified. "I'll be all right. This is just a lot, the way this is coming to-gether."

"I know." *And there's more,* he thought, but he didn't say that. Not yet.

He moved his bar stool closer to her and wrapped his arms around her and held her. She wasn't crying. He doubted that she'd let herself cry in a long time. But he could feel her fighting it with everything in her.

"Let go," he told her. "If you cry, it won't be the end of the world."

"I'll cry when I've found her. When I know for sure. Right now . . ." A pause, and then a strangled sound. "I can still hang on to hope."

His eyes prickled with tears, and he blinked them back.

"Jess," he said. "I want to discuss something with you."

She took a couple more deep breaths, then sat up. Her eyes were red, her nose was red. But she was not crying. "Sure," she said.

He looked at the timer. Still had another twenty minutes on the potatoes. He could get through this in twenty, he thought.

"You're in real danger," he said.

Somehow, she managed to pull a grin out of thin air. "They pay me for that. Really, they do."

"Not regular-line-of-duty danger, darlin'. *This* isn't what they pay you for. You've done your part, you've put them on the trail, you've given them info they couldn't have gotten any other way. But nobody is paying you to be stalked by some fucking sociopath."

"That I put up with because this is my case. And if Ginny really is involved, because it's more my case than anybody else's."

He took both her hands in his. "There's something we're missing in all of this. The killer keeps moving around us, and we're not sure how. If he gets around us one more time, you're lost." He felt his throat tighten, and the words that had no place in this discussion came out. "If anything happens to you, *I'm* lost."

She stared at him. "*You're* lost?"

"I don't want to talk about that. I want to talk about reasonable precautions."

Her eyes narrowed. "Fine. Such as . . . ?"

"The most reasonable thing you could do would be to back out of the stripping thing now. Work at HSCU on following leads, on putting together all the pieces that they have."

"They don't need me for that. They have people for that. They need me to get into the thick of this, to dance and look pretty and keep my eyes and ears open because they don't have anyone else to do that for them. Just me."

He hadn't expected her to take the suggestion well. He'd hoped, but he hadn't expected it. And . . . well, she hadn't.

"All right. Then come and live with me until this is over. I'll drive you to the club, I'll drive you back, I'll stay with you whenever you're not dancing, and we'll keep you safe that way."

She said, "Hank, this is sweet of you. It is. But look—if the killer realizes he cannot get to me, he's eventually going to kill some other girl. Fill in his six-by-six thing, pack his bags, and move on to some other city. And then this nightmare is going to start all over again." She leaned forward and looked up into his eyes. "Right?"

"We'll stop him," Hank said, but in fact, he did know that what she said had more than a grain of truth in it.

"As long as he's coming after me, we all know where to look, right? We all know who we have to watch."

"It doesn't matter. Because if I screw up this time, if I read things wrong, if I can't figure my way through the killer's twists . . . then you're going to be the one to die." He squeezed her hands. "You have to let us find another way to get this guy."

And she pulled away from him. "I'm not going to. I'm not going to make myself safe; I'm not going to hide away from everything I *can* do just so some other woman can die in my place. Some woman who might be somebody's mother or sister or wife or daughter. I'm not going to do that, Hank, and you shouldn't even think about asking me."

He stood up, angry. "There's a part of you, Jess, that thinks you deserve to die. That your sister's death is your fault, and that if you can't kill the killer, at least you can be dead, too." He clenched his hands into fists, and felt his stomach knot. "You think I haven't felt that all along? This guilt of yours? This totally unreasonable, totally stupid guilt from all the way back when you were twenty-one? That you've been carrying around on your shoulders like it was the world, and you were chained to it?"

She stepped up to him, right into his face. "I don't care what you see, and I don't care what you think. I have a job to do, and I'm going to do it."

"You're trying to kill yourself."

"You're full of shit."

"You're so scared to face the truth that you can't think straight. You want to believe that you have all these noble reasons for hanging on to this case and putting yourself in stupid, unnecessary jeopardy, but when it comes right down to it, you're in it to play Russian roulette with yourself. Get the killer or die trying—that's you. And there's a whole police force out there that can do exactly what you think you have to do alone. You're not the only good cop in Atlanta, Jess. Not by a long shot."

"Get out," she said. "I'm doing my job whether you like it or not. But I'll be damned if I'm going to take shit about the way I do it. Not from you, not from anyone." Her face was red, her fists knotted, and she looked like she wanted to kick down a wall. "You have no stake in how I do my job, Hank Kamian. You have no say in the risks I take, or why I take them, or what value I place on my own life. I won't put a partner in jeopardy. I won't get stupid. But no more women are going to die if I can do anything about it."

"Fine," he said. "People get what they want, Jess. And you want some dark, awful things. You want to be a martyr . . . well, that'll make your mother happy, won't it? You don't want my help; you want to be stupid. Then be stupid. I'm out of here."

He stalked to the door, turned back to her, and said, "Don't forget the potatoes."

He slammed the door behind him so hard it shook the light fixtures up and down the hallway.

chapter 16

The slamming of the door was like a shot of adrenaline. Jess stomped into the kitchen, muttering, "Don't forget the potatoes. Don't forget the fucking *potatoes?* Yes, Sarge; I'll jump right on that, Sarge; just what I want in my life is to have you tell me how to live it, Sarge."

The bags were in the way, and she had to have someplace to put the potatoes, didn't she? And, dammit, she was going to eat her steak with him or without him. She pulled one of the two slabs of meat—God, he'd paid a fortune for those steaks; they were really nice—out of the fridge, and everything inside jingled like Tinkerbell when Jess banged the door shut.

Steak. She knew how to make a damned steak. She'd show him. Broiler pan—Hank already had it laid out. Throw the steak on the pan, put the oven on broil, put the potatoes on the bottom shelf. Salt, pepper—there you were. She could do a steak.

She jammed the broiler pan and its single hunk of beef onto the top rack, then stood there staring at the oven, too angry to even move, until the steak started to sizzle. She realized she needed to clear space on the counter. The two bags Hank had brought with him were in her way. She tossed the first, but the second wasn't empty. In it she found two fat white candles, scented. A bottle of red wine. Chocolates.

And behind the bag, flowers sitting on the counter, arranged in a cut-glass vase, sweet-smelling and somehow homey.

Flowers? He'd brought her flowers?

And all of a sudden, her eyes were full of tears again.

The hell with that. He'd been trying to manipulate her. To get her to do what he wanted her to do. Get off the case, take a backseat, be safe, let more women die.

Except he hadn't given her the flowers first, had he? Hadn't lit the candles, put the big yellow box of candy in her hands, offered her a bunch of sweet butter-her-up nothings. He'd been saving those, she guessed.

For after she agreed with him.

Or something.

The possibility that she might have been a bit more graceful in turning down his offer to go stay with him occurred to her. The possibility that she had been, well, sort of a bitch about it . . . that also crossed her mind.

I could have been with Hank right now.

With two steaks broiling, with the wine and the chocolates sitting there waiting. With Hank with his arms around her, which had been both comforting and wonderful.

He didn't want her to get killed.

When looking for a man, that was, in fact, the sort of thing she'd hope one would care about. That she stayed alive from day to day. A man for whom that wasn't important wouldn't exactly be a great find.

Okay. So. She'd give him not wanting to see her die. But she wasn't mad at him because he didn't want her to get killed. She was mad at him because . . .

Because . . .

He wanted to keep her safe? Maybe, but if that was why she was so pissed off she'd rattled the refrigerator, it wasn't

a very good reason. Men wanted to keep their friends safe.
Women wanted to keep their friends safe. And he was her
friend. Friend. Yeah. Uh-huh.

Men didn't often ask friends to come live with them.
Offer to turn their lives completely upside down for friends.
Buy friends flowers. And chocolate.

Have wild, fantastic, mind-blowing, howl-at-the-moon
sex with friends.

So the odds were pretty good that he wasn't actually
thinking of her as a friend, precisely.

In which case, the protective urges were more under-
standable. Jess realized she smelled smoke. It took her a
second longer to get her head back to real time and discover
that the steak she'd been cooking—out of spite—was no
longer sizzling, but in the process of reducing itself to char-
coal.

"Shit!" She yanked it, and the ruined potatoes, out of the
oven, considered opening her window to clear the smoke,
and then considered again. Opening the window meant re-
moving the one barrier between her and the fire escape.

Shit, shit, damn.

So she could spend the rest of the night breathing smoke
and staring at the wonderful food she'd ruined, and feeling
guilty about being a complete jerk with Hank. He cared
about her. That was not a bad thing.

She didn't need to bother cooking herself another meal.
She had no appetite. That had walked out the door with
Hank. She cared about him, too. She didn't know where
they were headed—she couldn't be sure they were headed
anywhere, because when this case was over, her life was
going to go back to worse hours than she had at the moment, and to twenty to thirty cases on her desk all the time,
and how could she ask anyone to be part of that?

And the phone rang.

Be Hank, she thought, *so I can say I'm sorry.*

But it was Jim.

"Want a bit of good news?"

She was in too dark a mood for good news, but she said, "Sure."

Jim gave no sign that he noticed her lack of enthusiasm. "We found good, good evidence at Alton's place. Hank told you about Wayne Alton, right?"

"Yeah. He passed everything on."

"Good. He said he would. Anyway, we found another fourteen new girls in photos, none matching those found in Hemly's trophy stash. Plus more pictures of ones we found at Hemly's. Alton had pictures of the most recent two dead girls, along with jewelry, clothing, little hair clippings, and other trophies. A vial of blood. A bloody pair of handcuffs."

"Where was he hiding them?"

"Toilet tank in one of his dozen guest bathrooms. Alton had shut off the water in the toilet, drained it, and used it as storage."

"All right. Not the cleverest place in the world, but he probably didn't imagine anyone would ever look there." She sighed. "Any bodies at Alton's place?"

He sounded a lot less enthusiastic as he said, "We're still searching, but it doesn't look like we're going to find anything. Which is where this call comes in, actually."

No call without a catch. "Shoot," Jess said.

"Both Alton and Hemly are dead silent regarding Lenny, and their very expensive lawyers are running interference. What's worse, Lenny's whole cadre of lawyers caught wind of our interest in him, and the captain has been hovering over our heads like the angel of death, telling us that if we fuck up gathering the evidence on this, he will personally nail our balls to the wall. Lenny has friends in high places in this city; if everything we do with him is not pure as puppy love, his lawyers will break us on a technicality, and Northwhite, Hemly, and Alton will all three walk free."

"And my part in this is . . . ?"

"I got the transcript of your talk with Teri. It looks promising—if she can give us something solid on Lenny, we'll be able to get the judge to give us a search warrant. At the moment he's stonewalling us, refusing to consider Lenny's priors, or his proximity, or anything else. We think odds are good that he has the bodies his place. If you can get Teri to come through, we could break this thing wide open."

"I'll do. what I can. I'm not going to make promises." Jess stood by her narrow bed, wishing she and Hank were both in it. Wishing she'd done everything differently, and that she'd at least gotten the chance to see what Hank had planned for the evening. "I don't get the feeling that Teri's going to be talkative about Lenny as long as he's in a position to hurt her."

"Maybe not. Give it your best shot, Jess. We need you on this."

Jess had nightmares. Ginny, begging for rescue and Jess unable to find her, running through endless corridors past countless locked doors, listening to her sister screaming and begging for help while no one came.

And then jumping on a bus, and seeing the back of Ginny's head in a seat in front of her. Running forward, but for some reason not being able to reach Ginny.

Jess woke puzzled. The sun was sliding over the horizon, and she'd had a full night's sleep. Not good sleep, but sleep.

Something about buses nagged at her.

Buses. And Ginny on a bus.

She closed her eyes and tried to let her mind relax and play with those two puzzle pieces. Ginny. A bus.

Supposedly Ginny had gone missing from a bus. One of

her fellow dancers had taken her to a bus stop and seen her off to California.

Jess knew the dancer's name. Lori Wedder.

And as she thought about the bus, about Ginny, she was almost certain she'd seen that name somewhere. Recently. She couldn't remember where, though, or in what context. In an interview? One of the murder books, maybe? She could not have seen it someplace she would expect to find it, though. The murder books were out. If Lori Wedder's name had shown up there, Jess would have immediately made the connection. Lori Wedder was the last person who had seen Ginny alive. Or who had claimed to. If Lenny had actually killed Ginny, then Lori Wedder, who had managed to fall off the radar between the time Ginny vanished and the time Jess became a cop and started looking on her own, was lying.

Lori. Lenny. Lying.

And there it was. The click she'd needed.

In Teri Thomas's office, Jess had noticed the brag shelf she kept. Photos, posters, trophies. Almost everything had been about Stormy FoXXX. But not everything. There had been a few photographs, taken when Teri had been very young. Probably barely twenty-one. And one of them had been inscribed to her. It had been a picture of an old man with his arm around her waist. Jess had just skimmed past it at the time. It was small and faded, and the handwriting had been a messy scrawl.

Whatever she had seen, she'd registered only subconsciously. But if she closed her eyes, she could almost convince herself that those faded letters on that old photograph spelled out Lori Wedder.

Jess sat up, considering possibilities.

The picture had been of Teri; otherwise she wouldn't have kept it on that shelf.

And dancers changed their names sometimes. The

names they danced under, the names they worked under. Sometimes, if things got particularly messy, the names under which they lived their lives. Jess could not be sure that was what that messy, half-seen scrawl had said. But neither could she ignore the possibility that Teri might *be* Lori. It was an outside chance. But if it did say Lori Wedder, that fit. Teri was afraid of Lenny, and Lenny had worked with Lori, and Lori had seen Ginny last, and Ginny had loved Lenny, whom Jess believed had murdered her. If Lenny had murdered Ginny, then Lori had lied about seeing her safely onto a bus—which, if Lori was Teri, would give Teri a hell of a good reason to fear Lenny.

Of course, this was all going to fall apart if Jess went into Teri's office and saw that the fading letters spelled out something like Lisa Warner.

But if the photo had Lori Wedder's name on it, Jess had a few questions for Teri.

She got up to face the morning without Hank there. She faced flowers he hadn't had a chance to give her, and candles they hadn't lit, and wine they hadn't shared.

She should have called Hank last night. But she hadn't called him because she couldn't bear to talk to him over the phone and face the possibility of his rejection.

Which she'd earned. She'd been stubborn and rude and thoughtless, and hadn't looked at anything from where he was standing, and hadn't tried to understand his concern for her. She'd been a jackass. A bitch. That summed it up. She'd been a thoughtless jerk, and she wanted to do something for Hank to apologize. Something to let him know that he mattered. She'd considered buying a replacement steak, then asking him to come over while she broiled them, but that wouldn't fix the night before, and it wouldn't make him feel any better, either.

Not that she could cook worth a damn. Any attempt at

cooking on her part was likely to be mistaken for attempted assault.

She could, she thought, *buy* him breakfast. Biscuits and bacon as a peace offering, a way to get back to where they'd started. He wouldn't be coming over to her place. She could bet on that.

So she'd go over to his place. Grovel. Apologize. Admit she was wrong. She had been wrong. He'd only been trying to watch out for her. She'd take her dance stuff with her, and they could both leave from his place when it was time—and in the meantime, they could catch up on all the things they'd missed out on the night before because of her.

She showered quickly, dressed, threw things into a bag, and was out the door and on her way to pick up breakfast. Smiling. Hopeful.

She could fix this.

He'd had a horrible night. He'd sat in his car outside her place for a good twenty minutes, hoping Jess would either come after him, or call him, or something. But she didn't. And he'd been too mad at her to try to make up. He hadn't been trying to oppress her, or enslave her, or turn her into the little woman in the kitchen. God forbid. He'd been trying to save her life, and she was too stubborn to do anything but take offense.

He finally went home and, after a night of tossing and turning, managed to get a few minutes of restless sleep, but it didn't last long. He woke to the ringing of the phone beside his head.

He allowed himself a moment of hope before he looked at the caller ID, but it wasn't Jess. And the disappointment when Charlie said, "Hey, Hank, can you come by HSCU for a while before you and Jess start work this afternoon?" caught him like a punch in the gut.

That was life. A few days of happiness, followed by repeated kicks in the crotch. "I'll be there," he said.

Charlie met him at the door. "Jim is talking to a dancer who thinks she might have useful information for us," he said. "And both the FBI and the GBI liaisons are in there with the two of them. We stick any more cops in there with her, she's going to clam up. She was already nervous as hell. So he can't join us, but I want you to come down to the evidence room with me and hold a couple of photographs. We've already gotten everything we can from them. Now I want to see if you can give us your perspective."

They sat at a clean table outside the lockup, with the evidence signed out and the cop in charge of the room watching them with interest. Hank wore thin latex gloves. He closed his eyes and Charlie handed him a photograph.

"This is an old one," Hank said. "The killer has handled it a lot of times—likes it, likes the memories it brings. The girl . . . he had some new piece of equipment he tried out on her. And she gave him the thrill he was looking for. There's nothing of the girl here, though, except for the killer's perceptions of her. And those are mostly of quivering flesh and screaming."

"What was the equipment?"

"Something electrical. I don't know." Hank put the picture down. "Holding the thing is making me sick. I spent a whole lot of years not throwing up, and working with this monster, it's all I seem to do." He didn't say that when he held the picture, he could catch fringes of the killer thinking about Jess. Anticipating.

He opened his eyes and looked down at the photograph. The date on it put it eleven years earlier. The picture had been taken while the girl was still alive. She was naked except for high, high heels, down on her knees, handcuffed to a stripper's pole. Begging for her life. The expression of terror and desperation on her face burned into Hank's brain.

He was glad he couldn't feel her there.

Charlie was looking at him. "You okay?"

"No," Hank said. "This is . . . hell. This is the worst of these things we've ever done together. The girls' deaths are terrible. But the killer is . . . I don't know, Charlie. He feels like he's digging into my brain. He isn't crazy. Isn't confused. Isn't out of control. He's doing exactly what he wants to be doing, and he's enjoying it. And enjoying us not being able to catch him."

Charlie said, "We've had a lot like that."

Hank shook his head. "No, this is a whole new level of evil. I keep catching images of the killer deciding to do a set of public murders, to give himself a little excitement before he moves on. Some amusement." Hank searched through the sensations and images he'd been getting, trying to find the way to shape them into words. "He isn't afraid of getting caught, because the police have never even looked at him. Aren't looking at him now. He sees himself as so smart, so well insulated—so bulletproof—that no one will ever get close to him. He wasn't even afraid when he dumped the last girl, when Hemly was already in jail without bond."

"He's someone important. Powerful? Connections, maybe?" Charlie sighed. "But that doesn't make sense. You said he used the last girl as a diversion to draw us away from Goldcastle. That had to have been because he thought we were getting close to him."

Hank stood up and paced. "She *was* a diversion. But not the way we've been thinking. I think the last girl was actually bait to drag Wayne Alton into this mess."

"Doesn't work. We have hair and fiber evidence that matches Alton on every one of our bodies. He's our nonsecretor, incidentally. It'll take a while, but we're going to have DNA evidence. He left a fingerprint on Bethany Hertz's shoe. He has trophies in his house. He has no alibi for his whereabouts during the murder. We don't have to drag him into anything when he's running into it at full speed." Charlie stared at the line of photographs in their numbered evidence bags. "We're as solid on him as we are on Jason Hemly."

Hank sat back dawn, fists clenching and unclenching in frustration. "I don't *know*. I know what you have. But I know what I'm reading, too. It's like the fucker knows he's invisible, like no matter how hard we look he knows we aren't going to be able to see him."

Charlie's voice was mild. "We have means, motive, and opportunity for both of our suspects. We have previous behavior that suggests both of our probable killers are capable of committing these crimes. We have a likely suspect for the third leg in our killer triad, if we could talk to him or get a damned warrant to search his house. Or get one of his buddies to turn state's evidence on him, and let me tell you, Alton's and Hemly's lawyers are each pushing their clients to be the guy who gets the deal right now." Charlie was studying Hank with that basset-hound expression of his. "Plus Jess is hot to see Lenny hang. She thinks he killed her sister thirteen years ago, and I've gone over the transcript of that conversation she had with him, and I'm betting she's right." And he cleared his throat. "These photos you're touching come from our suspect's houses, and you're telling me that the killer touched them."

"I know," Hank said. "But all I can do is give you what I get and let you see if you can make sense of it. Give me another photo."

He closed his eyes, and Charlie put a second Polaroid in his hand.

"New picture. Killer present; I can still feel the girl's death on his hands. This picture was taken after he killed her, before he buried her. He's thinking she should have lasted a little longer."

"I don't see how she could have," Charlie said, his voice tight.

Hank opened his eyes, turned over the picture. A girl, her jugular veins intact, stared out of the photo from eyes gone dull and heading toward milky. Bruised, torn, sprawled, her expression panicked, she didn't look anything like the posed and composed, prettily dressed corpses the killer dumped in public. Her body had been through hell—Hank could see blistered burns, tiny knife cuts, fresh brands. Though nothing that would constitute a fatal wound.

"How did she die?" he asked.

Charlie said, "We don't know. We have to find the buried bodies before we'll be able to find out. The biggest surprise we got when we found the photographs, though, was how completely the killer's MO has changed. No dress-up, no bleeding out, no bath and makeup and fancy hair. The ones he buried go into the ground naked except for their shoes. He doesn't do anything with their faces; usually their eyes are still open."

Hank shoved the photo back at Charlie and dropped his head onto his arms.

"What?"

"I have a sharp image of Jess in the hands of this monster. Eyes open, going into the ground. Dirt falling on her face. It isn't Jess I'm seeing, though. It's her twin sister. And the killer wants to finish with Jess, because it makes everything round and tidy and complete." He felt sick. He was fighting nausea, the shakes, cold gut-check fear.

He heard Charlie say, "You're taking this pretty hard, man. You and Jess have something going on?"

Face still against his arms, Hank muttered, "Not anymore." He wasn't sure if Charlie heard him or not.

chapter 17

Jess wished she'd stayed in bed. Hank wasn't home. No-body at the dojo knew where he was, or when he might be back. She was determined not to talk to him over the phone, because she needed for him to be able to see her face-to-face, to realize that she was genuinely sorry about the way she'd acted—and it was hard to convey that over the phone. For her, at least.

She called the surveillance team and asked them if they were available to head in early, but they weren't.

She considered going in without backup, just to have some time to talk to Teri, but she decided this wasn't the day to be that stupid. She needed to get anything Teri said on tape, just in case. And she didn't feel like running into Lenny without backup and becoming the next dead dancer because she had decided not to follow protocol.

So she ended up back in that dismal yellow hole in the wall she was inhabiting, with enough cold breakfast for two people, and not enough appetite for one. If she'd needed to have her nose rubbed in everything that was wrong with her life, the day seemed to be more than willing to provide.

Jim called. "Checking in," he said. "I spent most of last night awake, running back through Northwhite's record and history. From Northwhite's extensive rap sheet, I discov-

ered that his first adult offense was statutory rape of his
stepsister, whose name was Lori Wedder. Wedder's mother
filed charges against Northwhite shortly before she and
Lenny's father split up, but then dropped them. Northwhite,
still going by his birth name of Mitchell Devon Leonard,
would have been eighteen at the time, Wedder fifteen. We
don't have anything on why the charges were dropped. The
mother has vanished since then, so we can't ask her. According to the notes on your sister's missing-persons file,
Lori Wedder is also the name of the girl who took her to the
bus station."

Jess felt a sharp thrill of connection. Jim added, "I
thought it was interesting that by the time Wedder was
twenty-three and Northwhite, by then going as Mitch
Devon, was twenty-six, the two of them were working in
the same strip club. And that Wedder formed a significant
part of Northwhite's alibi when your sister went missing."

"How so?"

Jim said, "If no one saw your sister get on the bus, then
the time of Virginia's disappearance could have been days
earlier."

"No, it couldn't have," Jess said. "Because I talked to
Ginny on the phone only a few hours before Wedder said
she took Ginny to the bus station. Much as I don't want to
be, *I'm* part of Northwhite's alibi. Ginny could only have
gone missing during the twenty-four hours between when I
called her to talk, and when she didn't show up at my
mother's the next day as she'd promised."

"Shit. I was hoping this meant that Northwhite and Wedder were working in collusion."

Jess said, "They still might have been. And I may be
onto something valuable regarding Wedder."

"Since she disappeared not long after your sister did,
anything would be useful."

"I think a photo in Teri Thomas's office is made out to

Lori Wedder. The photo was old, the writing was bad, and the ink and everything else were faded. And I might also be misremembering what I think I saw. But if the photo is of Teri, and I'm sure it must be, and if it's made out to Lori Wedder, we might have found our missing girl."

"So go in and talk to Teri Thomas."

"I will," Jess said. "As soon as the surveillance team is ready."

"Thomas going to be there today?"

"She's always there," Jess said.

"Then they'll be ready," Jim told her.

Hank decided to get to Jess's a little before she was scheduled to leave. Technically, he didn't have to have any contact with her until he walked into the club, and then only if either he or she needed to exchange information. But he wanted to see her. He didn't know what he could say that would make things better. *I'm sorry I'm trying to save your life? I'm sorry I'm afraid for you?* He didn't see where either of those were going to go over well. He wasn't sorry, either. He was just sorry she was so upset with him. But he wanted to say something.

Only she wasn't there. Her car wasn't in the parking space, and when he went upstairs, he could feel her touch on the doorknob, leaving. On her way to the club.

So he drove in, feeling more frustrated and angry with every passing minute.

Jess was right in front of him as he walked through the doors, talking to the greeter, an earnest expression on her face. Her hair cascaded over her shoulders and the front of her blouse, honey gold and straight, swinging with every gesture. Her gold blouse was see-through, her bra beneath it black and sparkling, her short-short skirt metallic gold with black trim. Her legs were bare, and he could remem-

ber what they felt like draped over his shoulders and shoved
apart by his thighs, and his mouth went dry.

Jess glanced in his direction. Gave him the same
professional-friendly smile she would have given any other
customer walking through the door, then returned her attention to the greeter.

He'd wanted something special. Some little acknowledgment that he wasn't just anybody. That she wasn't angry
with him, that the two of them were still the two of them.
But he didn't get it. He could tell himself she was undercover, that he couldn't expect her to break cover for him.
But that didn't change what he wanted.

He handed his money to the greeter, then walked past
Jess into the ballroom, wanting her and beginning to despise himself for wanting her.

"I *need* to talk to Teri right away," Jess was saying. "It's
an emergency, Kate."

Hank found an excuse to lean against a pillar in the ballroom but out of sight.

"Gracie, she's out today," the greeter said. "She called in
this morning, said she'd gone out to eat last night with
friends and this morning she can't get away from the toilet.
She said she's sure she'll be feeling well enough to be here
tomorrow. Maybe even later today. But Louella is taking
care of everything right now."

He could hear Jess's exasperated sigh. "Today of all
days," she said.

"To tell you the truth, though, I don't think she'll be in
tomorrow, either," Kate said. "I don't think any of us will
be."

And Jess said, "Oh?"

"Not because of her. Because of him."

"Lenny?"

"The police were already here this morning, wanting to
talk to him. He told them if they didn't have a warrant, they

couldn't look through his office or his home, and if they had any other questions, they could talk to his lawyer."

"Then he's taken care of it," Jess said.

"The cops are going to be back. Some of the girls are saying Lenny's the third killer. I bet the police end up shutting us down today."

"You think?"

"Cops in and out of here, Lenny with lawyers practically living in his office, Teri in a panic over the number of dancers quitting. I think so." A blast of music drowned out what she said next. Hank moved closer and heard, ". . . too, because this is the only place I've ever worked where anybody gave a shit about the dancers. You go to other clubs, there's nobody like Teri or Louella to take care of you."

"I like them."

"They're special. Both of them. As sleazy as this place can get, it would be a million times worse without them."

"I've got to go," Jess said. "I need to get to work."

"Yeah. I have another week before I can even start physical therapy on my leg—I really miss the dancing money. Being a greeter pays nothing."

"Hang in," Jess said. "You'll get through this."

"You, too. Give your brother a hug from me." Hank heard Jess's footsteps start toward him. "Oh! Gracie! I almost forgot. Someone sent you a little stuffed bear. It's backstage, waiting."

"A stuffed bear?" She laughed. "Well, that's better than candy, I guess."

Hank stepped in front of her as she came around the corner, and said, "We need to talk."

And she smiled at him, a sad, worried smile that was nothing like what he'd expected. "*I* need to talk," she said, her voice low and hurried, "and you need to let me. I owe you an apology. But . . . we can't right now. I have to get in touch with Teri—I think she could give us the info we need to get a search warrant for Lenny." She backed away, flashed him a dancer's smile, and said, "I haven't forgotten I owe you that lap dance, sweetie. I'm going onstage in a few minutes, but I'll catch you when I get back. Wait for me, okay?"

"Forever," he said. That was supposed to have been in character—a drooling promise from Hank the Stripper Groupie. But when he said it, Hank the Guy in Love with Jess was the one who spoke.

Jess danced. Most of the regulars had cleared out early on. The ghouls who'd taken their places for a few days, hoping for another murder so they'd be able to tell the neighbors the next day that they'd talked to that dead girl the night before, had thinned out as well. The place felt empty, and that made dancing harder. Fewer eyes watching her made each pair that remained more personal somehow. More invasive, hungrier and more desperate. The empty seats spilled shadows across the floor; the missing dancers had taken most of the air in the place with them when they left. A ghost storm rumbled in between the drumbeats, a falling barometer of fear that left everyone in the place slicked with cold sweat.

No one was pretending any longer. The noise and the greed and the frantic laughter and the desperate reaching out couldn't cover over the ghosts anymore. Jess could almost feel them watching her—dead girls crying out for vengeance, for justice. Ginny was among them. Maybe Ginny was first among them.

And that, too, drained her, left her weak and shaky when she needed to be strong. The hole in her life that was Ginny, that had been Ginny for so long, ached in every breath she drew, in every step she took.

She couldn't think about her sister often, because Ginny gone was half of Jess, but gone. All her childhood dreams and hopes, all her shared tribulations and memories could never be shared again with the one other person to whom they had meant so much.

Jess had prayed for so long that she would find her way to Ginny, that Ginny would be okay, that they could somehow put back together the friendship that some siblings were lucky enough to share. She had prayed that whatever had gone wrong between them, it would not turn out to be irreparable.

Now believing herself close at last to the truth behind Ginny's disappearance, she could no longer hold out hope that she would find her sister alive. The truth would hurt. The pain would go on, the emptiness that by the end of this was going to last forever.

But the storm was about to break. Something big was about to happen. And maybe, even if it didn't take away the pain, the truth would clean the wounds. Maybe, just maybe, Jess would be able to return her mother's other child to her, and that aching, grieving, hollow hope would leave behind something that resembled peace.

Jess talked. She circulated. She watched. She kept checking backstage, hoping that Teri would show up. Lenny apparently left sometime after Jess arrived.

She watched Hank watching her, too. She could see pain in his eyes—pain that she'd put there. They had to talk. Had to work things out between them.

She wasn't sure if he'd forgive her for being so impossible. She'd had her points—she couldn't quit doing her job because it was dangerous, and she couldn't walk away from this chance to find her sister now that she might finally have it. But she hadn't even tried to understand what he'd been saying. Or how what she was doing might look to him.

She had to believe he'd forgive her. She loved him. She shouldn't have let herself fall for him, but she felt like she'd had as much choice in the matter as she'd had in the color of her eyes. She had been made for him, he had been made for her, and the two of them not working out would be an inconceivable cosmic injustice.

She stopped by his table once and sat with him. "I'm going to have to get rid of an anonymous gift someone left for me backstage," she said. "Need to make sure it lands in the Dumpster out back, nicely wrapped in a brown paper bag. I want to get it to the forensics team. I suspect it's from Lenny, which might make it useful."

"You up for supper and company tonight?"

"I am." She rested her hand atop his. "I'm sorry about last night. Really sorry."

He said, "Me, too. I shouldn't have stormed out the way I did."

"Yes, you should have. I earned it. We'll talk. We'll get this worked out, Hank. You . . . I . . . ." She felt like she was going to choke up if she said anything more. This wasn't the time or the place.

"I'll pick us up supper on the way to your place. How do you feel about pizza?"

"I haven't eaten much of anything in days. Bring two, cover them in meat and cheese, and make them extra large."

He laughed, his half smile beautiful to her. "A woman after my own heart."

"I'll see you at my place, then?"

"I'll leave when you do. We should get there at about the same time."

Jess got out late, walked back to the Dumpster, and tossed her bagged teddy bear into it.

The floor manager accompanying her said, "Didn't like the present?"

"Didn't like the person who left it for me."

"Ah," he said, and walked her to her car. Behind her, the undercover cop in the Dumpster would be quickly tossing it out to the luckier senior cop who was loitering around outside the Dumpster.

In her rearview mirror, Jess saw Hank pull out of the parking lot right behind her. She watched him until he veered off to pick up their pizzas.

The rest of the way home, she traveled alone.

She pulled into the parking lot at the crappy by-the-month rental community, and stared at her run-down building, and thought, *I'm not alone because men are jerks. I'm not alone because no man would understand the importance of what I do and find ways to fit me into his life. I'm alone because it's easier to make excuses than to make changes. And if I keep making excuses, I'm going to die alone.*

Except she didn't know how to make the changes she needed to make.

She sat in the car, staring at the puddles of light her headlights threw against the cracked, faded siding. At the shadows they made in the moth-eaten shrubbery. At the overflowing Dumpsters sitting beside the seedy units, at the towels and blankets and aluminum foil being used as curtains by tenants, at the piles of dog crap in the weedy grass.

This moment was a snapshot of who she was—of the path she walked voluntarily. Her mission mattered—it mattered as much as it ever had. But did that mean she had to sacrifice everything else for it? She was going to spend the rest of her life alone if the answer to that question was yes. And she desperately did not want her mission to be the only thing in her life.

Work to home. Home to work.

Without even a cat waiting for her.

Or a goldfish.

Or a plant.

Because work took everything she had.

She turned off the ignition. She'd go inside, and in a few

minutes Hank would come along and those awful yellow walls would fade away, replaced by his life and his warmth and his humor. By his touch.

For tonight, things would be better. But how did she keep them better? She'd taken only one other chance on a man, and she had been the one to give up and walk away. In retrospect, he hadn't been the right man. He'd been like a crosstown bus. If she'd wanted another like him, one would have been along in ten minutes.

Hank, though . . . Hank was magic, and if she couldn't figure out how to fix her life to fit him into it, another Hank wouldn't be along in ten minutes. Or ten years. Or ever.

She got out of the car, took the fire-exit stairs rather than the elevator up to her room because it was late and she didn't want to find herself in an elevator with anyone, and walked down the seedy chipped-linoleum-floored hallway to her room.

Unlocked the door. Opened it.

The lights were off, when she always left them on. But some light spilled into the room from the dim hallway; she could see enough by that to have adrenaline kick her hard.

Everything she owned was scattered around the room. From her first glance into the dark studio, she could tell that almost everything had been torn to shreds.

Jess had her backup gun on her ankle. She reached down, pulled the weapon from its holster, and thumbed off the safety. Stepped into the room, elbowed the light switch on, kept the handgun raised as light flooded the place.

The studio apartment was empty; the bathroom door hung off its hinges, and from the doorway she could see every bit of space clearly. She didn't touch anything. Didn't want to take a chance of screwing up fingerprints.

No one was in the apartment. No one was out on the back fire escape.

A knife stuck out of the wall two feet above the daybed.

It might have been the one the vandal had used to slice up the mattress. It pinned an index card–sized piece of paper in place.

Jess walked over to it, keeping her attention on both entrances to the apartment—the window and the door.

I KNOW WHERE YOU LIVE.

Yeah. No shit, she thought.

Her cell phone was clipped to the waistband of her jeans. She pulled it off and dialed Jim.

"Got a threatening note in my apartment. And the place has been trashed. I need you and backup over here at light speed."

"You safe?"

"Secure for the moment," she said. "The place is empty except for me. I'm armed. And Hank should be here with pizza any minute."

"The cavalry and I will be right behind him." On the other end of the connection, Jim sighed, and she could hear him mutter, "Yeah, baby, you're going to have to go home. Case I'm working on just hit another snag."

She heard a female voice complaining bitterly. Then Jim was back.

"By the way," he said, "are you *ever* going to let me get some fucking sleep?"

"Apparently not."

When she hung up, she called Hank. "Someone hit my apartment," she said.

"I'm about seven minutes out at current speeds. I'll punch it," he said.

He beat the APD by three minutes. Hank clearly had a good understanding of the art of quantum driving.

Jess met him in the hallway, and she wasn't sure if he looked that pale because the lights in the hallway were flickering, buzzing fluorescent monstrosities, or because he was scared.

She got sure fast. "What the hell happened to your car?" he asked, and her mouth went dry and all the air whooshed out of her lungs.

"What do you mean, what happened to my *car*? My *apartment* got hit."

"So did your car," he said. "The tires are slashed, the windshield wipers and the antenna are broken off and gone, the doors have been jimmied open and the seats have been ripped apart."

"On my . . . car?"

She'd been calm about the apartment. It wasn't hers; nothing in it had really belonged to her—it had all belonged to Gracie. But the car was *her* car.

She loved that car. There'd been less than seven hundred of them made, and hers had been in good shape. Not mint, but everything on it was original, and it had been *hers*. She'd hunted it down, bargained for it, babied it, got it running. She'd loved it.

Suddenly she was shaking. She wasn't the cop at a crime scene anymore. She lost her distance. All of a sudden she was the victim, with somebody coming after her. She couldn't say the killer was after Grace anymore. She couldn't separate them out. In that moment, she and Grace stopped being two separate people, and the reality that *she* was in danger—that she personally had someone who planned to kill her, hit her hard.

Her knees wobbled, and Hank pulled her into his arms. "I've got you," he said.

He walked her out to the parking lot, and let her see what the bastard had done to her car.

"Can you tell who did this?" she asked him. "Was it the killer, or someone else?"

"The same person who killed the dancers did this."

Which meant the killer had to have been in the bushes watching her sit in her car before she got out. Watching her walk across the parking lot. He had to have had a chance to grab her right there, right then, when her mind was on Hank and not on protecting herself. It could have been all over, she could have been gone, and they could have never found her again.

Jim and Charlie came down to the parking lot to talk to her, Hank said, "She's going to be staying with me until you catch this guy."

Jess looked up at him. "Am I?"

"Yes." Hank's voice made it clear that he would not accept alternative suggestions. At the moment, she didn't feel like making them.

Jess's attention was on the car. She couldn't stop looking at it.

The slashed car seat and the tossed and scattered batting could have been her. She kept seeing those long cuts in the upholstery, kept transferring them to her body. Seeing blood—her blood—in puddles on the pavement. Seeing long rips in her. She knew what rips in people looked like. She knew only too well the way skin pulled apart and left gaping holes filled with dark, bubbling blood.

More cop cars were in the parking lot, lights flashing, and uniformed APD officers were combing the apartment complex hoping to catch the bastard before he got away clean. Detectives walked from door to door, knocking.

For a moment, Jess felt nine years old again, down at the bottom of the public swimming pool with Ginny, with both of them holding their breath and watching legs and arms flashing overhead. The screams and laughter sounded like they were coming from another world, drifting down to the bottom in little shivery fragments. She heard people talking all around her. But all the sense behind the words was gone.

It would have been easy to stay there, to let herself be

the victim. But victimhood was never productive. Never useful, neither to the victim nor to anyone else. Jess needed to think, not feel. She needed anger, not fear. She needed focus. She needed to catch the son of a bitch who was doing this, and nail him to a wall.

She realized that Hank had been watching her. "Back with me, sweetheart?" he asked.

She looked at him steadily, and gave him a cold, angry smile. "Bet on it. Let's get this guy."

chapter 18

The long night got longer. Hank and Jess stood eating pizza straight out of the box off the back of Hank's car while he and Jess answered questions.

By the time the two of them got to his place and climbed into bed, the sun was already well on its way up the sky.

They lay togther, touching, not speaking. He drifted toward sleep. At which point she said, "I hate to admit this, but I'm scared."

"You'd be foolish not to be."

"It's not the kind of scared you get when someone has a gun pointed at you, though. That's . . . immediate. Right there, right then, either you're going to live or you're going to die, but it isn't going to follow you around. This is . . . well, he's after me. Some part of me believes that even if I shed Gracie and turn back into Jess, he'll keep coming. Because this is about Ginny, and she's part of Jess, not Gracie."

She sounded so rational. He wanted to tell her that he loved her, that he would slay dragons for her, that the bastard coming after her would have to go through him to get to her, and he had a lot of practice taking apart bastards who were coming straight at him. But she didn't seem like she needed to be rescued right then. She was talking, but in a funny way, she was still very much in control of the situation.

So he locked his arms around her and told her all those things in his mind, and willed her to understand.

All he said out loud was, "I won't let him."

"You can't be with me all the time."

"Watch me."

She laughed. The Jess laugh. The I-am-bigger-than-this-disaster laugh. He loved that about her. That she could walk through, if not hell, then at least some version of purgatory, and laugh on the other side.

He kissed the back of her head, and the smell of her hair went straight to his brain, like a drug. Patent that stuff and Viagra would be old news, he thought.

She moved against him, sliding her butt back against the erection he'd been trying to keep from happening—and once it happened, trying to pretend wasn't there—and she said, "Not so tired after all, huh?"

And he sighed. "I'm a pig, clearly," he said.

She made a soft cat-purr sound in the back of her throat, and rubbed harder.

"You're not a pig. And I want you, too," she told him, rolling over and wrapping her arms around him.

He kissed her, and sighed. "Good." He kissed her a little harder, and she arched against him, and he thought, *Well, yeah, I want you. Only I want you to be mine,* all *mine, only mine, from now until forever. With nobody and nothing I have to share you with.*

She bit his earlobe, and he groaned and said, "You're making it hard for me to be a gentleman right now."

"I don't want you to be a gentleman." Her voice was hoarse in his ears. "Show me I'm still alive."

That he could give her. Did give her. And after, when she lay against his chest, curled warm and soft against him, he stroked her hair and watched her sleep, and thought, *This is*

*what I want. Jess is who I want for the rest of my life. And
how do I keep her? If I don't protect her, I'll lose her. If I do
the things that I know would protect her, she'll push me
away. How do I do this? How do I get us past this?*

Bloodred tunnel walls pushed in on Jess, and someone
was chasing her. She was running. Turning left, turning
right, but whoever was coming up behind her was quicker
than she was. She tried to run faster, but her feet were mired
in the dream air that flowed thick as clotting blood, that
clogged her lungs, that weighed her down.

The floor tilted up and became a hill, rose steep and then
steeper, and she fled slower, ever slower, while behind her
the ground leveled back for the hunter who came after her,
smoothing the way for him. And then a light reached out to
her. Bright and white and welcoming, straight ahead, and
for a moment her feet grew wings and she shot forward
while the hunter lumbered. To a door. She touched the door
and grabbed the doorknob, which seemed to grab her back;
but the light around her was blue-white, clean, and it
burned away the clotted air of the tunnels below and behind. She pulled on the door, and it resisted her. She pulled
harder, and the air began to thicken around her again.

She was not free.

Had not earned her way free.

She yanked and hammered and tried to shout for someone on the other side to let her in, knowing, believing that
freedom lay on the other side if she could only reach it, but
something on the other side fought against her, would not
give her safe haven, and she tried to scream, but no sound
would come out of her mouth, and then whatever was on
the other side of the door released its hold on the knob, and
the door flew open and brilliant blue-white light focused
like a spotlight on a girl on the other side. Lovely and
young, with long pale hair and pale blue eyes and pale full

lips, until the pretty peeled away, fell in sheets and clumps and clods to leave a dead girl standing. Long dead, blue and white as the light, her blond hair lank and matted, her eyes gone, turned into sunken dark holes that still saw. Dressed in the ballet dress made by her mother, facing her still living mirror image.

Jess screamed, "Ginny!"

In a voice at home only in hell and nightmares, Ginny answered, *"Run!"*

Hank shook her. "Wake up, wake up!" Jess lay rigid beside him, growling in the back of her throat. "Wake up. It's a dream."

Jess opened her eyes and stared at him, not seeing him. His fingertips fed him her pain and her guilt and her grief just as they'd filled him with the bloodred shapes of the nightmare.

"What the hell was that?" he asked her.

"I found Ginny," she told him, her voice as hoarse as if she had spent hours screaming.

He pulled her close and held her.

Jess said, "All these years she's been calling to me to find her. In my nightmares, she's always close—but always out of reach. She's been begging me to fix everything, to find her, to bring her home."

"I know," he said. "You told me."

"You don't understand. In all the years I've been looking for her, even in my dreams, *this is the first time I ever found her.* And she told me to run. Not to save her, not to take her home. All she said was, 'Run.'"

He pulled her tight against his chest and murmured something in her ear.

And her phone rang. She hadn't even shaken off the cobwebs of nightmare that still clung to her, and the caller ID on her cell phone told her that Charlie was already tracking her down. She'd had two hours of sleep.

He said, "Hey, Jess, I'm the bearer of bad news. We need you to work right away. It's crucial."

"You're kidding," Jess said. Hank raised eyebrows at her.

"Not kidding," Charlie said. "Your car, your apartment, that stuffed animal—forensics said the killer left nothing. But this is the first time Lenny hasn't had an alibi when something like this was happening. He lost his tail, and we have no idea where he was until he showed up at his place around three A.M. But we shut down the club. And a minute ago, Teri got here. She's upset. She's packing up her office right now. We need you in here as fast as possible. See if you can get her to connect him to anything—*anything*—related to this case. We're waiting outside the judge's office; if you can get her to give us something solid, the judge will give us a search warrant on Lenny. Find out why she's scared of him. Tell her what happened to your place last night. See if she'll connect the dots."

"All right," she said. "I'll come out from undercover?"

Jess listened to the long pause at the other end. "No. Not yet. She looks like she's edgy around cops today—stay in character for a while yet. Take your badge and wear your sidearm out of sight in case there are still parts of this we're missing. If someone else in the club poses a danger, you may need to break cover. And tell Hank to come, too. When we get the go-ahead, I'm going to need him up in Lenny's office."

"Got it."

When Jess got off the phone, she gave the rundown of the conversation to Hank, and said, "I need to have you drive me to my condo to get my badge and my service weapon." She grinned a little when she said it. "I think we have our guy. The judge is willing to work with us this morning—that might mean Lenny's friends have decided he's too much of a liability to keep protecting."

Hank frowned. "You think Teri actually knows anything that will give you Lenny?"

"I'm not sure. She knows more than she's admitted to up to now. Whether it's what we need or not . . ." Jess shrugged.

They dressed quickly—Jess in running shoes and jeans and a loose shirt that would cover her handgun without leaving a line. It felt so good to be back in her regular off-duty clothes again. Her feet were practically singing.

Hank kept staring at her as they dressed. "You seem so . . . different."

"Same old me," she told him.

"No. In spite of everything that's been happening to you over the last couple of days, you seem really happy."

"We're going to get him," she said, smiling. "I have this gut feeling that we're about to get our break."

Hank walked her down to his car—her personal was in the police parking lot as evidence, and she couldn't drive the Crown Vic and stay undercover. She'd pick up her work car as soon as she could. She had no idea when she'd get her own car back, though.

She watched Hank while he drove. Something was wrong. He wasn't saying something.

"What's bothering you?"

He started the car, then glanced over at her. "Not sure."

"Okay . . . what do you *think* might be bothering you?"

He grinned a little. "You're painfully persistent."

"Yes."

"Right. Well. There are things about Lenny that don't fit for me."

"I know. I'm pretty confident, though."

"I know you are. Between us, we'll get to the truth of it, though."

Jess grinned. "We will. We're going to break this one. Today, I think. I believe."

"I hope this really is the breakthrough everyone thinks it is." He made a face as he pulled into traffic. "And I don't like you going into that place without me right there with you."

She turned and smiled at him. "It'd be a little hard to make that look natural. Don't worry, though. I have the wire. The transmitter is in my purse. I'm armed. Charlie says our guys are searching the club, and standing by to get the warrant that will let them search Lenny's office. And even if something happened to all of them simultaneously, there's a team of well-trained cops sitting in a utility van in the parking lot across the street who can reach me in about sixty seconds." She reached over and patted his hand. "Don't worry. I'll be fine."

"All right," he said. "If you say so. I know you're a big girl. You can take care of yourself. I know."

"You'll have to pretend to be a customer until we get the warrant," she told him. "Once we have that, it won't matter if anyone knows either of us is working the case. But until then, just in case someone who could mess this up is watching, hang tight out here."

"I know." He gave her one hard hug. "Promise me you'll stay out of trouble. I don't want anything to happen to you."

This was a bad time for what she wanted to say next. It ought to wait, she thought. But she realized that she knew, without a doubt, how she felt about him. About them.

And she said, "Hank?"

"Yeah?"

"I . . . I love you."

The smile that illuminated his face right then could have lit the world. He wrapped her tight in his arms. "Really? You do? You're sure?"

"I'm sure."

"Because I love you, too."

"So . . . I get to keep you?"

"Always."

Jess walked down the peach-painted corridor, her running shoes squeaking loudly in the silence. Most of the backstage lights were off. She could hear cops talking, but without the dancers and the customers and the music, the place felt empty. Jess could smell good coffee brewing, though, and Teri's door was open; light spilled into the hallway, warm and friendly.

Teri sat in the middle of boxes and piles of paper. She looked tired. She wasn't wearing makeup, her hair was back in a plain ponytail, and she wore slacks and a pullover that didn't flatter her. For the first time, Jess could look at Teri and believe she really was in her mid-forties.

"Hey, Jess. Come on in. Have a seat."

Jess glanced over at the pictures on Teri's brag shelf. They were all there, but she couldn't read the one she wanted to see from that distance, and couldn't think of a reason why she would want to see it right then. If she got a chance to look at it, she'd take it. But even if she didn't, she still had her interview from the night before to go on.

Excited, Jess settled into the chair across from Teri's desk.

"Picked up your stuff yet?" Teri asked.

"No. I didn't even know the club was closed until I got here. They let me in to get my things out of my locker, but I thought I'd come in and say good-bye first."

Teri gave Jess a wan smile. "Yeah. I'd hoped you would stop by. I wanted to give you a little money for your brother before you left."

Her brother. Right. Jess focused on being Gracie. "You don't have to do that. We'll manage. How are *you?*"

"I'll live. Goldcastle is probably out of business," Teri

said. "I should have sold my shares sooner, but the place was doing so well. Who figured something like all of this would happen? And the second it does, you couldn't sell the stock to save your life. As it stands, I'm out a couple million bucks, but I have other investments. I'll be all right." She shrugged. "On a more personal level, I've been better. But I've been worse, too. I'm going to get out of this town, though. Start over someplace new." Teri had been pulling photographs off her bottom shelf and carefully layering them into a cardboard box. She turned to Jess. "How are *you?*"

"Not so good," Jess said.

Teri raised an eyebrow.

"First, I'm running on two hours of sleep and I feel like hammered rat crap."

Teri laughed. "Ouch. That's not good."

"Second, someone destroyed everything I own last night. Wrecked my apartment, tore up my car. And left a note stuck to my wall with a knife."

Teri sat up straight and stared at Jess. "Someone . . . did *what?*"

"Took a knife, ripped up everything in my apartment, tore the inside of my car apart. Left me a typed note saying, 'I know where you live.' Yesterday someone left a teddy bear for me here. The bear was left anonymously backstage—customers never send anonymous gifts. When I asked the police about it, they said it could have been related."

Teri seemed frozen. She sat staring past Jess, and Jess could see the muscles in her jaw working. And then, under her breath, she said, "That lying son of a bitch." Barely loud enough that Jess could hear her, but Jess had good hearing.

Teri didn't meet Jess's eyes. Instead, she got down on the floor and started gathering up more pictures.

Hiding.

And Jess thought, *Bingo.*

"Who, Teri?" she asked. "Who's a lying son of a bitch?"

Teri stayed behind the desk. Frames clattered into a box. "The one who tore up your place. And your car. Of course."

"You know who did it, don't you?"

Silence, except for the packing of pictures.

"Teri?"

Teri stood up, and Jess could see tears running down her cheeks. "He swore it wasn't him, that the one time it happened it was an accident. But lately, I've seen the way he watches some of the dancers. And . . . oh, God. You, too. He watches you."

"Who?"

"Lenny."

"Lenny Northwhite?"

"Is there another Lenny?" Teri asked, her voice dark and grim.

"I just wanted to make sure," Jess said. "There's more, isn't there?"

Teri said, "I have to have a cup of coffee. You want one?" She managed an unconvincing smile and held up her hands. They were shaking. "Look at this. I'm a leaf." Teri definitely needed a distraction to calm her down.

"Coffee. Sure," Jess said. "I could stand a cup right now."

"I should go out and tell those cops out there what I know. But I just . . . I can't. . . . Not by myself."

"Tell me," Jess said, knowing that at that moment, Jim and Charlie were holding their breath for testimony that could get them their warrant. "I'll listen. And then if you want, I'll go with you and keep you company while you tell them."

Teri stood with her back to Jess, pouring two cups of coffee from the coffeemaker.

She turned around, handed Jess a cup, took one herself.

Sat looking older every minute. Older, and more scared. "Lenny killed a girl. A lot of years ago . . ." She closed her eyes. "He said it was an accident. That they were having sex, that they got carried away, that they'd done a lot of drugs, he passed out, and when he woke up, she was dead. He came to me, and told me that he needed my help. He was in trouble already for a lot of things he'd done. Not one of the good ones, Lenny. He told me that he didn't want to go to prison, that this had been an accident, but that no one would believe it was an accident. That he'd go to jail." A pause. "I *wanted* him to go to jail."

Jess felt her heart pounding. They had Lenny. They *had* him.

"Why did he come to you?"

A bitter smile. "I'm his stepsister," Teri said. "His father married my mother for a while. Lenny spent most of the time they were married sneaking into my bedroom at night and raping me. Doing horrible things to me. When the police got involved, he told them that I'd seduced him. By that time I'd started to develop a reputation at school—the girl who would, you know? I would have done anything with anyone to wipe his touch off of my skin, and there had already been quite a few boys. And not always one at a time. Word spreads. It spread enough that my own mother dropped the charges she brought against him. They found all sorts of boys who were willing to testify that I was a nasty girl. My mother was so humiliated she disowned me. Dumped me on my real father. That was a disaster. Anyway, the cops believed him, and Lenny convinced me that if I ever told anyone otherwise, he'd kill me." She shrugged. "Not like they would have believed me."

"Oh, God."

"When I was seventeen, I ran away from my father's home. Lenny caught me and reminded me that I wasn't going anywhere. That he would hunt me down and kill me if I took off. He got my father's permission to have me move in with him—and I went along, because Lenny had pictures of me. Doing . . . some dreadful things. If I didn't go along with it, he said he'd send them to my mother.

"So I went along. My mother thought bad things of me, but I just couldn't stand the idea of her having pictures that proved it. I ended up living with Lenny for a few years, and during those years he owned me." She shuddered. Sipped her coffee.

Jess took a sip, transfixed by Teri's horror story, and by the knowledge that it was wrapping a giant noose around Lenny's neck. The judge would be hearing everything she was hearing.

"I danced in the club where he worked. I did parties. I did his friends. And he took lots and lots of pictures. Lenny loves pictures. One day he took our little family album in to a porn producer, and told the guy I'd do the same things on camera, and the producer jumped right on that, so to speak. For a while, Lenny claimed to be my manager."

Jess waited.

"And then one night he came into my room and hauled me out of bed." Teri took a long drink of her coffee. "I thought . . ." She shook her head. "It doesn't matter what I thought. He dragged me into his room, and there was a dead girl in his bed. His girlfriend. I knew her as Andromeda. That might have been her real name, but it probably wasn't."

Jess nodded, but now she could hardly breathe. This was Ginny's story all of a sudden. Andromeda the dancer, Lenny's girlfriend—her sister. And her hands started to shake. She rested them on her lap, clutching the coffee cup like it was her lifeline.

Teri swallowed. "Lenny stuck a gun to my head. Told me that I was going to bury the girl, and he was going to take pictures."

Jess whispered, "Oh, my God." This time when she said it, it wasn't for effect. All hope was gone. For sure, for certain. Jess would never see Ginny again.

Teri's free hand twisted at her hair, restless, seemingly independent of the rest of her body. Teri looked everywhere but at Jess. "Yeah. So. So I . . . helped him. He looked . . . crazy. He hadn't been bluffing when I was fifteen and he said he'd kill me if I told anyone the truth. And he wasn't bluffing with that gun. If I hadn't helped him, he would have killed me right then. We buried the girl under his house. In the crawl space. And he got his pictures. Evidence, he said, that I was an accomplice."

Jess just nodded. She couldn't say anything.

Teri kept talking, oblivious to Jess's distress. "When he turned his back on me—just for a second—I stole two of those pictures, and stuck them in a safe-deposit box. I knew where the body was buried, and it was under his house, and I had proof a dead girl was there. And it might have been me burying the girl, but somebody had to be taking those pictures. That was my leverage to get out of Lenny's house, out from under his thumb. To get free of him. But I couldn't shake him completely. He had the other pictures, and he never let me forget it."

"Does he still live in the same place?" she asked.

"Oh, no. We were both poor back then. He lived in a crappy little house inside the Perimeter." Jess closed her eyes and forced herself to take a deep breath. She wanted to cry. Part of her, knowing they'd found Ginny's killer and the killer of so many other women, wanted to cheer, too. Neither response would fit the situation, and she couldn't drop out of character yet. She took a big gulp of coffee and said, "Why didn't you get away from him?"

And Teri smiled. "Lenny has this saying he likes: Keep your friends close, but your enemies closer. He keeps me close because I could hurt him. He likes to remind me that he can hurt me more. From time to time he comes by with those pictures, tells me that he needs an alibi. That he's gotten in trouble with someone or other, and that I'm going to swear that he was with me. Or wherever he tells me he was."

Teri closed her eyes and rubbed at her temples with long, slender fingertips. "He'll say that he hit a parked car and he thought someone might have seen him, and he couldn't afford the ticket. Or something like that. I don't suppose I ever believed him—not really—but I never thought he was killing women." She took another long swallow of her coffee, and Jess took one, too. Matching gestures. Mirroring body language. Giving Teri the subliminal cues that would make it easier for her to open up to Jess.

"I bought into this place when it was still just a concept. By the time it was up and running, Lenny blackmailed me into making him the manager. We've been here for a few years. And even now, I don't know how it ever came to this."

Jess considered all of the times over the years that Teri could have come forward. Could have explained things to the police. Could have afforded a good lawyer. People got used to keeping secrets, of course. Did stupid things out of habit, once the reason the habit developed in the first place had passed. Compounded the lie without thinking.

Teri and Jess drank their coffee in silence.

After a while, Teri said, "Thanks for listening, Gracie. I can't believe I was so stupid for so long. I hope I get a chance to make things right."

Jess nodded.

And then she looked up at Teri, realizing she felt weak. Queasy. Feeling the shape of the room getting slippery around the edges.

Teri was watching her. Smiling at her.

Jess tried to say something, but her tongue felt like lead in her mouth. "What . . ." was all she managed to get out.

And the smile on Teri's face grew broader. She lifted up the bug that Jess had planted under the edge of Teri's desk that first day. Carefully and silently, Teri laid the bug on top of her desk. She sighed. Typed something into her computer. Rattled papers. Turned pages.

And then she stood and walked over to Jess, who watched her coming but couldn't move. Teri slid a hand down the front of Jess's shirt, fondled her breast, and said, "I . . . kept a diary. Of those years with Lenny. Could you . . . look over it for me? See if you think the police would find it useful?"

She gave Jess's nipple a little twist, then crouched down in front of her. And in a voice that to Jess sounded like a passable imitation of her own voice, Teri said, "Sure, Teri. If it'll help."

Then Teri leaned in and kissed Jess on the lips—a deep, lingering kiss. And in Jess's ear, she whispered, "Later, you and I will do . . . everything you can imagine. And a lot of things I'll bet you can't."

The almost-empty coffee cup rolled out of Jess's hand, down to the Persian rug on Teri's floor. Spilled coffee on Jess's leg, and she could feel that it was hot, but she couldn't respond. And the cup didn't even make a sound when it hit. Jess tried to understand why it had fallen. She could hear pages turning, but neither she nor Teri was turning them. She looked at Teri, who returned to her computer and twisted the monitor around so that Jess could see it— iTunes on, one track on the playlist titled "Turning Pages," and the little endless-loop icon at the bottom of the screen. And then, able only to move her eyes, she stared at Teri rolling that big wheeled costume trunk of hers toward Jess. Jess thought she ought to scream, but it was too much effort. Her eyelids weighed five hundred pounds apiece, and they were closing inexorably in spite of how hard she fought to keep them open. Even her arms and legs wouldn't twitch. Still, she ought to say . . . something.

Teri stopped the trunk beside the chair Jess sat in, opened the lid, and in a move startling in its speed and efficiency, levered Jess from the chair into the box, and folded her into it. Dropped Jess's purse in with her. Shoved a frilly pink tulle costume over Jess, and lowered the lid silently.

Jess knew the transmitter was right there in her purse. Jess was wired. She was within range. The building was full of cops. All she needed to do was say one word.

Say the word, and help would come running . . . flying . . . with one word . . . *any* word. . . .

chapter 19

Jim headed for the crawl space beneath the west wing of Leonard Northwhite's mansion, where it looked to Hank like half the cops in the city, plus state cops and Feds, had descended.

Hank followed Charlie inside and upstairs, where one of the cops said Lenny was waiting for them. Hank couldn't help but notice the yellow-tape border across the door the uniformed cop pointed to.

Leonard Northwhite sat in a chair at a desk in a bright, sunny home office, with an old manual typewriter in front of him. He had a gun in his lap, and late-afternoon sunlight streaming through the broken window behind his head that illuminated the streaks and spatters of blood and bits of brain and bone like hell's version of stained glass.

Charlie stared at dead Lenny and whistled.

Hank edged close to the desk, crouched down, and studied a long letter typed and laid out there—three whole pages that detailed the sex-and-murder ring that had met at Lenny's house, that noted where the bodies were buried, and that confessed that he, Leonard Northwhite, regretted his part in the enslavement, torture, rape, and ritual murder he, Jason Hemly, and Wayne Alton had regularly committed over the years. Lenny's letter said that he could no longer live with himself. That he was going to end it all.

Hank read the note without touching anything, noticing especially that Lenny had conveniently remembered to implicate his alleged accomplices.

Following the apology and guilt-sharing section of the letter, Lenny apologized to his stepsister. He apologized to the families of the dead dancers. He apologized to Hemly and Alton for drawing them into his snuff-dance cabal.

"For a guy who doesn't know how to use the shift key or English grammar, he's a remarkably good speller," Hank said. "And for a suicide, he sure is a chatty bastard."

Charlie looked sidelong at him. "You're in the wrong line of work."

"Oh?"

"I was thinking the same things myself."

"But the bodies are down there under the house, right?" That was the first thing the first diggers had reported when Jim and Charlie arrived. It had taken them all of two minutes to locate thirty-six graves. "All are filled in, but one doesn't seem to have a body in it. The first one, by date, has a nametag but the guys can't find any corpse. Name on the empty one is Andromeda Callisto."

"Jess's sister. And Teri told us where he actually buried *her* body." Charlie said, "Six rows of six." Charlie walked around the messy room, keeping to the narrow strip cleared by Forensics, looking at things. "Just like you said."

"Not quite," Hank said. "I thought one grave would still be open."

They looked around the room a bit longer. "And for such a neat killer, Northwhite sure is a slob about everything else," Hank added. "What can I touch, Charlie?"

Charlie tossed him a pair of thin latex gloves, then pulled a notebook out of his jacket. "Start with Northwhite. Only touch one spot on him—I'll note the spot and anything else that you touch in here so that we can give the list to Forensics."

Hank put the gloves on, then reached out and rested two fingers on Lenny's T-shirt-clad shoulder, bracing himself for the roil of desperate, dark emotions and physical anguish that always surrounded violent death: for the wash of pain, for the fear and guilt and grief and rage. These were the markers of both murder and suicide that twisted his stomach and make his knees weak.

Yet Hank stood there, his fingers resting on Lenny's shoulder, and all he got was a guy drinking beer from a long-necked bottle and having a friendly discussion with a dishy brunette.

"Charlie?"

Charlie was watching him. "What is it?"

"This is seriously fucked-up."

"How?"

"Well . . ." Hank frowned. "First off, he didn't kill himself."

Charlie nodded. "I'm not surprised. That note was a bit too helpful to be real. Wonder which member of their little circle it didn't mention?"

Hank said, "That's not it. Going by what I feel here, he wasn't murdered, either."

Charlie turned and stared at him.

"He is *dead*," Charlie noted. "Brain spattered over the back wall and window, teeth chipped from the muzzle in the mouth. He's not sleeping there."

"Well, yeah. But somehow he seems to have missed the whole pain-and-violence part. The last thing he was here for was a cold beer and a visit from a beautiful woman."

"You always get their pain, their fear. . . ."

"Except for the girl in the parking lot. The last one, who didn't quite fit. Remember I told you she didn't know she was being murdered? Or even suspect she was in danger?

She felt like this. She was being offered a role in a movie, and death sneaked up on her and she never seemed to notice. And with Lenny-boy, the last thing he was here for was a beer and a girl."

Charlie said, "Beer and a girl, huh? Hey, there are worse ways to go. But . . ." He looked around the crime scene and shook his head. Lenny had clearly not had a "beer and a girl" ending.

"Yeah," Hank said. "He managed to sleep through that part of the movie." And he and Charlie stared at each other, and Charlie said, "The beer," and Hank looked down at the trash can beside his left foot. It was empty. He looked at the desktop. He said, "Not here. Would any of the tech guys have taken a beer bottle from the scene?"

"Not yet. We're still photographing and measuring—" And Charlie said, "Fuck. Bet we'll find Rohypnol in his blood." And then he was out the door and yelling downstairs, "I gotta have someone get blood on this guy *now!*" Swearing the air blue as he waited for a Forensics tech to appear. "The girl," he said. "The girl who was with him for the beer is the one who killed him. Who typed the letter. Oh, fuck, oh, fuck . . ." When the tech came in, he said, "We're looking for Rohypnol. But just in case, also screen for ketamine or GHB, any new knockout drugs you folks haven't had time to give us in-service on yet."

She nodded.

Charlie couldn't stand still. He shifted from leg to leg like he needed to run. His hands clenched and unclenched. "Where's the ME? Did he suggest a time of death?"

She said, "Medical examiner is downstairs looking at dead dancers and talking to Jim. And Jim said to tell you that from the dates on the grave markers, none of the bodies was killed more recently than six years ago, and that the two bodies the ME has already exhumed would seem to confirm that. But the medical examiner said this guy was fresh. No later than four o'clock this morning."

Hank, like Charlie, wanted to start running. Because the person who killed Lenny had also killed the dancers. And that person was the woman who'd given him the beer.

He tried to reframe all the reads he'd done without his initial assumption that the killer was a man. That had been such an easy assumption to make. The killer was a man because there was semen on every scene. Fiber evidence. Trauma, rape, torture.

Now that he knew to read for a woman, maybe he could get something useful. The killer had touched the typewriter. Had typed a long, long note. So Hank moved beside the desk, careful not to step outside of the marked traffic lanes in the room, and said, "I'm going to touch the letter *E* key," he said, and watched Jim write that down in the notebook.

Charlie walked over to stand beside him. Stood there for a moment, sketching the desk and its contents. And muttered, "Shit, the letter. That proves he didn't kill himself."

Hank didn't ask for a clarification. Because the murderer was there, right with him, full of rage and glee and giddy amusement and sick, twisted pleasure. Typing while standing over a dead guy, getting a real thrill from the stink of blood and the fact that she had finally killed him—this stepbrother whom she had relentlessly pursued when she was still a teenager, whom she had eventually lured into her bed, and whom she had blackmailed and used for years. She was thrilled that she didn't need him anymore, that her exit strategy was perfect.

And that she would have the last piece of her personal game soon. The killer saw herself as the goddess with the golden eyes, untouchable and magnificent, and she had only one act remaining in this drama of hers.

Jess.

"Charlie," Hank said, "Jess is with Ekaterina Thomas right now. And I think Thomas is the killer."

"Jess is in a building full of cops, and with the under-cover team listening in on everything she says." Charlie looked worried. But he said, "She'll be okay. Still . . ." He ran down the stairs, yelling for Jim.

Jim shouted, "Over here. You know what? The deed to this house is in Lori Wedder's name. Also known as Teri Thomas." He paused, looking from Charlie to Hank. "What's wrong?"

Charlie said, "Unless Lenny could type after he was dead, he didn't kill himself."

Jim's expression didn't change at all. "Explain."

"There are no blood spatters on the letter. Not a drop. But there are blood spatters on everything else."

"Shit."

"Hank got a read on the person who killed Northwhite," Charlie continued.

Jim turned to Hank. "Talk to me."

"Teri Thomas."

"Christ. Northwhite's stepsister. That makes a sick sort of sense, I guess. But only if Thomas was sleeping with Hemly, Alton . . . and maybe Northwhite while she was killing dancers. At least the last handful." He frowned. "Can't check with Northwhite, but Alton and Hemly would be easy enough to ask."

Charlie said, "You suggesting she obtained semen, fiber, skin, and hair samples from each of them, planted evidence where they lived, and came over here to bury her bodies without Northwhite catching on? Seems like a hell of a stretch."

Jim said, "Try this on. She owned this house first, buried thirty-five women here, with a thirty-sixth grave commem-orating Ginny. And then she gave this place to Lenny, and bought herself a new place. With a *new* crawl space."

Hank nodded. "Which is where we'll find thirty-five more bodies. And one open grave."

Jim said, "Fits what Hank has been saying all along. That none of those three men felt like the killer to him."

Charlie turned and stared at Hank. "You *have* been saying that. But how would it work? She'd have to use . . . what . . . unlubricated condoms for her semen samples; liquid nitrogen to store them; have some way of collecting body hair and skin—say epithelial tissue from the inside of a cheek. And considering how much she and Lenny despised each other, I don't see her getting anything fresh from him."

"But if she had a way, the rest of it sort of fits. Alton told Jess that he and Teri were close. We have that on one of the transcripts. Remember?" Jim chewed on the inside of his cheek.

"She could have gotten the samples the same way she got Lenny to fall asleep while she killed him. She could have drugged them. In the middle of sex, or after. "Hey, honey, want a beer?" They wake up later, they're none the wiser."

"What about Hemly?" Charlie said. "We have anything that would indicate she was seeing him?"

"*Screw Hemly.* What about Jess?" Hank's mouth dried and his bowels clenched. He unhooked his cell phone from his belt and one-punch dialed the surveillance team. "How's Jess doing?" he asked the guy who answered.

"She's been reading in there for about half an hour." A pause. "Lump says more like forty-five minutes. I can hear Thomas rustling around in the background. But neither of them is talking."

Hank handed the phone to Charlie. "Something's wrong. Tell them to go check on her," he said. "Now. They say they can hear both of them in there, but nobody has said anything for about forty-five minutes."

"Oh, Christ," Charlie said, and identified himself, and told the guy who'd answered the phone to go check on her. Hank started toward Charlie's cruiser, with Charlie sidling along behind, and Jim bring up the rear, the cell phone pressed to his head.

Hank felt a wash of cold run through him. "I don't think we have much time. We need to get over there. Fast."

And then Charlie said, "The room is empty. A recorded loop on Thomas's computer was feeding the bug in the room the background noises."

All three men turned and ran out of the building.

Hank was the fastest. He reached Charlie's car first, dove into the backseat, and strapped on his belt.

He could still feel the killer's touch on his fingertips. He could feel her hunger, her desire, her rage. And the laughter. That was what scared him most. He could still feel her laughing inside his head.

"Where does Ekaterina Thomas live?"

Jim, riding shotgun, said, "We'll have that in a minute. I'm calling now."

Charlie was driving, and that, Hank thought, was a good thing. Charlie might be a guy with a job that didn't require a lot of hard driving, but even on good days he raced like a low-flying fighter pilot. He would get them there much faster than the more prudent Jim.

HSCU came back with Teri's address, but the traffic gods weren't with them. Teri lived in Buckhead, which was close enough that the three of them would be first responders, but the lunch rush hour was on. Charlie put on the lights and sirens.

"You're going to have to turn them off before we get to her house," Hank said. They rocketed down the long drive and out into traffic, with Jim feeding directions to Teri's house into his ear. "This bitch has a ritual she does with her victims, and she doesn't kill them until late in the ritual.

She thinks Jess is just another victim right now—she doesn't have any reason to hurry. But if she hears sirens coming or hears her address called over a scanner, she's going to kill Jess first, then run. She won't hesitate, and she won't take chances."

"That a hunch?" Jim asked.

"I've been soaking in her fucked-up mind since you brought me into this case. I'd bet everything I own on it."

They stayed off I-85 because at that hour it was a long parking lot, but surface roads, business traffic, and construction were all working against them, too.

The sense Hank had of all the other murders Teri committed told him that they *had* time.

But his gut kept insisting that they didn't.

chapter 20

"You're awake, sweetheart," a sultry voice murmured in Jess's ear.

Jess lay facedown on glossy wood flooring, her head pounding, her stomach churning, her mouth burning with bile. She groaned and tried to move, but her arms, stretched over her head, wouldn't respond. She turned her head to look up, and a hazy face swam into view.

Female. Long black hair. Pale whiskey-brown eyes.

"Teri?" Jess shook her head, trying to clear it. Trying to make sense of where she was, of what was going on. "What's . . . where are we?"

Her tongue slurred and stumbled over the words. She didn't remember drinking—had she and Teri gone drinking? Barhopping? Jess hadn't been drunk in years, but this felt like a bad hangover. And she couldn't *think*.

"Help me up, would you?" she managed to say.

Teri laughed. "After all the trouble I went to getting you there, Jess? I don't think so."

That was wrong. Teri should have helped her, but something about what Teri had said was wrong, too.

Name.

Yes, name.

Teri should have called her Grace. Or Gracie.

And then Jess remembered that she was in trouble. From Teri. Teri wasn't a friend.

But why not?

"You're going to dance for me," Teri said.

And Jess remembered the coffee. And she remembered the costume trunk.

Teri continued, "I so wanted to fuck you. Like I did your sister; she was my first. I was thirty, and she was twenty-one, and I was so excited. But she slept through it all because I gave her too much stuff. She died before I could kill her. I was so disappointed. But, see, I didn't know what I was doing then. I know now."

Teri's hand was stroking in little circles around the small of Jess's back. "Andi was my friend. And I fell in love with her. And then she went and fell in love with Lenny. *Lenny.* That pig. He really did fuck me when I was fifteen, but only because I lured him into it. I couldn't stand his dad, and I wanted them out of our house." Teri's hands ran up and down the backs of Jess's legs, and she could hear Teri's breath quickening. "And then poor old Lenny woke up after a night he couldn't remember, and there was his beloved Andromeda, dead underneath him. Where I put her when I was done with her, when his party boys were gone. And me standing over him with lots of photographs of him on a naked dead girl. I owned Lenny after that."

She laughed softly. "Know when I fell in love with you? When I saw you standing in my office in that tan silk skirt." Teri made a little sound in the back of her throat, and her hands began kneading Jess's buttocks. "Oh, God, you feel good," she whispered.

Jess became uncomfortably aware that she was naked. She didn't say anything. She tried to figure out how to get her hands out of the padded leather handcuffs and away from whatever it was that was keeping her arms stretched over her head. That was forcing her facedown onto the polished wood floor.

"You *were* sisters, weren't you? You and Andi? You dance alike, you move alike, you sound alike. And God, you look alike. But I could never be sure. It doesn't matter to me, you know. It won't change the way this ends. But . . . if you *are* sisters, it would be so perfect."

She was dizzy and woozy and queasy, and having the killer fondling her was not helping anything.

So Jess compartmentalized. Let one part of herself listen to Teri while pretending she couldn't feel anything Teri was doing. She put the bulk of her attention on figuring out an escape.

Jess didn't answer Teri's question about Ginny. Teri said, "If you don't talk to me now, you will later. I'll make you tell me." And she laughed. She kept touching, and kept talking. "When I met you, I'd already started getting ready to move on. Dropped my first few public kills. But I hadn't found my perfect finale yet.

"And then you walked into my office, and—perfect. You the perfect omega for my unfortunately flawed alpha." She leaned her face so close to Jess's that her breath brushed Jess's cheek. And she whispered, "The finale was going to be private. Just for you and me, darling. Only you and I would ever have the secret—and you'd never tell."

Jess said, "You think?"

Teri laughed. "I *know.* I took such pains to be sure." She straddled Jess's calves, and Jess felt lips, and then teeth, on her ass. And then a tongue licking its way up the small of her back. "Alpha and omega," Teri said in between bites.

Jess tried to kick, but Teri had her lower legs over the backs of Jess's, holding them down. And Jess was still too weak to be effective.

Teri scooted up Jess's legs. Hands slid around to grope and squeeze her breasts, that goddamned tongue kept licking, and Jess thought, *Bitch, if this room will stop spinning for a minute, I am going to rip you into pieces.*

But then Teri stopped, and sighed, and stood up. Her voice turned businesslike. "I *wanted* to fuck you. Wanted to spend all day and all night making you realize that you wanted me. Loved me. That I was better for you and better with you than any man could ever be. I wanted to make you beg, baby. I wanted to hear you scream. Because your sister never did. She slept through all the fun."

Jess's badge and empty shoulder holster dropped to the floor in front of her face, and Jess's empty stomach spasmed and flipped.

Teri said, "Unfortunately for both of us, what I found when I undressed you put us on a whole different timetable. Who would have thought that you were a police detective? Or that the APD could field such a convincing stripper?"

"You need to let me go," Jess said.

"Because you were wired?" Teri nodded. "I already figured that out. I knew the police were recording us. I just didn't know you were one of them. I wish I'd figured that out before I put you in the trunk and brought you home. The gun and badge gave me a few bad moments, I confess."

Jess tried to move forward or sit up, and discovered that the thing forcing her hands above her head had been the stripper's pole to which Teri had handcuffed her.

"I found your transmitter. Figured the belly-button jewel had to be the wire. Very nice. And the transmitter in the purse—well, that was clumsy, but the police have planted transmitters all over the club, too, so I knew what I was looking at. I have no idea what the range on those things is, but in case they go very far, I've disposed of both. You do have some rather nasty rips in the skin around your navel as a result." Teri leaned down and gave her a cold, hard smile. "On the bright side—if you're inclined to look at it that way—you won't have to suffer with them for long."

"You kidnapped me," Jess said. She managed to get her legs under her and struggled to a kneeling position. "So HSCU will know you're the one they're looking for."

"Oh, they'll figure it out eventually," Teri agreed. "Right now, I guarantee you they're still marveling over Lenny and the thirty-five dead girls beneath my old house. I owned that place for six years before I told Lenny to live there. I suppose they'll find Lenny's and my shared house, where the true thirty-sixth for that square is buried. Your sister."

Jess glared up at Teri.

"As for your colleagues finding you in time to help you . . . well, don't count on that. Or on any justice for your death. I'm going to disappear. Become someone else, doing something else. Different job, but same hobby. Everything's in place."

Hank had told them all along they had the wrong people—that the men they'd arrested had not been killers. She wished she had a chance to tell him that she was sorry she'd doubted him. She wished she had a chance to do a lot of things. If she had it to do over again, she would change her priorities. Make a place in her life for him, make sure that place stayed at the top. She would not neglect the one bit of joy and magic that had found a way into the dark spaces of her life. If she had the chance.

But she was unlikely to have another chance.

Jess could hear a police scanner in the background. She frowned, studying Teri, wondering how soon Teri intended to kill her, and wondering how she could buy more time. Wondering if she could somehow earn herself a second chance. She couldn't let herself think about Ginny—about what this monster had done to Ginny. Because if she didn't focus, Teri was going to do the same thing to her.

"How did you do it?"

"Do what? Kill them all? Keep it such a secret?" Teri reached down and ran a finger down Jess's spine. "Dance for me and I'll tell you. We have a little time. No one is coming to get you yet."

"Dance?"

"The dance is always my finale. After all the sex, after all the fun, after all the begging and pleading, my sweethearts get one last private dance. As long as they keep dancing, I let them live. When they fall . . . well . . ." She held up an enormous hypodermic syringe—big enough that Jess could see the 50cc marking at the top—and Jess saw that it was full of something cloudy and brownish. "Well, you don't want to fall. This is horrible stuff, a horrible way to die. And once I've injected it, it will take you about an hour to die. Meanwhile, it will take me a mere three minutes to vanish from the face of the planet, never to be seen again. It doesn't matter how close your colleagues get. I've planned for this moment for years. I've practiced. I'll have no problem leaving. But for now, you can buy yourself a little more life. A few more minutes. As long as you keep dancing."

The leather handcuffs were too tight to slip out of. Jess had tried folding her thumbs into the palms of her hands to make her hands no wider around than her wrists, but Teri had strapped the cuffs on tight enough that nothing short of amputation was going to get her out of them without a key.

"So start dancing, sweetheart. Remember, your hands are my hands. The pole? Well, that's me."

Jess got to her feet, still wobbly and sick. Discovered that Teri had put her in shoes so high they were crippling.

But . . . dance or die.

The pain in her feet drove straight up her legs; she felt as if she were standing on nails. She wondered if she could knock the pole loose and try an escape, but one look eliminated that hope. Teri had bolted it to the wood floor and to a massive wood beam in the ceiling overhead. The pole wasn't going anywhere. Neither was Jess.

Teri had walked away while Jess was getting up—she'd moved off the little stage in the round and down to a lone theater chair bolted to the floor in front. If Jess moved within range, the stiletto heels were sharp enough to make a good weapon—but with Jess's arms cuffed around the pole so that her hands hung useless in front of it, she had no way to get leverage for a balanced kick. Balancing put her in a position of weakness. She'd have one attack. No matter what the outcome of her attack, she would lose her balance and fall to the floor, leaving her wide open for Teri's follow-up, the poison-filled needle.

So Jess bought time. She swung her hips a little. Balancing. Desperate.

In the background, the music Teri chose played—Elvis Presley singing the suddenly creepy "Are You Lonesome Tonight?" Beneath that, the usual chatter on the police band. Nothing over the scanner indicated that she'd been missed or that help might be on the way. Jess kept moving.

And Teri said. "But you asked . . . how did I do it? Let's see. Until I went public, I called dancers I wanted into my office when I'd scheduled them for a two-day weekend or when they were getting ready to go on tour. I'd use various pretexts—having heard about a movie part, having a feature spot opening up in the schedule, discussing a rumor that they were whoring on the side. Anything that worked. They'd come in, I'd give them a cup of coffee, dump them into my trunk, roll them to my van, and they would disappear from the world." She smiled. "Nothing could have been easier. And no one ever suspected a thing. Taking women you work with works just fine when no one realizes they're missing for months. Or more. When I decided I wanted to move out of the area, though, I decided I didn't want to leave without making a splash. That would be . . . dull. Taking chances at getting caught is part of the fun. So I made nice to Lenny just long enough that he and I could play the same games we played when I was fifteen. This time, though, instead of getting pictures, I just saved hair, and used condoms." She winked. "Unlubricated, of course. You claim an allergy to chemicals, men will fall all over themselves to jump through the hoops that will hang them. Oh, and skin from the inside of his cheek. He might have felt a little funny about donating that for my collection, but he was as easy to drug back then as he was last night."

Jess, dancing on feet that were in agony, stumbled. The music segued to Boyz II Men singing "End of the Road." Jess righted herself, finding Teri's sound track creepier by the minute. She watched Teri glance at the hypodermic she held. That had been too close.

"Nice save," Teri said. "And I gave Jason Hemly a bunch of freebies at both his place and mine. His so I could plant pictures and mementos, mine so I could save condoms. Same thing with Wayne Alton. That's the only thing I have ever loved about men. If you'll do anything they can imagine, and you'll do it for free, they'll come back as long as you'll let them and never think to ask why. I had keys to their places, full access—and every once in a while, just to be sure they didn't get the silly idea that they should change their locks, I'd show up by surprise, call them to come home, and be naked and ready when they'd get home." She laughed. "I *still* have their keys. Isn't it great what a trip around the world will get you?"

"That's sick."

"Oh, come on. It was brilliant. And it was funny. Don't tell me you people hadn't been going insane trying to figure out why your serial-killer victims had three different DNA samples in them. Getting all excited when my paid witnesses told you what they saw. When you found evidence."

Jess kept dancing. She used the power of silence—let it hang there.

And after a moment, sure enough, Teri said, "I'm surprised your question wasn't 'Why?' actually. I would think the thing you'd really want to know would be what changed me, twisted me, turned me into a killer."

"No," Jess said. "I couldn't be less interested in that."

And for an instant, Teri's composure cracked. Then she said, "Liar. You have to be wondering what forces could drive a woman to kill seventy-seven other women. Well, including you." She laughed. "Plus Lenny, of course, but I consider his death a public service. So, your real question is *why*, isn't it?" And she smiled with evident self-satisfaction.

Jess swallowed her fear. "No." She kept moving, though no one could call what she was doing dancing. She was simply not falling down.

Teri's eyebrows went up.

Through her pain, maintaining her balance as best she cold, Jess said, "*Nothing* drove you to kill all those women. You *chose* to be the piece of shit who did that. That's all."

"That's not true," Teri said. "My stepfather molested me. Studies show that women who are sexually abused—"

Jess cut her off. "I'm sure you've found ways to rationalize it to yourself. But no matter what happened to you, worse things have happened to other people—people who didn't use personal pain and tragedy as an excuse to destroy others." She swallowed against pain and nausea, and she kept moving. No help was coming. The pain in her feet was becoming more than she could ignore. She was going to fall. She had . . . minutes. Maybe less.

Jess needed the bitch to move into range before she fell over and couldn't get back up. She was going to have one really lousy shot at saving herself, and she had to get it while she was still on her feet. She said, "You're common sidewalk shit, that's all. You used what happened to you as an excuse—but you would have been the same disgusting animal if nothing at all had happened to you. Shit, through and through."

"I'm a goddess," Teri said, walking toward Jess and the stage with that damned hypodermic in her left hand—and with Jess's gun in her right. "And now you're going to worship me."

chapter 21

Jim and Hank and Charlie found the house. Big stone walls. Gates leading to the front walk and the driveway—the driveway gate was open. One small break, Hank thought.

Hank got out of the car. He touched things Teri would have touched: the gate, the mailbox. And he felt the mind of the killer wrap around him. This was her lair—this was a place of death, and he could see it, smell it, hear it, feel it. Could taste it like poison on his tongue. Could hear the obscene laughter of a gloating killer everywhere: in the shadows and the way the light fell through the ancient live oaks and glinted off the koi in the fishpond. The killer's plans shivered beneath his skin; the images bored into his brain. Now that he was on the property, he could feel where Teri had taken her other victims. And he could feel where she would take Jess.

What he didn't know was how much time remained. If any.

Teri might have had an hour and a half alone with Jess. She'd probably had less; he had to hope she hadn't caught any breaks in traffic on her way home. How much of a hurry was she in to kill Jess and leave?

Hank jumped back into the car and pointed Charlie down the brick drive to the left. "That's the way she went," he said. It was a blind left—trees and azalea bushes and a lot of fat Christmas-tree pines blocked the view of what lay ahead. After they'd made the turn, though, the driveway straightened out, and terminated in an attractive little wooden cottage that lacked either a garage door or any windows, but that featured a van blazoned with Goldcastle advertising backed against the doorway.

"Ram it," Hank yelled. "Teri keeps the door barred when she has someone in there with her. The only way we're getting in there in time is by going through a wall."

Jim shouted, "Do it!"

"What the hell—it's only a pension," Charlie said, and the next instant the front of the Crown Vic smashed into the front of the van, and the rear end of the van crashed through the front wall of the building. Hank was moving before the car came to a complete stop, yanking off his seat belt, kicking his door open, jumping free, running for the van and the hole it had made. He went up and over the still-sliding van, threw himself onto his belly to squeeze under the hole in the wall, and dropped to the ground to one side before the police cruiser's other door had even had a chance to slam.

Charlie would be right behind him. But Hank's gut insisted that every second was going to count.

The van came to rest with its rear end angled against the front of the stage.

Hank caught a flash of Jess—warm blond hair and stark-naked body—handcuffed to a stripper's pole. Falling. Struggling back to her feet. Still alive.

And a brunette in skintight jeans and a lacy white skintight blouse, holding a syringe in one hand and pointing a gun at Hank with the other.

That would be Teri, he thought, as his world narrowed down to the gun and what he would have to do to control it.

He heard the brunette say, "I recognize you. You're the one she's been fucking." The gun barrel moved from him to

Jess. Teri's voice stayed calm. "Don't move or I'll kill her now."

Hank judged distances and angles between himself and the gun. A diversion would help—of course, Charlie or Jim bursting through the wall and shooting the murdering bitch would help a hell of a lot more.

Without warning, Jess kicked high, her long leg arcing through the air with incredible speed, connecting with the gun and the hand, and

—muzzle flash—

—explosion—

—the brunette staggered—

—the inertia from the kick or possibly the impact from a bullet crashed Jess over the side of the stage, where she dangled, hanging by the handcuffs around her wrists, helpless—

—and Hank launched himself across the wreckage of the wall and whatever had been in the place before the van and the cop car landed there, and sprang onto the stage in one vault, bellowing to get Teri to focus on him and draw her fire away from Jess, because he had no time to think, to weigh, to measure; he had time only to act. Behind him, he heard Charlie shout, "Drop the gun and put your hands in the air."

And Teri swung the gun around, shot Charlie, no hesitation, and Hank heard a cry of pain. Charlie. Hit.

Jim yelled, "Get down!" Only Hank couldn't get down to clear the shot for Jim. The bitch's gun pointed dead at him.

He threw himself into a flying tackle. His body remembered that same move once before, hitting his team member on the battlefield, and again he felt the weight of one body toppling, heard screaming again and couldn't tell if it was then or now, him or someone else. He felt like he was two places at once—once as a grenade went off and the pain fought with the shouts of the other three Rangers running in to get him out, get him to safety. And the other—this moment, facing a killer with a gun and a huge, gleaming needle.

He ripped the gun away from her, slid it across the floor, rolled away to clear a shot for Jim.

Teri lunged at him. Screaming. That massive hypodermic syringe in her hand.

Coming straight at him, her teeth bared in a feral grin.

And Jess shouted, "Mine," and Hank felt the bullet go over him, and Teri jammed the needle into his right shoulder at the same instant that her face disappeared in a circle of blood.

Teri flopped, dead, on top of him.

Hank pulled away from her and she toppled back, and he felt the syringe yank out of him.

But fire already burned inside of him. He stared at the syringe. Half-empty. Which meant that half of whatever had been in there was in him.

He crawled to Jess, ignoring spreading fire. She hung from the stage, the padded handcuffs not giving at all, naked, with her service weapon once again in her hand. Blood covered her face, and she stared up at him.

"You got her?" Hank asked.

Jess growled. "Yeah. I got her. Gun landed in my reach. She was going to kill you with whatever was in that needle."

Hank smiled at Jess, ignoring the pain, knowing that Teri had killed him, and that he simply hadn't fallen down yet. But Jess had done everything a human being could do to keep that from happening. "It was a good shot," he said.

And she told him, "I didn't think you would find me."

"I *had* to find you," he told her. "I love you."

She stared up at him, and her face was a wonder. "I love you, too. With everything in me. I will love you forever."

He wanted more time. He wanted to hear her tell him that again, but the burning in his blood was getting worse, spreading through his body. He nodded to the handcuffs. "Where's the key?"

"I don't know."

Most handcuff keys were interchangeable. Jim would have one. Charlie would have one. One of them ought to work.

And then Hank remembered *Charlie*. Almost to his twenty, wanting to get out and be with his family. Shot. Hank could still hear him groaning, so Charlie was still alive. But how badly was he hurt? "I'll be right back," he told Jess, and jumped off the wrecked stage, and clambered over bits of wall and fallen roof to Charlie. Shot through the arm, bleeding heavily, with Jim beside him, calling for backup. Hank breathed a sigh of relief. Charlie didn't look too bad.

"Handcuff key, Jim," Hank said. "Fast. And an ambulance. Bitch hit me with whatever poison she was going to kill Jess with. I don't know how long I've got. Jess is okay, though."

Jim fumbled for the key while he kept the pressure on Charlie's wound.

Charlie said, "I can get my key, Jim. Just tell Dispatch what happened."

So Jim passed on the news that Hank had been poisoned.

Hank saw dismay on both Jim's and Charlie's faces.

"You're going to be okay, aren't you?" Charlie asked.

Hank, whose whole body felt like it was on fire, said, "Probably used up my last life this time." He managed a left-shoulder shrug, though even that hurt like hell. Charlie pulled out a handcuff key and handed it to him.

Hank went back to Jess. When the handcuffs fell off her wrists, Jess collapsed. Hank caught her and pulled her close and sagged to the floor with her, and she said, "I'm all right. Have to get out of these shoes, that's all."

He turned Jess around to face him. "She poisoned me," he told her. He was having a hard time breathing, and his stomach was starting to churn, and his skin felt like it was bubbling off his body. "I wanted to thank you. For everything. For . . . bringing the light back to my life."

"No. You can't die," she told him. "You can't."

He slid out of his shirt and wrapped it around her. "Not much I can do about it," he said. "Or you, either. Just hold me until it's over."

"No," she said. "You can't die. I won't allow it." She wrapped her arms around him, and buried her face against his chest. He stroked the back of her hair.

Last mission, he thought. But that was okay. He'd done his part, and Jess had done her part. The killer was dead in a corner. He was going to follow the bitch into oblivion, but what mattered was that the good guys had stopped the killer. They'd won. And Hank wasn't dying alone. Jess was with him, holding him, and he loved her, and she loved him. He could have lived with that, if he'd gotten to keep her. He could die with it, too.

He'd lived so that he mattered. So had she. They'd done all right.

He kissed her.

"Stay with me," she said. "Hold on."

"I'm right here." The pain was horrible. It was like being doused in gasoline and lit with a match, but he could hear the scream of sirens, and they were getting closer.

Sounding close.

Right on top of him, in fact. *Any minute,* he thought, *I'm going to keel over dead, and Jess is going to be stuck with the irony of help being so close.*

Then paramedics were wrapping Jess in a blanket, and

Jess was clutching Hank's hand and her eyes were full of tears.

And they were riding in the back of the ambulance, with one paramedic starting an IV on him and putting an oxygen mask over his face and marking the place where Hank said the needle went in.

Pain ate him alive; the angels hovered over him singing something sweet and shimmery. Jess, glued to his side, hung on to his hand. He kept from screaming in agony only by reminding himself that he didn't want that to be the last thing Jess remembered about him.

Still dying.

But still not dead.

And the pain was hell. He'd never felt worse. But it wasn't changing. He couldn't feel it intensifying. He couldn't feel himself getting numb and fading away, either. And, for that matter, he couldn't see any tunnel or any white light, and the angels started to sound suspiciously like some sixties girl group singing under the wail of the sirens.

"Jess," he said as they pulled up to the emergency entrance, "I think that bitch might have mixed up a defective batch of whatever it was in that needle of hers."

And then he and Jess were inside, with lab techs everywhere and a guy with a portable X-ray machine and a doc doing a local on him and then sticking a big-ass needle attached to a big-ass syringe into the same spot the bitch had hit—a particularly tough bit of scar tissue—and Hank was by that time suspicious of the whole dying thing, even if he did feel sick as hell.

The doc waved the syringe—half-full of brownish liquid—in his face and said, "Bet you've never been grateful for these scars before."

"Not really," Hank said. "Can't say I ever got much pleasure from them."

"They saved your life today," the doc said. "Encapsulated the poison, kept almost all of it out of your bloodstream, assuming the syringe the paramedics brought in with them was completely full when she hit you with it. Lab's going to be hours getting a complete breakdown on everything she had in there, but what they've called up to us so far would have been enough to kill you three times over, had it been able to go anywhere."

Jess stood beside him, holding his left hand. Smiling. It was the sort of smile that would see a man safely through hell and lead him all the way to heaven. And she said, "See, I told you that you couldn't die. We're supposed to be together."

Hank could still hear those angels somewhere in the background. They didn't sound so much like Patti and the Blue Belles anymore. They seemed to be cheering. Or maybe that was Jim and Charlie and the handful of paramedics on the other side of the curtain.

"We are. So marry me already."

She said, "I thought you'd never ask."

As weddings went, it was odd. Jess wore an emerald-green dress—one she had to consider, at last, part of a dream come true. Her bridesmaids were strippers, Hank's groomsmen were martial artists, and Jess's mother was the only family member either of them had there. But Jim gave her away. Jess was almost certain that Jim was hitting on her mother, something Jess was trying hard not to think about. And the bride's side of the chapel had a record turnout of men in dress uniform. Her colleagues were celebrating one of their own at the same time that they were saying good-bye.

Hank's side of the little chapel held his employees,

grateful students, friends from the Rangers—and more cops. His family and her family, such as they were.

At the reception, one of Hank's students caught the garter. Jess didn't toss her bouquet, though she did pull a flower from it and throw that.

And then they were finished. "You ready to get out of here?" Hank asked her.

"I've been ready since we got here."

They were on their way to the airport, but before the honeymoon, Jess had one final stop to make.

Hank pulled the car into the cemetery and they both got out, Jess carrying her bouquet.

They walked hand in hand to a new grave with a little metal marker where the stone would one day be.

Jess knelt beside the grave and pressed the bouquet's plastic handle into the freshly laid sod.

"You should have had one of these, too," Jess said to Ginny. "So you can have mine. I miss you so much, and I would never have found him without you. But I would never have found you without him, either."

She rested one hand on the sod. "It's over, and the monster who did this has had as much justice as she ever could have had. If some part of you is still here . . . know that it's done. And I'm moving on, now. I did what I set out to do. I brought you home. Now I'm . . . going to find out if I can be a mother. Maybe teach little kids to dance. I can't pick up where you and I left off, but I've found out that I wouldn't want to. Hank is better than any life you or I could have imagined for ourselves when we started out. And I would never have met him without you. And would have never appreciated him without everything that had come before."

She stood, and Hank stepped behind Jess and wrapped his arms around her.

Hank said, "Thank you, Ginny. From both of us."

They stood there for a while, not moving, watching the breeze blow the bouquet's ribbons around.

And then Jess and Hank turned and slowly walked away, into the bright future they had bought and paid for with a past of shattered dreams.

Penguin Group (USA)
is proud to present
GREAT READS—GUARANTEED!

**We are so confident that you will love
this book that we are offering a
100% money-back guarantee!**

If you are not 100% satisfied with
this publication, Penguin Group (USA)
will refund your money!
Simply return the book before
September 1, 2005 for a full refund.

**With a guarantee like this one,
you have nothing to lose!**